BEWARE OF PITY

STEFAN ZWEIG was born in 1881 in Vienna, a member of a wealthy Austrian-Jewish family. He studied in Berlin and Vienna and was first known as a poet and translator, then as a librettist and biographer. His stories and novellas were collected in 1934. Zweig travelled widely, living in Salzburg between the wars, and enjoying literary fame. In 1934, with the rise of Nazism, he briefly moved to London, taking British citizenship. After a short period in New York, he settled in Brazil where, in 1942, he and his wife were found dead in bed, in an apparent double suicide.

STEFAN ZWEIG

BEWARE
OF PITY

Translated from the German by
Phyllis and Trevor Blewitt

PUSHKIN PRESS
LONDON

Revised edition published in 2003

First published in 2000 by
Pushkin Press
123 Biddulph Mansions
Elgin Avenue
London W9 1HU

First published in Germany by S Fischer Verlag
First published in Great Britain 1939
Translation copyright © Atrium Press, 1982

British Library Cataloguing in Publication Data:
A catalogue record for this book is available
from the British Library

ISBN 1 901285 49 9

Set in 10 on 12 Baskerville
and printed by Compass Press

AUTHOR'S NOTE

A SHORT EXPLANATION may perhaps be necessary for the English reader. The Austro-Hungarian Army constituted a uniform, homogeneous body in an Empire composed of a very large number of nations and races. Unlike his English, French, and even German *confrère*, the Austrian officer was not allowed to wear mufti when off duty, and military regulations prescribed that in his private life he should always act *standesgemäss*, that is, in accordance with the special etiquette and code of honour of the Austrian military caste. Among themselves officers of the same rank, even those who were not personally acquainted, never addressed each other in the formal third person plural, *Sie*, but in the familiar second person singular, *Du*, and thereby the fraternity of all members of the caste and the gulf separating them from civilians were emphasized. The final criterion of an officer's behaviour was invariably not the moral code of society in general, but the special moral code of his caste, and this frequently led to mental conflicts, one of which plays an important part in this book.

STEFAN ZWEIG

THERE ARE TWO KINDS
OF PITY

*One, the weak and sentimental kind, which is
really no more than the heart's impatience to be
rid as quickly as possible of the painful emotion
aroused by the sight of another's unhappiness,
that pity which is not compassion, but only an
instinctive desire to fortify one's own soul against
the sufferings of another; and the other, the only
kind that counts, the unsentimental but creative
kind, which knows what it is about and is determined to hold out, in patience and forbearance, to
the very limit of its strength and even beyond.*

INTRODUCTION

"TO HIM THAT HATH, to him shall be given." These words from the Scriptures the writer may safely restate as: "To him that hath told much, to him shall much be told." Nothing is further from the truth than the only too common notion that the author's fantasy is incessantly at work within him, that his invention has an inexhaustible and continuous fund of stories and incidents upon which to draw. In reality he need only, instead of setting out to find, let himself be found by, characters and happenings, which, in so far as he has preserved the heightened capacity for observing and listening, unceasingly seek him out as their instrument of communication. To the person who has over and over again tried to trace human destinies, many tell their own story.

The following story was related to me almost entirely in the form in which I here present it and, moreover, in most unusual circumstances. One evening when I was last in Vienna, tired after a very full day, I sought out a restaurant on the outskirts of the city which I imagined had long since ceased to be fashionable and was but little frequented. No sooner had I entered it, however, than I was made disagreeably aware of my mistake. As I passed the first table, an acquaintance jumped up with every sign of genuine pleasure—I, to be sure, did not respond with equal warmth—and invited me to join him. It would be untrue to say that this importunate gentleman was in himself an impossible or unpleasant fellow; he was merely one of those embarrassingly convivial souls who collect acquaintances as assiduously as children collect postage-stamps and are therefore peculiarly proud of every fresh addition to their collection. To this good-natured eccentric—in his spare time an erudite and competent archivist—the whole meaning of existence lay in the modest satisfaction derived from being able to remark with airy nonchalance at the mention of any name that received mention from time to time in the Press: "A close friend of mine," or "Ah, I met him only yesterday!" or "My friend A tells me, and my friend B thinks," and so on throughout the entire alphabet. His friends could always count on him to applaud loudly at their first nights, he would ring up every actress the morning after the show to offer his congratulations, he never forgot a birthday, he forbore to mention disagreeable Press notices and invariably drew attention to the favourable ones out of genuine friendliness. Not at all a bad fellow, then, for he was genuinely anxious to please and was delighted if one so much as asked a small favour of him, or better still, added a fresh specimen to his cabinet of curiosities.

But there is no need to describe friend "Also-present"—the name by which this variety of good-natured parasite within the variegated species of snob is generally known in Vienna—in greater detail, for everyone is familiar with the type and knows it is impossible to repel its touching and inoffensive advances without being brutal. Resigning myself to my fate, therefore, I sat down beside him, and a quarter of an hour had passed in idle chatter when a man entered the restaurant—tall and striking on account of the contrast between his fresh, youthful complexion and an intriguing greyness at the temples. Something about the way he held himself immediately betrayed the ex-officer. My neighbour jumped up eagerly to hail him with the assiduity so typical of him. The newcomer, however, responded with indifference rather than politeness, and scarcely had the waiter dashed up and taken his order when friend "Also-present" turned to me and said in a low whisper: "Do you know who that is?" Knowing of old the pride he took in triumphantly displaying any even moderately interesting specimen from his collection, and fearing long-winded explanations, I merely uttered a perfunctory "No," and continued to dissect my *Sachertorte*. This apathy on my part merely had the effect of increasing the celebrity-monger's excitement; screening his mouth cautiously with his hand, he breathed in an undertone: "Why, that's Hofmiller of the Commissariat. You know, the fellow who won the Order of Maria Theresa in the war." Since this information did not seem to bowl me over as he had hoped, he began, with the fervour of a patriotic school primer, to enlarge upon all the valiant deeds performed by Captain Hofmiller in the war, first with the cavalry, then on an observation flight over the Piave, when he had shot down three planes single-handed, and finally with a machine-gun company, when for three days he had occupied and held a sector of the front—all this accompanied by a mass of detail (which I omit) and punctuated the whole time by exclamations of boundless astonishment that I should never have heard of this paragon, upon whom the Emperor Charles had in person conferred the most rare of all decorations in the Austrian army.

Involuntarily I yielded to the temptation to glance across at the other table so as to see for once at close quarters a duly and historically certified hero. But I encountered a hard, indignant look that seemed to say, "So that fellow's been talking a lot of rot about me, has he? You won't find anything to look at here." Whereupon he slewed his chair round with an unmistakably hostile movement and flatly turned his back on us. Somewhat abashed, I looked away, and from now on avoided so much as a glance at the cloth on his table. Shortly afterwards I took leave of my good gossip, noticing, however, as I left, that he immediately went over to his hero's table, no doubt to give him as glowing an account of me as he had given me of him.

That was all—a mere exchange of glances. And I should have forgotten all about this fleeting encounter, but it so happened that the very next day, at a small party, I once more found myself face to face with this forbidding gentleman. In evening dress he looked even more striking and elegant than in the informal tweeds of the day before. We both had some difficulty in suppressing a faint smile, that significant smile that passes between two people who, in a fairly large group of people, share a closely guarded secret. He recognized me, as I did him, and we were probably both equally irritated or amused at the thought of our unsuccessful celebrity-monger of the day before. At first we avoided speaking to each other, and in any case it would have been useless to try to do so, for a heated discussion was already going on all around us.

The subject of this discussion will easily be guessed when I mention that it took place in the year 1937. Future historians of our epoch will one day record that in the year 1937 almost every conversation in every country of this distracted Europe of ours was dominated by speculation as to the probability or improbability of a new world war. Wherever people met, this theme exercised an irresistible fascination, and one sometimes had a feeling that it was not the people themselves who were working off their fears in conjectures and hopes, but, so to speak, the very air, the storm-laden atmosphere of the times, which, charged with latent suspense, was endeavouring to unburden itself in speech.

Our host, a lawyer by profession and dogmatic by nature, opened the discussion. Employing the usual arguments, he put forward the usual airy nonsense: the present generation, he said, knew all about war and would not let itself be tricked so innocently into the next war as it had been into the last. At the very moment of mobilization the guns would be pointed in the wrong direction, for ex-soldiers like himself in particular had not forgotten what was in store for them. I was annoyed by the smug assurance with which, at a moment when in thousands and hundreds of thousands of factories explosives and poison gas were being manufactured, he dismissed the possibility of a war as lightly as he might flip the ash off his cigarette with a tap of his forefinger. One should not always let the wish be father to the thought, I protested with some firmness.

The ministries and the military authorities who ran the whole war machine had likewise not been sleeping, and while we had been befuddling ourselves with Utopias, they had taken full advantage of the interval of peace in order to organize the masses in advance and have them ready to hand, at half-cock, so to speak. Even now, while Europe was at peace, the general attitude of servility had, thanks to modern methods of propaganda, increased to unbelievable proportions, and one ought boldly to face the fact that from the very moment when the news of mobilization came hurtling through the loud-speakers no opposition could be looked for from any quarter. The grain of dust that was man no longer counted today as a creature of volition.

Of course they were all against me, for, as is borne out by experience, the instinct of self-deception in human beings makes them try to banish from their minds dangers of which at bottom they are perfectly aware by declaring them non-existent, and a warning such as mine against cheap optimism was bound to prove particularly unwelcome at a moment when a sumptuously laid supper was waiting for us in the next room.

14

And now, to my surprise, the gallant hero of the day before entered the lists in my support—the very man in whom my false intuition had led me to suspect an opponent. Yes, it was sheer nonsense, he declared vehemently, to try nowadays to take into account the willingness or unwillingness of human material, for in the next war all the actual fighting would be done by machines, and men would be reduced to no more than a kind of component part of the machine. Even in the last war he had not met many men at the front who had either unequivocally acquiesced in or opposed the war. Most of them had been whirled into it like a cloud of dust and had simply found themselves caught up in the vast vortex, each one of them tossed about willy-nilly like a pea in a great sack. On the whole, more men had perhaps escaped into the war than from it.

I listened in astonishment, my interest particularly aroused by the vehemence with which he now went on: "Don't let us deceive ourselves. If in any country whatever a recruiting campaign were to be launched today for some utterly preposterous war, a war in Polynesia or in some corner of Africa, thousands and hundreds of thousands would rush to the colours without really knowing why, perhaps merely out of a desire to run away from themselves or from disagreeable circumstances. But as for any effective opposition to a war—I wouldn't care to put it above zero. It always demands a far greater degree of courage for an individual to oppose an organized movement than to let himself be carried along with the stream—individual courage, that is, a variety of courage that is dying out in these times of progressive organization and mechanization. During the war practically the only courage I came across was mass courage, the courage that comes of being one of a herd, and anyone who examines this phenomenon more closely will find it to be compounded of some very strange elements: a great deal of vanity, a great deal of recklessness and even boredom, but, above all, a great deal of fear—yes, fear of staying behind, fear of being sneered at, fear of independent action, and fear, above all, of taking a stand against the mass enthusiasm of one's fellows. It was not until later on in civil life that I personally realized that most of those reputed to be the bravest at the front were very questionable heroes—oh, please don't misunderstand me!" he said, turning politely to our host, who was pulling a wry face. "I do not by any means except myself."

I liked the way in which he spoke, and I had an impulse to go up to him, but at that moment our hostess called us in to supper and, since we were placed far apart at table, we had no further opportunity of talking to each other. Not until the party broke up did we run into each other, in the cloakroom.

"I believe," he said with a smile, "we have already been indirectly introduced by our mutual patron."

I also smiled. "And, what is more, very thoroughly."

"I expect he made me out to be no end of an Achilles, and no doubt he was as proud as a peacock of my Order."

"That's about it!"

"Yes, he's damned proud of it—just as he is of your books."

"A rum customer. But I've met worse. By the way—if you've no objection, I'll walk along with you."

We walked along together. Suddenly he turned to me.

"Believe me, I'm not talking for effect when I say that for years nothing has been a greater bore to me than this Maria Theresa Order of mine—it's far too conspicuous for my liking. I must admit, to be quite honest, that when it was awarded to me out there at the front I was, of course, absolutely bowled over. After all, I'd been brought up as a soldier, and as a cadet I'd heard this Order spoken of as something almost legendary, this one Order which comes the way of perhaps no more than a dozen men in every war—a positive bolt from the blue. Why, for a young chap of twenty-eight that sort of thing means a devil of a lot. All at once you find yourself standing before the whole brigade, everyone gazes up reverently as something suddenly sparkles out on your breast like a little sun, and His Majesty, the Emperor, that unapproachable deity, shakes you by the hand and congratulates you. But a distinction of that kind, you know, only had any sort of point in our military world; and when the war was over, it seemed to me ridiculous to have to go about for the rest of my life labelled as a hero, just because on one occasion I had acted with real courage for twenty minutes—probably no more courageously than thousands of others, except that I had had the good fortune to be noticed, and the perhaps still more astounding good fortune to come back alive. By the end of a year I was fed to the teeth with stalking about like a walking monument, seeing people wherever I went stare at the little metal disc and then let their gaze travel in awed admiration up to my face; in fact, my exasperation at being so eternally conspicuous was one of the reasons why, at the end of the war, I left the army and entered civilian life."

He strode along more vigorously.

"I say one of the reasons, but the chief reason was one that you may be able to appreciate even more. The chief reason was that I myself had become thoroughly sceptical as to my claim to be called a hero and of my heroism. After all, I knew better than all these strangers who gaped at me that the man behind the Order was anything but a hero, was even definitely the reverse—one of those who only rushed headlong into the war in order to extricate themselves from a desperate situation, men who were running away from their responsibilities rather than patriotic heroes. I don't know how you writers feel about it—to me, at least, to live in a halo of glory seems unnatural and unendurable, and I felt genuinely relieved when I was no longer obliged to strut about with my heroic history writ large on my uniform. Even to this day it annoys me when people rake up my glorious past, and I may as well confess to you that I was very nearly on the point yesterday of coming over to your table and telling that chattering fool he'd better find someone else to brag about. The awed look you gave me kept riling me for the rest of the evening, and I had a good mind, just in order to give that fellow the lie, to compel you to hear from my own lips by what tortuous paths I attained to the status of a hero. It's a very odd story, and yet it may serve to show that courage is often nothing but inverted weakness. Incidentally, I wouldn't mind telling you the whole story straight out here and now. Something that goes back a quarter of a century in a man's life no longer concerns him, but quite another person. Have you time? And it wouldn't bore you, would it?"

Of course I had time, and we paced up and down the now deserted streets far into the night. I have only made a few changes in his narrative (I need scarcely add it was not related to me at a single interview), such as putting Uhlans instead of

Hussars, to conceal the identity of the various garrisons, and, of course, changing the names of people and places. But in no instance have I added anything essential of my own invention, and it is not I but the man who lived the story who now narrates it.

BEWARE OF PITY

THE WHOLE THING began with a blunder on my part, an entirely innocent piece of clumsiness, a *gaffe*, as the French call it. Then followed an attempt to put things right; but if you try to repair a watch in too much of a hurry, you're as likely as not to put the whole works out of order. Even today, now that years have gone by, I am unable to decide exactly where my sheer *gaucherie* ended and my guilt began. I dare say I shall never know.

I was twenty-five at the time and a second lieutenant in the −th Regiment of Imperial Uhlans. I cannot claim ever to have been particularly keen about soldiering or felt it to be my vocation. But when you get four growing boys with voracious appetites and two girls in the family of an Austrian official, and there's barely enough to feed them, you don't bother much about their inclinations, but push them out at an early age into the treadmill of a profession, so that they won't be a charge on the household any longer than necessary. My brother, who even at his first school swotted so hard that he ruined his eyesight, was sent to a seminary for priests; I was packed off, because of my sturdy physique, to a military academy. From that point onwards the thread of life spins itself out mechanically, there's no need to do any more lubricating. The State sees to everything. In a few years, out of a pale, adolescent youngster it fashions, free of charge, after the prescribed military pattern, an ensign with a downy moustache, and hands him over, ready for use, to the army. One day, on the Emperor's birthday, according to the usual custom, I was discharged from the academy, not yet eighteen years old, and shortly afterwards the first star flashed out on my collar; thus the first stage was reached, and now the successive stages of promotion could reel themselves off mechanically at suitable intervals, to end up with gout and a pension. That I should enter the cavalry of all things, the most fashionable and expensive arm of the service, was by no means my personal wish, but a caprice on the part of my Aunt Daisy, who had married my father's elder brother as his second wife on his leaving the Ministry of

21

Finance for a more remunerative post as the president of a bank. At once rich and snobbish, she could not bear the thought that anyone connected with her who happened also to be called Hofmiller should "disgrace" the family by serving in the infantry; and since she made me an allowance of a hundred crowns a month to indulge this whim, I had to make a show of humble gratitude to her on every possible occasion. Whether it was to my liking to serve in the cavalry or, indeed, to enter the army at all, no one had ever considered, I myself least of all. Whenever I was in the saddle I felt fine, and my thoughts did not travel far beyond my horse's neck.

In November 1913, the year when my story opens, some order or other must have passed from one department to another, for before you could say Jack Robinson our squadron was trans-ferred from Jaroslau to another small garrison town on the Hungarian frontier. It is of no importance whether I call the little town by its right name or not, for two buttons on a uniform could not more closely resemble each other than does one Austrian provincial garrison town another. In one as in the other the same military establishments: barracks, a riding-school, a parade-ground, an officers' mess, and in addition three hotels, two cafés, a pâtisserie, a wine-bar, a dingy music-hall with faded soubrettes who, as a side-line, most obligingly divide their attentions between the regular officers and the volunteers. Everywhere soldiering entails the same busily empty monotony; hour after hour is mapped out in accordance with inflexible, antediluvian regula-tions, and even one's leisure does not seem to offer much in the way of variety. In the officers' mess the same faces, the same con-versation; at the café the same games of cards and billiards. Sometimes one is amazed that the good God should trouble to give the six or seven hundred roofs of a little town of this sort the background of a different sky and a different countryside.

My new garrison had, it is true, one advantage to offer over the former one in Galicia; it was a stopping-place for express trains, and was situated on the one hand near Vienna and on the other at no great distance from Budapest. Anyone who had money—and there are no end of wealthy fellows in the cavalry, to say nothing of the volunteers, who are either aristocrats or sons of industrialists—might, if he could get off, take the five o'clock train to Vienna and be back again at half-past two in the morning by the night express: time enough, that is, to do a theatre, to saunter about the Ringstrasse, to play the cavalier and keep a look-out for chance *amours*; some of the officers were even in the enviable position of keeping a flat or some kind of *pied-à-terre* for such purposes. Unfortunately, such diverting escapades were beyond the scope of my monthly allowance. The only amusements left me were the café or the pâtisserie, where, since the stakes at cards were usually too high for me, I was reduced to playing billiards, or chess, which was cheaper still.

And so one afternoon—it must have been somewhere about the middle of May, 1914—I was sitting in the pâtisserie with our local apothecary and deputy mayor, who from time to time took me on at chess. We had long since finished our customary three games, and were chatting away out of sheer inertia—what was there to do in this boring hole?—but the conversation was already petering out like a smouldering cigarette-end. Then, suddenly, the door opened, and a billowing skirt swept in a gust of fresh air and a pretty girl: brown, almond eyes, dark complexion, superbly dressed, not a bit provincial, and, what was more, a new face in this God-forsaken monotony. But alas! the elegant nymph did not vouchsafe us a glance as we looked up in awed admiration; briskly and spiritedly, with firm athletic tread, she walked past the nine little marble-topped tables straight to the counter, where she proceeded to order cakes, pastries and liqueurs by the dozen. I was immediately struck by the very obsequious way in which the proprietor bowed to her; never had I seen the back-seam of his swallow-tails arched so tautly. Even his wife, the buxom, overblown provincial beauty, who was accustomed to accept the attentions of us officers in the most perfunctory manner (we were often in debt for all kinds of little trifles until pay-day came round), rose from her seat at the cash desk and almost dissolved in treacly politeness. While the worthy proprietor was entering her order in his book, the pretty young lady carelessly nibbled at a few chocolates and made conversation with Frau Grossmaier: but as for us, who were, I fear, craning our necks with unseemly eagerness, we were not accorded so

23

much as the bat of an eyelash. Naturally the young lady did not burden her pretty hands with a single parcel; everything, Frau Grossmaier humbly assured her, would be sent at once without fail. Nor did it even enter her head to pay at the cash desk like us ordinary mortals. We all realized at once that here was a quite unusually grand, distinguished customer.

As, her order completed, she turned to go, Herr Grossmaier rushed forward to open the door for her. My friend the apothecary also got up to bow most respectfully as she swept past. She acknowledged the courtesy with regal graciousness—devil take it, what velvety deep-brown eyes!—and I could scarcely wait until, overwhelmed with sugary compliments, she had left the shop, to begin pumping my companion about this swan in our duck-pond.

"You mean to say you don't know her? She's the niece of ... (I shall call him Herr von Kekesfalva, although that was not his real name) Kekesfalva. Surely you know the Kekesfalvas?"

Kekesfalva—he threw down the name as though it were a thousand-crown note and looked at me as if expecting me to echo as a matter of course, "Kekesfalva! Ah yes, of course!" But I, a recently transferred subaltern, dropped into this new garrison only a few months since—I in my innocence knew nothing of this most mysterious goddess and politely asked for further information, which my companion proceeded to impart with all the complacent pride of a provincial, far more long-windedly and in greater detail, of course, than I shall retell it here.

Kekesfalva, he explained, was the richest man in the whole neighbourhood. Practically everything belonged to him, not only the Kekesfalva estate—"you must know the house, you can see it from the parade-ground, the yellow house to the left of the high-road with the flat tower and the huge park"—but also the big sugar-factory on the road to R, the saw-mill in Bruck and the stud-farm in M; they all belonged to him, and six or seven blocks of houses in Budapest and Vienna as well. "Yes, you'd scarcely believe that we can count such colossally rich people among our neighbours. Why, he lives like a grandee. In winter in the little palace in the Jacquingasse in Vienna, and in the summer in various watering-places; he only keeps his house here open for a few months in the spring, but lord, what style he lives in!

Quartets from Vienna, champagne and French wines, everything tip-top, the best of everything." And incidentally, if I cared, he'd be only too glad to give me an introduction, for—with an expansive and complacent gesture—he was on the best of terms with Herr von Kekesfalva, had had frequent business dealings with him in the past and knew that he was always glad to welcome officers to his house. A word from him and I should receive an invitation.

Well, and why not? One positively suffocated in this stagnant duck-pond of a provincial garrison town. By now one knew all the women on the promenade, knew each one's summer hat and winter hat, best dress and everyday dress, they were always the same. And one knew their dogs and their maids and their children, one had passed and repassed them time after time. One knew all the culinary arts of the fat Bohemian mess cook, and one's palate was gradually being dulled by the sight of the everlastingly unvaried menu at the hotel. One knew by heart every name, every sign-board, every notice in every street, every shop in every building and every show-window in every shop. By now one knew almost as precisely as Eugen the head waiter at what time His Worship the magistrate would appear in the café; on the stroke of half-past four he would sit down in the window corner on the left and order a *café mélange*, whilst the notary in his turn would come in exactly ten minutes later, at four-forty, take a cup of tea with lemon—blessed variation!—because of his poor digestion, and, puffing away at the everlasting cheroot, retell the same old jokes. God, one knew every face, every uniform, every horse, every driver, every beggar in the whole neighbourhood, one knew even oneself to the point of satiety! Why not break away from the treadmill for once? And then, that pretty girl, those deep-brown eyes! And so I told my patron with feigned indifference (no over-eagerness before this conceited vendor of pills!) that it would be a pleasure, to be sure, to make the acquaintance of the Kekesfalva family.

And lo and behold! my valiant apothecary had not been pretending. Two days later, swelling with pride, he handed me a printed card on which my name had been neatly inscribed; and this invitation-card informed me that Herr Lajos von Kekesfalva requested the pleasure of the company of *Herr Leutnant* Anton Hofmiller at dinner at eight o'clock on Wednesday of the following week. One wasn't dragged up in the gutter, thank God, and knew what was proper in such circumstances. So on the following Sunday morning I got myself up in my very best—white gloves and patent-leather shoes, my face perfectly shaved, a drop of eau-de-Cologne on my moustache—and drove out to pay my courtesy call. The butler—old, discreet, well-cut livery—took my card and murmured apologetically that the family would be extremely sorry to have missed the *Herr Leutnant*, but they were all at church. So much the better, said I to myself. Paying one's first call, whether official or private, is always a ghastly business. At any rate, you've done the right thing. You'll go to dinner on Wednesday evening, and let's hope you'll have a good time. That settles that, I thought, until Wednesday evening. But it was with genuine delight that two days later, that is to say, on the Tuesday, I found that a visiting-card with the corner turned down had been left for me at the barracks by Herr von Kekesfalva. Capital, I thought to myself, these people have irreproachable manners. Fancy their repaying my call within two days—and I a mere junior officer. Why, a General couldn't wish for greater consideration and courtesy. And I now looked forward with really pleasurable feelings of anticipation to the Wednesday evening.

But from the very start Fate played me a dirty trick—one really ought to be superstitious and pay more heed to little omens. At half-past seven on the Wednesday evening there was I all dressed up—dress uniform, new gloves, patent-leather shoes, trousers creased as sharp as a razor-blade—and my batman was just smoothing out the folds of my cloak and giving me a last look over (I always needed him for that, for I had only a small hand-mirror in my ill-lit little room), when there came a knock at the door. It was an orderly, to say that the officer on duty, my friend Captain Count Steinhübel, requested me to hurry over to him in the guard-room. Two Uhlans, probably blind drunk, had been brawling, and the upshot was that one of them had hit the other over the head with the butt of his rifle. And now the clod was lying there bleeding, unconscious, his mouth wide open. They didn't know yet whether his skull was broken or not; the

regimental doctor had cleared off to Vienna on leave, the
Colonel was not to be found, and in his desperation poor old
Steinhübel, curse him, had sent the orderly haring off for me, me
of all people, to get me to give him a hand while he looked after
the injured man. So now I had to take down the evidence and
send orderlies flying all over the place to hunt up a civilian doctor in the café or somewhere else. What with all this it was now
a quarter to eight, and I could see that there was no chance of
my getting away for another quarter or half an hour. Confound
it all, this filthy business *would* happen today, today of all days,
when I was invited out to dinner. I looked more and more impatiently at my watch; impossible to arrive punctually if I had to
hang about here another five minutes. But duty's in our very
bones, it comes before any private obligation; I simply couldn't
go away. And so I did the only thing possible in this damnable
situation, which was to send my batman in a cab (that little item
cost me four crowns!) to the Kekesfalvas to beg them to excuse
me if I were late, but I had been unexpectedly detained on duty,
and so on and so on. Fortunately the hullabaloo in the barracks
didn't last much longer, for the Colonel appeared in person with
a doctor who had been dug out from somewhere or other, and I
was able to slip away.

But now came a further bit of bad luck. Today of all days there
was no cab in the Rathausplatz, and I had to wait until they had
telephoned for a carriage. And so when at long last I landed up
in the great entrance hall of the Kekesfalva house, the minute
hand of the clock on the wall was already pointing down verti-
cally; it was exactly half-past eight instead of eight, and I could
see that the cloakroom was bulging with overcoats. I could tell,
too, by the manservant's somewhat embarrassed expression that
I had arrived too late—disagreeable, very disagreeable, for such
a thing to happen on one's first visit.

Nevertheless the manservant—white gloves now, tails, stiff shirt
and stiff features—reassured me by saying that my batman had
delivered my message half an hour ago, and conducted me to the
salon—four-windowed, hung with red silk, ablaze with crystal
chandeliers, a marvel of elegance, I had never seen anything
more magnificent. But alas to my confusion it turned out to be

completely deserted, and from the next room I could distinctly hear the cheerful clatter of dishes. How vexing, how vexing, I thought to myself, they're already at table.

Well, anyhow, I pulled myself together, and the moment the manservant threw open the folding-doors I stepped forward to the threshold of the dining-room, clicked my heels smartly and bowed. The whole company looked up; ten, twenty pairs of eyes, strange eyes all of them, inspected the latecomer, who, far from self-assured, stood framed in the doorway. An elderly gentleman, doubtless the master of the house, immediately rose, hurriedly laid aside his napkin, came towards me and held out a welcoming hand. Not at all what I had imagined him to be, this Herr von Kekesfalva, not in the least the country squire with twirling Magyar moustaches, round-faced, plump and rubicund from good living. Behind gold-rimmed spectacles a pair of somewhat tired eyes floated above grey pouches, his shoulders seemed slightly hunched, his voice sounded wheezy, as though he were troubled by a cough; one would have taken him, if anything, for a scholar, with his slender, delicate features, which ended in a scanty, white goatee. The old gentleman's exceptional kindliness was extraordinarily reassuring; no, no, he said, cutting short my excuses, it was for him to apologize. He knew only too well the sort of thing that cropped up in the army, and it had been particularly kind of me to send him a special message; it had only been because they had not been sure when to expect me that they had already started dinner. But now I must take my place without further delay. He would introduce me to all the guests individually later on. But first, he said, leading me to the table, I must meet his daughter. A young girl in her teens, delicate, pale, fragile like himself, looked up from a conversation, a pair of grey eyes glanced shyly at me. But I only caught a fleeting glimpse of slender, restless features, and bowed first to her, then collectively right and left to the other guests, who were obviously glad not to have to lay down their knives and forks in order to go through the tedious ceremony of a formal introduction.

For the first two or three minutes I still felt thoroughly ill-at-ease. There was no one there from the regiment, not a single fellow-officer, not a single acquaintance, not even one of the town bigwigs; nothing but strange, utterly strange faces. The guests seemed for the most part to be landowners or officials of the neighbourhood with their wives and daughters. But mufti, mufti everywhere, not a single uniform but mine. My God! how was I, clumsy, shy fellow that I was, to make conversation with all these strangers? Fortunately I had been given a very good place. By my side sat the brown-eyed, proud beauty, the pretty niece, who had, after all, it appeared, noticed my admiring gaze in the pâtisserie, for she smiled at me kindly as at an old acquaintance. Her eyes were like coffee-beans, and, when she laughed, they really did seem to crackle like roasting beans. She had charming, translucent little ears beneath luxuriant dark hair; like pink cyclamen nestling in moss, I thought. She had bare arms, soft and smooth; they must be like peeled peaches to the touch.

It was good to be sitting beside such a pretty girl, and the fact that she spoke with a soft Hungarian accent made me almost fall in love. It was good to be dining in so dazzlingly bright a room at such an elegantly laid table, a footman behind me, before me the most marvellous food. My neighbour on the left, too, who for her part spoke with a slight Polish intonation, seemed to me, if somewhat massive, not unattractive. Or was it only the wine that made me think so—the bright gold, blood-dark wine and sparkling champagne which the footmen in white gloves behind poured out positively extravagantly from silver carafes and broad-bellied bottles?

Yes, indeed, my honest apothecary had not been boasting idly. The Kekesfalvas lived like princes. Never had I eaten such good food, never let myself dream that one *could* eat such good, such superb food. Ever more delicious, more costly delicacies came floating along on an inexhaustible succession of dishes: pale-blue fish, crowned with lettuce and surrounded by slices of lobster, swam in golden sauces; capons rode on broad saddles of piled-up rice; puddings blazed blue in burning rum; towering ice-bombs, tier upon tier; sweet and many-hued, fruits that must have travelled half round the world nestled against each other in silver baskets. There was no end to it all, no end, and then at last a veritable rainbow of liqueurs, green, red, white, yellow, cigars as thick as asparagus shoots, and delicious coffee.

A marvellous house, an enchanting house—a thousand blessings on my excellent apothecary! A bright, a happy, an uproarious evening! I did not know whether I felt so released, so free because to right and left and opposite me the others too now had sparkling eyes and were talking in raised voices, because they too had thrown dignity to the winds and were talking away vivaciously on all sides—at any rate, my usual shyness had vanished. I rattled on without the slightest constraint, I paid court to both my fair neighbours at once; I drank, I laughed, I gazed about me with wanton, carefree eye, and although it may only have been by chance that from time to time my hand brushed gently against the lovely bare arms of Ilona (for this was the name of the delicious niece), she seemed by no means to take it amiss; she too relaxed, transported, liberated like the rest of us by this Lucullan feast.

Gradually—wasn't it, after all, because of the unusually good wine, Tokay and champagne one upon another?—I felt a lightness come over me that bordered on exuberance, almost on boisterousness. I still lacked something to complete my bliss, to lift me completely out of myself, to carry me away; and what it was for which I unconsciously yearned, became gloriously clear to me the very next moment, when from a third room, beyond the salon—the butler had unobtrusively reopened the folding-doors—came soft music, the very music for which my heart was craving: dance music, at once rhythmic and soft, a waltz, lilted by two violins, echoed sadly by a sombre cello, rapped out in sharp staccato by a piano. Music, yes, music, that was the one thing that had been lacking! Music; and perhaps one would waltz to it, let oneself soar, fly through the air, become more blissfully aware than ever of one's lightness. The Villa Kekesfalva must be an enchanted house; you had only to dream and—hey presto!—your wish was fulfilled. As we now got up, pushed back our chairs and went couple by couple—I gave Ilona my arm and once more felt her cool, soft, voluptuous skin—into the salon, we found all the tables cleared away as though by magic and the chairs placed round the walls. The parquet floor was a smooth, brown, shining mirror, a heavenly skating-rink for the waltz, and from the next room the unseen orchestra spurred us on.

I turned to Ilona. She laughed and understood. Her eyes had already said "Yes," and in a moment we were whirling round, two couples, three couples, five couples, over the smooth parquet, while the more cautious and the more elderly looked on or chatted. I loved dancing, and, what is more, was a good dancer. Our bodies interlocked, we floated along; I felt I had never danced better in my life. I asked my other neighbour for the next waltz; she too danced superbly, and my senses reeled as, bending over her, I breathed the perfume of her hair. Ah, she danced wonderfully, everything was wonderful, I had not been so happy for years. I scarcely knew where I was, I felt like embracing everyone, saying something kind, some word of thanks to each one of them, so light, so rapturous, so blissfully young did I feel. I went whirling from one to the other, I talked, I laughed, I danced, and, carried away on the stream of my own happiness, I lost all sense of time.

Then suddenly—I chanced to look up at the clock. It was half-past ten, and I realized with a start that here had I been dancing and talking and joking away for almost an hour and, idiot that I was, I had not yet asked my host's daughter to dance. I had only danced with my neighbours and two or three other ladies, those who had taken my fancy, and had forgotten all about the daughter of the house. What boorishness, indeed, what discourtesy. But quick, we must put that right straight away.

To my horror, however, I could no longer remember exactly what the young girl looked like. I had only bowed to her for a moment as she sat at table; all I could recall was something delicate and frail, and then the curious glance of her grey eyes. Wherever could she be? As the daughter of the house she surely could not have gone away? Uneasily I inspected all the women and girls seated round the walls: not one of them resembled her. At last I went into the third room, where, hidden by a Chinese screen, the musicians were playing, and breathed a sigh of relief. For there she was—why, of course it was she—delicate, slender, in a pale blue gown, sitting between two old ladies in the corner of the boudoir behind a malachite-green table, on which stood a shallow bowl of flowers. Her slender head was inclined a little as though she were listening with her whole soul to the music, and it was the warm pink of the roses that drew my attention to the transparent pale gleam of her brow beneath the heavy auburn hair. But I did not allow myself time for further observation. Thank God, I said to myself with a sigh of relief, I've tracked her down. It's not too late for me to make up for my omission.

I went up to the table—the music rattled on in the next room—and bowed a polite invitation to dance. A startled pair of eyes stared up at me in amazement, the lips remained parted in the very act of speaking. But she made not the slightest movement to follow me. Had she not understood? So I bowed again, my spurs jingling softly as I said: "May I have this dance, *gnädiges Fräulein*?"

What now happened was appalling. The bowed head and shoulders jerked backwards, as though to avoid a blow; the blood came rushing to the pale cheeks; the lips, parted the moment before, were pressed sharply together, and only the eyes stared fixedly at me with an expression of horror such as I had never before encountered in my whole life. The next moment a shudder passed through the whole convulsed body. With both hands she levered, heaved herself up by the table so that the bowl on it rocked and rattled; and as she did so some hard object, either of wood or metal, fell clattering to the ground from her chair. She continued to hold on with both hands to the sway-ing table, her body, light as a child's, still shaking all over; yet she did not run away, she clung more desperately than ever to the heavy table-top. And again and again that quivering, that trem-bling, ran through her frame, from the contorted, clutching hands to the roots of her hair. And suddenly there burst forth a storm of sobbing, wild, elemental, like a stifled scream.

By now the two old ladies had closed in upon the trembling creature; they seized hold of her, caressed, fondled and tried to soothe her, gently unloosing her hands, her clutching hands, from the table. She sank back into her chair. But the weeping went on, grew, if anything, more vehement, breaking forth again and again, like a gush of blood, like a hot agony of vomiting, in spasm after spasm. If the music behind the screen were to stop even for a moment, the sound of the sobs would be bound to reach the ears of the dancers.

I stood there aghast, looking an utter fool. What—what on

earth had happened? Helplessly I looked on as the two old ladies endeavoured to calm the sobbing girl, who now, in an access of shame, had buried her head on the table. But ever fresh paroxysms of weeping, wave after wave, shook the slender frame and set the bowl on the table clattering. I stood rooted to the spot, an icy coldness in my limbs, my collar choking me as though it were a burning rope.

"I beg your pardon," I stammered at length in an undertone into the empty air—both the women were comforting the sobbing girl, neither had eyes for me—and retreated, feeling quite dizzy, into the salon. No one there had, apparently, noticed anything, the couples were still whirling tempestuously, and I felt I must hold on to the doorpost, for the room was reeling round me. What had happened? Had I done something awful? My God, I must have drunk too much, drunk too quickly at dinner, and now intoxicated had made some frightful blunder.

The music stopped, the couples separated. The prefect of the district released Ilona with a bow, whereupon I rushed up to her and, to her amazement, dragged her almost roughly aside. "Please help me! For Heaven's sake help me, do explain to me!"

Obviously Ilona had imagined I had pulled her over to the window in order to whisper some pleasantry to her, for her eyes grew suddenly hard; I must, I suppose, in my agitation, have looked either pitiable or terrifying. My pulses racing, I told her the whole story. And, strange, she flared up at me, the same utter horror in her gaze as in that of the girl in the other room.

"Are you mad? Don't you know? Didn't you see?"

"No," I stammered, crushed by this fresh and equally incomprehensible look of horror. "See *what?*—I don't know anything. It's the first time I've been here."

"Surely you noticed that Edith ... is lame? ... Didn't you see her crippled legs? Why, she can't move two steps without crutches ... and you ... you ca—... "—she quickly suppressed an abusive epithet—"You go and ask the poor child to dance ... oh, it's horrible, I must go to her at once ... " "No!" In my despair I seized Ilona by the arm. "Just a moment, just a moment ... you must make my apologies. I couldn't possibly know ... I only saw her at dinner, just for a second ... please do explain to her ... "

But Ilona, fury in her gaze, had snatched her arm away and was hurrying into the next room. My throat constricted, my mouth dry with nausea, I stood on the threshold of the salon, which whirled and buzzed and hummed with its (to me suddenly intolerable) laughing, gaily chattering couples, and thought: another five minutes and they'll all know of my *gaffe*. Five minutes, and scornful, censorious, ironic looks from all directions will paw me over from head to foot; tomorrow my boorish behaviour will be gossip for the whole town, a savoury morsel for hundreds of tongues, delivered with the early morning milk at the front door, bandied about in the servants' quarters and passed on to the cafés, the offices. Tomorrow the whole regiment will know of it.

At this moment I glimpsed as through a mist the girl's father. Looking somewhat dejected—did he know already?—he was coming across the room. Could he be coming towards me? No—anything rather than meet him now. I was suddenly seized by a panic fear of him and of them all. And without knowing exactly what I was doing, I stumbled to the door that led out into the hall and out of this hellish house.

"Is the *Herr Leutnant* leaving us already?" asked the astonished manservant, with a gesture of respectful incredulity.

"Yes," I answered, aghast the moment the word was out of my mouth. Did I really wish to leave? And the very next moment, while he was taking my coat off the peg, I realized clearly that I was committing a fresh and perhaps even more inexcusable act of stupidity by decamping in this cowardly fashion. But it was too late now. I could not give him back the coat, I could not possibly, now that he was opening the front door with a perfunctory bow, go back to the salon. And so I suddenly found myself standing outside the strange, accursed house, the wind blowing cold in my face, my heart hot with shame, my breath coming in gasps as though I were suffocating.

This was the ill-fated blunder which started the whole thing. Now, when in cold blood and at a distance of many years I look back on the simple incident which gave rise to the whole catastrophic chain of events, I must, in justice to myself, affirm that I blundered entirely innocently into the unfortunate error; even the cleverest and most sophisticated of mortals might have committed the *gaffe* of asking a crippled girl to dance with him. But in the first rush of horror I thought of myself not merely as an arrant bungler, but as a cad, a criminal. I felt as though I had struck an innocent child with a whip. The whole thing could, after all, have been put right with a little presence of mind; it was only by rushing away then and there like a criminal, without making any attempt to apologize—no sooner had I felt the first breath of cold air on my face outside the front door than this was immediately obvious to me—that I had irrevocably made a mess of the whole thing.

I cannot describe my state of mind as I stood outside the house. Behind the lighted windows the music died away; no doubt the musicians were merely breaking off for an interval, but in my guilty and overwrought state I feverishly imagined that it was because of me that the dancing had stopped. Everyone would now be crowding into the little boudoir to comfort the sobbing girl; all the guests, the women, the men, would, one and all, be inveighing against the reprobate who had invited a crippled child to dance and then, having played his dastardly trick, beat a cowardly retreat. And tomorrow—I could feel the cold sweat breaking out under my cap—my shameful behaviour would be gossiped about and decried all over the town. I could just imagine how my fellow-officers, Ferencz, Mislywitz and above all Jozsi, that confounded wag, would come up to me, smacking their lips. "Well, Toni, this is a fine way to behave. Once you're let off the lead you go and disgrace the whole regiment!" For months this ragging and sneering would go on in the officers' mess; at our mess table every piece of idiocy on the part of any one of us was chewed over for the next ten or twenty years, every asininity immortalized, every joke fossilized. Today, after the lapse of sixteen years, they still tell the hoary old story of how Captain Wolinski came back from Vienna and boasted of having made the acquaintance in the Ringstrasse of Countess T and having spent the very same night with her in her flat; of how two days later the newspapers reported the scandalous story of a maid who, having been dismissed by the Countess, had swindled a number of shops and indulged in all sorts of amorous adventures by passing herself off as her former mistress; and how the wretched Casanova had been obliged, moreover, to put himself in the hands of the regimental doctor for three weeks. Anyone who once made himself a laughing-stock in the eyes of the regiment remained so forever; there was no forgetting, no forgiving, there. And the more I figured the whole thing out, the more frenzied and absurd did my ideas become. At that moment of folly it seemed to me a hundred times easier to give one quick pull on the trigger of my revolver than to live through the hellish torments of the next few days, the impotent waiting to discover whether my comrades already knew of my disgrace and whether the secret whispering and sniggering were not already going on behind my back. Oh, I knew myself only too well. I knew that I should never have the strength to hold out once the mocking and sneering and gossiping got under way.

How I reached home that night I no longer know. All I remember is wrenching open the cupboard in which I kept a bottle of slivovitz for visitors and tossing down three half-tumblersful to get rid of the horrible feeling of nausea in my throat. Then I threw myself down on the bed, fully dressed, and tried to think things out. But just as flowers grow in more tropical luxuriance in a hothouse, so do wild and frenzied ideas flourish in the darkness. Confused and fantastic, they shoot up out of the sultry soil into garish lianas which choke the breath out of one's body, and with the swiftness of dreams the most fantastic hallucinations take shape and chase hither and thither round the overheated brain. Disgraced for life, I thought to myself, hounded out of society, sneered at by my fellow-officers, gossiped about all over the town. Nevermore would I be able to set foot outside my room, nevermore venture out into the streets, for fear of meeting one of the people who knew of my crime (for it was as a crime that in that first night of emotional tension I looked upon my simple blunder; myself I looked upon as hunted and pursued by universal ridicule). When, eventually, sleep came, it can only have been a light, fitful sleep, during which my fears were still feverishly at work within me. For directly I opened my eyes I was confronted by the angry childish face, I could see the twitching lips, the hands convulsively clawing at the table, I could hear the

noise of falling pieces of wood, which I now realized must have
been her crutches, and I was overcome by an insane fear that the
door might suddenly open and—black coat, white-edged waistcoat, gold-rimmed spectacles—the girl's father with his scanty,
neatly trimmed goatee come stumping up to my bed. In my fear
I jumped up. And as I stared at myself in the mirror, and saw the
sweat of sleep and fear upon my features, I felt like smacking in
the face the blundering fool behind the pale glass.

But fortunately by now it was day; steps clattered along the
corridor and carts rattled on the cobble-stones below. And when
daylight comes in at the window you think more clearly than
when you are muffled up in the malignant darkness that delights
in creating spectres. Perhaps, I said to myself, it's not such a bad
business after all. Perhaps no one noticed it. *She*, of course, that
poor pale creature, the helpless cripple, she will never forget it,
never forgive. Suddenly a consoling thought flashed across my
mind. Hurriedly combing my tousled hair, I struggled into my
uniform and rushed past my dumbfounded batman, who called
after me plaintively in his halting Ruthenian German: "*Herr
Leutnant, Herr Leutnant*, coffee ready."

I tore down the steps of the barracks, and shot so quickly past
some Uhlans who were standing about half-dressed in the courtyard that they had no time to spring to attention. At one bound
I had left them behind and was outside the gate; from there I ran
straight to the flower-shop in the Rathausplatz. In my impetuosity
I had, of course, entirely forgotten that shops did not open at
half-past five in the morning, but fortunately Frau Gurtner dealt
in vegetables as well as flowers. A cart of potatoes stood half-
unloaded before her door, and no sooner had I rapped briskly
on the window than I could hear her pattering down the stairs.
I invented a hasty excuse. Yesterday, I said, I had completely
forgotten that today was the birthday of a very dear friend of
mine. In half an hour's time the regiment would be riding out,
and so I should like some flowers to be sent at once. Flowers,
quickly, then, the finest that she had! Whereupon the plump
shop-woman, still in her night-jacket, shuffled off in her worn-
out bedroom slippers, opened the shop, and displayed her crown
jewel, an enormous cluster of long-stemmed roses. How many

did I want? All, all of them, I said. Should she just tie them up as they were, or would I prefer her to put them in a nice basket? Yes, yes, a basket. All that was left of my month's pay went on this magnificent purchase; at the end of the month I should have either to go without my evening meal and my visits to the café or else to borrow money. But at this moment that was a matter of indifference to me; if anything, I was actually glad that my foolishness was going to cost me dear, for all the time I felt a kind of malicious desire to punish myself thoroughly, blunderer that I was, to make myself pay through the nose for my twofold doltishness.

So now all was well, wasn't it? The most lovely roses, beautifully arranged in a basket, to be delivered without fail. But at this point Frau Gurtner came running excitedly after me down the street. Where, then, and to whom, was she to send the flowers? The *Herr Leutnant* had said nothing about that. Oh yes, threefold dunderhead that I was, in my agitation I had forgotten all about that. To the Villa Kekesfalva, I instructed her, remembering, fortunately, thanks to that horrified exclamation of Ilona's, the Christian name of my wretched victim: Fräulein Edith von Kekesfalva.

"Ah yes, of course, the Kekesfalvas," said Frau Gurtner with pride. "Our best customers."

And, one more question—I had already turned to rush off— did I not want to send a few words with them? A few words? Oh, I see! The name of the sender. Of the donor. How else was she to know who had sent the flowers?

So once more I entered the shop. Taking a visiting-card, I wrote on it: "With apologies." No—that was impossible. That in itself would be a fourth piece of folly. Why should I remind her of my blunder? But what else was I to write? "With sincere regrets." No, that wouldn't do, either; she might think I was sorry for *her*. Best to write nothing, nothing at all.

"Just put my card with the flowers, Frau Gurtner, just the card."

Now I felt relieved. I hurried back to barracks, gulped down my coffee and got through the morning's drill somehow, perhaps a little more absently and less calmly than usual. But in the army no one pays much attention if a lieutenant comes on duty in the morning with a bit of a hang-over. How many there are who come back, after a riotous night in Vienna, so tired out that they can scarcely keep their eyes open, and fall asleep while trotting briskly along. As a matter of fact, it suited my book very well just then to have my whole time taken up with shouting words of command, inspecting my men and then riding out. For my military duties to some extent kept at bay my uneasiness; the disquieting memory was still, it was true, drumming behind my temples, and I still felt as though an acrid sponge were lodged in my throat.

But at noon, just as I was about to go over to the officers' mess, my batman came running after me with an eager "*Panje Leutnant!*" He held in his hand a letter, a longish rectangle— English paper, blue, delicately scented, a coat of arms elegantly embossed on the back, the envelope addressed in a fine pointed hand, a woman's hand. Hastily tearing it open, I read:

"*Sincere thanks, my dear HERR LEUTNANT, for the undeserved present of lovely flowers, with which I was, and still am, delighted. Do please come to tea with us on any afternoon that suits you. Do not trouble to let us know. I am—alas!—always at home.*—EDITH V. K."

A delicate hand. Involuntarily I recalled how the slender childish fingers had gripped the edge of the table, remembered how the pale face had suddenly flushed purple, as though claret had been poured into a glass. I read the few lines again, and then a second and a third time, and breathed a sigh of relief. How discreetly she had glossed over my gauche behaviour. At the same time how skilfully, how tactfully, she herself had alluded to her infirmity. "I am—alas!—always at home." It would be impossible to grant forgiveness more tastefully. Not a hint of annoyance. A load fell from my mind. I felt like a prisoner in the dock who has fully expected to be sentenced to lifelong imprisonment, when the judge rises and announces, "Discharged." I should have to go there soon, of course, to thank her. Today was Thursday—so I should pay my call on Sunday. Or no, better make it Saturday.

But I did not keep my word. I was too impatient. I was haunted by the desire to know that my guilt was once and for all wiped out, to put as speedy an end as possible to the disquietude aroused in me by the uncertainty of the situation. I was still racked by the fear lest in the officers' mess, at the café, or elsewhere, someone would broach the subject of my mishap, "Well, and how did things go off at the Kekesfalvas'?" I wanted to be able to reply in calm superior tones, "Charming people. I had tea with them again yesterday,"—so that everyone might see at once that I wasn't in bad odour. Oh, to be able to write off the whole wretched affair. Oh, to be done with it. And the result of this state of mental agitation, moreover, was that on the very next day, that is, the Friday, while I was strolling along the promenade with Ferencz and Jozsi, my best friends, I suddenly found myself resolving that I would pay my visit that very day. I curtly took leave of my somewhat astonished friends.

It was not a particularly long walk to the Kekesfalvas', half an hour at the most if one stepped out briskly. First five tedious minutes through the town, then along the somewhat dusty highroad which led also to our parade-ground, and every inch of which our horses by this time knew so well that we could let the reins hang slackly. Half-way along this road, by a little chapel on a bridge, a narrower, shady avenue of old chestnut trees branched off to the left—a private avenue which was little used either by pedestrians or carriages and which followed without impatience the leisurely meanderings of a sluggish little stream.

But, oddly enough, the nearer I approached the little *Schloss*, the white walls and the wrought-iron gate of which were by now visible, the more quickly did my courage evaporate. Just as, on arriving at the very door of the dentist's, one seeks for some excuse to retreat before ringing the bell, so now did I long to make a hurried escape while there was yet time. Must it really be today? Should I not regard the whole disagreeable affair as finally settled by the young girl's letter? Involuntarily I slowed down my pace; there was, after all, still time to turn back. One is always glad to make a detour when one shrinks from going straight to one's objective, and so, crossing the little stream by a rickety plank, I turned off from the avenue into the fields, with the idea of first walking round the house from the outside.

The house behind the high stone wall revealed itself as a two-storeyed, rambling edifice in late Baroque style; it was painted, after the old Austrian fashion, a so-called Schönbrunn yellow, while the windows were furnished with green shutters. Separated from it by a courtyard, a few smaller buildings, obviously the servants' quarters, the estate offices and the stables, abutted on the park, of which I had seen nothing at all that first evening. Only now, peering in through the oval openings in the vast wall, did I realize that the house was not, as I had been led to believe by the interior, a modern villa, but a regular country-house, a nobleman's country-seat of the old style, such as I had now and again seen in Bohemia when riding past on manoeuvres. The only remarkable feature of the house was the curious square tower, slightly reminiscent in its shape of an Italian *campanile*, which thrust itself up into the sky in somewhat incongruous fashion—perhaps the remains of an earlier *schloss*. I now remembered that I had frequently noticed this watch-tower from the parade-ground, but had taken it to be the church tower of some village or other, and only now did it occur to me that the usual "bulb" of the tower was missing and that the curious cubic structure had a flat roof, which served either as a sun terrace or an observatory. The more certain I became of the feudal, traditional character of this country-seat, the more uncomfortable did I feel; it was in this house of all houses, where the conventions must undoubtedly be rigidly observed, that I had gone and made such an ass of myself on my first appearance.

But at length, having walked right round the outer wall and reached the gate again from the other side, I screwed up my courage, walked along the gravel path between a double row of pollarded trees to the front door and lifted the heavy chased bronze knocker, which, in accordance with old custom, served the purpose of a bell. A moment later the butler appeared. Strange, he did not seem at all taken aback by my unannounced visit. Without inquiring further or taking the visiting-card which I held in my hand, he invited me, with a polite bow, to wait in the salon, saying that the ladies were still in their room, but would come in a moment; there seemed to be no doubt, then, of my being received. He led me into the house as though my visit

41

were expected; with renewed uneasiness I recognized the red-tapestried salon in which we had danced that first evening, and a bitter taste in my mouth reminded me that next door must be that room with the fateful corner.

At first, it is true, cream-coloured folding-doors, with delicate gold ornamentation, hid from sight the scene, so vivid in my memory, of my *gaffe*, but after a few moments I could hear, on the other side of the door, chairs being drawn up, hushed whispers, and a discreet coming and going which betrayed the presence of several people. I tried to employ the time of waiting in surveying the salon: rich furniture, Louis Seize, to the right and to the left old Gobelin tapestries and, between the french windows that gave directly on to the garden, old pictures of the Grand Canal and of the Piazza San Marco, which seemed to me, novice though I was in these matters, to be extremely valuable. It is true that I did not form a very clear picture of any single one of these art treasures, for I was listening with eager attentiveness to the noises in the next room. There was a faint clatter of plates, a door banged, and now I fancied too—a cold shudder ran down my spine—that I could hear the unrhythmical dry tap-tap of crutches.

At last an as-yet invisible hand pushed open the folding-doors from inside. It was Ilona, who now came towards me. "How nice of you to come, *Herr Leutnant!*" she said, and conducted me straight into the only-too-familiar room. In the same corner, on the same chaise-longue, behind the same malachite-green table (why repeat a situation so painful to me?), sat the crippled girl, a voluminous white fur rug spread over her lap so that her legs were invisible—evidently I was not to be reminded of "it". With obviously studied friendliness Edith smiled me a greeting from her invalid's corner. Nevertheless it was a painful moment for both of us, this renewal of our acquaintance, and I could tell at once, from the constrained manner in which, with some effort, she held out her hand to me across the table, that she too was thinking of "it". Neither of us succeeded in finding the first word to break the ice.

Fortunately Ilona hurriedly interjected a question into the suffocating silence.

"What may we offer you, *Herr Leutnant?* Tea or coffee?"

"Oh, just whichever you like," I replied.

"No—whichever you prefer, *Herr Leutnant!* Please don't stand on ceremony, it's all the same to us."

"Well, then, coffee, if I may," I decided, and was glad to find that my voice did not sound too husky. Damned clever, that, of Ilona to have bridged the first moment of tension with such a practical question. But it was ruthless of her to leave the room now to order tea, for I, to my discomfiture, was left alone with my victim. It was high time now to say something, to make conversation at all costs. But there was a lump in my throat and there must have been a trace of embarrassment in my gaze; I did not venture to look in the direction of the sofa, for fear she might think I was staring at the rug which concealed her crippled legs. Fortunately she showed herself to be more composed than I, and she opened the conversation with a certain excitable vehemence of manner which I remarked in her for the first time.

"Won't you sit down, *Herr Leutnant?* There, draw up that arm-chair. And why don't you take off your sword—we're going to keep the peace, aren't we? Put it on the table or the window-ledge ... wherever you wish."

I drew up a chair somewhat formally. I still found it impossible to look about me quite freely. But she came energetically to my rescue.

"I really must thank you again for the exquisite flowers ... they're wonderful. Just see how lovely they look in the vase. And then ... and then ... I must apologize too for my stupid out-burst. It was frightful the way I behaved ... I couldn't sleep the whole night, I was so ashamed. You meant it so kindly ... how could you possibly have had any idea? And besides,"—she suddenly gave a shrill, nervous laugh—"besides, you really had guessed my inmost thoughts ... I had sat down there purposely to watch the dancers ... and just as you came up to me I was longing for nothing so much as to join in ... I'm quite crazy about dancing. I can watch other people dancing for hours on end—watch them until I can feel within myself their every movement ... yes, really, every movement. And then it's not *they* who are dancing, I myself am spinning, swaying, yielding, letting

43

myself be led, be whirled along … you've probably no idea how foolish one can be … After all, as a child I was a good dancer and simply adored dancing … and whenever I dream nowadays, it's of dancing. Yes, silly as it sounds, I dance in my dreams, and perhaps it's a good thing for Papa that … that … happened to me, or else I'd certainly have run away from home and become a dancer … There's nothing I have such a passion for. It must be wonderful to thrill, to hold, to stir hundreds and hundreds of people with one's body, with one's movements, with one's whole being, evening after evening … it must be glorious … By the way, just to show you how crazy I am … I collect pictures of great dancers. I have them all—Saharet, Pavlova, Karsavina. I have photographs of them all, in all their roles and poses. Just a moment, I'll show you them … there, they're in that little box over there … there, near the fireplace … in the little Chinese lacquer box"—her voice grew suddenly querulous with impatience—"no, no, no, there on the left by the books … oh, how clumsy you are! … Yes, that's it"—at last I had found the box and taken it to her. "Look, this one, the one on the top, is my favourite picture, Pavlova as the dying swan … ah, if only I could follow her about, if only I could see her, I believe it would be the happiest day of my life."

The door behind us through which Ilona had left the room began to move gently on its hinges. Hastily, as though caught out in some piece of mischief, Edith closed the box with a sharp, resounding snap.

"Not a word in front of the others of what I've told you. Not a word," she said, as though rapping out an order.

It was the white-haired manservant with the beautifully trimmed mutton-chop whiskers who was discreetly opening the door; behind him Ilona was wheeling in a rubber-tyred tea-trolley piled with good things. She poured out, then came and sat down by us; I immediately felt my self-assurance return. A welcome subject of conversation was provided by the huge Angora cat, who had crept in noiselessly with the tea-trolley and was rubbing himself with unconstrained familiarity against my legs. After I had admired the cat, I was subjected to a cross-fire of questions: how long had I been here, how did I like the new garrison, did I know Lieutenant So-and-so, did I often go to Vienna? And involuntarily I found myself taking part in a natural, easy conversation, in the course of which the painful tension imperceptibly vanished. Gradually I even ventured to take occasional sidelong looks at the two girls. The one was completely different from the other: Ilona, already a woman, full-blooded, well-developed, voluptuous, healthy; beside her, Edith, half child, half young woman, about seventeen or eighteen, still appeared somehow immature. Curious contrast: one would have liked to dance with the one, to kiss her; the other one wanted to spoil as an invalid, to pet and make a fuss of, to protect and, above all, to soothe. For a strange restlessness emanated from her. Not for one moment were her features in repose; now she looked to the left, now to the right, now she leaned back as though exhausted; and she spoke as nervily as she moved in jerky, staccato tones, without pausing for breath. Perhaps, I thought to myself, this lack of restraint, this restlessness, is a compensation for the enforced immobility of her legs; perhaps, too, the result of a perpetual state of semi-fever, which quickens the tempo of her gestures and her speech. But I had little time for observation. For with her blunt questions and her light, volatile manner of talking she had a way of focusing attention completely on herself; and to my surprise I found myself taking part in a really enlivening and interesting conversation.

This went on for an hour, perhaps even an hour and a half. Then all of a sudden the shadow of a figure loomed up from the salon, and someone entered the room cautiously, as though fearing to disturb us. It was Herr von Kekesfalva.

"Please, please, stay where you are," he urged me, realizing that I was about to rise out of politeness, and then bent down to plant a fleeting kiss on his daughter's forehead. He was again wearing the black coat with the white-edged waistcoat and the old-fashioned stock (I never saw him in anything else). With those eyes that peered out circumspectly from behind gold-rimmed spectacles he looked like a doctor; and he might indeed have been a doctor at a patient's bedside as he cautiously took a seat beside the crippled girl. Strange, the moment he appeared, the room seemed to take on a more melancholy aspect; the anxious way in which every now and then he cast searching, tender, side-long glances at his daughter checked and muted the flow of our hitherto unconstrained chatter. Too soon he became aware of our constraint and made an attempt to get the conversation going again. He too asked about my regiment, about the Captain, and inquired about the former Colonel, who was now a divisional chief at the War Ministry. He seemed for years to have had amazingly detailed knowledge of the affairs of the regiment, and I don't know why, but I had a feeling that he had some definite purpose in stressing his particularly intimate acquaintance with each individual senior officer of the regiment.

Another ten minutes, I thought to myself, and I can take my leave unobtrusively. But at this moment there was another gentle tap on the door, and the butler entered noiselessly, as though he were bare-footed, and whispered something in Edith's ear. She immediately flew into a temper.

"Tell him to wait. Or no, tell him to leave me in peace altogether today. Tell him to go away. I don't need him."

We were all embarrassed by the violence of her outburst, and I rose with a disagreeable feeling that I had stayed too long. But she burst out at me as peremptorily as at the manservant:

"No, stay. It's nothing, nothing at all."

Her imperious tone really bordered on rudeness. Her father too seemed to feel uncomfortable, for with a helpless, troubled expression he admonished her:

"Edith!"

And now she herself realized, perhaps because of his distress, perhaps because I was standing there in embarrassment, that her nerves had got the better of her, for she suddenly turned to me.

"Do forgive me, but Josef could perfectly well have waited, instead of bursting in like that. It's only the usual daily torture—the masseur who gives me remedial exercises. The most utter nonsense—one, two, one, two, up, down, down, up; and that, if you please, is going to put me right. The latest discovery of our dear doctor, and a quite superfluous form of torment. Useless, like everything else!"

She looked at her father challengingly, as though holding him responsible. In some embarrassment, for he was obviously ashamed in front of me, the old man bent over her.

"But my child ... do you really think that Dr Condor ... ?"

He broke off, however, for her mouth had begun to work and her nostrils were quivering. It was in just this way that her lips had trembled on that fateful evening, and I began to dread a fresh outburst. But suddenly she blushed and murmured submissively:

"All right then, I'll go, although there's no point in it, absolutely no point. Excuse me, *Herr Leutnant*, I hope you'll come again soon."

I bowed and was about to take my departure, but she had already changed her mind about my going.

"No, stay with Papa while I march off." Those last words, "march off", were as sharp and staccato as a threat. Then she picked up the little bronze bell that stood on the table and rang it; it was only later that I noticed that bells of this kind were placed within her reach on all the tables all over the house, so that she could always call someone to her at a moment's notice. The bell rang out sharp and shrill and on the instant the butler, who had discreetly made himself scarce, reappeared.

"Help me," she ordered him and threw off the fur rug. Ilona bent down to whisper something to her, but "No!" she indignantly snapped at her friend, obviously in a state of agitation. "Josef shall help me up. Then I can walk by myself."

What happened now was frightful. Bending over her, the butler seized her frail body under the armpits with an obviously practised grip and lifted her up. Holding with both hands on to the arms of the chair, she stood there erect, and measured each of us with a challenging look; then, feeling for the two sticks that were hidden beneath the rug, she pressed her lips firmly together, raised herself on to the crutches and—tap-tap, tap-tap— stamped, swayed, heaved herself forward, contorted and witch- like, while the butler held his hands out behind her to catch her should she slip or collapse. Tap-tap, tap-tap, tap-tap—first one foot and then the other, and between each step there was a faint clanking and squeaking as of tautly stretched leather and metal; evidently—I did not dare to look at her poor legs—she was wearing some kind of mechanical supports on her ankles. My

47

heart was constricted as by an icy grip during this forced march, for I immediately realized why she had so demonstratively refused to be helped or to be wheeled out in her invalid chair: she wanted to show me, me in particular, to show all of us, that she was a cripple. She wanted, out of a kind of mysterious vindictiveness born of despair, to torture us with her torture, to arraign us, the hale and hearty, in the place of God. But it was this very challenge, this frightful challenge, that made me feel— and a thousand times more acutely than on the occasion of her outburst of despair when I had asked her to dance—how immeasurably she must suffer from her helplessness. At last—it seemed an eternity—she had swayed and stumbled the few paces to the door, heaving, hurling and throwing herself violently from one crutch to the other with the whole weight of her slender body. I could not bring myself to look closely at her, for the hard dry sound of the crutches, their tap-tap, tap-tap on the floor each time she took a step forward, the grating and slithering of the metal supports, and, too, the hollow sound of her laboured breathing, agitated me so excessively that I felt my heart beating against the very stuff of my uniform. She had left the room, and I listened breathlessly until behind the closed door the terrible noise grew fainter and fainter and finally died away.

Only now did I dare to look up. The old man—I had not noticed it—must have got up quietly in the meantime and was gazing intently out of the window, gazing out somewhat too intently. In the uncertain light I could see only the silhouette of the bowed figure, but the shoulders quivered in a series of vibrating lines. He too, the father who saw his child torture herself in this way day after day, he too had been shattered by this sight.

The air between the two of us was deathly still. After a few minutes the dark figure at last turned round and came softly up to me with uncertain tread as though walking over slippery ground.

"Please don't be offended with the child, *Herr Leutnant*, for being a little brusque, but ... you don't know how much she's had to go through in all these years ... always some new treatment, and the whole thing is so terribly slow. I can understand her being impatient. But what are we to do? After all, we must try everything, mustn't we?"

The old man had come to a halt before the deserted tea-table. He did not look at me as he spoke, but kept his eyes, which were almost concealed by the greyish lids, trained rigidly on the table. As though in a dream he dipped into the open sugar-bowl, seized a lump, twirled it between his fingers, stared at it blankly and put it down again; one might almost have thought he had been drinking. He was still unable to withdraw his gaze from the tea-table; some particular object seemed to rivet his attention. Absently he picked up a spoon, put it down again and then said, as though to the spoon:

"If you only knew what the child used to be like. She was on the move all day long, rushing up and down the stairs all over the place until our hearts were in our mouths. When she was only eleven she would gallop right across the meadows on her pony, no one could keep up with her. We were often afraid, my late wife and I, she was so reckless, so high-spirited, so agile, everything came so easily to her. One had a feeling that she had only to spread out her arms and she would fly. And to think that that should happen to *her*, *her* of all people ... "

The parting in the thin white hair sank lower and lower over the table. The restless hand still rummaged amongst the objects that lay about on the table, this time picking up, instead of the spoon, an idle pair of sugar-tongs and drawing curious round runic characters on the table with it (he was afraid to look at me, out of a feeling of shame, I knew, out of embarrassment).

"And yet, how easy it is even today to make her happy. She can take a childish pleasure in the slightest little thing. She can laugh at the silliest joke and get excited over a book. I wish you could have seen how delighted she was when your flowers came and she threw off the fear that she had insulted you ... You have no idea how acutely sensitive she is about everything ... she feels everything more deeply than the rest of us. I'm quite sure no one is more wretched than she herself at having behaved with such lack of self-control ... But how is she ... how is she to control herself? How is the child to possess her soul in patience when the whole thing is so slow, how keep from complaining when God has so afflicted her, and she has done nothing ... no harm to anyone?"

He continued to stare at the imaginary figures which his trembling hand was now sketching in the empty air. And suddenly he let the sugar-tongs fall with a clatter. It was as though he had started up and had only just realized that he had been speaking not to himself, but in the presence of an utter stranger. In a quite different voice, a waking, distressed voice, he began to stammer out an awkward apology.

"Forgive me, *Herr Leutnant* ... I can't think why I'm bothering you with our troubles. It was only because ... it just came over me ... and I just wanted to explain to you ... I don't want you to think badly of her ... to ... "

I don't know how I summoned up the courage to interrupt the stammering, embarrassed old man and to go up to him. But suddenly I found myself taking his hand, the hand of this complete stranger, in both my own. I said nothing. I only seized the cold bony hand which, out of shyness, he involuntarily drew back, and squeezed it. He stared at me in astonishment, his spectacles flashed as he jerked his head obliquely upwards, and an uncertain gaze timidly sought out mine. I was afraid he was going to say something. He said nothing, but the black, round pupils dilated, as though on the point of overflowing. I too was conscious of a profound emotion such as I had never before experienced, and to escape from it I bowed hurriedly and left the room.

In the hall the butler helped me on with my coat. Suddenly I felt a draught at my back. I knew without turning round that the old man had followed me and was standing in the doorway; he evidently felt impelled to thank me. But I did not want to be made to feel embarrassed. I behaved as though I had not noticed that he was standing behind me. Quickly, my pulses racing, I left the tragic house.

The next morning—a pale mist still hung above the houses, and the windows were all shuttered to guard the good sleep of the townsfolk—our troop rode out, as on every morning, to the parade-ground. At first we ambled at a jog-trot over the uncomfortable cobble-stones; still somewhat drunk with sleep, stiff and sullen, my Uhlans swayed in their saddles. Soon we had ridden along the four or five streets of the little town; on reaching the broad high-road we broke into a gentle trot and turned off to the right across the open fields. "Gallop!" I ordered my squadron, and at one breathless bound the snorting horses were off. They recognized at once the soft, springy turf, the clever beasts; there was no further need to urge them on, we could let the reins hang slackly, for scarcely had they felt the pressure of our legs than they were off like the wind. They too craved excitement and distraction.

I rode on ahead. I am passionately fond of riding. I could feel the blood flowing from my hips, coursing through my relaxed limbs in a warm, pulsating, life-giving stream, while the cold air whistled round my brow and cheeks. Marvellous morning air: one could still taste the dew of the night in it, the breath of the loosened soil, the smell of the blossoming fields; one was enveloped in the warm, sensuous steam of snorting nostrils. I was always thrilled afresh by this first morning gallop, which so agreeably shook up one's fusty, drowsy body and chased away one's stupor as though it were a suffocating fog; the feeling of buoyancy which bore me along automatically expanded my lungs, and with mouth wide open I drank in the rushing air. "Gallop! Gallop!" I felt my eyes brighten, my senses quicken, and behind me I could hear the rhythmic clank of the swords, the spasmodic snorts of the horses, the faint creaking of the saddles as they rose and fell, the even thud of the hoofs. It was one single Centaurian body, this charging group of men and horses, carried along by one single impetus. On, on, on, gallop, gallop, gallop. Ah, to ride thus, to ride thus to the ends of the earth! With a secret, proud feeling that I was the Lord and Creator of this exhilaration, I turned round in my saddle from time to time to glance at my men. And suddenly I saw all my good Uhlans had a new expression on their faces. The Ruthenian sullenness, the lethargy, the sleep had been wiped from their eyes as though it were a layer of soot. Feeling my gaze on them, they drew themselves up in the saddle and answered with smiling lips the joy in my eyes. I could tell that, like me, these dull peasant lads were stirred to rapture by the exhilaration of this whirlwind speed, this anticipatory dream of human flight. They all felt as blissfully as I the animal joy of being young, of at once expending and renewing their strength.

But suddenly I gave the order: "Tro-o-ot!" With an astonished jerk they all tugged at the reins, and like a machine that has been sharply braked the whole column resumed a lumbering trot. Somewhat nonplussed, they kept casting furtive glances in my direction, for as a rule—they knew me and my passion for riding— we galloped at full tilt right across the meadows to the regimental parade-ground. But I felt as though an invisible hand had tugged at my reins; I had suddenly remembered something. I must unconsciously have caught sight of the *Schloss* on the horizon to my left: the white rectangle of its walls, the trees in the garden and the roof of the tower. And like a pistol-shot the thought flashed through my mind: perhaps someone can see you from over there; someone whose feelings you wounded with your passion for dancing, whose feelings you are wounding once again with your passion for riding; someone with crippled, fettered legs, someone whom it hurts to see you flash past like a bird. At any rate, I suddenly felt ashamed of careering along like this, so full of health, so unimpeded, so free. I was ashamed of my far too physical happiness as of some undeserved privilege. I made my disappointed lads ride behind me through the meadows at a slow, cumbrous jog-trot. They were hoping against hope, I could tell without looking at them, for the word of command that would send them charging off again.

The very moment, it is true, that I was seized by this strange inhibition, I realized that to mortify oneself in this way was stupid and useless. I realized that there was no point in denying oneself a pleasure because it was denied another, in refusing to allow oneself to be happy because someone else was unhappy. I realized that all the time one was laughing and cracking silly jokes, somewhere in the world someone was lying at the point of death; that misery was lurking, people starving, behind a thousand windows; that there were such things as hospitals, quarries and coal-mines; that in factories, in offices, in prisons countless thousands toiled at every hour of the day, and that it would not relieve the distress of a single human being if yet another were to torment himself needlessly. Were one to attempt, I was quite certain, to visualize the misery that existed at any one time all over the world, there would be an end of one's sleep and the smiles would die on one's lips. But it was never the suffering that one pictured to oneself, that one imagined, that stunned and devastated one; it was only what one had seen in the flesh with eyes of compassion, that stirred and shattered one. In the midst of my exaltation I had seemed to see, as near and real as in a vision, the pale distorted features of the crippled girl, had seen her drag herself across the room on her crutches, heard the tap-tap and the clanking and creaking of the concealed supports on the helpless limbs; and in a moment of dismay, as it were, without thinking, without reflecting, I had pulled in the reins. It was of no use my now saying to myself: what good does your riding along at a stupid trot instead of at a tempestuous, exhilarating gallop do anyone? For a blow had been struck at some place or other in my heart in the neighbourhood of my conscience; I no longer had the courage to experience, in all the freedom of vigour and health, the joys of the body. Slowly, sleepily we trotted along towards the coppice that led to the parade-ground, and it was not until we were completely out of sight of the *Schloss* that I roused myself and said: nonsense! Enough of this stupid sentimentality! I gave the order: "Gallop!"

It all began with that sudden pull at the reins, which was, so to speak, the first symptom of the strange poisoning of my spirit by pity. At first I felt only dimly—just as one does when one is ill and wakes up light-headed—that something had happened, or was happening, to me. Hitherto, in my circumscribed life, I had simply lived for the day. I had bothered only about what my friends, my superiors, found amusing or important, but I had never taken a personal interest in anything, nor had anyone in me. Never yet had anything actually moved me profoundly. My family affairs were settled for me, my profession, my career was mapped out and defined, and this freedom from responsibility— only now did I realize it—had, without my knowing it, been very agreeable. And now suddenly something had happened in me, *to* me—nothing that was apparent on the surface, nothing that had any appearance of being real. And yet that one angry look, that moment when I had perceived in the eyes of a crippled girl hitherto undreamed-of depths of human suffering, had rent something asunder within me, and I now felt a sudden warmth streaming through my being, precipitating that mysterious fever that was, and continued to be, as inexplicable to me as an illness always is to the sufferer. I realized that I had stepped outside the fixed circle of the conventions within which I had hitherto lived securely and had entered a new sphere, which, like all that is novel, was at once exciting and disquieting: for the first time I saw an emotional abyss opening out before me, to survey which, to hurl myself down into which, seemed in some inexplicable way alluring. But at the same time an instinct warned me against yielding to such wanton curiosity, and said, "Enough. You have made your apologies. You have cleared up the whole silly business." But, "Go and see her once more," another voice whispered within me. "Feel that shudder run down your spine once more, that trickle of fear and expectation." And, "Keep away," came the warning again. "Don't force your company on her, don't intrude on her. These extravagant emotions will be too much for you, simpleton that you are, and you'll make an even worse fool of yourself than the first time."

Surprisingly enough, the decision was taken from me, for three days later I found a letter from Kekesfalva lying on my table, asking me whether I would care to dine with them on Sunday. Only men were to be present this time, among them Lieutenant-Colonel von F. from the War Ministry, of whom he had spoken to me, and, of course, his daughter and Ilona would be particularly pleased to see me. I am not ashamed to admit that this invitation made me, if anything a shy and retiring young man, very proud. They had not forgotten me, then, and the remark that Lieutenant-Colonel von F. was coming seemed, moreover, to indicate that Kekesfalva (I realized at once that it was out of a feeling of gratitude) was discreetly trying to secure influential friends for me.

And indeed I had no need to repent of having instantly accepted the invitation. The evening turned out to be a really pleasant one, and I, a mere subaltern, about whom nobody in the regiment bothered very much, was conscious of encountering quite unusual cordiality on the part of these elderly and distinguished gentlemen; evidently Kekesfalva had gone out of his way to draw their attention to me. For the first time in my life I was treated by a superior officer of high rank without any trace of condescension. Lieutenant-Colonel von F. inquired whether I was happy in my regiment and what were my prospects of promotion. He told me not to hesitate to call on him if I went to Vienna or needed his help at any time. The notary, a bald-headed, cheerful man with a good-natured, beaming moon of a face, invited me to his house; the director of the sugar-factory repeatedly addressed his conversation to me and what different conversation it was from that in our mess, where I was obliged to endorse every opinion expressed by a superior officer with a "Just so, sir!" Far sooner than I had expected an agreeable feeling of self-assurance stole over me, and in half an hour's time I was joining without constraint in the conversation.

Once again dishes were served that I had known hitherto only from hearsay or the boasting of well-to-do fellow-officers: caviar, icy-cold and delicious, which I tasted for the first time, venison pasty and pheasant, and, one after another, those wines that so pleasantly titillated the senses. I know it is stupid to let oneself be impressed by such things. But—why deny it?—it was with positively childish vanity that I, an insignificant young greenhorn, enjoyed dining in such Lucullan fashion with these eminent elderly gentlemen. Good lord, I kept thinking, good lord, Vavrushka should be here to see all this, and that lousy fellow who's always been bragging to us about the princely meals he and his friends have had at Sacher's in Vienna. They should jolly well come to a house like this for once, and then they'd open their eyes and mouths wide. Yes, if only they could see me sitting here so cheerily, the beastly dogs in the manger, could see the Lieutenant-Colonel from the War Ministry drinking my health, could see me deep in a friendly discussion with the director of the sugar-factory, and could hear him remark quite seriously, "I say, how well-informed you are!"

Black coffee was served in the drawing-room, brandy made its bow in huge, big-bellied ice-cold glasses, accompanied by a whole kaleidoscope of liqueurs, and those marvellous fat cigars, of course, with the imposing bands. In the midst of the conversation Kekesfalva bent over me to ask whether I would prefer to join the gentlemen at cards or to stay and chat with the ladies. The latter, of course, I declared with alacrity, for I should not have felt altogether easy at risking a rubber with a Lieutenant-Colonel from the War Ministry. If I won, I might perhaps annoy him; if I lost, then goodbye to my month's allowance. And then, too, I remembered that I had only twenty crowns on me.

And so, while the card-table was being put out in the adjoining room, I sat down by the two girls, and oddly enough—was it the wine or my own good spirits that cast a glamour over everything?—they both of them seemed to me today to be looking uncommonly pretty. Edith did not look so pale, so sallow, so sickly as when I had last seen her. Had she put on some rouge in honour of her guests, or was it really the general animation that had brought a flush to her cheeks? At any rate, there was no sign of the drawn, tremulous line round her lips or the petulant twitching of her brows. There she sat in a long pink gown; no rug, no coverlet concealed her infirmity, and yet I and the rest of the company were in too good a mood to think of "it". As for Ilona, I even had a faint suspicion that she was slightly tipsy, so brightly did her eyes twinkle, and when, with a smile, she threw back her lovely rounded shoulders, I positively had to draw back to withstand the temptation of touching her bare arms as though by accident.

After so excellent a dinner, with a brandy at the back of my throat sending glorious warmth throughout my body, a fat cigar in my mouth, its smoke tickling my nose deliciously, and two pretty, vivacious girls beside me, I should have been the dullest of clods had I found any difficulty in chatting away gaily. I know that I am usually a good conversationalist, except when inhibited by my confounded shyness. But this time I was somehow or other in tip-top form, and I chattered away with real animation. Of course, they were only silly little stories that I regaled them with: the latest happenings in barracks, the story, for instance, of how, the week before, the Colonel, wishing to send off an express letter in time to catch the mail to Vienna, had sent for an Uhlan, a regular Ruthenian peasant lad, and impressed on him that the letter must go off to Vienna at once, whereupon the dolt had dashed off post-haste to the stables, saddled his horse and galloped off along the high-road to Vienna! If we hadn't rung up the next garrison and let them know, the silly ass would actually have done the whole eighteen hours' ride to Vienna. Lord knows I didn't bore them and myself with a lot of profound and clever stuff, I really only retold the most humdrum stories, barrack-room yarns and so forth, but to my infinite astonishment, I amused the two girls no end, and they never stopped laughing for a moment. Edith's laugh sounded particularly exuberant with its high, silvery note and occasional shrill treble, but her gaiety must quite genuinely have come from within, for the skin of her thin cheeks, transparent and delicate as porcelain, took on a warmer and warmer hue; a flush of health, of positive prettiness, lit up her face, and her grey eyes, as a rule somewhat steely and hard, sparkled with childish delight. It was good to look at her when she forgot her fettered body, for at such moments her movements became more and more relaxed, her gestures more natural; she leaned back at her ease, she laughed, drank, drew Ilona down to her and put her arm round her shoulders. There was no denying that they both enjoyed my escapades famously. It is always encouraging for a talker to find that he is being a success, and a whole string of stories that I had long since forgotten came back to me. Usually shy and embarrassed, I now discovered in myself a boldness quite new to me; I made them laugh and laughed with them. The three of us giggled together in the corner like school-children.

And yet, whilst I was joking and laughing away like this, seemingly entirely absorbed in our jolly little group, I was all the time half unconsciously, half consciously, aware that I was being watched by a pair of eyes. A pair of eyes that was gazing at me from over a pair of spectacles, from the card-table, and the look in those eyes was a warm happy look which increased my own feeling of happiness. Stealthily, for I imagine he felt ashamed in the presence of the others, the old man peered across at us from time to time over his cards, and once, when I caught his eye, he gave me an intimate, friendly nod. At that moment his face shone with the radiant intentness of one listening to music.

And so it went on, with never a pause in our chatter, until nearly midnight, when further delectable refreshments were served, drinks and heavenly sandwiches. And, strange to say, I was not the only one who fell to with a will. The two girls also helped themselves liberally, they too drank freely of the lovely, heavy, dark, old English port. But at last the time came to say farewell. Edith and Ilona shook me by the hand as though I were an old friend, a dear, trusted comrade. Of course I had to promise them to come again soon, the next day or the day after. We were all to be taken home in the car, and I went out into the hall with the three men. The butler was helping the Lieutenant-Colonel on with his things, and I was getting my own coat, when suddenly I felt someone trying to assist me into it. It was Herr von Kekesfalva, and in my bewilderment (for how could I, a mere youngster, let myself be waited on by the old gentleman), I mutely protested. "*Herr Leutnant*," he whispered in shy, urgent tones in my ear. "Oh, *Herr Leutnant!* You don't know, you can't imagine, how happy it has made me to hear the child really laugh again. She gets so little pleasure in life. And today she was just as she used to be before ... " At this moment the Lieutenant-Colonel joined us. "Well, are we going?" he smiled at me kindly. Of course Kekesfalva did not venture to go on talking in front of him, but suddenly I could feel the old man stroking my sleeve, very, very gently and shyly, as one might caress a child or a woman. There was infinite tenderness, infinite gratitude in the very reserve and reticence of his shy gesture. I felt that it conveyed so much happiness and so much despair that once again I was quite overcome, and as, with respectful bearing befitting a subaltern, I walked down the three steps to the car with the Lieutenant-Colonel, I had to pull myself together so that no one should remark my emotion.

I could not go to sleep at once that night; I was too agitated. Insignificant as the reason for this might appear objectively, for all that had happened, after all, was that an old man had tenderly stroked my sleeve, that one restrained gesture of heart-felt gratitude had sufficed to cause some emotional spring deep down within me to well up and overflow. There had been in that tentative caress a tenderness of such chaste and passionate ardour as I had never yet encountered even in a woman. For the first time in my life I had received an assurance that I had been of use to someone on this earth, and my astonishment at the thought that I, a commonplace, unsophisticated young officer, should really have the power to make someone else so happy knew no bounds. I ought perhaps, in order to explain the intoxication that lay for me in this sudden discovery, to stress the fact that nothing had so weighed on me from childhood up as the conviction that I was an utterly superfluous individual, uninteresting to other people and at most an object of indifference. As a cadet at the military academy I had never been more than an average, a completely unimpressive scholar, I had never been one of the specially popular, specially favoured ones, and it had been just the same later on in the regiment. I was profoundly convinced that were I suddenly to disappear, to fall from my horse, let us say, and break my neck, my fellow-officers would no doubt remark "Pity about him," or "Poor Hofmiller!" but in a month's time no one would really miss me. Another man would be put in my place, would be given my mount, and others would perform my duties just as well or just as badly as I myself. And just as I had fared with my fellow-officers, so had I fared with the few girls with whom I had had liaisons in the two garrison towns in which I had been stationed: at Jaroslav a dentist's receptionist, at Wiener Neustadt a little seamstress. Anna and I had gone out together; I had taken her to my room on her free day, and given her a little coral necklace on her birthday; we had exchanged the usual tender phrases, and no doubt been sincere. Nevertheless, when I had been transferred, we had both rapidly found consolation elsewhere. For the first three months we had exchanged the usual letters and then had both formed fresh attachments; the only difference in her case being that in moments of tenderness she had called the other man "Ferdl" instead of "Toni". All over and done with, forgotten, but never hitherto had I, a young man of twenty-five, been carried away by an intense, passionate emotion, and I myself had expected and demanded no more of life than to be able to perform my duties decently and correctly and in no way to create a bad impression.

But now, however, the unexpected had happened, and I surveyed myself with amazement and startled curiosity. What was this? Could it be that an ordinary young fellow like me had power over other people? That I, who had not fifty crowns to call my own, was able to give a rich man more happiness than all his friends? That I, Lieutenant Hofmiller, could be of help to someone, a comfort to someone? That if I went and spent an afternoon chatting to a lame, tormented girl, her eyes brightened, new life came into her cheeks, and a household that was over-cast with gloom was flooded with light because of my presence?

In my excitement I walked so rapidly through the dark streets that I grew quite warm. My heart swelled so within me that I felt like tearing open my coat. For a fresh, a second surprise, emerging out of the first, forced itself on my consciousness: the surprising discovery, which was even more intoxicating, that it had been so easy, so incredibly easy, to gain friendship of these strangers. What was it I had done, after all? I had merely shown a little sympathy, had spent two evenings, two delightful, jolly, exhila-rating evenings, at the house—and that had been enough. How stupid, then, to idle away one's leisure time day after day at the café, playing boring games of cards with dull-witted companions, or strolling up and down the promenade. No, from now on no more of this torpid existence, this beastly lounging about. And so, as I strode more and more rapidly through the soft night, I, a young man suddenly awakened to life, resolved with real fervour that from now on I would change my way of life. I would go less often to the café, would give up playing billiards and that wretched *tarock*, would have done once and for all with all those efforts to kill time that were of no earthly use to anyone and only blunted my own intelligence. Instead, I said to myself, I shall go often to see that poor sick girl, shall even take the trouble to see that I always have something diverting or agreeable to tell the two of them; we'll play chess together or pass the time in some other pleasant way. The very resolve to help and from now on to be of use to others inspired me with a kind of enthusiasm. In my elation I felt like singing, like doing something quite crazy. It is never until one realizes that one means something to others that one feels there is any point or purpose in one's own existence.

This was how it came about that during the next few weeks I spent the latter part of the afternoons, and as a rule the evenings as well, at the Kekesfalvas'. Very soon these friendly chats became a habit and, what is more, a form of indulgence that was not without its dangers. What a temptation for a young man who from childhood up had been buffeted about from one military institution to another unexpectedly to find a home, a home after his heart, instead of bleak barrack-rooms and smoke-filled mess-rooms. When, at half-past four or five, my duties finished, I strolled out there, my hand would no sooner lift the knocker than Josef would delightedly throw open the door as though he had seen me coming through a magic spy-hole. In all sorts of delightful, obvious ways I was made to realize that I was regarded as one of the family. Every one of my little weaknesses and predilections was anticipated and encouraged; my favourite brand of cigarettes was always laid out ready for me, the book that on my last visit I had happened to say I should like to read I would find lying, as though by chance, the pages carefully cut, on the little stool; one particular armchair opposite Edith's chaise-longue was regarded incontestably as "my" chair—trifles, mere nothings, all these, to be sure, but such things as imperceptibly cast a homely warmth over a strange room and, without one's being aware of it, cheer and lighten the spirit. There I would sit, feeling more at ease than ever I did among my comrades, chatting and joking away as the mood took me, realizing for the first time that any form of constraint fetters the true forces of the spirit and that the real measure of a man is only revealed when he feels entirely at his ease.

But yet another, far more mysterious, factor was responsible for the fact that I found the daily company of the two girls so exhilarating. Ever since I had been sent, at an early age, to the military academy, that is to say, for the last ten or fifteen years, I had lived continuously in a masculine, a male environment. From morning till night, from night till morning, in the dormitory at the military academy, in camp, in barracks, in the mess and on the march, in the riding-school and in the class-room, always and always I had breathed an air that reeked of the male, first of boys, then of grown lads, but always of men, men; I had grown used to their virile gestures, their firm, noisy tread, their guttural voices, their tobacco-like smell, their free and easy ways and sometimes coarseness. To be sure, I was extremely fond of most of my fellow-officers, and could not really complain that my feelings were not reciprocated. But there was one exhilarating element that this male atmosphere lacked; it contained, as it were, insufficient ozone, insufficient power to rouse, invigorate, stimulate, quicken, electrify; and just as our excellent military band despite its exemplary rhythm and swing, nevertheless remained a brass band, its music therefore harsh, blaring, depending solely for its effect on rhythm, because it lacked the delicately sensuous tones of stringed instruments, so did even our jolliest times in barracks lack that element of subtlety which the presence or even the mere proximity of women invisibly adds to all social intercourse. Even when, as fourteen-year-old cadets, we had promenaded two by two through the town in our smart gold-laced uniforms and had come across other lads flirting or chatting idly with girls, we had felt regretfully that because of our monastic incarceration our young lives had been violently robbed of something that was every day permitted to our contemporaries as a matter of course, in the streets, in the parks, in railway trains and in dance-halls: the untrammelled enjoyment of the society of young girls. We, segregated, imprisoned behind iron bars, stared at these short-skirted imps as though at enchanted beings, dreaming of even a single conversation with a girl as of something unattainable. Deprivation of that kind is not easily forgotten. The fact that, later on, swift and, for the most part, cheap adventures with all kinds of accommodating wenches came our way, by no means compensated for those sentimental boyish dreams, and I could tell by the gauche and clumsy way in which I stammered and stuttered whenever I happened to be introduced to a young girl in society (although I had by this time slept with a dozen women) that long years of deprivation had impaired, robbed me of, my naïve and natural ease of manner.

And now all of a sudden that unavowed yearning to form for once a friendship with young women, instead of with moustachioed, male, uncouth fellow-officers, was being fulfilled in the most perfect way. Every afternoon I sat, completely at home, with the two girls; the limpidity, the femininity of their voices, gave me a sense (I cannot express it otherwise) of positively physical wellbeing, and it was with a feeling of almost indescribable happiness that for the first time in my life I enjoyed complete freedom from shyness in the presence of young girls. For the specially happy thing about our relationship was the fact that, because of the unique circumstances, there was none of the galvanic tension which is as a rule inevitably present when two young people of opposite sexes spend a long time in each other's company. During the long hours when we sat chatting together there was a complete absence of that hot-house atmosphere that usually makes a *tête-à-tête* in the half-darkness so dangerous. At first, I am bound to admit, the full voluptuous lips, the plump comely arms of Ilona, the Magyar sensuousness revealed in all her soft, lithe movements, had excited me, young fellow that I was, in the most agreeable fashion. More than once I had had to steel my hands against the desire to crush the warm, soft creature with the laughing black eyes just once in my arms and cover her with kisses. But Ilona had confided to me right at the very beginning of our acquaintance that she had been engaged for two years to a law student in Beskeret and was only waiting for some improvement in Edith's condition, or her complete recovery, to marry him—I gathered that Kekesfalva had promised his poor relation a dowry should she wait until then. And besides, of what crudeness, what perfidy would we not have been guilty if, without being really in love, we had indulged in furtive kissing and hand-holding behind the back of the pathetic creature who was fettered so helplessly to her invalid chair. Ilona's initial sensuous, tantalizing attraction very soon ceased to trouble me, and whatever I was able to feel in the way of affection was concentrated more and more fervently on the hapless creature with whom life had dealt so harshly, for, inevitably, in the secret chemistry of the emotions the feeling of pity for a sick person is imperceptibly bound up with tenderness. To sit by the lame girl, to cheer her with my conversation, to see her wan, restless mouth soothed by a smile, or at those moments when, yielding to a fit of temper, she would start up impatiently, to reduce her to shamefaced submission by a mere touch of the hand and to receive in return a grateful look from her grey eyes—such little intimacies incidental to my platonic friendship with this helpless invalid made me happier than the most passionate love-affair with another woman could have done. Thanks to these mild spiritual up-heavals, I discovered—for how much fresh knowledge had I already to thank these last few days—tender zones of feeling hitherto completely unknown and unsuspected.

Unknown and unsuspected tender zones of feeling—but also, it must be admitted, very dangerous ones! For, despite the most resolute efforts, it is never possible for a relationship between a healthy person and an invalid, a free person and a prisoner, to hang fire for ever. Unhappiness makes people vulnerable, incessant suffering unjust. Just as in the relations between creditor and debtor there is always an element of the disagreeable that can never be overcome, for the very reason that the one is irrevocably committed to the role of giver and the other to that of receiver, so in a sick person a latent feeling of resentment at every obvious sign of consideration is always ready to burst forth. One had constantly to be on one's guard against overstepping the scarcely perceptible boundary beyond which sympathy, instead of sooth-ing, only hurt her the more. On the one hand, pampered as she was, she demanded to be waited on by everyone like a princess and cosseted like a child; on the other hand this very consideration for her was likely to embitter her, since it made her more acutely aware of her own helplessness. If, for instance, one obligingly pushed the little stool nearer to her to spare her the effort of having to reach out for book or cup, she would flare up, her eyes flashing: "Do you imagine I can't look after myself?" Just as a caged animal sometimes, for no apparent reason, will attack the keeper whom it usually fawns upon, so from time to time she was seized with a malicious desire to shatter at one blow the serenity of the atmosphere by suddenly referring to herself as "a wretched cripple". At such moments of tension one had to keep a tight hold on oneself in order not to upbraid her unfairly for her can-tankerousness.

But to my own astonishment I found the requisite strength again and again. In some mysterious way, once one has gained an insight into human nature, that insight grows from day to day, and he to whom it has been given to experience vicariously even one single form of earthly suffering, acquires, by reason of this tragic lesson, an understanding of all its forms, even those most foreign to him, and apparently abnormal. I refused, therefore, to be put off by her occasional fits of rebellion; on the contrary, the more unfair and unwarranted were her outbursts, the more did they move me; gradually, too, I realized why my visits, my presence, were so welcome to Edith's father and Ilona, to the whole household. Long protracted suffering is apt to exhaust not only the invalid, but the compassion of others; violent emotions cannot be prolonged endlessly. Edith's father and Ilona certainly shared to the full the sufferings of the poor impatient invalid, but by now their capacity for suffering was to some extent spent, they had become resigned to it. They regarded the invalid as an invalid, her lameness as a fact; they now waited with downcast eyes until the brief nerve-storms had played themselves out. But they were no longer appalled as I was appalled each time afresh, and because I was the only one to whom her suffering was a continually fresh source of consternation, I came to be the only one in whose presence she was ashamed of her lack of control. I had only to say, when she lost her self-control, "My dear Fräulein Edith" and the grey eyes would be lowered obediently. She would blush, and one could tell that she would have liked to run away from herself; but her crippled legs fettered her to her chair. And I could never take leave of her without her saying in a certain pleading way that shook me to the core, "You *will* come tomorrow, won't you? You're not angry with me because of all the stupid things I said today?" At such moments I felt a kind of obscure amazement at the thought that I, who had, after all, given her nothing except my sincere sympathy, should possess so much power over another person.

But it is the way of young people that each fresh piece of knowledge of life should go to their heads, and that once uplifted by an emotion they can never have enough of it. As soon as I discovered that my ability to feel pity was a force that not only stirred me myself positively pleasurably, but extended its beneficent influence beyond my own personality, a strange metamorphosis began to take place within me. Ever since I had first allowed this capacity for sympathy to enter into my being, it seemed to me as though a toxin had found its way into my blood and had made it run warmer, redder, faster, pulsate and throb more vigorously. All of a sudden I could no longer understand the slothful torpor in which I had hitherto lived as though in a grey, insipid twilight. A hundred and one things to which I had never even given a passing thought began to excite me and to occupy my thoughts. All around me I perceived, as though that first glimpse into the sufferings of another had given me a fresh, a keener, a more understanding eye, things that engaged my attention, thrilled me, shook me. And since this whole world of ours is crammed, street upon street, room upon room, with poignant tragedies, drenched through and through with burning misery and distress, my days were passed from morn till night in a state of heightened attentiveness and expectation. Strange—I found, when trying new mounts for the regiment, that all of a sudden I could no longer, as formerly, give a stubborn horse a savage blow over the crupper without a pang, for I was guiltily aware of the pain I was causing and the weals seared my own skin. Or, again, I would find myself digging my nails into the palms of my hands when our testy Captain struck a poor Ruthenian Uhlan a resounding blow in the face with his clenched fist for saddling a horse badly, and the lad stood there rigidly at attention, his hands pressed to his sides. The soldiers standing about would either stare or laugh vacuously, but I, I alone, would see the hot tears of shame spring to the lashes of the dull-witted lad beneath his lowered lids. All of a sudden, too, I found I could no longer stand the ribald jokes in the officers' mess at the expense of clumsy or awkward comrades; ever since I had realized in the person of the weak, defenceless Edith the torture of helplessness, I was revolted by any act of brutality and moved to pity by any form of helplessness. Countless trifling things that had hitherto escaped my attention I now noticed, ever since chance had squeezed into my eyes those first hot drops of sympathy; little, simple things, but each of them with the power to move and stir me deeply. It struck me, for instance, that the woman at the tobacconist's shop where I always bought my cigarettes held the coins that I handed to her remarkably close to the thick lenses of her spectacles, and I was immediately troubled by a suspicion that she might be suffering from cataract. The next day, I thought, I would ask her about it very tactfully and perhaps ask Goldbaum, our regimental doctor, to be so kind as to examine her. Or it occurred to me that the volunteers had of late been pointedly cutting that little red-haired chap K, and I remembered having seen in the newspaper (how could *he* help it, the poor lad?) that his uncle had been sent to prison for embezzlement; I made a point of sitting by him in the mess and entered into a lengthy conversation, immediately perceiving from his look of gratitude that he knew I was doing it simply to show the others how unsporting and caddish their behaviour was. Or I would put in a word for one of my troop whom the Colonel had ordered four hours' fatigue duty.

Again and again, day after day, I found fresh opportunities for indulging, trying out, this passion that had suddenly possessed me. And I said to myself: from now on, help anyone and everyone so far as in you lies. Cease to be apathetic, indifferent. Exalt yourself by devoting yourself to others, enrich yourself by making everyone's destiny your own, by enduring and understanding every facet of human suffering through your pity. And my heart, astonished at its own workings, quivered with gratitude towards the sick girl whom I had unwittingly hurt and who, through her suffering, had taught me the creative magic of pity.

Well, I was soon to be awakened from romantic emotions of this kind, and pretty thoroughly too. We had been playing dominoes one afternoon, and then had talked and whiled away the time so agreeably that we none of us noticed how late it was. At length, at half-past eleven, I looked up in dismay at the clock and hurriedly took my leave. But as Herr von Kekesfalva accompanied me out into the hall, we heard from outside a humming and droning as of thousands and thousands of bumblebees. The rain was drumming on the eaves in a regular downpour. "The car will take you home," Kekesfalva reassured me. That was quite unnecessary, I protested; the thought that the chauffeur should, solely on my account, have to dress again at half-past eleven and get out the car, which had already been put away in the garage, was really distressing to me. (All this consideration for, entering into the feelings of, others was entirely novel to me; I had only acquired the habit during these last few weeks.)

67

But, after all, there was considerable temptation in the thought of whizzing home comfortably in a soft, well-sprung coupé in foul weather like this instead of trudging for half an hour, dripping wet, along the muddy high-road in thin shoes; and so I gave in. Despite the rain, the old man refused to be deterred from seeing me to the car and putting the rug over my knees. The chauffeur started up, and we raced off homewards through the pelting rain.

It was wonderfully comfortable and luxurious, speeding along so noiselessly and smoothly in the car. Nevertheless, as we now turned off towards the barracks—we had reached the town in an incredibly short time—I knocked on the glass partition and begged the chauffeur to stop when he reached the Rathausplatz. Better not drive past the barracks in Kekesfalva's elegant coupé, I thought. I knew it didn't look well for a subaltern to come rolling up like a Grand Duke in a posh car and be assisted out of it by a chauffeur in livery. That kind of showing off was not regarded with favour by the bigwigs, and my own instinct, besides, had long told me to mix my two worlds as little as possible—the luxurious world of the Kekesfalvas where I was a free man, independent, pampered, and the other world, the world of duty, in which I had to keep my place, in which I was a poor devil who felt himself lucky if the month had thirty instead of thirty-one days. Without my knowing it, one side of me was reluctant to have anything to do with the other; sometimes I was no longer able to decide who was the real Toni Hofmiller, the one who was a mere subaltern or the one who spent his time at the Kekesfalvas.

The chauffeur drew up obediently in the Rathausplatz, two streets away from the barracks. I got out, turned up my collar and was about to walk rapidly across the wide square. But just at that moment the storm burst forth with redoubled fury, and the wind rained wet blows full in my face. Better, therefore, to wait a few minutes in the shelter of a house-door before running across the two streets to the barracks. Or, to be sure, the café was still open and I could sit there in safety until the heavens had emptied the contents of their largest watering-can. The café was only six doors away, and lo and behold, behind the dripping window-panes there was still a glimmer of gas-light. Perhaps some of my comrades were still squatting round our table; it would be a splendid opportunity to set things right, for it was high time I put in an appearance again. Yesterday, the day before yesterday, the whole of this week and last week I had absented myself. Really, they had every reason to be fed up with me, for even if one is fickle, one should at least observe the formalities.

I opened the door. In the front half of the café the lights were already extinguished for reasons of economy, newspapers were lying about all over the place, and Eugen, the head waiter, was counting the takings. Only in the billiard-room at the back could I still see a light and the glimmer of polished uniform buttons. Yes, by Jove, there they still were, those everlasting *tarock* players, Jozsi, Ferencz, and Goldbaum, the regimental doctor. Evidently they had long since finished their game, and were merely lolling about in that familiar state of café inertia in which one is afraid to make a move; and so it was a regular godsend for them that my arrival should break in upon their boredom and lethargy.

"Hallo ... here's Toni!" announced Ferencz to the others, and, "What an honour for our lowly dwelling!" exclaimed the regimental doctor, who, as we used to chaff him, suffered from quotation diarrhoea. Six sleepy eyes blinked up and smiled at me. "*Servus! Servus!*"

I was pleased that they were so glad to see me. Really capital chaps, I thought to myself. Haven't held it against me at all that I've made myself scarce all this time without a word of apology or explanation.

"Black coffee," I ordered the sleepy waiter who came shuffling up, and settled into my chair with the inevitable, "Well, what's the latest?" with which every conversation opened whenever we met.

Ferencz puffed out his cheeks until his round face seemed more moon-like than ever, his twinkling eyes almost disappearing in his rosy apple cheeks; slowly, doughily, his mouth opened.

"Well, the *very* latest," he said with a comfortable grin, "is that your Lordship has deigned once more to grace our humble hovel with his noble presence."

And the regimental doctor leaned back and began to declaim from Goethe: "Mahadöh, the god of earth, for one last time

came down below, to take upon himself thy form, and feel with
thee both joy and pain."

All three looked at me with sardonic amusement, and I felt my
heart sink into my boots. Better make my escape quickly, I
thought, before they begin to ask me why I have stayed away all
this time and where I have just come from. But before I could
collect my wits Ferencz winked in an odd way and nudged Jozsi.

"Look there!" he said, pointing under the table. "What d'you
think of that? Patent-leather shoes, if you please, in this lousy
weather, and full regimentals. He's a lad, is our Toni, he's dug
himself in nicely. They do themselves proud, I'm told, out there
at the old Manichaean's. Five courses every evening, the apothecary tells me, caviare and spring chicken, real Bols and choice
cigars—very different from our hogwash at the old pub. Oh yes,
I tell you, we've all underrated our Toni, he knows a thing or
two!"

Jozsi at once backed him up. "The only thing is, he's a poor
sort of pal. Yes, my dear Toni, instead of saying to your old
buffer out there, 'See here, old boy, I have a couple of smart
friends, frightfully decent, jolly fine fellows, don't eat with their
knives either, I'll bring 'em along some time'—instead of that, he
thinks to himself, let 'em go on swilling their filthy Pilsner and
peppering their throats to a frazzle with their wretched goulash!
Jolly way of behaving, I must say! Everything for himself and
damn-all for the others. Oh well, I suppose you've at least
brought me a nice fat Upmann. In that case, you're let off for
today."

They all three laughed and smacked their lips. But I blushed
crimson from my collar to my ears. For, devil take it, how could
that confounded Jozsi have guessed that Kekesfalva had, as usual,
slipped one of his best cigars into my pocket as I was leaving?
Could it be sticking out between the buttons of my tunic? If only
the fellows didn't notice. In my embarrassment I forced a laugh.

"Why, of course—an Upmann! The best is good enough for
you, my boy. 'Fraid you'll have to make shift with one of our so-
called Egyptians." And I offered him my cigarette-case. But even
as I did so my hand drew back with a jerk. The day before yesterday had been my twenty-fifth birthday; the girls had somehow

managed to find it out, and at dinner, as I had lifted my table-napkin from my plate, I had felt something heavy wrapped up in it: a birthday present of a cigarette-case. But Ferencz had already spotted the new acquisition—in our little set the most trifling incident was magnified into an event.

"Hallo, what's this?" he growled. "A new piece of equipment!" He promptly took the cigarette-case out of my hand (how could I prevent him?), fingered it, examined it, and finally weighed it in the palm of his hand. "I say," he said across the table to the regimental doctor, "this seems to me to be the real thing! Come along, have a good look at it—your governor deals in this kind of thing, I'm told, and you ought to know something about it."

Goldbaum, who was the son of a Jewish goldsmith in Drohobycz, clamped his pince-nez on to his somewhat fleshy nose, took the cigarette-case, weighed it, examined every facet of it and rapped on it with his knuckles in the manner of an expert.

"Genuine!" he pronounced at last. "Real gold, embossed and damned heavy. Would stop the teeth of the whole regiment! Value about seven or eight hundred crowns."

After this verdict, which astonished me myself, for I had supposed it to be gold-plated, he passed the case on to Jozsi, who handled it much more reverently than the two others (what respect we poor devils had for anything expensive!). He gazed at it, admired himself in it, fingered it, finally opened it by the jewelled clasp and gave a melodramatic start.

"Hallo—an inscription. Listen, just listen to this! 'To our dear friend Anton Hofmiller on his birthday. Ilona, Edith.' "

All three of them now stared at me. "The devil!" breathed Ferencz at last. "I must say you choose your friends well these days. My compliments! You'd have got a metal match-box case from me and have considered yourself deuced lucky!"

I felt a constriction at the throat. Tomorrow the whole regiment would know the wretched story of the gold cigarette-case and would have learned the inscription by heart. "Let's have a look at it, that swagger case of yours," Ferencz would say in the officers' mess, just to get a rise out of me, and I should have to display it *gehorsamst* to the Captain, *gehorsamst* to the Major, and perhaps, even, *gehorsamst* to the Colonel. They would all weigh it in their hands, estimate its value, and chuckle ironically at the inscription; then would come the inevitable ragging and cross-questioning, and it would be impossible for me to be offensive in the presence of my superior officers.

In my embarrassment, and in order to bring the conversation to a speedy close, I inquired: "Well—any of you chaps feel like another game?"

At this their good-humoured chortles turned to hearty laughter. "What d'you think of that, Ferencz?" said Jozsi, nudging him in the ribs. "That's rich! At half-past twelve, when the place is shutting, he wants to begin playing *tarock.*"

And the regimental doctor leaned back, comatose and comfortable: "Well, well, a happy man pays no regard to time."

They laughed and went on savouring the stale joke for a while. But now the head waiter came up with a diffident air. "Time, gentlemen!" he pleaded. We walked together—the rain had abated—to the barracks and there shook hands and said good night. Ferencz patted me on the back. "Nice to have you back with us," he said, and I could tell that he meant it quite sincerely. Why, then, was I so furious with them? They were, after all, jolly decent chaps, all of them, without a trace of envy or malice. And even if they did rag me a little, they didn't mean anything by it.

They really hadn't meant it unkindly, the good chaps; all the same, their idiotic gaping and whispering had destroyed something in me that could never be restored: my confidence. For until now my strange relationship with the Kekesfalvas had in some wonderful way increased my self-esteem. For the first time in my life I had felt myself to be someone who gave, who helped; and now I had been made to realize how others regarded this relationship, or rather, how it was bound to be regarded from outside by those ignorant of the underlying circumstances. For what could they know of this subtle craving to be stirred by pity to which I had fallen a prey as though—I cannot express it otherwise—to some dark passion? To them it seemed beyond question that I had gained an entrée to this luxurious, hospitable household solely in order to insinuate myself into the good graces of the rich, to save myself the expense of evening meals and to cadge presents. They did not in their hearts hold this against me, they did not grudge me, good fellows that they were, the warm corner, the choice cigars; they obviously did not think—and it was precisely this that riled me—that there was anything in the least dishonourable or shabby in letting oneself be fêted and pampered by these "suckers", for in their view we cavalry officers were merely conferring an honour on an old moneybags by sitting down at his table. There had been not the faintest element of disapproval, therefore, in Ferencz's and Jozsi's admiration of my gold cigarette-case; on the contrary, they had even felt a certain respect for me for knowing how to make my Maecenas shell out. What really vexed me was that I began to doubt my own motives. Wasn't I, after all, really behaving like a sponger? Ought I, as an officer, as an adult person, to let myself be dined and wined evening after evening? That gold cigarette-case, for example—I ought never to have accepted it, nor the silk scarf that had recently been pressed on me when there had been a storm raging out of doors. A young man of my age should not allow people to slip cigars in his pocket to smoke on the way home, and tomorrow, by God, I must talk Kekesfalva out of that idea of his of getting me a new mount. Only now did it occur to me that the day before yesterday he had murmured something about my brown gelding (which, of course, I was paying for by instalments) not being up to scratch, and there he was right. But to let him lend me a three-year-old from his stables, a famous racehorse, which would do me credit—that wouldn't do at all. Lend—yes, I knew what he meant by that. He was trying to buy me, to pay cash down for my sympathy, for my entertaining company, just as he had promised Ilona a dowry simply to get her to stay and nurse his poor child. And I, simpleton that I was, had almost fallen into his trap without realizing that I was becoming a downright sponger.

Nonsense, I told myself once more, and remembered how the old man had timidly stroked my sleeve, how his face lit up every time I entered the house. I remembered the affectionate brotherly-sisterly relationship that existed between me and the two girls; they never seemed to notice if I happened to drink a glass too much, or if they did notice it, they were only too glad that I should feel at my ease in their company. Nonsense, crazy nonsense, I kept repeating to myself, nonsense—why, the old man was fonder of me than my own father.

But of what use is any amount of self-persuasion and self-encouragement once one's inner equilibrium has been shaken? I felt that Jozsi's and Ferencz's good-natured ragging had shattered my spontaneity. Do you really go there only out of pity, out of sympathy for these rich people? I kept asking myself. Are you not actuated to a certain extent by vanity, a desire for a good time? In any case, I must get the whole thing straight. No one shall say that I have forced myself on them. And as a preliminary measure I resolved in future to space my visits out and decided that the very next day I would omit my usual visit to the Kekesfalvas. The next day, therefore, I stayed away. The moment I came off duty I strolled across to the café with Jozsi and Ferencz, where we read the papers and played the inevitable game of *tarock*. But I played damned badly, for there was a round clock let into the panelled wall right opposite me—twenty past four, half-past four, twenty to five, ten to five—and instead of keeping my mind on the cards, I counted the time. Half-past four, that was the time I usually arrived for tea; it was always laid out ready, and if ever I were a quarter of an hour late, they would greet me with, "Has anything happened?" My punctual arrival had become such a matter of course that they counted on it without fail; no doubt they too would now be glancing up at the clock just as uneasily as I myself, and waiting and waiting. Wouldn't it, after all, be politer at least to telephone to say I was not coming? Or better, perhaps, send my batman ...

"I say, Toni, your playing's a scandal; do pay attention!" fumed Jozsi, giving me a furious look. My absent-mindedness had cost him the game. I pulled myself together.

"I say, can I change places with you?"

"Certainly, but why?"

"I don't know," I lied; "I think it's the din in this hole that's getting me down."

Actually it was the clock, which I was trying not to look at, and the relentless movement of the minute hand. My nerves were on edge, my thoughts were straying, and I kept on worrying as to whether I ought not to go to the telephone and make my excuses.

For the first time I began to perceive that true sympathy cannot be switched on and off like an electric current, that anyone who identifies himself with the fate of another is robbed to some extent of his own freedom.

But devil take it, I scolded myself, I am under no obligation to do the half-hour's trudge out there every day. And in response to the secret law of mental association which makes a man in a temper unconsciously vent his spleen on some completely inno-cent person, just as a billiard ball transmits the impact of the cue to another ball, my displeasure was now directed, not against Jozsi and Ferencz, but against the Kekesfalvas. Let them wait for me for once. I'd show them that I was not to be bought with presents and attentions, that I was not going to turn up to the minute like a masseur or a gym instructor. One should never create precedents; a habit was liable to become a duty, and I was not going to tie myself down. And so in my pig-headedness I sat on and on in the café for three and a half hours, until half-past seven, merely in order to prove conclusively to myself that I was entirely at liberty to come and go as I pleased, and that good food and choice cigars were a matter of complete indifference to me.

At half-past seven we all got up to go. Ferencz had suggested a stroll along the promenade. But no sooner had I emerged from the café in the wake of my two friends than I was conscious of a swift glance from a familiar pair of eyes as their owner hurried past. Wasn't that Ilona? Of course. Even had I not, only the day before yesterday, admired the wine-red dress and the panama trimmed with the broad ribbon, I should have recognized her from behind by the supple swaying of her hips as she walked. But where was she off to in such a hurry? This was not walking, it was racing. In any case, I must follow the pretty bird, however swiftly it might wing its way.

"Just a moment!" I said, taking leave of my bewildered friends somewhat brusquely and hurrying after the swinging skirt, that was by now across the road. For I was overjoyed at running into Ilona in my own world.

"Ilona, Ilona, stop, stop," I called after her; she was going at a tremendous pace. At length she stopped, without betraying the least sign of astonishment. She had, of course, seen me as she had flashed by.

"This is capital, Ilona, meeting you in the town like this. I've so often wanted to take you for a walk round our august city. Or shall we go to the old pâtisserie, and sit there for a while?"

"No, no," she murmured in some confusion. "I'm in a hurry. They're expecting me at home."

"Well, then, they can wait five minutes longer. If the worst comes to the worst I'll even give you a letter of excuse to take along with you so that they won't put you in the corner. Come along, and don't look at me so sternly." I wanted to take her arm. For I was honestly delighted at meeting Ilona, Ilona of all people, who was so pretty, so presentable, in my other world. But she was still rather on edge.

"No, I really must go," she said hastily. "The car's waiting for me over there." And, indeed, there was the chauffeur saluting us respectfully from the Rathausplatz.

"But at least you'll allow me to escort you to the car?"

"Well, of course," she murmured with remarkable testiness. "Of course . . . and by the way . . . why didn't you come this afternoon?"

"This afternoon?" I asked, deliberately dragging out my words as though to jog my memory. "This afternoon? Oh yes—it was a silly business, this afternoon. The Colonel wanted to buy a new mount and so we all had to go along with him and have a look at it and try it out." (This incident had actually happened a month ago. I'm really an appallingly poor liar.)

She hesitated and was about to make some retort. But why was she tearing at her glove, why was she tapping the ground so restlessly with her foot? Then she burst out: "Won't you at least come back with me to dinner?"

Be firm, I said quickly to myself. Don't give in. Hold out for one day at least. "What a pity!" I said with a regretful sigh. "I should have loved to come. But today's all booked up, we've got a reunion this evening, and I can't miss it."

She gave me a keen look—odd that she had the same impatient lines between her brows as Edith—and said not a word, I don't know whether out of intentional rudeness or embarrassment.

The chauffeur opened the door for her, and slamming it to, she asked through the window: "Are you coming tomorrow?"

"Oh yes, tomorrow of course." And the car drove off.

I wasn't very pleased with myself, I can tell you. Why had Ilona been in such a hurry, why had she been so embarrassed, as though she were afraid of being seen with me, and why had she driven off so impetuously? And then, too, I ought at least to have sent my regards to her uncle and some little message to Edith; after all, they'd done me no harm. But, on the other hand, I was pleased with my reserved behaviour, I had stood my ground. Now at least they couldn't say that I tried to thrust myself on them.

Although I had promised Ilona to turn up the following after-noon at the usual time, I thought it advisable to ring up before-hand. Better adhere strictly to the formalities, they were safeguards. I wanted it to be quite clear that I never forced my company on anyone in the house. I wanted from now on to make sure that every time I went I was expected, and expected with pleasure. This time there was certainly no need for me to have any lingering doubts on that score, for Josef awaited me at the door. "The *gnädiges Fräulein* is out on the tower and has left word that the *Herr Leutnant* should go straight up," he informed me in urgent, officious tones. "I don't believe the *Herr Leutnant* has been up there yet," he added. "He will be astonished to find how lovely it is."

He was right, good old Josef. I had actually never been up to the terrace at the top of the tower, although the curious and some-what mysterious building had frequently aroused my interest. Originally, as I have said, the turret of a *Schloss* that had long since fallen into ruins or been pulled down (even the girls did not know its exact history), the ponderous square tower had stood empty for years and now served as a store-room. As a child Edith had often, to the consternation of her parents, clambered up the somewhat rickety ladders to the attic at the top, where bats flapped sleepily about amongst piles of old lumber and one's every step on the old mouldering floor-boards sent dust and dirt flying up in thick clouds. But it was because of its very mysteriousness, its uselessness,

that the odd, imaginative child had specially selected this aban-
doned loft, the grimy windows of which offered an uninterrupted
view of the distant countryside, as a hiding-place and play-room.
When, however, she had been struck down by illness and could
no longer hope ever again to climb up to the romantic lumber-
rooms—her legs at first being completely paralysed—she had
felt as though she had been robbed of some precious treasure.
And her father would often see her gazing up at that beloved and
now suddenly lost paradise of her childhood. In order to give her
a surprise, Kekesfalva took advantage of the three months which
Edith spent at a German sanatorium to commission a Viennese
architect to reconstruct the old tower and to build a spacious
terrace at the top; and by the autumn, when she was brought
back because there had been no marked improvement in her
condition, the lofty tower had been provided with a lift which
was as roomy as that in a sanatorium, and enabled the child to
be taken up to her beloved watch-tower in her invalid chair
whenever she liked. Thus the world of her childhood was unexpectedly restored to her.

The architect, it is true, who had had to carry out the work in
a hurry, had paid less attention to purity of style than to technical
convenience; the bare cubic structure which he had clapped on
to the rugged square tower, would, with its straight, geometrical
lines, have been more in keeping with a harbour or a power-
station than with the comfortable florid Baroque curves of the
little *Schloss*, which must surely have dated back to the time of
Maria Theresa. But in essence it fulfilled Kekesfalva's hopes.
Edith, it transpired, was completely entranced by the terrace,
which in such unhoped-for fashion delivered her from the con-
finement and monotony of her sick-room. From this, her very
own, tower she could survey through her binoculars the vast
expanse of flat countryside, watch all that went on in the neighbourhood, sowing and reaping, work and play. After her long
period of seclusion she was once more linked with the world; she
would gaze out hour after hour from her tower at the toy of a
railway which, with its little wisps of smoke, wound its way
through the countryside; no vehicle on the road escaped her idle
curiosity, and, as I learned later on, she had followed many of

our rides, manoeuvres and parades with her telescope. Out of a curious feeling of jealousy, however, she kept this remote belvedere of hers, her private world, hidden from the eyes of all visitors to the house, and I realized from the impulsive enthusiasm of the faithful Josef that he considered the invitation to visit this usually inaccessible retreat a mark of special favour.

He suggested taking me up in the lift, and I could see how proud he was at being entrusted with the sole control of this expensive conveyance. But when he told me that a spiral staircase, lit on every floor by stone windows, also led up to the terrace, I refused his offer, picturing to myself how delightful it must be to see, as one climbed from landing to landing, wider and wider stretches of countryside opening out before one's eyes. And each of the small unglazed apertures did indeed offer a fresh and ever more enchanting view. A windless, transparently hot day hung like a golden web over the summery countryside. The smoke curled above the chimney-tops of the scattered houses and farm-steads in almost motionless rings; I could see—every contour seemed to be cut out of the steel-blue sky as though with a sharp knife—the peasants' thatched cottages with the inevitable storks' nest on the eaves, and the duck-ponds in front of the barns, which gleamed like polished metal. And in amongst it all, in the wax-coloured fields, tiny Lilliputian figures, dappled cows grazing, women weeding and washing, lumbering ox-drawn wagons, and little carts scurrying hither and thither among the neat checker-board of fields. When, after climbing the ninety-odd steps, I reached the top, my eyes were able to roam at will over the whole vast sweep of the Hungarian plain to where a thin streak, probably the Carpathian mountains, gleamed blue on the far-off, hazy horizon, and to my left shone out, neat and compact, our little town with its globular church tower. With the naked eye I could recognize our barracks, the town hall, the school, the parade-ground; and for the first time since my transfer to this garrison I became aware of the unassuming charm of this out-of-the-way corner of the world.

But it was impossible for me to yield myself up in tranquillity to this friendly vista, for the moment I reached the flat terrace I had to prepare myself to confront the invalid. At first I could see

no trace of her; the wicker chaise-longue in which she was resting had its broad back turned towards me, and like some brightly-
coloured shell, completely concealed the slender form. The table
beside it, on which stood a pile of books and an open gramophone, was all that revealed her presence. I hesitated to approach
her from behind; if she were resting or dreaming she might perhaps be startled. I therefore walked right round the terrace so as
to come upon her face to face. But as I crept circumspectly round
to the front I noticed that she was asleep. Her slender body had
been carefully tucked up, a soft rug wrapped round her feet, and
on a white pillow rested, a little to one side, and framed in light
auburn hair, her childish, oval face, to which the now sinking
sun lent an amber-golden glow of health.

Involuntarily I paused and utilized this moment of hesitancy
to survey the sleeping girl as though she were a picture. During
all the time we had spent together I had never actually had an
opportunity of looking straight at her, for, like all sensitive and
hyper-sensitive people, she put up an unconscious resistance to
letting herself be observed. Even if, when one was talking to her,
one's gaze rested on her merely by accident, the little angry furrow
would appear between her brows, her eyelids would flutter, her
lips twitch; not for an instant was it possible to catch a glimpse
of her profile in repose. But now, as she lay there with closed
eyes, I could scrutinize at my leisure (and I felt as though I were
committing an impropriety, a rape almost) the somewhat angular
and, so to speak, as yet unfinished features, in which the childish
was mingled in the most fascinating way with the womanly and
the frail. The lips, slightly parted as though she were thirsty,
breathed gently, but even this tiny effort caused her thin, childish
breast to rise and fall, and, as though exhausted, drained of
blood, the pale face, nestling in the auburn hair, sank back on
the pillow. I stole cautiously nearer. The shadows under the
eyes, the blue veins on the temples, the reddish transparency of
the nostrils, revealed what a thin and colourless outer shell it was
that protected the alabaster-pale flesh from the outside world.
How sensitive must one be, I thought to myself, for one's nerves
to throb so close beneath the surface, to be so exposed; how
immeasurably must one suffer if one had such an airily light,

elfin body, which seemed made to soar, to dance, to float, and were yet cruelly chained to the heavy, solid earth. Poor, fettered creature! Once again I felt that hot welling up of emotion within me, that painful, exhausting and yet wildly exciting gush of pity which overwhelmed me whenever I thought of the unfortunate creature. My hand trembled and I yearned to stroke her arm tenderly, to bend over her and to pluck a smile, so to speak, from her lips the moment she awoke and recognized me. A craving to display tenderness, an emotion that was inevitably mingled with my pity whenever I thought of her or looked at her, urged me to draw nearer to her. But I must not disturb this sleep, which kept her from herself, from the dread reality of her existence. It is a most wonderful thing to be close, to be near to the sick during their sleep, when all their feverish thoughts are held captive, when they are so completely oblivious of their infirmity that sometimes a smile lights upon their parted lips as a butterfly upon a delicate leaf, a smile foreign to them, a smile which does not belong to them, and which, moreover, is scared away on the very moment of awaking. What a mercy, I thought, that the crippled, the maimed, those whom Fate has cheated, at least in sleep have no knowledge of the shapeliness or unshapeliness of their bodies, that there at least that kindly deceiver, the dream, reveals their form to them as a thing of beauty and symmetry, that at least in the nebulous world of slumber the sufferer can escape the curse to which he is physically chained. What moved me most at this moment, however, were the hands which lay crossed on the coverlet, the dimly-veined, outstretched hands with their fragile, slender knuckles and tapering bluish nails— tender, bloodless, powerless hands, just strong enough, perhaps, to stroke little creatures, such as doves and rabbits, but too weak to clutch, to grasp anything. How is it possible, I thought with dismay, to beat off suffering with such feeble hands? How struggle against, seize, hold anything? And it almost repelled me to think of my own hands, those firm, heavy, muscular, strong hands which could control the most refractory horse with a tug at the reins. Involuntarily I found my gaze now resting on the rug, which lay, shaggy and heavy, far too heavy for this airy, insubstanial creature, across the thin knees. Beneath this opaque covering the impotent legs—I did not know whether they were smashed, crippled or merely atrophied, and I had never had the courage to ask—lay lifeless, stretched taut in that steel or leather contraption. I remembered how at each step the cruel apparatus hung like a dead weight on the crippled limbs, how she was condemned to drag the repulsive, clattering, grinding things for ever along with her—she so tender, so delicate, she of all people, she to whom one felt that floating and leaping and soaring aloft would come more naturally even than walking.

I could not suppress a shudder at the thought, and so violent was the tremor that ran through my frame that my spurs jingled. It must have been an infinitesimally small, scarcely audible sound, this silvery jingle, but it seemed to penetrate the thin veil of her sleep.

She still did not open her eyes as she drew a long, uneasy breath, but her hands began to stir; gradually they unclasped, the fingers stretched, tautened themselves, as though awaking with a yawn. Then her lids fluttered tentatively and her eyes darted about her in surprise.

Suddenly her gaze fell upon me and became set in a fixed stare; the message had not yet been transmitted from the purely optical field to the sphere of conscious thought and memory. But then with a start she was wide awake, she had recognized me, and the blood gushed crimson to her cheeks. Once again it was as though red wine had been poured into a crystal glass.

"How stupid of me!" she said with a frown. She clutched nervously at the rug which had fallen off her knees, and drew it closer to her as though I had surprised her in a state of nudity. "How stupid of me. I must have dozed off for a moment." And her nostrils began—how well I knew the signs of the oncoming storm—to twitch. She looked at me challengingly.

"Why didn't you wake me straight away?" she asked. "You shouldn't stare at a person who's asleep. It's not done. People always look ridiculous when they're asleep."

Thoroughly upset at having annoyed her by my considerateness, I tried to save the situation by making a feeble joke. "Better to be ridiculous when asleep," I said, "than ridiculous when awake."

But by now she had levered herself up by both elbows. The furrows between her brows deepened, and her lips began to quiver and tremble ominously. She gave me a sharp, searching look.

"Why didn't you come yesterday?"

This attack was too sudden for me to be ready with an easy answer, and before I had time to reply she went on inquisitorially:

"Surely you must have had some special reason for letting us sit and wait for you? Otherwise you would at least have rung."

Idiot that I was not to have foreseen this question and had my answer pat. I fidgeted from one foot to the other and stammered out the hoary old excuse about our having suddenly had an inspection of remounts. I had hoped to slip away by five o'clock, but unfortunately the Colonel had wanted to put one more horse through its paces, and so on and so on.

Her gaze, grey, severe and sharp, rested on me. The more I beat about the bush, the more impatient she became. I could see her fingers drumming on the arm of the chair.

"I see," she finally said in cold, hard tones. "And how did this touching story of the inspection end? Did the Colonel buy the horse after all?"

I realized that I had got myself into a deuce of a hole. She hit the table once, twice, thrice with her glove as though to work off the nervous tension in her fingers. Then she looked up menacingly.

"Let's have an end of all these ridiculous lies. Not a word of what you've been telling me is true. How dare you try and fob me off with a lot of nonsense."

The glove beat more and more violently on the table. Then she hurled it resolutely away from her in a wide arc.

"It is all a lot of twaddle. All of it! You were *not* in the riding-school, there was *no* inspection of remounts. At half-past four you were sitting in the café, and to the best of my knowledge that's not the sort of place where horses are broken in. Don't try to fool me. Our chauffeur happened to see you playing cards on the stroke of six."

I was still tongue-tied. But she was suddenly off on a new tack.

"And incidentally, what need is there for me to beat about the bush with you, either? Am I, simply because you tell me an untruth, to play hide-and-seek with you? *I'm* not afraid to tell the truth. Well, then, you may as well know—it was not by chance that our chauffeur saw you in the cafe; I sent him into town on purpose to inquire what had become of you. I thought perhaps you were ill or that something had happened to you, because you didn't even telephone and ... oh, for all I care you're at liberty to think I'm hysterical ... I can't stand being kept waiting ... I simply can't stand it ... and that's why I sent our chauffeur. But they told him at the barracks that the *Herr Leutnant* was perfectly all right and was enjoying a game of *tarock* at the cafe, and then I asked Ilona to go and find out why you were treating us with such scant courtesy ... to find out whether I had offended you yesterday ... I sometimes let myself go in a really quite irresponsible way ... There, you see—*I'm* not ashamed to admit all this to you ... whereas *you* trot out all these piffling excuses! Don't you feel yourself how paltry it is to tell such wretched lies?"

I was about to answer—I believe I should even have had the courage to tell her the whole wretched story of Ferencz and Jozsi—but she went on impetuously:

"No more trumped-up stories, please—no fresh lies, I can't do with any more. I'm stuffed up with lies till I'm absolutely sick. They're dished up to me from morning to night. 'How *well* you're looking today, how splendidly you're walking today ... really you're much, *much* better.'—That's how they try and drug me day in, day out, and no one seems to realize that I'm being suffocated. Why don't you tell me straight out that you had no time to come yesterday, and no inclination either? We haven't taken out a subscription in your company, and nothing would have pleased me better than if you had rung up and left a message to say you were not coming, but were going out on the spree somewhere with your friends. Do you think I'm so silly that I can't understand your sometimes getting fed up with playing the Good Samaritan here day after day, can't realize that a grown man would rather go for a ride or take his sound legs for a walk than sit about by an invalid's chair? There's only one thing that disgusts me, one thing I can't stand, and that is excuses, humbug, lies—I'm fed to the teeth with them. I'm not so stupid as you all think, and I can stand quite a lot of frankness. A few days ago we engaged a new charwoman in place of the old one who had died, and the very first day she was here, before she had talked to anyone—she saw me being helped across to an arm-chair on my crutches. She dropped her scrubbing brush in horror and screamed out: 'Lord Jesus, such a rich, distinguished young lady ... being a cripple!' Ilona went for the poor, honest creature like a wild thing; she was going to dismiss her and throw her out on the spot. But I, I *liked* it, the woman's horror did me good, because, after all, it is honest, it is human, to be horrified at see-ing such a sight all of a sudden. I promptly gave her ten crowns and she went off to the church to pray for me. The whole day I felt glad, yes, positively glad, at knowing at last what others *really* feel when they see me for the first time ... But you, all of you, you always think you've got to spare my feelings with your false sense of delicacy, and you fancy you're being kind to me with your beastly consideration ... But do you think I haven't eyes in my head? Do you think I can't detect behind your chatter, your stuttering and stammering, the same horror and discomfiture as was felt by that good woman, that one *honest* person? Do you imagine I don't see your embarrassed, dismayed looks when I pick up my crutches, don't see how you hurriedly make conver-sation so that I shan't notice? Just as though I didn't know you all through and through, you and your Valerian drops and sugar, sugar and Valerian drops, that utterly disgusting muck! I know perfectly well that you heave a sigh of relief when you've shut the door behind you and left me lying there like a corpse ... I know perfectly well how you turn up your eyes and sigh, 'The poor child!' And all the time you're so jolly pleased with your-selves for having given up one or two hours to cosseting the 'poor invalid'. But I don't want your sacrifices. I don't want you to feel you have to dole out your daily dose of pity—I don't care two straws for you all and your precious pity—once and for all, I tell you, I can do without your pity. If you want to come here, then for heaven's sake come, and if you don't, well then don't, but for God's sake be frank and let us have no more of your stories about remounts and trying out new horses. I cannot ... I cannot stand these lies and your revolting indulgence any longer." Quite beside herself, she had positively shouted the last few words at me, her eyes smouldering, her face livid. Then suddenly her fury subsided. Her head fell back as though exhausted on the chair, and only gradually did the colour return to her still quivering lips.

"Well, that's that!" she said in a low tone, as though ashamed. "I had to say that some time. And now it's all over and done with. Let's not talk of it any more. Give me ... give me a cigarette."

And now something strange happened to me. I am as a rule tolerably controlled and have firm, steady hands. But this unexpected outburst had so shattered me that I felt as though my limbs were paralysed; I had never felt so stunned in my life. Laboriously taking a cigarette out of my case, I handed it to her and lit a match. But my fingers trembled so violently that I could not hold the match steady, and the flame flickered in the empty air and went out. I had to light a second match, and this too swayed unsteadily in my trembling hand before her cigarette was lit. My obvious clumsiness must have made her realize the state I was in, and it was in quite another, a surprised, disquieted voice that she now asked me gently:

"Whatever is the matter with you? You're trembling ... What ... what is upsetting you so? ... What is all this to you?"

The tiny flame of the match had gone out. I sat down in silence.

"How could you let my stupid prattle upset you so?" she murmured in really troubled tones. "Papa is right. You are really a ... a very ... a very strange person."

At that moment there was a faint droning noise behind us. It was the lift, on its way up to the terrace. Josef opened the gate, and Kekesfalva stepped out with that guilty, shy air of his, that droop of the shoulders that for some reason was always more noticeable whenever he approached his crippled daughter.

Naturally I got up to greet Kekesfalva. He gave me an embarrassed nod and bent down to kiss Edith on the brow. Then there was a strange silence. Everyone in that house seemed to sense everything about everyone else. The old man must immediately have been aware of the dangerous tension between the two of us, for he hovered about uneasily with downcast eyes. I could see he would have liked to run away. Edith made an effort to break the ice.

"Just fancy, Papa, this is the first time Lieutenant Hofmiller has been up to the terrace!"

"Yes, it's wonderful up here," I said, conscious as I spoke of the pitiful banality of my words, and then relapsed into silence. To hide his embarrassment, Kekesfalva bent over Edith's chair.

"I'm afraid it will soon be too chilly for you up here. Hadn't we better go downstairs?"

"Yes," replied Edith. It was a welcome relief to all of us to have to busy ourselves with various trifles, such as collecting the books, wrapping Edith in her shawl, ringing the bell that here, as everywhere else in the house, lay ready to hand on the table. In two minutes' time the lift came droning up and Josef wheeled the invalid's chair cautiously into it.

"We'll be down in a moment," said Kekesfalva, waving to her affectionately. "Perhaps you'll change for dinner? In the meantime Lieutenant Hofmiller and I can take a little stroll round the garden."

The manservant closed the lift door, and the invalid chair sank into the depths below as though into a crypt. The old man and I involuntarily averted our gaze. We were both silent, but suddenly I became aware that he was timidly approaching me.

"If you don't mind, Lieutenant, there's something I'd like to talk over with you ... that is, I'd like to ask you a favour ... Perhaps we might go over to my office in the estate buildings? I mean, of course, only if you wouldn't mind ... Otherwise we can, of course, instead go for a walk in the park."

"But it's an honour, I assure you, Herr von Kekesfalva," I replied.

At that moment the lift came droning up again to take us down. We descended, and then walked across the courtyard to the estate building. It struck me how stealthily Kekesfalva made his way past the house, how he seemed to hug the wall, to make himself small, as though afraid of being caught. Involuntarily— I could not help it—I found myself walking behind him with equally noiseless stealthy tread. At the end of the low building, which would have been the better for a fresh coat of whitewash, he opened a door and ushered me into his office, which proved to be hardly better furnished than my own room in barracks: a cheap desk, shabby and rickety; old, discoloured wicker chairs; and on the wall, over the torn wallpaper, one or two charts which had evidently not been in use for years. Even the musty smell reminded me unpleasantly of our own garrison offices. At the first glance—how much I had learned to grasp in these last few days—I realized that this old man showered luxuries and comforts on his child alone, and stinted himself like a thrifty peasant. I had noticed for the first time as he walked ahead of me how shabby and shiny his black coat was at the elbows; he must have been wearing it continuously for the last ten or fifteen years.

Kekesfalva pushed forward the capacious armchair uphol-stered in black leather, the only comfortable chair in the room. "Sit down, *Herr Leutnant,* do sit down," he said with a certain tender insistence in his tone, bringing up one of the doubtful-looking wicker chairs for himself before I could forestall him. Now we sat close to one another; he could, he *must* begin, and I waited in an odd state of agitation to hear what favour this rich man, this millionaire, could have to ask of me, a poor subaltern. But he kept his head obstinately lowered, as though he were casually examining his shoes. I could hear the breath coming heavily and painfully from the bowed chest.

At length he raised his forehead, which was beaded with sweat, and removed his clouded spectacles; deprived of its usual flashing screen, his face looked different, more naked as it were, more pitiful, more tragic; as is so often the case with short-sighted people, his eyes looked duller and more weary than when seen through the magnifying lenses. I thought I could tell too, from the slight inflammation round the lids, that the old man slept lit-tle and slept badly. Once more I could feel that warm surging up of emotion within me; my pity, I now knew, was gushing forth. Suddenly I felt I was no longer sitting opposite the rich Herr von Kekesfalva, but an old man weighed down with sorrow.

Clearing his throat, he now began in a husky voice that was still imperfectly under control: "I want to ask you a very great favour, *Herr Leutnant* ... I know, of course, I have no right to trouble you. You scarcely know us ... besides, you can refuse, of

88

course you can refuse. Perhaps it is presumptuous of me, importunate, but from the very first moment I met you I have felt confidence in you. You are, one feels it straight away, a good man, a man always ready to lend a helping hand. Yes, yes, yes"—I must have made a gesture of protest—"you *are* a good man. There is something about you that inspires confidence, and sometimes ... I feel as though you had been sent from ... "—he stopped short, and I could tell that he had been going to say "from God", but had not had the courage—"sent to me as someone to whom I can speak frankly. Besides, it's not a very big thing that I want to ask of you ... but here am I rambling on without even asking you whether you're willing to listen to me."

"Why, of course."

"Thank you. When one is old, one has only to look at a person to know him through and through. I know a good man when I see one. My wife taught me that, God rest her soul ... That was the first tragedy, her being taken from me, and yet I keep telling myself that it was perhaps better that she did not live to see the tragedy that befell the child ... she could not have borne it. You know, when the whole thing began, five years ago ... I had no idea then it would last so long ... How ever could one imagine that one day a child could be just like other children, running about and playing and dancing about like a top ... and then all of a sudden it should all be over, over for *ever*? ... And then, we've all been brought up to respect doctors, we read in the papers of the miracles they're able to perform, they can stitch up people's hearts and graft new eyes on to them, we're told ... And so it was only natural that I should think that they could do a simple thing like curing a child—a child that was born healthy, mark you, that had always been healthy—in no time. That was why I wasn't very alarmed at first, for I never believed, never for a moment, that God could do such a thing, that He could afflict a child, an innocent child, for ever. If it had happened to *me*— well, my legs have carried me about for long enough, what further need have I of them? And then, I've been by no means a good man, I've done a lot of wicked things, I've even ... But what was I saying? ... Yes, yes, if it had happened to me, I could have understood. But how could God go so wide of the mark and strike the wrong one, an innocent creature? How are the likes of us to comprehend that the legs of a living creature, a child, should suddenly go *dead*, just because a mere nothing, a bacillus, the doctors said, and imagined they were saying something that made sense ... But bacillus is only a word, when all's said and done, an excuse, but that other thing—that's real, the fact that a child should lie there, her legs suddenly rigid, unable to walk or move any longer, and that one should have to stand helplessly looking on ... That's something one cannot, one *cannot* comprehend."

With a vehement gesture he wiped the sweat from his rumpled hair with the back of his hand. "Of course I made inquiries of every possible doctor ... Wherever there was a famous doctor to be found, I went to see him. I got them all to come here, and they held forth and talked Latin and discussed and held consultations; one tried one thing and one another, and then they said they hoped, and they trusted, and took their fees and departed, and things were left just where they were. That is to say, there has been some improvement, as a matter of fact considerable improvement. At first she had to lie flat on her back and her whole body was paralysed, whereas now at least her arms and the upper part of her body are normal and she can walk alone on crutches ... *some* improvement, yes, *considerable* improvement—I mustn't be unfair—there certainly is ... But none of them has effected a complete cure. They have all shrugged their shoulders and counselled patience, patience, patience. Only one of them has persevered with her, only one. Dr Condor ... I don't know if you've ever heard of him?"

I was obliged to say that I had never heard the name.

"Of course, how could you be expected to know him? You're in perfect health, and he's not one of those who throws his weight about. He doesn't hold a university post. I don't believe he has a big practice, either ... that is, he isn't out for a big practice. He is really a remarkable, a most uncommon man. I don't know exactly how to explain it to you. He's not interested in ordinary cases, the kind that can be treated by any sawbones ... he's only interested in severe cases that other doctors give up with a shrug of the shoulders. I can't, of course, uneducated as I am, affirm that Dr Condor is a better doctor than other doctors.

I only know that he is a better *man*. I got to know him first when my wife was ill, and I saw how he fought for her life. He was the only one who refused to give up hope until the very last, and I realized then that here was a man who lived and died with every one of his patients. He has—I don't know if I'm expressing myself properly—he has a kind of passion to get the better of an illness. He's not actuated, like other doctors, by ambition to make money and a name for himself. He doesn't think of himself, but of others, of those who are suffering. Oh, he's a wonderful man."

The old man had worked himself up into a state of excitement, and the eyes that had been so tired took on a fierce brilliance.

"A wonderful man, I tell you, who would never leave a soul in the lurch; he looks upon every case as a solemn duty. I know I'm not able to express myself very well, but it seems as though he feels guilty whenever he's unable to do anything—*personally* guilty—and for that reason you won't believe it, but I swear to you it's the truth—on one occasion when he failed to do what he'd set out to do—he had promised a woman who was going blind that he'd put her right—and then, when she really did go blind, he married her. Just fancy, a young man marrying a blind woman seven years older than himself, not beautiful and without any money, an hysterical creature, who is now a burden to him and is not the least bit grateful ... That shows, doesn't it, what kind of man he is, and you'll understand how happy I am to have found such a man, who looks after my child as I do myself. I have remembered him in my will ... if anyone can help her, he can. God grant he may. God grant it!"

The old man clasped his hands as though in prayer. Then he drew his chair up nearer to me. "And now listen, *Herr Leutnant*. I want to ask you a favour. I've told you how sympathetic this Dr Condor is. But, you see, just because he is such a good man, I feel uneasy. I'm always afraid, you see ... I'm always afraid that out of consideration for my feelings he won't tell me the truth, the whole truth. He's always promising me and assuring me that there's definite improvement, constant improvement, and that the child will eventually get quite well. But whenever I ask him point blank how long it will take, he is evasive and merely says, 'Patience, patience'. But I *must* have certainty. I am an old, a sick man, and I must know if I shall live to see her recover, and if she is ever going to get well, quite well ... No, believe me, *Herr Leutnant*, I *can't* go on like this. I *must* know, I can't bear this uncertainty any longer."

Overcome by his agitation, he rose and took three vigorous, rapid paces to the window. I had seen him like this before. Always when the tears rushed to his eyes he would turn away abruptly like this. He too refused to be pitied—how like *her* he was! His right hand fumbled clumsily in the back pocket of his pitiful old black coat and drew out a handkerchief, but it was in vain that he pretended he had only been wiping the sweat from his brow, for I could see only too clearly the reddened lids. Once, twice, he paced up and down the room; I could not tell whether the groans I heard issued from the rotting floorboards or from the decrepit old man himself. Then, like a swimmer about to plunge, he took a deep breath.

"Forgive me. I didn't mean to talk about it all. What was I going to say? Oh yes, tomorrow Dr Condor is coming again from Vienna—he made an appointment over the telephone. He comes every two or three weeks to see how things are going. If it rested with me I wouldn't let him go away at all; he could stay here in the house and I would pay him whatever he wished. But he says he needs a certain perspective so as to judge the progress of his patient, so as to ... a certain perspective, so as to ... yes, what was I saying? ... I know. He is coming tomorrow, and he'll examine Edith in the afternoon; he always stays to dinner afterwards and goes back by the night express. And it occurred to me that if someone were to ask him casually ... a complete stranger, who had nothing to do with the whole thing, whom he doesn't even know ... were to ask him ... quite casually, as it were ... just as one asks after an acquaintance ... ask him how things were going with regard to Edith's illness, and whether he thought the child would ever really be cured at all—*quite* cured, I mean—*completely* cured, and how long he thought it would take ... I have a feeling that he wouldn't lie to you. He has no need to spare your feelings, he need not scruple to tell *you* the truth. When he talks to me he may be keeping something back; after all, I am the child's father, I am an old, sick man, and he knows how it tears at my heart. But you must not, of course, let him suspect that you have talked to me about it. You must touch upon the subject *quite* casually, just as a stranger might make inquiries of a doctor. Will you ... will you do this for me?"

How was I to refuse? There in front of me, his eyes swimming, sat the old man, waiting for my assent as though for the Last Trump. Naturally I promised all he asked. His hands shot out towards me.

"I knew it. I knew it when you came back that time and were so kind to the child, after ... well, you know. I knew at once that here was a man who would understand me ... the very man to ask him for me, and I promise you, I swear to you, not a soul shall know, either before or afterwards, neither Edith, nor Condor, nor Ilona. Only *I* shall know what a tremendous service you have done me."

"But it's no trouble at all ... it's a mere trifle."

"No, it is not a trifle ... it is a great ... a *very* great service you're doing me ... a *very* great service indeed, and if ... "—he hunched his shoulders slightly and his voice seemed to tail off— "if I for my part can ever ... ever do anything for you. Perhaps you have ... "

I must have recoiled (was he going to offer to pay me on the spot?), for he went on hurriedly in the stammering tones that in his case always betrayed profound agitation:

"Oh no, don't misunderstand me. I don't mean ... I don't mean anything material ... I only mean ... I mean ... I have good connections. I know a whole crowd of people at the various ministries, at the War Ministry too, and it's always a good thing these days to have someone at the back of one. That's all I meant, of course. For everyone there may come a time ... that was all ... that was all I was going to say."

The timid way in which he offered me his help made me feel ashamed. The whole time he had not glanced up at me once, but had, as it were, addressed his own hands. Now for the first time he looked up uneasily, groped for the spectacles that he had laid aside, and settled them on his nose with trembling fingers.

"It might be better," he murmured, "if we were to go across to the house now, or ... or Edith will be wondering why we've been away so long. One has, unfortunately, to be terribly on one's guard with her; since she has been ill, her senses seem to have become more acute than other people's; as she lies there in her room she knows everything that goes on in the house. She knows what one is going to say almost before one has opened one's mouth. So, you see, she might ... that is why I suggest we had better go across to the house before her suspicions are aroused."

We walked over to the house. Edith was already waiting in the salon, in her chaise-longue. Scarcely had we entered the room than she threw us a sharp, keen look out of her grey eyes, as though trying to read on our brows, to guess from our somewhat sheepish, hang-dog expressions, what we had been talking about. And since we made no sort of reference to it, she was noticeably monosyllabic and aloof for the rest of the evening.

A "trifle", I had called Kekesfalva's request that I should inquire as casually as possible of a doctor whom I had not yet met what were the prospects of the crippled girl's recovery; and, looked at dispassionately, it really was a small thing he was asking me to do. But I can scarcely describe how much this unexpected commission meant to me personally. There is nothing that so raises a young man's self-esteem, that so contributes to the formation of his character, as for him to find himself unexpectedly confronted with a task which he has to accomplish entirely on his own initiative and by his own efforts. Responsibility had often come my way before, of course, but it had always been connected with the carrying out of my military duties, with tasks that I had to perform as a junior officer on the orders of my superiors and within the framework of certain narrow and circumscribed limits: duties such as commanding a troop, taking charge of a transport, buying mounts, settling quarrels amongst my men. All these orders and the execution of them were a normal part of army life. I had merely to follow certain written or printed instructions, and when in doubt to apply to an older and more experienced officer, in order to carry them out satisfactorily. Kekesfalva's request, on the other hand, was not addressed to the officer in me, but to that "inner" me who was as yet only vaguely known to myself, whose capacities and limitations I had yet to discover.

The fact that in his distress an almost complete stranger had selected me, me of all people, from among all his friends—this confidence in me gratified me more than all the praise I had hitherto received from superiors or friends.

A certain consternation, it was true, was mingled with my gratification, for I once more realized how unimaginative and passive my sympathy had been until now. How could I have been a constant visitor to this house, week in, week out, without ever having asked the most natural of all questions: is this poor girl always going to be a cripple? Cannot medical science find some cure for this condition of the limbs? It was quite disgraceful of me—not once had I inquired of Ilona, of Edith's father, of our regimental doctor; I had accepted her infirmity quite fatalistically as a fact. Now, therefore, the anxiety that had tormented her father for years was like a knife at my heart. What if the doctor really could release this child from her sufferings? What if those poor fettered limbs should be able to stride out freely once more, if this creature whom God had forsaken should once more be able to dance, to leap, to soar, blissfully and joyfully, in the wake of her own laughter? The very thought intoxicated me; it was delightful to imagine how the two of us, the three of us, would gallop across the fields on horseback; how instead of waiting, a prisoner in her room, for my arrival, she would be at the door to greet me, and be for ever happy and carefree. Impatiently I counted the hours, more impatiently perhaps than Kekesfalva himself, until I could ply the strange doctor with questions; no decisive moment in my own life had ever been of such importance to me.

The next day, therefore (I had specially arranged to get off duty), I turned up earlier than usual at the Kekesfalvas. Ilona received me. The doctor from Vienna had arrived, she told me; he was with Edith now, and was apparently giving her an especially thorough examination. He had been here for two and a half hours already, and Edith would probably be too tired afterwards to come and join us, so I should have to put up with her company—that was, she added, if I had nothing better to do.

From this remark I realized to my delight (it always bolsters up one's vanity to know oneself to be the only one to share a secret) that Kekesfalva had kept his word and not told her of our plan.

I stayed, of course. We played chess to amuse ourselves, and it was some considerable time before the sound of the footsteps that I was so impatiently awaiting was audible in the adjoining room. At last Kekesfalva and Dr Condor entered, deep in conversation, and I had some difficulty in suppressing a certain dismay, for my first impression of Dr Condor, as I stood facing him, was profoundly disappointing. It is true that whenever we have been told a great many interesting things about a person whom we have not yet met, our visual fantasy conjures up a picture of him beforehand, dipping liberally into the storehouse of our most precious and most romantic memories. In order to picture to myself a talented doctor such as Kekesfalva had described to me, I had confined my imagination to those characteristics which the average producer and theatrical wig-maker exploit to present the typical stage doctor: a spiritualized countenance, a keen and penetrating eye, an impressive bearing, a scintillating wit—again and again we fall hopelessly into the foolish error of thinking that Nature sets a special stamp on outstanding individuals so that they may be recognized at a glance. My heart sank, therefore, when, to my surprise, I found myself bowing to a stocky, plump little man, short-sighted and bald, his crumpled grey suit smothered in cigarette-ash, his tie askew; when, instead of the keen glance of the diagnostician, I encountered a listless and almost sleepy gaze behind a pair of cheap steel pince-nez. Before Kekesfalva had time to introduce us, Condor offered me a small clammy hand and promptly turned away to help himself to a cigarette. He stretched lazily.

"Well, well, here we are. I may as well tell you straight away, my dear friend, that I'm ravenous. It would be splendid if we could have something to eat fairly soon. If dinner's not yet on the way, maybe Josef could get me a snack to be going on with, a sandwich or something of the sort." Lowering himself expansively into an armchair, he went on: "I never can manage to remember that there's no restaurant car on this particular afternoon express. Another instance of our true Austrian inefficiency. Ah, splendid!" he interrupted himself, bobbing up quickly as Josef slid back the folding doors of the dining-room. "One can always count on you to be punctual, Josef. And I must also give your chef his due. What with all this confounded rushing about, I didn't manage to get a bite of lunch."

Thereupon, without further formality, he stumped across to the table, sat down without waiting for us, and, stuffing his table-napkin down his shirt-front, began hurriedly—and somewhat too noisily for my liking—to guzzle down his soup. Not a word did he address either to Kekesfalva or to me while thus energetically engaged. His whole attention seemed to be taken up by his food, although his short-sighted gaze rested simultaneously on the bottles of wine.

"Capital! Your famous Szomorodner—and what's more, '97. I remember sampling that last time I was here. That alone is enough to make one come racing out here to see you. No, Josef, don't pour it out yet, I'd rather have a glass of beer first . . . that's right . . . thank you."

He emptied his glass at a draught and then, helping himself to an enormous portion of the dish that was quickly offered him, he fell to in leisurely and comfortable fashion. Since he appeared to be entirely oblivious of our presence, I had ample opportunity of observing this gourmand in profile. I discovered, to my great disappointment, that this man who had been so enthusiastically held up to my admiration had the most *bourgeois*, homely features imaginable: a full moon of a face, pitted with little holes and disfigured with pimples, a bottle nose, a nebulous chin, reddish cheeks covered with a strong stubble of beard, a short bull neck—in fact, everything that went to make up what is known in Viennese dialect as a *sumper*—a good-natured, roistering sort of fellow, without a thought above eating and drinking. As he sat there comfortably eating away, his waistcoat crumpled and half-unbuttoned, he looked the part to the life. Gradually the indefatigable gusto with which he chewed away began to get on my nerves—it may have been because I remembered the courteous and polite way in which I had been treated at this very same table by the Colonel and the factory owner, perhaps also because I felt somewhat doubtful of ever being able to extract from this glutton, who held his glass of wine up to the light before rolling it over on his tongue, a precise answer to the kind of intimate question I had to ask.

"Well, what's the news in your part of the world? Is the harvest going to be up to scratch? Not too dry during the last week or so, not too hot? I read something about it in the papers. And the factory? Are you people in the sugar cartel going to put the prices up again?" It was with such casual, and I might almost say idle, questions, which really needed no answer, that every now and again Condor interrupted his hurried chewing and gorging. He seemed persistently to ignore my presence, and although I had often heard of the rudeness of the typical doctor, a certain rage began to spring up within me at this good-humoured boor. Out of sheer pique I maintained an obstinate silence.

Dr Condor, however, refused to be incommoded in the very slightest by our presence, and when we finally moved across to the salon, where our coffee was waiting for us, he threw himself with a grunt of satisfaction into Edith's chair, which was equipped with all sorts of special gadgets, such as adjustable arms, ashtrays and so forth, and had a revolving bookcase within easy reach of it. Since anger makes one not only malign but sharp-sighted, I could not help noticing with a certain satisfaction as he lolled there how stumpy were his legs with their untidy socks, how flabby his paunch; and in order to demonstrate how little disposed I for my part was to make his closer acquaintance, I slewed my chair round so that my back was actually turned to him. Completely unruffled, however, by my ostentatious silence and by Kekesfalva's nervous pacing up and down—the old man danced about incessantly to see that the doctor had all he wanted in the way of cigars, matches and brandy—Condor helped himself to no less than three cigars from the cabinet, placing two of them by his coffee-cup as a reserve supply; and no matter how willingly the deep armchair accommodated itself to his body, it seemed as though he could never be comfortable enough. He fussed and fidgeted about until he had found the most satisfactory position possible. When he had finally finished his second cup of coffee he gave the grunt of satisfaction of a well-fed animal. Revolting, I thought to myself, revolting. But at this point he suddenly stretched his limbs and blinked ironically across at Kekesfalva.

"Well, St Lawrence on the grill, apparently you grudge me my good cigar, for you just can't wait any longer for me to give my report. But you ought to know me by now. You know I don't like mixing shop with food—and besides, I really was *too* frightfully hungry, *too* tired. I've been on the go continuously since half-past seven this morning, and I felt as though not only my stomach, but my head, were left high and dry. Well then"—he took a long pull at his cigar and blew out a ring of blue smoke—"well then, my dear friend, let us get down to business. Everything is quite satisfactory—walking exercises, stretching exercises, all going very well indeed. Perhaps even a shade better than when I saw her last. As I have said, we may be very satisfied. The only thing is"—he took another pull at his cigar—"her general state of mind, what one may term her psychical condition, as regards that, I found her—now don't be alarmed, I beg you, my dear friend—I found somewhat of a change in her today."

Despite his warning, Kekesfalva was terribly alarmed, and I could see the spoon he held in his hand beginning to shake.

"A change ... what do you mean ... what kind of a change?"

"Now come—a change is a change. I didn't say, my dear friend, a change for the worse. Don't attach a meaning to my words that isn't there ... I don't know myself for the moment what's the matter, but *something's* not quite as it should be."

The old man continued to hold the spoon in his hand. Apparently he had not the strength to put it down.

"What ... what's not quite as it should be?"

Dr Condor scratched his head. "Ah, there you have me. If only I knew. But in any case, don't get upset. We're speaking quite academically and with no nonsense, and I should like to state once again, quite categorically: the change in her did not seem to me to be connected with her illness, but with herself. Something, I don't know what, was not quite right today. I had a feeling for the first time that in some way or other she had slipped from my grasp." He took another pull at his cigar, then switched the gaze of his alert little eyes over to Kekesfalva. "It's best, you know, for us to approach the matter quite frankly. We have no need to beat about the bush with each other and can lay all our cards on the table. Well then, my dear friend, tell me quite frankly and honestly, I beg you: have you in your eternal

99

impatience called in another doctor? Has Edith been examined or treated by anyone else in my absence?"

Kekesfalva flared up as though he had been accused of something monstrous. "Good God, Doctor, I swear to you by my child's life! ... "

"All right ... all right ... spare me your oaths." Condor quickly interrupted him. "I believe you without all that. That's settled. *Peccavi!* I've simply gone wide of the mark, made a wrong diagnosis; that can happen, after all, to the most famous specialists. How stupid of me ... And I could have sworn that ... oh well, it must be something else that's wrong ... but it's strange, very strange. May I?" He poured himself a third cup of black coffee.

"Yes, but what's wrong with her? How has she changed? What do you mean?" stammered the old man, dry-lipped.

"My dear friend, you really make things very difficult for me. There's absolutely no need to worry, you have my word again for it, my word of honour. If it were anything serious I wouldn't, you may be sure ... in front of a stranger ... I beg your pardon, *Herr Leutnant,* I don't mean it unkindly, I only mean ... I wouldn't discuss it from an armchair, so to speak, while comfortably sipping your good brandy—by the way, it really is excellent brandy."

He leaned back again in his chair and for a fraction of a second closed his eyes.

"Yes, off the cuff it's difficult to explain this change in her. Very difficult, because it is something that lies on the borders of what is explicable. But if at first I supposed that another doctor had been interfering in the case—I *really* don't think so any longer, Herr von Kekesfalva, I swear to you—it was because today for the first time something between Edith and myself was not functioning properly—the usual contact was lacking ... Wait a moment ... perhaps I can put it more clearly. During the course of a long period of treatment a certain, definite contact is established between a doctor and his patient. Perhaps it is putting it too crudely to call it a contact, which, after all, in the last resort denotes something physical. In this relationship there is a strange mixture of trust and mistrust, the one works against the other, a mixture of attraction and repulsion, and of course the mixture varies from one visit to the next—we are used to that. Sometimes the patient seems to the doctor to be different, and sometimes the doctor seems to the patient to be different; sometimes they understand each other at a mere glance, at others they talk to each other at cross-purposes ... Yes, these ups and downs are very, very odd; one can't pin them down, much less measure them. Perhaps one can best explain it by a comparison, even at the risk of its being a very crude comparison. Well then—with a patient it's just the same as when you've been away for a few days and you come back and sit down at your typewriter. To all intents and purposes it works exactly as it always did, functions just as admirably as ever; but all the same, something that you can't define tells you that someone else has been using it in your absence. Or just as you, *Herr Leutnant*, doubtless notice a difference in your horse when someone else has borrowed him for a couple of days. Something's not quite right about his gait, his bearing, he has somehow got out of your control, and yet you, probably, are equally unable to define exactly where the difference lies, so infinitesimal is it ... I know these are very crude comparisons, for the relation of a doctor to his patient is, of course, a far more subtle thing. I should be hard put to it—I tell you frankly—to explain what it is about Edith that is different since my last visit. But something—and it annoys me to think that I can't put my finger on it—is the matter, something about her is different."

"But how ... how does it show itself?" gasped Kekesfalva. I saw that all Condor's adjurations had failed to reassure him, and his brow was beaded with sweat.

"How does it show itself? Well, in trifling things, imponderabilia. Even while I was going through the remedial exercises with her, I noticed she was putting up resistance against me; before I could even begin to examine her, she protested that it was quite unnecessary, that everything was just the same as usual, whereas as a rule, she *waits* with the greatest impatience for my report. Then, when I suggested certain exercises, she made disparaging remarks, such as, 'Oh, they're no use!' or 'They're not going to do much good.' Now, such remarks are, I admit, unimportant in themselves—the outcome of ill-temper, frayed nerves—but until now, my dear friend, Edith has never said such things to me. Well, perhaps she was merely in a bad mood—that can happen to anyone."

"But ... there's really no change for the worse, is there?"

"How many more protestations must I make? If there were anything in the least wrong, I, her doctor, would be just as worried as you, her father, and I am, as you see, not worried in the slightest. On the contrary, this rebellion against me doesn't altogether displease me. Admitted—your young daughter is more cantankerous, more headstrong, more impatient than a few weeks ago—probably she's been giving *you* a few hard nuts to crack. But such a revolt points, on the other hand, to a certain strengthening of the will to live, the will to recover; the more vigorously and more normally an organism begins to function, the more forcibly will it eventually get the better of its illness. Believe me, we doctors are not so immoderately fond of 'good', submissive patients as you may think. They are the ones who least help us to help them. To us, vigorous and even frantic resistance on the part of a patient can only be welcome, for, strangely enough, these apparently unreasonable reactions sometimes have more effect than our most miraculous remedies. I repeat, therefore— I am not in the least worried. If, for instance, one were thinking of starting her on a new course of treatment, one could now expect her to make great efforts; maybe this would be the appropriate moment to bring into play the psychical forces which in her case are so decisive. I don't know"—he raised his head and looked at us—"if you quite get my meaning."

"Of course," I said involuntarily. It was the first word I had addressed to him. It all seemed to me so obvious and plain.

But the old man did not stir. He sat there rigid, gazing into space with unseeing eyes. I felt that he had not understood a word of what Condor had been saying, for the simple reason that he did not want to understand it: because his whole attention, all his fears, were concentrated on the question: will she ever be cured? Soon? When?

"But ... but ... what treatment?"—he always stammered and stuttered when he became agitated—"What new treatment? You said something about some kind of new treatment ... What new treatment are you thinking of trying?" (I noticed at once how he leaped on the word "new", as though therein lay a spark of hope.)

"Leave that to me, my dear friend. Let me decide what I shall try and when I shall try it. Just don't press me, don't keep expecting me to work miracles. Your 'case', as we doctors so disagreeably put it, is, and will continue to be, my major concern. We shall come through all right."

The old man gazed at him in troubled silence. I could see that it was only with difficulty that he refrained from putting one more of his futile and persistent questions. Condor must also have been affected by the strained silence, for he suddenly rose.

"Well, I think that's all for today. I have given you my impressions, anything more would be sheer mumbo-jumbo and quackery. Even if Edith should actually get somewhat more irritable in the next few days, don't be alarmed. I shall soon put my finger on what is wrong. There's only one thing for you to do, and that's to try not to hover round the invalid looking so worried and anxious. And then one more thing: you must take great care of your own nerves. You're looking rather washed out, and I'm afraid that all this worrying and fussing is only sapping your own strength more than is fair to your daughter. The best thing you can do is to start by going to bed early tonight and taking a few Valerian drops before going to sleep, so that you will wake up fresh tomorrow. That's all. That brings my visit to an end for today. I'll just finish this cigar, then I'll be off."

"You're really ... really going already?"

Dr Condor was firm. "Yes, my dear friend. That's enough for today. I still have another, somewhat jaded, patient to attend to this evening, and I've prescribed a long walk for him. Just take a look at me. I've been on the go without a break since half-past seven this morning. I spent the whole morning in hospital—we had a strange case there ... but don't let's talk of it ... After that I had the train-journey, then I've been here the whole afternoon, and we doctors of all people need to get some fresh air in our lungs every now and again so as to keep our heads clear. So please don't send for your car today, I'd rather stretch my legs. There's a glorious full moon. Of course I don't want to take this young man away with me. If, despite your doctor's orders, you mean to stay up, I expect he'll keep you company for a while longer."

Immediately, however, I remembered my mission. No, I declared eagerly, I had to be on duty particularly early next morning, and I ought in any case to have left long since.

"Well then, if you've no objection, we can walk along together."

And now Kekesfalva's ashen-grey eyes lit up for the first time. He too had remembered.

"And I think I'll go straight to bed," he said in a tone of unexpected submissiveness, stealing a look at me behind Condor's back. The reminder was unnecessary, for I could feel my pulses beating against my cuffs. I knew that the time had come for me to fulfil my promise.

No sooner had Condor and I stepped outside the front door than we involuntarily came to a halt at the top of the flight of steps leading to the garden for it was an astonishing prospect that met our gaze. While we had been indoors, we had been too preoccupied to think of looking out of the window; and now the complete transformation that had come over the scene took our breath away. An enormous full moon, a smoothly polished silver disc, hung motionless in the starry heavens, and whilst the air, warmed by the heat of a sunny summer's day, blew sultry upon our faces, a magic winter seemed, thanks to the dazzling radiance of the light, to have suddenly descended upon the world. The gravel gleamed like freshly fallen snow between the double row of trees which, with their dark shadows, flanked the path; gleaming now like glass in the light, now like mahogany in the darkness, they stood there in ghostly rigidity. Never can I remember having felt the moonlight to be so eerie as here in the utter stillness and immobility of this garden drowned in a flood of icy brilliance. So deceptive was the spell of this seemingly wintry light, that instinctively we trod warily on the shimmering flight of steps, as though we were walking on slippery glass. As we made our way along the snowy gravel path, we were suddenly no longer two but four, for ahead of us walked, clearly outlined in the crystal-clear moonlight, our shadows. I found my gaze resting on the two persistent dark companions who, like moving silhouettes, traced out before us our every movement, and it afforded me some satisfaction—one's feelings are sometimes curiously childish—to see that my shadow was longer, slimmer, I might almost say "better", than the plumpish, squat shadow of my companion. I felt my self-assurance somewhat reinforced by this evidence of my superiority. I know that it takes a good deal of courage to admit such naïveté to oneself. For one's emotional state is always determined by the most odd and accidental things, and it is precisely the most superficial factors that often fortify or diminish our courage.

We reached the gate without exchanging a single word. In order to close it, we were obliged to look back. The front of the house, a single block of glittering ice, shone as though painted with bluish phosphorus, and this gleaming façade was so dazzling that it was impossible to tell which of the windows was lit from within and which from without, so brilliant was the light shed upon it by the exuberant moon. Not until the gate banged to was the silence broken; and as though encouraged by this earthly sound in the midst of the spectral silence, Condor turned to me with an ease of manner which I had not hoped for.

"Poor Kekesfalva!" he said. "I keep on reproaching myself for having perhaps been too brusque with him. I know, of course, that he would have liked to keep me hours longer and to ask me a hundred and one questions, or rather the same questions a hundred times over. But I just couldn't stand any more. It's been an awful day—patient after patient from morning till night, and moreover cases in which one makes no headway."

By this time we had turned into the avenue, the trees of which with their shadowy network of foliage were massed together to screen the moon's rays. All the more glaringly did the icy-white gravel shine out in the middle of the roadway, and we both walked along this bright channel of light. I did not feel that a reply on my part was called for, but Condor seemed quite oblivious of my presence.

"And then there are days, you know, on which I just can't stand his insistence. The difficult thing, you know, in our profession, is not the patients; in the end one learns how to manage them, one develops a certain technique. And after all, if patients grumble and plague us with their questions, that's simply a part of their condition, just as much as a temperature or a headache. We count in advance on their being impatient, we take it as a matter of course, we're prepared for it, and we have certain soothing phrases and white lies ready to hand, just as we have sleeping draughts and analgesics. But the people who make life so unendurable for us are the relatives, the friends who, so to speak, interpose themselves between doctor and patient and are always clamouring to know the 'truth'. They all behave as though their patient were the only person on earth who was ill and as though one ought to give all one's attention to him, to him alone. I don't really take Kekesfalva's questioning amiss, but, you know, when that sort of thing becomes chronic, one's patience sometimes gives out. Ten times over I've told him I have a serious case just now in town, and that it is a matter of life and death. And although he knows that, he telephones day after day and pesters and pesters me, and tries to wring some hope from me at all costs. And all the time I know as his doctor how bad it is for him to get worked up like this. I'm far more worried than he suspects, far more. A good thing he doesn't know how bad matters are."

I was dismayed. Matters were bad, then? Condor had quite frankly and spontaneously given me the information I was expected to worm out of him. Profoundly disturbed, I pressed him further:

"Forgive me, *Herr Doktor*, but you'll understand how upsetting this is for me ... I had no idea Edith was in such a bad way."

"Edith?" Condor turned to me in utter astonishment. He seemed for the first time to realize that he had been talking to someone else. "What d'you mean? Edith? I haven't said a word about Edith ... You've completely misunderstood me. No, no, Edith's condition is really quite stationary—*unfortunately*, still stationary. It's Kekesfalva I'm worried about, more and more worried every day. Hasn't it struck you how much he's changed in the last few months? How ill he looks, how he's deteriorating from week to week?"

"I really cannot judge that. It is only during the last few

weeks that I've had the honour of knowing Herr von Kekesfalva and ... "

"Ah—quite so. Forgive me ... in that case you can't have noticed ... But I, who've known him for years, was really alarmed today when I happened to glance at his hands. Hasn't it struck you how transparent and bony they are? When one has frequently seen the hands of dead people, you know, that sort of bluish colour on a living hand always dismays one. And then too—I don't much like those bursts of sentimentality; the slightest emotion brings the tears to his eyes, the colour leaves his cheeks the moment he begins to worry. It is precisely on men like Kekesfalva, who have in the past been so energetic and ruthless, that giving way to their feelings has such a grave effect. Unfortunately it's not a good sign when hard men suddenly go soft—yes, I don't even like to see them grow kind-hearted all of a sudden. Of course, I've been meaning for a long time to give him a thorough examination, only I can't really trust myself to get down to it. For, good God, if one were ever to put the idea into his head that he himself were ill, and the idea, into the bargain, that he might die and leave his child behind a cripple— why, it simply won't bear thinking of. He's undermining his own health in any case with this eternal brooding, this frantic impatience ... Really, *Herr Leutnant*, you misunderstood me—it's not Edith, but *he* who is my chief concern ... I'm afraid the old man's not long for this world."

I was appalled. I'd never dreamed of such a thing. I was twenty-five years old at the time and I had never yet seen anyone near to me die. So I could not at first grasp the idea that someone with whom I had just been dining, talking, drinking, might the very next morning be lying stiff and stark in his winding-sheet. I realized, too, from a sudden slight stab at the heart, that I had come to be really fond of the old man. In my agitation and embarrassment I tried to make some sort of rejoinder.

"How ghastly!" I said, quite distractedly. "Absolutely ghastly. Such a distinguished, such a generous, such a kind-hearted man too—the first real nobleman, the first genuine aristocrat I've ever met."

And now a surprising thing happened. Condor came to such

an abrupt halt that I, too, involuntarily pulled up short. He looked at me fixedly, his glasses flashing as he veered round sharply. He took several deep breaths before asking me in tones of utter amazement:

"A nobleman? ... An aristocrat? ... Kekesfalva? Forgive me, *Herr Leutnant* ... but do you really mean that seriously ... what you said about his being a real Hungarian nobleman?" I didn't quite understand his question, but I felt I had said something foolish. So I replied in an embarrassed tone:

"I can only judge from my own personal experience, and to me Herr von Kekesfalva has at all times shown himself to be most well-bred and gracious ... we've always heard Hungarian landowners referred to in the regiment as particularly overbearing ... But ... I ... I never met a more gracious person ... I ... I ... "

I lapsed into silence because I felt that Condor was still peering closely at me. His round face gleamed in the moon-light, the pince-nez, behind which I could only indistinctly see his eyes, looked twice their size; and this gave me an uncomfortable feeling of being a struggling insect under a very powerful microscope. Standing there facing each other in the middle of the road we would have presented a curious picture to any passer-by. Then, lowering his head, Condor strode on and murmured as if to himself:

"You really are ... an odd fellow, if you'll forgive my saying so—I don't mean it in a bad sense. But it's very odd, you know, you must yourself admit, very odd ... You've been coming to the house now, so I hear, for some weeks. And what's more, you live in a small town, a little hen-coop of a place, where there's a terrific amount of cackling into the bargain—and you take Kekesfalva for an aristocrat! Do you mean to say you have never, amongst your fellow-officers, heard certain ... well, I won't say, derogatory—but let's say remarks to the effect that the less said about his nobility the better? Surely someone has passed that on to you?"

"No," I said vehemently, realizing that I was beginning to get angry (it's not pleasant to be labelled as "curious" and "odd"). "I'm sorry—nothing has ever been passed on to me. I have never discussed Herr von Kekesfalva with any of my friends."

"Odd!" murmured Condor. "Odd! I always thought he was exaggerating when describing you. And I may as well tell you frankly—it's obviously my day for making false diagnoses—I was a little suspicious of his enthusiasm ... I couldn't really believe that you only went to the house because of that first little mishap, and then went again and again simply out of sympathy, out of friendliness. You've no idea how the old man is exploited, and I had made up my mind (why shouldn't I tell you?) to find out what it actually is that takes you to the house. I thought to myself, either he's a—how shall I put it politely?—a scheming young fellow, who is trying to feather his nest, or, if he does go there in good faith, he must be very young emotionally, for it is only on the young that the tragic and dangerous exerts so curious an attraction. Incidentally, the instinct of really young people in that respect is nearly always right, and you were absolutely on the right track ... Kekesfalva is really quite an exceptional person. I know perfectly well all the things that can be said against him, and it seemed to me, if you'll forgive my saying so, somewhat funny your referring to him as a nobleman. But, if you will believe someone who knows him better than anyone else here, there's no need for you to feel ashamed of having shown him and that poor child so much friendliness. You needn't let whatever anyone says bother you; it really doesn't apply to the touching, pathetic, moving person that Kekesfalva is today."

Condor had been striding along without looking at me as he said all this. It was only after some time that he once more slackened his pace. I felt that he was reflecting, and did not like to disturb him. We walked along side by side for another four or five minutes in complete silence. A carriage came towards us; we had to step aside, and the clod of a driver stared curiously at the strange couple, the lieutenant and the little, plump, bespectacled gentleman, who were silently walking along the highway together so late at night. We let the carriage pass; and then Condor suddenly turned to me.

"Listen, *Herr Leutnant.* Things half done and hints half given are always bad; all the evil in the world comes from half-measures. Perhaps I've let slip too much already, and I should not, in any case, like you to be shaken in your generous outlook. On the other hand, I've aroused your curiosity too much for you not to make inquiries of other people, and I am, unfortunately, bound to fear that the information you get will not be very favourable. And then, too, it's an impossible situation for anyone to go on visiting a house without knowing who the people are—probably you wouldn't feel any too easy about going there again now that I've inadvertently gone and upset you. If it would really interest you, therefore, to learn more about our friend, I'm at your disposal."

"Why, of course it would."

Condor took out his watch. "A quarter to eleven. We still have two full hours. My train doesn't go until one twenty. But I hardly think the road is the place to talk of such matters. Perhaps you know of some quiet corner where we can speak freely?"

I reflected. "The best place of all would be the Tiroler Weinstube in the Erzherzog Friedrichstrasse. It has little alcoves where one is left undisturbed."

"Splendid! The very place for us," he answered, and once more quickened his pace.

Without another word we continued on our way down the road. Soon the first houses of the town could be seen lined up on each side of us in the bright moonlight, and, as luck would have it, we did not meet any of my friends in the now deserted streets. I do not know why, but I should have found it disagreeable to be cross-questioned the next day about my companion. Ever since I had been caught up in this strange entanglement I had anxiously concealed every thread that might indicate the way into the labyrinth which, I felt, was drawing me down into ever fresh and more mysterious depths.

The Tiroler Weinstube was a cosy little place, with just a suggestion of ill-repute. Situated in a little out-of-the-way, winding, ancient alleyway, it was the bar of a third-class hotel which was in particular favour with us officers because of the porter's accommodating habit of deliberately forgetting to trouble guests who required a double room—even in the middle of the day—with all the formalities of registration. A further guarantee that a veil of discretion would be drawn over one's hours, long or short, of amorous dalliance was provided by the thoughtful arrangement whereby one had no need, in order to reach one's trysting-place above, to use the conspicuous main entrance (a small town has a thousand eyes), but could, without embarrassment, approach the stairs directly from the bar and thus make one's way unobtrusively to one's discreet goal. The full-bodied Terlaner and Muscatel wines, however, which were served in the bar of this dubious little place were beyond reproach, and every evening the townsfolk would sit happily together at the solid bare wooden tables and, over a few glasses of wine, discuss, with greater or less vehemence, the usual affairs of the town or of the world. All round this rectangular, somewhat tawdry room, the unchallenged domain of the worthy drinkers whose only business here was their wine and dull-witted conviviality, was built in, a step higher, a gallery of so-called "boxes", separated from each other by fairly thick, sound-proof partitions, and quite superfluously decorated with poker-work designs and homely drinking mottoes. Heavy curtains shut off these alcoves so completely from the rest of the room that they might almost have been called *chambres séparées*, and, indeed, to a certain extent, too, they served as such. Whenever the officers of the garrison wished to amuse themselves with a few girls from Vienna without being seen, they would reserve one of these 'boxes', and our Colonel, usually a stern disciplinarian, had even expressly approved this wise procedure, whereby civilians were prevented from seeing too much of the carousing of his young officers. The supreme law of the establishment, moreover, was discretion; on the express orders of the proprietor, a certain Herr Ferleitner, the waitresses, who were dressed in Tyrolese costume, were strictly forbidden ever to raise the sacred curtains without clearing their throats noisily beforehand, or in any other way to disturb the gentlemen of the regiment unless expressly summoned by a ring of the bell. Thus both the dignity and the frivolities of the army were most admirably guarded.

It could not often have been recorded in the annals of the little bar that a customer had occupied one of the alcoves merely for the purpose of having a private chat. But I felt it would be disagreeable for us to be disturbed by either the greetings or the curiosity of fellow-officers, or to have to jump smartly to attention if a senior officer entered the bar. I found it unpleasant enough to have to cross the main room in Dr Condor's company—what *badinage* would I not be subjected to next morning were I to be seen hiding myself away in such intimate seclusion with a strange, plump gentleman!—but the moment we entered the bar I noticed with extreme satisfaction that it was as deserted as such a place always is at the end of the month in a small garrison town. No one from our regiment was there, and we had our choice of the alcoves.

Evidently in order to prevent the waitress from bothering us again, Condor immediately ordered two litres of white wine, paid for it on the spot and tossed the girl such an enormous tip that she disappeared for good with a grateful "Your very good health, sir!" The curtain fell, and it was only indistinctly that from time to time we caught the sound of a laugh or a few words from the tables in the middle of the room. We were completely sealed up and secure in our little cell.

Condor poured out the wine into the tall, long-stemmed glasses. I realized from a certain hesitancy in his movements that he was inwardly cogitating all that he was going to tell me (and possibly, too, not tell me). When eventually he turned to me, the sleepy, comfortable look which had so annoyed me earlier on in the evening had completely disappeared. His gaze was now concentrated and alert.

"Perhaps we had better begin at the beginning and for the moment leave our aristocratic friend Herr Lajos von Kekesfalva completely out of the picture. For when my story begins no such person existed. There was no landed proprietor in a long black coat, with gold-rimmed spectacles, and no Hungarian nobleman. There was only, in a wretched little village on the Hungarian-Slovak frontier, a keen-eyed, narrow-chested little Jewish lad called Leopold Kanitz, familiarly referred to, I believe, as Lämmel Kanitz."

I must have started or in some other way betrayed my extreme surprise, for I was prepared for anything but this. But Condor went on in smiling, matter-of-fact tones:

"Yes, Kanitz—Leopold Kanitz, I can't change that. It was

only much later that on the recommendation of a Minister the name was so sonorously Magyarized and decked out with a prefix of nobility. You have probably overlooked the fact that a man with influence and good connections, who has lived in this country for a long time, can grow a new skin, can have his name Magyarized and sometimes even acquire a title. A young fellow like you can't be expected to know that; and besides, a great deal of water has flowed under the bridge since that puny creature, that keen-eyed, wily young Jewish lad minded the peasants' horses or carriages whilst they were drinking in the inn, or carried the market-women's baskets for them in return for a handful of potatoes.

Kekesfalva's father, or rather Kanitz's father, then, far from being an aristocrat, was the poverty-stricken, be-ringleted Jewish landlord of a wayside tavern just outside the town. The woodcutters and coachmen looked in there every morning and evening to warm themselves with a glass or two of *kontuschowska* before or after their drive through the Carpathian frost. Sometimes the fiery liquid went too quickly to their heads; at such times they would smash chairs and glasses, and it was in a brawl that Kanitz's father received his death-blow. A number of peasants who had arrived tipsy from the market started a scrimmage, and when old Kanitz, in order to save his few sticks of furniture, tried to pull them apart, one of them, a great hulking brute of a coachman, hurled him so violently into the corner that he lay there groaning. From that day on he spat blood, and a year later he died in hospital. He left no money whatever, and the mother, a plucky woman, managed to support herself and her small children by taking in washing and acting as a midwife. As a sideline she went out hawking, and Leopold carried her packages on his back. In addition, he scraped together a few *kreutzers* wherever he could. He got a job at the local shop, and went on errands from village to village. At an age when other children are still playing happily at marbles he knew exactly what everything cost, where and how one bought and sold things, how one made oneself useful and indispensable, and, what was more, he found time to pick up a few scraps of knowledge. The rabbi taught him to read and write, and he was so bright

113

that by the age of thirteen he was able to do occasional clerical work for a lawyer, and to do accounts and fill up tax forms for the little shopkeepers in return for a few *kreutzers*. To save light, for every drop of oil was an extravagance for the poverty-stricken household, he sat night after night by the signal-lamp at the level-crossing—the village had no station of its own—and pored over torn or discarded newspapers. Even at that time the old people of the village wagged their beards approvingly and predicted that this lad would make his way in the world.

How he managed to leave the Slovak village and get to Vienna I don't know. But when he appeared in this district at the age of twenty he was already an agent for a reputable insurance firm, and, indefatigable as ever, combined with his official function a hundred and one other little jobs. He became what is known in Galicia as a "factor", a man who trades in everything, acts as middle-man for everything, and in all sorts of ways bridges the gap between supply and demand.

At first people tolerated him. Soon they began to take notice of him and even to need him. For he knew everything and was an expert on everything; was there a widow, for example, who was trying to marry off her daughter, he would come out in the role of marriage broker; was there someone who wanted to emigrate to America and needed information and papers, Leopold would procure them. In addition, he bought and sold old clothes, clocks, antiquarian pieces, valued and exchanged land and goods and horses, and when an officer wanted a loan, he always managed to procure it for him. His knowledge and his sphere of operations widened from year to year.

With that sort of energy and tenacity a man can make money in all sorts of ways. But real fortunes are only made as the result of a special relation between receipts and expenditure, between earnings and out-goings. This, then, was the other secret in the rise of our friend Kanitz: in all those years he spent as good as nothing, apart from the fact that he supported a whole string of relations and paid for his brother's studies. The only money he really spent on himself went in the purchase of a black coat and those gold-rimmed spectacles which you know so well and by means of which he won for himself amongst the peasants the reputation of being a "scholar". But long after he had become affluent he continued to pose in the district as a little agent. For "agent" is a wonderful word, an all-embracing cloak, which covers a multitude of sins, all sorts of things, and Kanitz concealed behind it, above all, the fact that he had long since ceased to be a middleman, and was now an entrepreneur and capitalist. It seemed to him to be more important and more sensible to become rich than to be regarded as rich (one might have thought he had read Schopenhauer's wise paralipomena with regard to what one *is* or merely *represents* oneself to be).

The fact that a man who is at once hard-working, clever and thrifty will sooner or later make money seems to me to be so obvious as to require no particular philosophical meditation; and there does not seem to be anything particularly admirable in his doing so; after all, we doctors know better than anyone that at decisive moments a man's banking account is of very little use. The thing that really impressed me about friend Kanitz from the start was his positively demonic determination to add to his knowledge at the same time as his fortune. Whole nights in trains, every free moment while travelling, in hotels, on expeditions, he read and studied. He studied all the text-books on both commercial and industrial law so as to be able to act as his own lawyer, he followed all the auctions in London and Paris like a professional antiquarian, and he was as versed as a banker in the intricacies of investments and financial transactions. And so it followed as a matter of course that his business assumed more and more grandiose proportions. From the peasants he turned to the farmers, from the farmers to the great aristocratic landed proprietors; soon he was negotiating the sale of whole harvests and forests, building factories, founding syndicates, and finally even securing certain army contracts. The black coat and the gold-rimmed spectacles were now to be seen more and more frequently in the ante-rooms of the Ministries. But still—and by this time he had a fortune of a quarter of a million, perhaps half a million crowns—the people here in this part of the world still took him to be an insignificant agent and still greeted little Kanitz extremely casually, until at last he pulled off his big coup and at one blow was transformed from Lämmel Kanitz into *Herr* von Kekesfalva."

Condor broke off. "What I have told you so far, I know only at secondhand. The story that follows, however, I had from him himself. He told it me after the operation on his wife, while we sat waiting in a room at the sanatorium from ten o'clock at night until dawn. From this point on I can vouch for every word, for at such moments a man does not lie."

Slowly and thoughtfully Condor sipped his wine before lighting a fresh cigar—I think it was the fourth he had smoked that evening, and it was this incessant smoking in particular which made me realize that the exaggeratedly comfortable, jovial manner he assumed in the role of doctor, his drawling way of talking and apparent nonchalance, were all part of a technique specially adopted to enable him to sort out his impressions (and perhaps to observe his patients) at leisure. He took several pulls at his cigar, sucking at it almost drowsily with his thick lips and gazing at the smoke with almost dreamy interest. Then he pulled himself up sharply.

"The story of how Leopold Kanitz became lord and master of Kekesfalva begins in a slow train from Budapest to Vienna. Although he was forty-two by this time, and his hair was already greying at the temples, our friend still spent most of his nights travelling—the avaricious are thrifty with time as well as money—and it goes without saying that he invariably travelled third. An old hand at the game, he had developed a certain technique for night journeys. First of all, he would spread out over the hard wooden seat a plaid rug that he had picked up at an auction. Then he would hang the inevitable black coat carefully on the peg, and put his gold-rimmed glasses away in their case, take out of his canvas travelling-bag—he never aspired to a leather one—a woolly dressing-gown, and finally tilt his cap over his face to keep the light out of his eyes. All these preparations complete, he would snuggle up in the corner of the carriage, for he had long since become accustomed to dozing off even in a sitting position. That a man has no need of a bed for the night and of comfort for sleep, little Leopold had learned as a child.

But on this occasion our friend did not fall asleep, for there were three other people besides himself in the compartment, and they were talking shop. And when people talked shop, Kanitz could never keep his ears shut. His thirst for knowledge had diminished as little with the years as his thirst for possessions; the two were no more to be rent asunder than are a pair of pincers.

He was just on the point of dozing off when the mention of a sum of money made him start like a horse at the sound of a bugle-call. 'And would you believe it, it was really only through his blasted stupidity that the lucky swine made sixty thousand crowns at one swoop!' Sixty thousand? Who? What? How? In a flash Kanitz was wide awake; it was as though an icy-cold shower had driven the sleep from his eyes. Who had earned sixty thousand, and how? He must find out at all costs. Of course he took good care not to let his three fellow-travellers know that he was eavesdropping. He pulled his cap even lower over his forehead, so that its shadow should completely cover his eyes and the others should think he was asleep; then, cunningly and cautiously making use of each jolt of the carriage, he edged nearer to them, so as not to lose a word, despite the rattling of the wheels.

The young man who had been talking away with such vehemence and had let out the trumpet blast of indignation which had caused Kanitz to prick up his ears was, it transpired, a clerk in the office of a Viennese lawyer, and in his anger at his employer's amazing luck he continued to hold forth in excited tones:

'And the joke is that the fellow bungled the whole thing from start to finish. Because of a piffling little court case that brought him in fifty crowns at the most he was a day late in getting to Budapest, and in the meantime the silly cow had let herself be soft-soaped right up to her ears. The whole affair had gone off marvellously—an incontestable will, perfect witnesses from Switzerland, unimpeachable medical evidence that the old girl Orosvár had been in full possession of her faculties when she had made her will. The gang of great-nephews and connections by marriage would never have got a brass farthing in spite of the scurrilous stories that their lawyer managed to get into the evening newspapers, and so dead certain was my muttonhead of a chief that, because the case was not to come on until Friday, he went back without a qualm to Vienna for a silly little court case. In the meantime that artful dodger Wiezner got at her by paying her a friendly visit—what d'you think of that, the lawyer on the other side! The half-witted cow went all hysterical. "But I don't want such an awful lot of money, all I want is peace",,' he mimicked in some North German dialect or other. 'Ah, well, she's got her peace now, and the others, quite needlessly, have grabbed three-quarters of her inheritance! Without waiting for my chief to turn up, the silly cow of a woman agreed to a settlement out of court, the most idiotic settlement there ever was. She signed away a good half of her fortune with one stroke of the pen'."

"And bear in mind, *Herr Leutnant*," said Condor, turning to me, "that during the whole of this philippic our friend Kanitz sat rolled up in the corner like a hedgehog, his cap pulled right down over his eyes, not missing a single word. He realized at once what it was all about, for the Orosvár case—I'm using another name, because the real one is too well known—was at that time front-page news in all the Hungarian newspapers, and was a really fantastic affair. I'll give you a brief account of it.

The old Princess Orosvár, already fabulously rich when she came from the Ukraine, had outlived her husband by a good thirty-five years. She was as hard as nails and as wicked as they make 'em, and ever since her only two children had died in one night of whooping-cough she had hated all the other Orosvárs with a deadly hatred for having outlived her own poor brats; and it seems to me quite credible that it should have been out of sheer spite and a malicious desire not to let her impatient nephews and great-nieces inherit her fortune that she should have lived to be eighty-four. Whenever any of the relatives who were waiting so eagerly for her death turned up to see her, she would refuse to receive them, and even the most cordial letter from any member of the family was thrown unanswered into the wastepaper basket. Misanthropic and eccentric ever since the loss of her children and her husband, she never spent more than a few months of the year in Kekesfalva, and no one visited her; the rest of the time she gadded about the world, lived in grand style in Nice and Montreux, dressed and undressed, had her hair done, her hands manicured and her face made up, read French novels, bought masses of clothes, went from shop to shop, haggling and cursing like a Russian market-woman. Naturally, her companion, the only person whose presence she tolerated, had by no means an easy life of it. Day after day the poor, quiet creature had to feed, brush and take out three loathsome, smelly terriers, play the piano to the old fool, read aloud to her, and let herself be bullied in the most vile manner for no reason at all. Sometimes, when the old lady had drunk more brandy or vodka than was good for her—a habit she had brought with her from the Ukraine—the poor young woman, it is said on the best authority, had even to put up with blows. In all the luxury resorts of Europe, Nice, Cannes, Aix-les-Bains and Montreux, everyone knew the bloated old woman with the enamelled pug-face and the dyed hair who, in a raucous voice, without caring who was listening, blustered like a sergeant-major at the waiters and grimaced at people whom she didn't like. Wherever she went there followed her like a shadow on these ghastly promenades—walking behind her with the dogs, never by her side—the companion, a thin, pale, fair-haired creature with frightened eyes, who, one could tell, never ceased to be ashamed of her mistress's vulgarity, and yet feared her as though she were the devil incarnate. In her seventy-eighth year the Princess Orosvár had a very severe attack of pneumonia in the hotel in Territet which the Empress Elizabeth so frequently visited. How the news found its way to Hungary is a mystery. But without any prearranged plan the relatives came rushing along, packed out the hotel, pestered the doctor for news, and waited, waited, for the old lady's death.

But spite is a wonderful thing for keeping people alive. The old virago recovered, and on the day when they heard that the convalescent was to come downstairs for the first time, the impatient relatives took their departure. Now the old lady had got wind of the over-solicitude of her would-be heirs, and with her usual malice had bribed the waiters and chambermaids to pass on to her every word they uttered. Her suspicions were confirmed. They had quarrelled like a pack of wolves as to who should have Kekesfalva, who Orosvár, who the pearls, who the estates in the Ukraine, and who the *palais* in the Ofnerstrasse. And so the battle royal began. A month later a letter arrived from a bill-broker in

Budapest, to the effect that he would be obliged to take pro-
ceedings against her great-nephew Deszä unless she could give
him a written assurance that he was one of the beneficiaries
under her will. This put the lid on everything. The Princess
telegraphed for her lawyer in Budapest, got him to draw up a
new will and, what is more—malice sharpens the wits—in the
presence of two doctors who expressly certified that she was in
full possession of her faculties. This will her lawyer took back
with him to Budapest, and for six years it was kept in a sealed
envelope in his office, for the old lady was in no hurry to die.
When at last the time came for it to be opened, it occasioned a
tremendous surprise. It appointed as principal beneficiary the old
lady's companion, a certain Fräulein Annette Beate Dietzenhof
of Westphalia, whose name, now heard for the first time, fell like
a thunderclap on the ears of all the relatives. Kekesfalva, Orosvár,
the sugar-factory, the stud-farm, and the *palais* in Budapest—all
were left to her; but the estates in the Ukraine and her assets in
cash the Princess had left to her native town for the building of
a Russian church. Not one of the relatives inherited so much as
a bean; meanly enough, she had expressly emphasized in her
will that she was passing over her relatives because 'they could
not wait for me to die'.

And now there was a really first-class hullabaloo. The relatives
yelled blue murder, rushed off to lawyers, and raised the usual
objections to the will. The testatrix, they alleged, had been of
unsound mind, for she had drawn up her will during a severe illness, and had been unduly influenced by her companion; there
was no doubt that the latter had cunningly gained a hold over
the Princess by the power of suggestion. At the same time they
attempted to raise the whole thing to the plane of a patriotic
question. Were Hungarian estates, they asked, which had been
in the possession of the Orosvárs since the time of Arpad, now
to pass into the hands of a foreigner, a Prussian, and the rest, if
you please, to go to the Orthodox Church? Budapest could talk
of nothing else, and whole columns of the newspapers were taken
up with the affair. But despite the outcry raised by the injured
relatives, their case was pretty hopeless. In two lower courts
judgment was given against them; unfortunately for them, both

the doctors in the case were still living in Territet and they reaffirmed the fact that the Princess had been in her right mind at the time of making the will. The other witnesses were also obliged to admit in cross-examination that, although the Princess had been eccentric during the last few years of her life, she had nevertheless been perfectly sane. All the usual lawyers' tricks, all the customary methods of intimidation, proved in vain; there was a hundred to one certainty that the higher court would not reverse the judgments given in Fräulein Dietzenhof's favour.

Kanitz had, of course, read the reports of the case, but he listened intently to every word, for he took a passionate interest in other people's financial affairs for the sake of what he could learn from them; moreover, he had known the Kekesfalva estate ever since he had been an agent.

'You can just imagine', the clerk went on, 'how livid my chief was to find on his return that the silly creature had let herself be led up the garden path. She had already signed away all her claims to the Orosvár estate, the *palais* in the Ofnerstrasse, and had let herself be fobbed off with the Kekesfalva estate and the stud-farm. She had obviously been particularly impressed by the sly dog's promise that she would be burdened with no further litigation, and that the relatives would even be magnanimous enough to pay her lawyer's fees. Now this settlement might still have been disputed in law, for it had not been signed in the presence of a notary public but only before witnesses, and it would have been as easy as winking to starve out the greedy gang, for they hadn't another cent, and couldn't possibly have stood the delay of taking the case to a higher court. Of course my chief, damn his eyes, should have given them a piece of his mind and contested the agreement in the courts in the interests of the beneficiary. But the gang knew the best way of getting round him—on the quiet they offered him a fee of sixty thousand crowns to keep his mouth shut. And since in any case he was furious with the silly creature for letting herself be done out of half a million in half an hour, he declared the settlement valid and raked in the money— sixty thousand crowns, what d'you make of that, for messing up the whole business for his client by going off to Vienna like that. Yes, you've got to be born under a lucky star; the Lord bestows

His gifts on the biggest scoundrels in their sleep! And now all she's got out of the millions left to her is Kekesfalva, and she'll go and chuck that away jolly soon, if I know anything about her, the silly fool.'

'What's she going to do with it?' asked his companion.

'Chuck it away, I tell you. Do something crazy, you may be sure. I've heard rumours, incidentally, that the sugar cartel is trying to get the factory out of her. The day after tomorrow, I believe, the managing director is going there from Budapest. And as for the estate, I believe a fellow called Petrovic, who used to be bailiff there, is going to lease it, but perhaps the sugar cartel will take that over as well. They've money enough. A French banker—I dare say you've seen it in the papers—is said to be planning a merger with the Bohemian sugar industry ... '

At this point the conversation turned to general topics. But our friend Kanitz had heard quite enough to make his ears burn. Few people knew Kekesfalva so well as he; he had been there twenty years before to insure the furniture. He knew Petrovic too, knew him very well from when he had first started in business. It was through his good offices that the scoundrel had always invested with a certain Dr Gollinger the fat sums he screwed out of the estate every year and put in his own pocket. But the most important thing of all was that Kanitz could still vividly recall the cabinet containing the Chinese porcelain, the sculptured glass and the silk embroideries which had been left by Prince Orosvár's grandfather, who had been Russian ambassador in Peking. During the lifetime of the Princess he, Kanitz, who alone was aware of their immense value, had tried to buy them for Rosenfeld in Chicago. They were *objets d'art* of the rarest kind, worth some two to three thousand pounds. The old lady, of course, had had no idea of the fabulous prices that were being paid in America for oriental *objets d'art*, and she had sent Kanitz about his business. She wasn't going to let anything go, she had said, he could go to the devil. If those articles were still there—Kanitz trembled at the thought—one could get them dirt cheap when the property changed hands. The best thing would be to secure an option on the whole of the furniture and effects.

Behaving as though he had just woken up—his three fellow-travellers had long since been talking of other matters—our friend Kanitz pretended to yawn, stretched himself and pulled out his watch. Two o'clock. The train would soon be stopping at this little garrison town. Hurriedly folding up his woolly jacket, he put on his everlasting black coat and tidied himself. At half-past two he got out of the train, drove to the Red Lion, and booked a room; it goes without saying that, like a general before a battle the outcome of which is uncertain, he slept very badly. At seven o'clock—there was not a moment to be lost—he got up and trudged down the avenue to Kekesfalva along which we've just walked. I must get there first, get there before anyone else, he thought. Settle everything before the vultures come flying along from Budapest. Quickly persuade Petrovic to let me know the moment there is to be a sale of the furniture. If the worst comes to the worst, join with him in bidding for all the household effects and make sure of getting the furniture when it comes to dividing up the spoils.

Since the death of the Princess very few servants had been kept on at Kekesfalva; and so Kanitz was able to creep in without difficulty and have a look round. A fine property, he thought to himself, really in admirable condition. The shutters freshly painted, the wails beautifully colour-washed, a new fence—aha, that fellow Petrovic knows why he has had so many repairs done, he gets a nice fat rake-off on every bill! But where was the fellow? The main gate turned out to be shut, and, loudly as he knocked, no one stirred in the courtyard. Confound it all, supposing the fellow had himself gone off to Budapest to come to terms with that simple-minded Dietzenhof woman?

Kanitz wandered impatiently from one door to another, shouted, clapped his hands—not a sign of anyone. At last, stealing in through the little side-door, he caught sight of a female in the conservatory. All he could see through the glass was that she was watering plants. Here was someone at last who could give him some information. Kanitz knocked sharply on the glass. 'Hallo!' he shouted, and clapped his hands to attract her attention. The female who was busied with the plants gave a start, as though caught out in doing something wrong, and it was some time before she ventured timidly to the door. A fair-haired, slender female, no longer in her first youth, dressed in a simple dark blouse and cotton apron, she stood there framed in the doorway, the garden-shears still held half-open in her hand.

'You keep one waiting long enough, I must say!' snapped Kanitz somewhat impatiently. 'Where on earth is Petrovic?'

'Who?' asked the thin young woman, with a troubled look, involuntarily taking a step backwards and hiding the garden shears behind her back.

'Who? Is there more than one Petrovic here? I mean Petrovic— the bailiff.'

'Oh, I beg your pardon ... the ... the bailiff ... oh, yes ... I've not yet seen him myself. He's gone to Vienna, I believe. But his wife told me she hoped he would be back before this evening.'

Hoped, hoped, thought Kanitz in irritation. Wait until evening! Waste another night at the hotel! More unnecessary expense, and even then one didn't know what was going to come of it.

'Bother! He *would* be away today of all days.' he murmured half to himself, and then, turning to the young woman, he asked: 'Is it possible to view the house in the meantime? Does anyone have the keys?'

'The keys?' she repeated in dismay.

'Yes, devil take it, the keys!' (Why is she hedging in this silly way? Probably she's been given orders by Petrovic not to let any-one in. Well, I suppose I'll have to give the frightened ninny a tip.) Kanitz immediately assumed a jocular air and went on in condescending tones:

'Come now, don't be so scared! I'm not going to steal any-thing. I only want to have a look round. Now then, out with it— have you the keys or not?'

'The keys ... of course I have the keys,' she stammered, 'but ... I don't know when Herr Petrovic ... '

'I've already told you I don't need Petrovic to go round the house. So don't let's have a lot of nonsense! D'you know your way about the house?'

She grew even more embarrassed. 'Well, I think ... I know my way to some extent ... '

A half-wit, thought Kanitz. What wretched servants this fellow Petrovic has about the place.

124

'Now then, let's get on with it, I haven't much time,' he bellowed.

He went ahead, and she followed—yes, actually followed, uneasily and diffidently. At the door leading into the house she hesitated again.

'Good God Almighty, look sharp and unlock it!' Why was the creature behaving so stupidly, so awkwardly? fumed Kanitz. While she was taking the keys from her shabby leather purse he inquired once more, to be on the safe side:

'What d'you actually do here?'

The frightened creature stood still and blushed. 'I am ... ' she began and immediately corrected herself. ' ... I was ... I was the Princess's companion.'

Our friend Kanitz was absolutely flabbergasted (and I can assure you it was very difficult to disconcert a man of his calibre). Involuntarily he stepped back a pace.

'You don't ... you don't really mean to say you're Fräulein Dietzenhof?'

'Why, yes,' she answered in the frightened tones of someone accused of a crime.

There was one emotion that Kanitz had never yet experienced in his life, and that was embarrassment. But for this one brief moment, as he stumbled blindly, as it were, upon the almost legendary Fräulein Dietzenhof, the heiress to Kekesfalva, he was acutely embarrassed. He instantly changed his tone.

'I beg your pardon', he stammered in confusion, hastily taking off his hat. 'I beg your pardon, *gnädiges Fräulein* ... But no one told me that you had already arrived. I had no idea. Please forgive me. I had only come to ... '

He hesitated, for now he had to think up a plausible pretext.

'It was only about the insurance. I was here several times some years ago in the late Princess's lifetime. Unfortunately I did not have the pleasure of meeting you, *gnädiges Fräulein*. It was only about that, about the insurance ... only to see that everything was still intact. It's our duty to do so. But there's no hurry.'

'Oh, it's quite all right, it's quite all right ... ' she said nervously. 'Of course, I know very little about such things. Perhaps you had better discuss the matter directly with Herr Peterwitz.'

'Certainly, certainly,' replied Kanitz, who had not yet entirely recovered his presence of mind. 'Why, of course I'll wait to see Herr Peterwitz.' (Why should I correct her, he thought.)

'But perhaps, *gnädiges Fräulein*, if it wouldn't be troubling you, I could take a quick look round, and then the whole thing could be settled straight away. I don't suppose anything's been changed?'

'No, no,' she said hurriedly, 'nothing at all has been changed. If you'd like to see for yourself ... '

'It's most kind of you, *gnädiges Fräulein*,' said Kanitz with a bow, and they both entered the house.

His first thought was for the four Guardis in the *salon*, which I expect you know, and the glass cabinet in the adjoining room, now Edith's drawing-room, with the Chinese porcelain, the tapestries and little jade figures. What a relief, everything was still there. Petrovic hadn't stolen anything; the dolt was more interested in making what he could on the sale of the oats, the clover, the potatoes, and on the contracts for repairs. Meanwhile Fräulein Dietzenhof, obviously anxious not to disturb the stranger on his restless tour of inspection, threw open the shutters. The light came pouring in, and it was possible to see through the tall French windows right out into the park. I must make conversation, thought Kanitz. Mustn't let her slip through my fingers. Must make friends with her.

'What a lovely view there is of the park!' he began, taking a deep breath. 'It must be marvellous to live here.'

'Yes, very nice,' she agreed submissively, but there was no real conviction in her tone. Kanitz realized at once that this scared creature had forgotten, if she ever knew, how to contradict flatly and only now did she add by way of amendment:

'It's true the Princess never felt really happy here. She always said that flat country made her feel melancholy. She really only liked the mountains and the sea. This district was too lonely for her, and the people ... '

Once more she broke off. I simply must make conversation, Kanitz reminded himself. Maintain contact with her.

'But you, I trust, are now going to stay with us, *gnädiges Fräulein*?'

'I?' Involuntarily she threw up her hands, as though to ward off something disagreeable. 'I? No, oh no! What should I do alone in a great house like this? Oh no, no, I'm going away as soon as everything has been settled up.'

Kanitz stole a furtive glance at her from the side. What a wisp of a thing she looked in this big room, the poor owner of Kekesfalva. Except that she was rather too pale and frightened, one might almost have called her pretty, the long slender face with the veiled lids made one think of a rain-drenched land-scape, the eyes seemed to be of a delicate cornflower-blue—soft, warm eyes, which did not dare to beam too brightly, but again and again shyly took refuge behind the lids. And as an experi-enced observer of human nature Kanitz realized at once that here was a being whose backbone had been broken: a creature without a will of her own, whom one could twist round one's lit-tle finger. Well then, make conversation, make conversation! Wrinkling his brow sympathetically, he went on:

'But what's going to become of this lovely property? An estate like this needs to be managed, and managed with a firm hand.'

'I don't know, I don't know.' She spoke with extreme nervous-ness. A tremor ran through her delicate frame. And at that moment Kanitz grasped the fact that this woman, who had for years been in the position of a dependant, would never have the courage to make an independent decision, and that she was terrified rather than pleased at the thought of having come into this inheritance, which lay like a great weight on her soul. In a flash Kanitz thought out the situation. It was not for nothing that in the last twenty years he had learned to buy and sell, to push and shove his way through life. One had to persuade the buyer into buying, dissuade the seller from selling: that was the first rule in the business of being an agent, and he immediately turned on the relevant patter. Rub in all the disadvantages, he thought. Perhaps in the end he might lease the whole estate from her and steal a march on Petrovic. Perhaps it was a stroke of good luck that the fellow happened to be in Vienna today. He assumed an expression of commiseration.

'How right you are! A large estate is always a great nuisance. You never get a moment's peace. Day after day you have to have rows with the bailiff and the staff and your neighbours, and then on the top of it all come the taxes and lawyers. Whenever people have an inkling that you've got even a little bit of property or money, they try to squeeze your last farthing out of you. You find you're surrounded by enemies, however well-disposed you are to everyone. It's no use, it's no use——every man becomes a thief when he smells money. Yes, unfortunately, you're right. You've got to rule over an estate like this with an iron hand, or you simply can't make a success of it. You have to be born to it, and even then it's one long, everlasting struggle.'

'Ah, yes,' she said with a sigh. He could tell that she was remembering something horrible. 'People are terrible where money's concerned. Terrible. I never knew that before.'

People? What did people matter to Kanitz? What did he care whether they were good or bad? He must rent the estate, and that as quickly and advantageously as possible. He listened and nodded politely, and while he listened and answered, another part of his brain was occupied in wondering how he could wangle the whole thing as rapidly as possible. Should he found a company to lease the whole Kekesfalva estate, the farms, the sugar-factory, the stud-farm? He would be perfectly prepared to sub-let it all to Petrovic and only keep the furniture and fittings. The main thing was to make an offer for the lease straight away and put the fear of God into her; she would take anything he offered her. She couldn't reckon up, she had never earned money and did not deserve to make a great deal of money. While every nerve and fibre of his brain was at work, his lips went on chattering apparently unconcernedly.

'The worst part of the whole thing is the litigation. It's no use being pacific, you're never done with quarrels and disputes. That's what has always frightened me off buying any kind of property. One long round of law suits, lawyers, negotiations, writs and scandals. No, better to live unpretentiously, to have security and not have to worry. You think that when you've got an estate like this it's something worth having, but in reality you're at the mercy of everyone, you never get a moment's peace. In itself it would be marvellous, this house, this lovely old property, marvellous … but to run it you need nerves of steel and an iron fist, or it's never anything but a burden to you.' She listened to him with bowed head. All of a sudden she looked up; a deep sigh seemed to come from the bottom of her heart. 'Yes, a terrible burden ... if only I could sell it!'"

Dr Condor paused abruptly. "I must break off my story at this point, *Herr Leutnant*, in order to make clear to you what that one short sentence meant in the life of our friend Kanitz. I have already told you that Kekesfalva related this story to me during the saddest night of his life, the night on which his wife died, at one of those moments, therefore, which a man lives through perhaps only twice or three times in his life—one of those moments when even the most reserved man feels a need to bare his soul to another man as to God. I can still see him clearly before me: we were sitting downstairs in the waiting-room of the sanatorium; he had moved up close to me and he poured out his story in low, vehement, excited tones. I felt that he was talking and talking in order to forget that his wife was dying upstairs, that he was trying to deaden his senses with an interminable spate of words. But at this point in his narrative where Fräulein Dietzenhof said to him: 'If only I could sell it!' he stopped dead. Just think of it, *Herr Leutnant*—even fifteen or sixteen years later he was so strangely agitated by the memory of that moment when the unsuspecting spinster admitted to him so impulsively that all she wanted was to sell Kekesfalva quickly, quickly, as quickly as possible, that he turned quite pale. Twice, three times, he repeated the sentence to me and with exactly the same emphasis, 'If only I could sell it!' For the Leopold Kanitz of those days had, with his quick powers of perception, immediately realized that the great business deal of his life was positively falling, as it were, into his hands, and that he had nothing to do but reach out and grasp it—that it was possible for him to purchase this wonderful property instead of merely renting it. And whilst he hid his stupefaction under a veil of idle chatter, the thoughts were racing through his brain. I must buy it, of course, he decided, buy it at once before Petrovic or the director from Budapest are hot on the scent. I mustn't let her slip through my fingers. I must cut off her retreat. I shan't go away until I am the owner of Kekesfalva. And with that mysterious capacity for keeping the mind working on two levels which comes to one at certain moments of high tension, he was on the one hand *thinking* of his own interests, and them only, while on the other he was *talking* to her with studied slowness against those interests.

'Sell ... yes, of course, *gnädiges Fräulein*, you can always sell ... selling in itself is an easy matter ... but to sell *advantageously*, that's an art. To sell advantageously, that's the important thing. To find someone who's honest, someone who knows the district, the land and the people ... someone who has connections with the place, not one of those lawyers—God forbid!—who try to involve you in useless litigation ... and then—very important in this particular case—you must sell for cash.

You must discover someone who won't give you bonds and promissory notes ... make certain of your money and get a proper price.' (And while he spoke he was working out sums in his head. I can go up to four hundred thousand crowns, four hundred and fifty thousand at the most; after all, there are the pictures, which are worth a good fifty thousand, maybe a hundred thousand, the house, and the stud-farm. I shall have to find out, though, if the place is mortgaged, and get her to tell me whether she has already had an offer. And suddenly he took the plunge.

'Have you, *gnädiges Fräulein*—forgive me for asking such an indiscreet question—have you a rough idea of the price? I mean, have you any kind of definite figure in mind?'

'No,' she answered helplessly, and gazed at him with troubled eyes.

Oh lord, that's bad, thought Kanitz. As bad as can be. These people who don't name a price are always the worst to do business with. They go running about to Pontius and to Pilate for advice, and everyone names a price and says his say and puts in his oar. If she's given time to take advice, it's all up. While this tumult was going on within him, however, he went on talking indefatigably.

'But you've surely worked out a *rough* idea, *gnädiges Fräulein* ... you must know, after all, whether the estate is mortgaged, and to what extent?'

'Mortgaged?' she repeated. Kanitz immediately realized that this was the first time she had ever heard the word.

130

'I mean, some kind of provisional valuation must have been made—if only for the purpose of assessing the estate duties. Did your lawyer—forgive me if I seem to be importunate, but I should like to advise you frankly—did your lawyer name no sort of figure?'

'The lawyer?' She seemed dimly to recall something. 'Oh yes, yes ... wait a moment ... yes, the lawyer did write something to me. Something or other about a valuation. Yes, you're right, it was in connection with the taxes, but ... but it was all drawn up in Hungarian, and I don't know Hungarian. That's right, I remember now, my lawyer told me to get it translated, and oh dear, in all the confusion it went right out of my head. All the papers must be over there in my case. I have a room over in the estate building I can't sleep in the room that used to be the Princess's. But if you'll really be so kind as to come across there with me, I'll show you everything ... that is to say'—she hesitated—'that is to say if I'm not troubling you too much with my affairs.'

Kanitz trembled with excitement. Everything was falling into his lap with a rapidity only encountered in dreams. She herself was going to show him all the documents, the valuation of the property, and that would give him the whip hand. He bowed humbly.

'I assure you it is a pleasure to me to give you advice, *gnädiges Fräulein*. And I think I may claim without exaggeration to have had some experience in these matters. The Princess'—here he was deliberately lying—'always came to me for advice on financial matters; she knew that my only concern was to advise her for the best.'

They went across to the estate building. Yes, indeed, all the documents concerned with the lawsuit were there, stuffed anyhow into a briefcase; the whole of the correspondence with her lawyers, the tax forms, the copy of the final settlement. She nervously ran through the documents, and Kanitz, breathing heavily as he watched her, could feel his hands trembling. At last she unfolded a paper.

'I think this must be the letter.'

Kanitz took the letter, to which was affixed a document in

Hungarian. It was a brief note from the Viennese lawyer.

'My Hungarian colleague informs me that, through the good offices of certain influential friends, he has succeeded in getting the estate assessed at a quite exceptionally low figure for the purpose of death duties. In my opinion the enclosed assessment corresponds only to about a third, and in the case of certain objects, indeed, only a quarter, of the real value.'

Kanitz seized the document with trembling hands. Only one thing in it interested him—the Kekesfalva estate. It was assessed at one hundred and ninety thousand crowns.

Kanitz turned pale. It was exactly what he had himself calculated, exactly three times the amount of this artificially low figure, that is to say, six to seven hundred thousand crowns, and the lawyer, moreover, had known nothing whatever of the Chinese vases. How much should he offer her now? The figures danced and swam before his eyes.

But the voice at his side was asking in anxious tones: 'Is it the right document? Can you understand it?'

'Of course,' said Kanitz with a start. 'Yes, oh yes ... Well then, the lawyer informs you that the value of Kekesfalva is a hundred and ninety thousand crowns. That is, of course, only the estimated value.'

'The estimated value? Excuse me ... but what does that mean?'

Now was the time to clinch matters, now or never. Kanitz tried to suppress his laboured breathing. 'The estimated value ... yes, the estimated value, there's always some uncertainty about it, it's ... always a very doubtful matter ... for ... the official valuation never quite corresponds to the real value for selling purposes. One can never rely—that is *definitely* rely—on getting the whole amount at which an estate is assessed. In some cases, of course, one can get it, in some cases even more ... but only in certain circumstances ... it's always a bit of a gamble, as in the case of an auction ... The estimated value is, after all, no more than a figure to go upon, a very vague figure, of course. One can assume, for example'—Kanitz trembled; not too little now and not too much—'if an estate like this, for example, is officially assessed at a hundred and ninety thousand crowns ... one may assume that ... that ... in the event of a sale one could at any rate get a hundred and fifty thousand. One could count on that at any rate.'

'How much did you say?'

Kanitz could feel the blood suddenly roaring and throbbing in his ears. She had turned to him with astonishing vehemence and asked the question as though only just able to control her indignation. Had she seen through his lying game? Ought he not, perhaps, to raise the sum quickly by another fifty thousand crowns? But an inner voice urged him: Try it on. And he staked all on one card. Although his pulses were drumming at his temples, he said, with a show of diffidence:

'Yes, I should expect *that* at any rate. A hundred and fifty thousand crowns, I should think one could quite certainly get that for it.'

But at that moment his heart almost stood still, and the pulses that had been thundering seemed to stop dead. For the poor unsuspecting creature at his side exclaimed in tones of genuine amazement:

' ... As much as *that?* Do you really think ... as much as *that?*'

And it was some time before Kanitz recovered his self-possession. He had to struggle to control his breathing before he could reply in tones of sober conviction: 'Yes, *gnädiges Fräulein*, I can almost stake my word on that. You ought at any rate to get as much as *that*'."

Once again Dr Condor broke off. At first I thought he was only pausing to light a cigar. But I noticed that he had all of a sudden grown restless. He took off his pince-nez, put them on again, smoothed back his scanty hair as though it were in his way, and looked at me; it was a long, uneasy, quizzical look. Then he leaned back abruptly in his chair.

"It may be that I have already told you too much, *Herr Leutnant*, at any rate more than I originally intended. But I trust you will not misunderstand me. If I have told you quite frankly of the trick by which Kekesfalva outwitted the poor unsuspecting creature, it is not, I assure you, because I want to prejudice you against him. The poor old man with whom we dined tonight, sick in mind and body, as we saw him, the man who has entrusted me with the care of his child and who would give the last farthing of his fortune to see the poor thing cured, that man is no longer, has long since ceased to be, the individual guilty of that shady transaction, and I should be the last to accuse him today. It is precisely at this moment, when in his despair he really needs help, that it seems to me important that you should learn the truth from me instead of hearing all sorts of malicious gossip from others. I beg you, therefore, to bear one thing clearly in mind—Kekesfalva (or rather Kanitz as he then was) did *not* go to Kekesfalva that day with the intention of getting this woman, so unversed in the ways of the world, to sell the estate to him for a song. He had only meant to pick up one of his little bargains in passing, and no more. This tremendous opportunity that came his way positively took him by *surprise*, and he would not have been the man he was had he not utilized it to the full. But you will see that subsequently the tables were to some extent turned.

I don't want to spin out my story more than necessary, and I'll skip some of the details. I will merely tell you that the hours that followed were the most tense, the most agitated, of his whole life. Just picture the situation to yourself: here you have a man who has hitherto been merely an insignificant little agent, an obscure dealer, and suddenly an opportunity to become immensely rich comes whirling his way like a meteor out of the sky. Within the space of twenty-four hours he would be able to earn more than he had earned hitherto in twenty-four years of the most exacting toil, the most wretched huckstering, and—tremendous temptation—there was no need for him even to run after this victim, to captivate her, to bemuse her; on the contrary, his victim was walking of her own free will into his snare, she was positively licking the hand that held the knife. The only danger lay in the fact that someone else might intervene. Hence he dared not let the heiress slip from his grasp for a single instant, dared not give her time to think. He would have to get her away from Kekesfalva before Petrovic returned, and while taking these precautionary measures he must not for one instant betray the fact that he himself was interested in the sale of the estate.

It was Napoleonic in its audacity, its perilousness, this plan to take the besieged fortress of Kekesfalva by storm before the relieving army approached. But chance is a willing accomplice of the man who is ready to venture all. A fact of which Kanitz himself was quite unaware had smoothed the path for him, and this was the extremely cruel and yet natural fact that the poor heiress had already been subjected to so many humiliations and encountered so much hatred in this *Schloss* which was now hers that she herself cherished one wish alone—to get away from it, away from it as quickly as possible. No envy is more mean than that of small-minded beings when they see a neighbour lifted, as though borne aloft by angels, out of the dull drudgery of their common existence; petty spirits are more ready to forgive a prince the most fabulous wealth rather than a fellow-sufferer beneath the same yoke the smallest degree of freedom. The staff of Kekesfalva had been unable to suppress their fury at the fact that this North German woman of all people, who, as they clearly remembered, had often had comb and brush thrown at her head when she was doing the irascible old Princess's hair, should now suddenly have become the owner of Kekesfalva and thus their mistress. On the news of the heiress's arrival Petrovic had taken the first train out of the place so as not to have to welcome her, and his wife, a common hussy who had formerly been a kitchen-maid at the *Schloss*, had greeted her with the words: 'Well, I dare say you won't want to stay with us—it won't be grand enough for you.' The houseboy had thrown down her suitcase outside the door with a loud crash, and she herself had had to drag it across the threshold, for Petrovic's wife had not lifted a finger to help her. There was no meal ready for her, no one bothered about her, and that night she was obliged to listen to conversation carried on in fairly loud tones about a certain 'legacy-hunter' and 'swindler'.

The poor, weak-spirited woman realized from this reception that she would never have a moment's peace in this house. It was for that reason alone—and of this Kanitz was quite unaware—that she readily agreed to his proposal that she should accompany him that very day to Vienna, where, he said, he knew a man who would be sure to buy the estate. He seemed to her to be a messenger from heaven, this grave, courteous, well-informed

135

man with the melancholy eyes. And so she asked no further questions, but gratefully handed over to him all the documents in the case, and listened with quietly intent blue eyes as he advised her with regard to the investment of the money she would get from the sale. She must only invest in something absolutely safe, in Government bonds. She must not entrust even a crumb of her fortune to a private individual; she must put everything in the bank, and a notary public must take over the administration of it. There was no point whatever in calling in her lawyer at this stage, for what was the business of a lawyer but to make simple things complicated? Yes, yes, he kept on interposing indefatigably, it was possible that she might obtain a higher price in three or four years' time. But think what expenses there would be in the meantime and what a lot of bother with the court and officials. And realizing from the look of alarm that once more came into her eyes what a horror this pacific creature had of courts and business matters, he went through the whole gamut of his arguments again and again, always ending on the same note: quickly, quickly! At four o'clock that afternoon, complete agreement established, they caught the Vienna express before Petrovic returned. The whole thing had been so tempestuous that Fräulein Dietzenhof had not even had an opportunity of asking this strange gentleman, whom she was entrusting with the sale of her entire inheritance, his name.

They travelled first class in the express—it was the first time that Kekesfalva had sat on the red velvet cushions. In Vienna he took her to a good hotel in the Kärntnerstrasse and booked a room there for himself also. Now on the one hand it was essential that Kanitz should that very evening have the deed of sale drawn up by his accommodating lawyer, Dr Gollinger, so as to get the whole thing put on a legally incontestable basis the very next day, and on the other he did not dare leave his victim alone for even a second. And so he hit upon what I must frankly admit was a brilliant idea. He suggested to Fräulein Dietzenhof that she should spend the evening at the opera, where a much-talked-of performance by a visiting company was billed, while he would see if he could not get in touch that very evening with the gentleman who, he knew, was looking out for a large estate.

Touched by so much solicitude, Fräulein Dietzenhof agreed with alacrity; he deposited her safely at the opera—she would not be able to budge now for four hours. He himself, meanwhile, dashed off in a cab—also for the first time in his life—to his crony, Dr Gollinger. He was not at home, but Kanitz routed him out of a wine-bar, and promised him two thousand crowns if he would draw up the agreement in all its details that very night and make an appointment with the notary for seven o'clock the next evening.

Kanitz—a spendthrift for the first time in his life—had kept the cab waiting outside the lawyer's house while they had been talking. Racing back in it to the opera, he arrived just in time to catch an enraptured Fräulein Dietzenhof in the foyer and escort her back to the hotel. And so a second sleepless night began for him. The nearer he approached his goal, the more was he racked by anxiety lest the hitherto submissive heiress might yet elude him. Getting out of bed again and again, he worked out in the minutest detail the tactics he was going to employ the next day to encircle the enemy. Above all, he must not leave her alone for a single moment. He must hire a carriage, and keep it waiting everywhere they went; they must never take a step on foot, lest she might run into her lawyer in the street. He must prevent her from looking at a newspaper, for there might be a paragraph about the settlement in the Orosvár lawsuit, and she might begin to suspect that she was being swindled a second time. But, as it happened, all these fears and precautions were needless, for the victim did not *want* to escape; she ran obediently after the wicked shepherd like a woolly lamb on a pink ribbon, and when, after a ghastly night, our friend entered the breakfast-room of the hotel in a state of utter exhaustion, she was sitting there, waiting patiently, in the same home-made gown. And now began a strange whirligig, our friend dragging poor Fräulein Dietzenhof round with him quite unnecessarily from morning to evening, so as to delude her into believing that all the spurious difficulties which he himself had so laboriously invented for her during his sleepless night were real.

I shall pass over the details, but he dragged her to his lawyer and from there telephoned all over the place about all sorts of other matters. He took her to a bank and asked for the manager in order to consult him with regard to the investment of her money and to open an account for her; he hauled her along to several mortgage banks and to an obscure real-estate broker's on the pretext that he had to obtain some information. And she went with him, she waited quietly and patiently in the ante-rooms while he carried on his sham negotiations. Twelve years of slavery in the service of the Princess had long since inured her to this waiting; it neither depressed nor humiliated her, and she waited, waited, her hands motionless in her lap, lowering the gaze of her blue eyes whenever anyone passed. She did whatever Kanitz asked, as patiently and obediently as a child. She signed documents at the bank without so much as glancing at them, and so unhesitatingly signed receipts for sums of money she had never received that Kanitz began to be assailed by the disturbing thought that this silly woman might perhaps have been equally satisfied with a hundred and forty or even a hundred and thirty thousand crowns. She said 'Yes' when the bank manager advised her to put her money in railway stock. 'Yes' when he suggested bank shares, and invariably looked across anxiously at her oracle Kanitz. It was clear that all these business formalities, these signatures and forms, indeed the mere sight of money, inspired in her a feeling of acute uneasiness that was yet tinged with awe, and that the one thing she longed for was to run away from all these puzzling transactions and to sit down in some quiet room again, to read, to knit or to play the piano, instead of being com-pelled, unpractical-minded and unsure of herself as she was, to face such weighty decisions.

But Kanitz drove her untiringly along on this round of spurious visits, partly in order to help her, as he had promised, to invest the purchase price of the estate in the safest way, partly in order to throw her into a state of confusion; and so it went on from nine in the morning until half-past five in the evening. In the end they were both so exhausted that he suggested they might go and sit down in a café. All the essentials were settled, the sale was as good as completed; she would have only to sign the deed of sale at the notary's at seven o'clock and to receive the purchase price. Immediately her face lit up.

'Ah, then I can go away tomorrow morning?' Her cornflower eyes beamed at him.

'Why, of course,' said Kanitz soothingly. 'In an hour's time you will be the freest person on earth and will have no more need to bother about money and property. Your investments will bring you in an absolutely safe six thousand crowns, a year. You can live anywhere in the whole wide world, wherever you like and as you like.'

Out of politeness he inquired where she meant to go, and her face, which the moment before had brightened, clouded over.

'I was thinking that it might be best if I went to my relatives in Westphalia. I think there's a train via Cologne in the morning.'

Kanitz immediately displayed tremendous zeal. He asked the waiter for the timetable, looked through the index, worked out all the connections. Express Vienna-Frankfurt-Cologne, change at Osnabrück. It would be best to take the nine-twenty, which arrived in Frankfurt in the evening, he said; he would advise her to spend the night there, so as not to get too tired. In his restless eagerness he went on turning over the pages and found an advertisement of a Protestant hostel. She need not bother about the ticket, he would see to that, and would also be sure to see her off in the morning. In the discussion of such little matters the time passed more quickly than he had hoped; and now at last he could look at the clock and remark: 'I say, we must be off to the notary's at once.'

Within the space of an hour the whole thing was settled. Within the space of an hour our friend had swindled the heiress out of three-quarters of her fortune. When his accomplice saw the name of *Schloss Kekesfalva* filled in on the agreement, saw, moreover, what a paltry sum was being paid for it, he screwed up one eye behind Fräulein Dietzenhof's back and winked admiringly at his old crony, as much as to say, 'Splendid, you dog. You *have* pulled off something this time!' The notary also gazed with interest from behind his glasses at Fräulein Dietzenhof; he had, of course, read in the newspapers of the struggle over Princess Orosvár's inheritance, and he was somewhat suspicious of this hasty resale of the estate. Poor creature, he thought, you've fallen into evil hands. But it is not the duty of a notary to

warn either seller or purchaser when witnessing the signatures to
a deed of sale. It is his job to stamp the deed, to fill it up, and to
see that the fees are duly paid. And so the good man merely
bowed his head—he had had to witness many a shady transaction
and set the seal of the imperial eagle upon it—neatly unfolded
the agreement and politely invited Fräulein Dietzenhof to sign
first.

The timid creature gave a start. She gazed irresolutely at her
mentor Kanitz, and not until he had encouraged her with a nod
did she step up to the table and write in her neat, clear, straight
German hand: 'Annette Beate Maria Dietzenhof'. Then it was
our friend's turn to sign. And therewith the whole thing was
settled: the document signed, the purchase price handed over to
the notary, the bank account named into which the cheque was
to be paid next day. With one stroke of the pen Leopold Kanitz
had doubled or trebled his fortune. From that moment he, and
he alone, was lord and master of Kekesfalva.

The notary carefully blotted the signatures. Then they all
three shook hands with him and walked down the stairs,
Fräulein Dietzenhof first, after her Kanitz, holding his breath,
and last of all Dr Gollinger, who, to Kanitz's extreme annoyance, kept poking him in the ribs from behind with his stick and
declaiming *sotto voce* in a beery voice: '*Scampus maximus, scampus
maximus*'. Nevertheless, Kanitz was by no means pleased when
Dr Gollinger took leave of him at the door of the building with
an ironically low bow, for now he was left alone with his victim—
and this really terrified him.

You must try, my dear Lieutenant, to understand this unexpected revolution in his feelings. I should not like to express it
sentimentally and say that our friend Kanitz's conscience had
suddenly been awakened—but ever since that stroke of the pen
the external situation between the two partners to the agreement
had utterly changed. Just think: during the whole of these two
days Kanitz, in the role of purchaser, had struggled against this
poor woman, in the role of vendor. She had been the opponent
whom he had had to encircle strategically, whom he had had to
close in upon and force into capitulation. But now the financial-
military operation had come to an end. Napoleon Kanitz had

won a victory, a complete victory, and this poor, quiet, simply dressed woman, who was walking beside him along the Walfischgasse, was no longer his opponent, his enemy. And, strange as it may sound, nothing oppressed our friend more at this moment of speedy victory than the fact that his victim had made his victory *too* easy for him. For when one does another person an injustice, in some mysterious way it does one good to discover (or to persuade oneself) that the injured party has also behaved badly or unfairly in some little matter or other; it is always a relief to the conscience if one can apportion some measure of guilt to the person one has betrayed. But Kanitz could not accuse this victim of anything, even the slightest thing; she had yielded herself up with bound hands and had never ceased, moreover, to cast unsuspecting, grateful looks at him out of her cornflower-blue eyes. What was he to say to her now? Congratulate her on the sale of the estate, that is, its loss? He felt more and more uncomfortable. I shall see her to the hotel, he thought quickly, and then the whole thing will be over.

But his victim had for her part also become visibly uneasy. Her gait too had changed; she was walking along thoughtfully, hesitantly. This change did not escape Kanitz's notice, although his head was lowered; he felt from the way in which she falteringly put one foot down after the other (he did not dare to look her in the face) that her mind was preoccupied with something. He was seized with panic. Now at last she has tumbled to it that I am the purchaser, he thought. She'll probably start upbraiding me now; she's probably already repenting her stupid haste and will go running off to her lawyer tomorrow.

But now at last—they had walked in silence down the whole of the Walfischgasse, side by side, shadow by shadow—she plucked up courage, cleared her throat and began:

'Forgive me ... but as I'm going away tomorrow morning I should like to settle everything up first ... I should like, above all, to thank you for the trouble you have taken and ... and ... to ask you to be so kind as to tell me frankly how much I owe you for all your trouble. You've lost so much time by seeing to all this for me and ... I'm leaving tomorrow morning ... I should like to settle everything up first.'

Our friend's footsteps faltered, his heart stopped beating. This was too much. He had not been prepared for this. He was assailed by the kind of disagreeable feeling one has when one has beaten a dog in anger and the poor creature comes crawling along upon its belly, looks up at one imploringly and licks the hand that has administered the cruel punishment.

'No, no,' he protested in genuine dismay, 'you owe me nothing, nothing at all.' And he could feel the sweat breaking out all over him. To him, to this man who always foresaw everything, who for years had learned to be prepared for every reaction on the part of a client, this was an entirely novel experience. During the hard years when he had been a little agent doors had been shut in his face, people had turned their backs on him, and there had been streets in his district which he had preferred to avoid. But that someone should actually thank him—that had never yet happened to him. And he felt ashamed in the presence of this, the first person to trust, to go on trusting him. He felt constrained to make excuses.

'No,' he stammered, 'good lord, no. You owe me nothing at all ... I wouldn't dream of taking anything. I only hope I've done the right thing and have acted entirely to your satisfaction. Perhaps it would have been better to wait, I'm afraid perhaps we might have ... might have got more if you had not been in such a hurry. But you wanted to make a quick sale, didn't you? And I think you've done the best thing. By God, I think you've done the best thing!'

He was able to breathe freely again; he became positively honest at this moment.

'A person like you who has no knowledge of business had much better have nothing to do with it. It's much better that a person like yourself ... should get a smaller, but safe sum. Don't'—he swallowed hard—'don't, I beg you, let yourself be put off by people who tell you later on that you have made a bad bargain, or have let the place go too cheaply. You'll always find people who'll come along after you've sold a thing and throw their weight about and say they would have given more, far more ... but when it comes to the point they never produce the cash. They'd have all got you tied up with a lot of bills of exchange or promissory notes and shares. Those would be no good to you, no good at all, I swear to you. You wouldn't be able to cope with them. To do business one must ... one must be hard as nails, and clever and cunning into the bargain ... and you're not that. For you it was better to have a smaller sum, but a safe sum. And your money *is* safe. I swear to you, as I stand here before you, the bank is a first-class one and your money is safe. You'll get your dividends regularly to the day and hour, nothing can go wrong. Believe me ... I swear to you ... it's better for you as it is.'

Meanwhile they had reached the hotel. Kanitz hesitated. I ought at least to treat her to something, he thought. Invite her out to dinner, or perhaps to a theatre. But she was already holding out her hand.

'I don't think I ought to keep you any longer ... I've been worried the whole day to think that you should have given up so much of your time on my behalf. For two whole days you've devoted yourself exclusively to my affairs, and I really have a feeling that no one could have been more self-sacrificing. Once again ... thank you very much. Never'—she blushed slightly— 'never has anyone been so kind to me, so helpful. I should never have thought it possible that I should have got this business off my hands so quickly, that everything would be made so easy and pleasant for me ... thank you very, *very* much.'

Kanitz took her hand, and as he did so he could not help looking up at her. Something of her habitual apprehension had been swept away by the warmth of her emotion. There was a warm glow on her usually too pallid and frightened features; she looked almost childlike with her expressive blue eyes and her grateful little smile. Kanitz sought in vain for words. But before he could speak she had said 'Goodbye' and walked away, light, graceful and confident; her gait was now quite different from what it had been, it was the gait of someone who had cast off a burden, someone liberated. Kanitz looked uncertainly after her, but the porter had already handed her the key of her room, and the page was showing her to the lift. The whole thing was over.

And so it was that the lamb took leave of the slaughterer. Kanitz, however, felt as though he had struck his own head with the axe. He stood there dazed for a few minutes, staring into the deserted foyer of the hotel. Finally the ebb and flow of the street carried him away, he did not know whither. Never yet had anyone looked at him like that, with such a human, such a grateful expression. Never yet had anyone spoken to him like that. That 'thank you very, *very* much' still rang in his ears. And this was the person he had plundered, betrayed. Again and again he came to a halt and wiped the sweat from his brow. And suddenly, outside the big glassware shop in the Kärtnerstrasse, along which he stumbled, reeled aimlessly, as though drunk with sleep, he found himself confronted by his own face in the mirror in the shop-window, and he stared at himself as one looks at the photograph of a criminal in the paper in order to find out what it actually is that is criminal about the features; the pugnacious chin, the ugly-looking lip, or the cruel eyes. He stared at himself, and catching sight of his own anxious, wide-open eyes, he suddenly remembered the eyes of the woman he had just left. Those are the kind of eyes one ought to have, he thought with a sudden shock, not red-rimmed, greedy, restless eyes like mine. Those are the eyes one ought to have—blue, luminous eyes, inspired by inner faith. (My mother used to look like that sometimes, he thought, on Friday evenings.) Yes, that was the kind of person one ought to be, a person who'd rather be betrayed than betray—a decent, guileless person. That's the only kind that's blessed by God. All my wiles, he thought, haven't made me happy. I'm still a lost soul who knows no peace. Leopold Kanitz walked on to the end of the street, a stranger to himself, and never had he felt more wretched than on this day of his greatest triumph. At length, because he thought he was hungry, he went into a café, and ordered something to eat. But every bite revolted him. I shall sell Kekesfalva, he brooded, sell it again straight away. What am I to do with an estate, I'm not a farmer? Am I, alone as I am, to live in a house of eighteen rooms and haggle with a lot of scoundrelly tenants? It was utterly stupid, I should have bought it for the mortage bank, and not in my own name ... Suppose she finds out, after all, that I was the purchaser? And besides, I shan't make a great deal out of it. If she's willing, I'll give it back to her, keeping only twenty or even ten per cent for myself. She can have it back any time she likes, if she repents of having sold it.

This idea took a weight off his mind. I'll write to her tomorrow, he thought, or, as far as that goes, I can even tell her tomorrow morning before she leaves. Yes, that was the right thing: to give her of his own free will an option on the repurchase. And now he thought he would be able to sleep in peace. But despite the two ghastly nights he had already had, Kanitz slept fitfully and uneasily on this night also. The cadence of that '*very*', that 'thank you *very* much', kept ringing in his ears; North German, out-landish as were her accents, they were yet so vibrant with sin-cerity that his very nerves tingled at the thought of them. No transaction in the last twenty-five years had occasioned our friend so much worry as this, the greatest, the luckiest, the most unscrupulous coup of his career.

By half-past seven Kanitz was already up and out in the street. He knew that the express via Passau left at nine-twenty, and he wanted to be in time to buy Fräulein Dietzenhof some chocolates or a box of *bonbons*. He felt impelled to make some gesture of recognition, and perhaps, too, he yearned to hear once again those words, so novel to him, 'thank you very much', uttered in those moving, outlandish accents. He bought a huge box of chocolates, the finest, the most expensive he could find. Even this did not seem to him fine enough as a parting present, and so he bought some flowers as well in the next shop—a great cluster of glowing red blooms. Both hands laden with his parcels, he returned to the hotel, and asked the porter to send them straight up to Fräulein Dietzenhof's room. But the porter, immediately ennobling him, as is the Viennese way, answered obsequiously: '*Bittschön, bittsehr*, Herr von Kanitz, the *gnädiges Fräulein* is already in the breakfast-room.'

Kanitz reflected for a moment. His leave-taking of Fräulein Dietzenhof yesterday had been such a moving experience that he was afraid lest a fresh meeting might destroy his pleasant memory of it. At length he made up his mind, and, the box of chocolates in one hand and the flowers in the other, he entered the breakfast-room.

She was sitting with her back to him. Even though he could

not see her face, there was something so touching about the unassuming, quiet way in which she sat there that in spite of himself he was deeply moved. Shyly he went up to her and hurriedly put down the flowers and the box of chocolates. 'A little something for the journey,' he said.

She started and flushed scarlet. It was the first time anyone had given her flowers. That is to say, one of the legacy-hunters had, it is true, once sent a few wispy roses up to her room in the hope of winning her over as an ally, but that rampant monster the Princess had immediately ordered her to send them back. And now here was someone bringing her flowers, and there was no one to forbid her to accept them.

'Oh, no,' she stammered, 'why should you do this? They're far ... far too lovely for me.'

She nevertheless gazed up at him gratefully. Was it the reflection of the flowers or the blood surging to her cheeks?—at any rate a pink glow once more suffused her embarrassed features, and she looked almost lovely at this moment, this girl who had left the first bloom of youth behind.

'Won't you sit down?' she said in her confusion, and Kanitz sat down awkwardly opposite her.

'So you're really going away?' he said, and in spite of himself his voice quivered with a note of genuine regret.

'Yes,' she said, lowering her head. There was no joy in this 'Yes', but no distress either. No hope and no disappointment. It was uttered in a tone of quiet resignation, without any particular emphasis.

In his embarrassment, and out of a desire to be of service to her, Kanitz inquired whether she had sent a telegram to announce her arrival. No, oh no, that would only frighten her people, they never got a telegram from one year's end to another. But surely they were near relatives? asked Kanitz. Near relatives— no, by no means. A kind of niece, the daughter of her late stepsister; the husband she did not know at all. They had a small farm, with an apiary, and they had written very kindly to say she could have a room there and stay as long as it suited her. 'But whatever are you going to do there, in that little out of the way place?' asked Kanitz.

'I don't know,' she answered with lowered eyes.

Our friend was gradually becoming agitated. There was such an air of emptiness and forlornness about this little creature, and she viewed herself and her future with such bewildered apathy, that he was reminded of himself, of his own unsettled, homeless existence. Her aimlessness brought home to him his own.

'But there's no point in that,' he said almost vehemently. 'One ought not to live with relatives, it's never a good thing. And then there's no need now for you to bury yourself in a little hole like that.'

She threw him a look at once grateful and sad. 'Yes,' she sighed, 'I'm a little frightened of it myself. But what am I to do?'

She spoke into empty space and then raised her blue eyes as though expecting him to give her some advice—those were the kind of eyes one ought to have, Kanitz had told himself the day before, and suddenly—he did not know how it happened—an idea, a wish, forced its way to his lips.

'Then why not stay here?' he said. And involuntarily he added in a low voice: 'Stay with me?'

She gave a start and stared at him. Only now did he realize that he had said something that he had not consciously wanted to say. The words had slipped out without his having, as usual, weighed them, thought them out, tested them. A wish that he himself had neither elucidated nor admitted to himself had suddenly been transmuted into speech, vibrant with meaning. It was only from the deep flush on her cheeks that he realized what he had said, and he was afraid that she might misunderstand him. As my mistress, she probably thinks. And so that she should not think for a moment that he meant to insult her, he added hastily:

'I mean—as my wife.'

She started abruptly. Her lips twitched, and he could not tell whether she was on the verge of sobbing or flying into a rage. Then she jumped up suddenly and ran out of the room.

This was the most terrible moment in our friend's life. It was only now that he realized the folly he had committed. He had slighted, offended, humiliated, a really kind person, the only person who had ever placed any trust in him, for how could he, already middle-aged, a Jew, shabby, ill-favoured, a huckster, a money-grubber, offer his hand to so inherently a distinguished, so refined a being. He was bound to admit that she was right to run away in such disgust. Good, he said grimly to himself. That serves me right. At last she has realized what I am, at last she has shown the contempt which is my due. It's better she should do that than thank me for my scoundrelly tricks. Kanitz was not in the least offended by her flight; on the contrary, he was—he admitted to me himself—positively *glad* at that moment. He felt that he had received his just punishment; it was only fair that she should from now on think of him with the contempt that he felt for himself.

But in a moment she reappeared in the doorway, her eyes wet with tears. She was in a state of terrible agitation; her hands trembled. She came up to the table. She had to hold on to the back of the chair with both hands before sitting down again. Then she sighed gently without raising her eyes.

'Forgive ... forgive my rudeness,' she said, 'in jumping up so suddenly. But I was so taken aback ... how can you? You don't know me ... you don't know me at all.'

Kanitz was too upset to find words. He only realized, in his shattered state, that she felt no vestige of anger, but only fear. That she was as taken aback by the absurdity of his sudden proposal as he himself. Neither of them had the courage to speak to the other, neither of them had the courage to look at the other. But she did not leave Vienna that morning. They stayed together from early morning till late at night. Three days later he repeated his proposal, and in two months they were married."

Dr Condor paused.

"Well, let's have one last drink. I've nearly come to the end of my story. I should only like to repeat—it is rumoured hereabouts that our friend cunningly made up to the heiress and trapped her into marrying him so that he could get the estate. But I must repeat that that is quite untrue. Kanitz, as you now know, had already made sure of the estate, there was no *need* for him to marry her, and his proposal was not dictated by the slightest trace of self-interest. The little agent would never have summoned up the courage to propose to this refined, blue-eyed young woman to further his own ends; he was, rather, in spite of himself, taken unawares by an emotion that was genuine, and, strangely enough, remained genuine. For of this absurd courtship was born an unusually happy marriage.

The union of opposites, in so far as they are really complementary, always results in the most perfect harmony; and the seemingly incongruous is often the most natural. The first reaction of this couple, so suddenly united, was, of course, to be afraid of each other. Kanitz trembled lest somebody should carry tales to her of his shady business deals and lest at the eleventh hour she might reject him with contumely. He therefore set to work with almost incredible energy to cover up all traces of his past. He gave up all his dubious practices, returned notes of hand at a loss to himself, and steered clear of his former cronies. He had himself baptized, chose an influential godfather, and managed, by putting down considerable sums of money, to purchase the privilege of substituting for the name 'Kanitz' the more aristocratic and euphonious one of 'von Kekesfalva'. And, as is usual in such cases, once the change was effected, the original name soon vanished without a trace from his visiting-card. But right up to the very day of the wedding he lived in a state of constant fear that today, tomorrow, or the day after, she might, in horror, withdraw her confidence from him. Whereas she, for her part, who day in, day out, for twelve years, had been accused of incompetence, stupidity, malice and narrow-mindedness, by that old monster her former mistress, whose devilish tyranny had shattered what self-confidence she had ever had, expected to be stormed at incessantly, sneered at, scolded, humiliated by her new lord and master. From the very outset she resigned herself to a life of slavery, as though to an inevitable fate. But lo and behold. Everything she now did was right; the man into whose keeping she had give her life thanked her every day afresh and treated her always with the same shy reverence. The young woman was astounded; she was not able to comprehend so much tenderness.

Gradually the girl who had already been, so to speak, half withered, blossomed out. She grew pretty, developed graceful curves. It was a whole year, two years, before she ventured really to believe that even she, the despised, the downtrodden, the oppressed, could be respected, loved like other women. And it was only when the child was born that real happiness began for the two of them.

During these years Kekesfalva threw himself into his work with renewed enthusiasm. The little agent had long since been left behind, and he began to cut a dash in the business world.

He modernized the sugar-factory, acquired an interest in rolling-mill near Wiener Neustadt, and pulled off that brilliant coup in connection with the alcohol combine which made such a stir at the time. The fact that he became rich, really rich now, made no difference to the couple's secluded, thrifty mode of life. They seemed to be anxious not to remind people too insistently of their existence, so seldom did they invite guests to the house, and the house that you now know seemed then incomparably simpler and more provincial—and, God knows, a much happier house than it is today.

Then came his first trial. For a long time his wife had suffered from internal pains. She went off her food, lost weight, and dragged herself about, looking more and more weary and exhausted. But, for fear of causing her overworked husband anxiety with regard to her own insignificant self, she pressed her lips tightly together whenever she had an attack and hid her pain. When, eventually, it proved impossible to conceal it any longer, it was too late. She was taken to Vienna in an ambulance to be operated on for what the doctors said was a gastric ulcer—actually it turned out to be cancer. It was at that time that I got to know Kanitz, and I have never seen a man in a more frenzied, more desperate state. He could not, would not, realize that the doctors were powerless now to save his wife; it seemed to him that it was only out of indolence, indifference, incompetence on the part of us doctors that we did nothing further, *could* do nothing further. He offered the specialist fifty thousand, a hundred thousand, crowns if he cured her. The day before the operation he wired for the leading specialists from Budapest, Munich and Berlin, in the vain hope of finding one who would say that she could be saved from the surgeon's knife. And I shall never in all my life forget the mad look in his eyes as he screamed at us, when the poor woman, as was only to be expected, died during the operation, that we were a pack of murderers.

That was his Damascus. From that day on a permanent change took place in this ascetic of the business world. A god whom he had served from childhood had ceased to exist for him—the god of money. Now only one thing on earth existed for him—his child. He engaged governesses and servants, had the house restored; no luxury was too much for the once-so-thrifty man. He trailed the nine-year-old, ten-year-old, child off to Nice, Paris, Vienna, pampered and cosseted her in the most ridiculous fashion, and, just as in the past he had thrown himself wildly into the pursuit of money, so he now threw money about with a kind of contempt. You were not so far wrong, perhaps, to call him aristocratic and generous-hearted, since for years now he has been inspired by a quite unusual indifference towards profit and loss; ever since he discovered that all his millions could not bring him back his wife, he has learned to despise money.

I shall not, for it is getting late, describe to you in detail the way in which Kanitz idolized his child. It was, after all, understandable, for she was growing up into an enchanting little person, a positively elfin creature, delicate, slender, light as thistle-down, with grey eyes that looked out on the world with bright, friendly gaze. From her mother she had inherited her shy sweetness, from her father her keen intelligence. Serene and lovable, she blossomed out in all that wonderful naturalness that is peculiar to only children whom Life has never treated with hostility or harshness. And only someone who knew the delight of the ageing man, who had never dared to hope that such a joyous, open-hearted creature could spring from his melancholy, sombre loins, could possibly gauge the extent of his despair when the second tragedy befell him. He could not, would not, believe— nor can he to this day—that this child of all children, *his* child, was to be permanently afflicted, maimed, and I shrink from disclosing all the mad and foolish things that he did in his wild desperation. I shall not go on to tell you how he drove all the doctors in the world crazy with his insistence, how he tried to bribe us all with the most fabulous sums to effect an immediate cure, how he rang me up every other day, for no reason but to pander to his own tearing impatience. A colleague of mine told me recently, in confidence, that the old man goes every week to the

University Library, and sits there amongst the students, pathetically copying all sorts of foreign words out of the encyclopedia,
and then ploughing for hours on end through the medical text-
books in the wild hope that he may be able to find something
that we doctors have overlooked or forgotten. I have heard,
again, from various other sources—you may laugh, but it is
always madness that first gives one an insight into the intensity
of a passion—that he has promised vast sums in the way of dona-
tions both to the synagogue and to the parish priest in the event
of his child's recovery. Uncertain to which God to turn, the forsaken God of his fathers or the new one, and pursued by the
dread fear of getting on the wrong side of either, he has pledged
himself to both.

You realize, don't you, that it is not by any means out of a love
of gossip that I am telling you all these somewhat ridiculous
details, but in order that you may understand what it means to
this afflicted, distracted, broken-down man to find someone who
will *listen* to him at all, someone whom he can feel really under-
stands his grief, or at least tries to understand it. I know he makes
things difficult for one with his obstinacy, his egocentric obsession,
which makes him behave as though his child's misfortune were
the only misfortune in this world of ours, which is, after all, brimful
of tragedies. But it is precisely at this moment, when his frenzy
of despair is beginning to make him ill, that he must not be left
in the lurch, and you are really—really, my dear Lieutenant—
doing a good deed by bringing a little of your youth, your vitality,
your lightheartedness into that tragic house. It is only for fear lest
you may be put off by other people that I have told you more of
his private affairs, perhaps, than is actually fair to him; but I
think I can rely on you to regard everything I have told you as
strictly between ourselves."

"Of course," I said mechanically, and those were the first
words that passed my lips during the whole of this story. Not
only did I feel stunned by his astounding revelations, which had
turned my whole idea of Kekesfalva inside out like a glove; but
I was also appalled at my own obtuseness and stupidity. To think
that I had been going about the world at the age of twenty-five
with such unseeing eyes! During all these weeks I had been a

daily visitor to the house, and, befogged by my own pity, I had refrained, out of a stupid feeling of delicacy, from ever asking either about Edith's illness or about the mother who was so obviously missed in the house, had never asked how this curious old man had come by his wealth. How could I have failed to see that those veiled, almond-shaped, melancholy eyes were not those of a Hungarian aristocrat, but that their keen yet weary gaze reflected the age-long tragic struggle of the Jewish race? How had I failed to perceive that in Edith yet other elements were mingled, how failed to realize that over this house hung the spectral shadow of a strange past? In a flash I now called to mind a whole series of minor incidents, remembered with what a frosty stare our Colonel had on one occasion dismissed Herr Kekesfalva's greeting, merely raising two fingers half-way to his cap, and how my friends had talked of the "old Manichaean". I felt as one does when the curtains in a dark room are suddenly drawn aside, and the sunlight is so blinding that everything swims purple before one's eyes and one reels in the dazzling glare of the almost inconceivable flood of light.

But, as though he had guessed what was going on in my mind, Condor leaned over me with almost professional solicitude, and his small, soft hand patted mine reassuringly.

"You couldn't possibly have known, *Herr Leutnant*; how could you? You have been brought up, after all, in a secluded world, a world apart, and you are, moreover, at the fortunate age when one has not yet learned to regard anything out-of-the-ordinary with immediate suspicion. Believe me, as an older man, I know there is no need to be ashamed of being taken in by life now and again; it is, if anything, a blessing not yet to have acquired that over-keen, diagnostic, misanthropic eye, and to be able to look at people and things trustfully when one first sees them. You could not otherwise have helped the old man and his poor sick child so splendidly. No, don't be astonished, and, above all, don't be ashamed—you have instinctively behaved in the best possible way."

Hurling his cigar-stump into a corner, he stretched himself and pushed back his chair. "But now I think it's about time for me to be going."

I also rose, although I still felt somewhat dizzy. For something strange was taking place within me. I was agitated in the extreme, was even plunged into a state of heightened awareness by all the astonishing things I had heard; at the same time I was conscious of a dull pressure on my brain, a pressure on a quite definite spot. I remembered clearly that while Condor had been talking I had wanted to ask him something, but had not had the presence of mind to interrupt him; there had been some question I had wanted to put at a particular point in his narrative. And now that I was free to ask any question I pleased, I could no longer remember what it was; it must have been swept away in the excitement of listening. In vain I tried to trace back the thread of the whole conversation—it was just as when you feel a quite specific pain in some part of the body and are yet unable to locate it. As we crossed the now half deserted public bar I was entirely taken up with the mental effort of trying to remember.

We stepped outside. Condor looked up. "Aha!" he said, smiling with some satisfaction. "I could tell the whole time that the moonlight was too bright. We're going to have a thunderstorm, and a pretty bad one too. We shall have to hurry."

He was right. The air, it was true, still hung motionless and sultry over the sleeping houses, but dark, ominous clouds were chasing across the sky from the east, shrouding from moment to moment the pale, dying moon. Half the sky was already completely darkened; black as a giant tortoise, the compact metallic mass surged forward, now and again spangled by distant summer lightning, and at each flash came a low reluctant growl, like that of an angry animal, from the background.

"In half an hour's time we shall be for it," pronounced Condor. "I at least shall reach the station without getting wet, but you, *Herr Leutnant*, you had better turn back, or you'll get a thorough wetting."

But I was dimly aware that I still had something to ask him, although I did not yet know what; the memory of it was drowned in dull blackness; just as the moon above us was drowned in chasing clouds. I could feel a certain thought hammering at the portals of my brain; it was like a persistent, gnawing ache.

"No, I'll risk it," I replied. "Let's look sharp, then. The faster we walk, the better. My legs are quite stiff."

Stiff legs—*that* was it, that was the clue. A light immediately flooded my consciousness. In a flash I knew what it was I had wanted to ask Condor all this time, what I *had* to ask him, what I had promised Kekesfalva to ask him. The whole time my unconscious had been busied solely with Kekesfalva's question: was the child incurable or not? Now I must put that question. And so, as we strode through the deserted streets, I began somewhat diffidently:

"Forgive me, *Herr Doktor* ... all you have told me is, of course, frightfully interesting to me ... frightfully important, I mean. And you will understand that for that very reason I should like to ask you something further ... something that has worried me for a long time, and ... after all, you're her doctor, you follow the case as no one else can. I'm a layman and can't have any real idea ... and I should very much like to know what you really think about it. I mean, is this paralysis of Edith's a passing illness, or is she incurable?"

Condor jerked his head up sharply, and his pince-nez flashed at me. Involuntarily I shrank from the vehemence of his gaze, which seemed to probe beneath my skin. Did he suspect that Kekesfalva had put me up to this? But the next moment he had lowered his eyes, and far from slackening his pace was striding out even more vigorously than before.

"Why, of course," he muttered, "I might have expected that. It always comes to that in the end. Curable or incurable, black or white. As though it were as simple as all that. Even 'well' or 'ill' are words that no self-respecting doctor should utter with a clear conscience, for where does illness begin and health end? And he should certainly avoid such expressions as 'curable' and 'incurable'. Of course they are very common, both of them, and one can't get along in practice without them. But you'll never get *me* to utter the word 'incurable'. Never! I know that it is to the most brilliant man of the last century, Nietzsche, that we owe the horrible aphorism: a doctor should never try to cure the incurable. But that is about the most fallacious proposition of all the paradoxical and dangerous propositions he propounded. The exact opposite is the truth. I maintain that it is precisely the incurable one *should* try to cure, and, what is more, that it is only

155

in so-called incurable cases that a doctor shows his mettle. A doctor who from the outset accepts the concept 'incurable' is funking his job, capitulating before the battle begins. Of course I know that it is easier, more convenient, to pronounce certain cases 'incurable' and, after pocketing one's fee, to turn one's back on them with a sigh of resignation—indeed, extremely convenient and profitable to concern oneself exclusively with those cases that have been shown to be curable, in which one can turn to page so-and-so of the medical text-book and find the whole treatment set out for one in black and white. Ah well, those that care to can go in for that kind of witch-doctoring. As for me, it seems to me as pitiable a thing as if a writer were only to attempt to say what had already been said, instead of trying to force into the medium of the spoken word the unsaid, nay, the unsayable; as though a philosopher were to expatiate for the ninety-ninth time on what has long been known instead of tackling the unknown, the unknowable. Incurable—that is, after all, only a relative, not an absolute, concept. For a progressive science such as medicine incurable cases are only so for the time being, within the time-limits of our own age, within the compass of our present knowledge, that is to say, within the limits of our restricted perspective. But it's not a question merely of the moment. In hundreds of cases where today we know of no cure, tomorrow, the day after, a cure may be found, for medical science is, after all, making tremendous strides. So for me, you see, I would have you note"—he said this irritably, as though I had offended him—"there are no incurable illnesses. On principle, I never give a case or a patient up, and no one will ever wring from me the word 'incurable'. The utmost that I would say in the most desperate case would be that an illness was 'not yet curable', that is to say, that contemporary science had not yet found a cure for it."

Condor was striding along so vigorously that I had some difficulty in keeping up with him. Suddenly he slowed down his pace.

"It may be that I am expressing myself in too complicated, too abstract terms. It's difficult to get these things sorted out when hurrying to catch a train. But perhaps an example will serve better to illustrate what I mean, a very personal example, more-over, and one associated for me with a very painful experience. Twenty-two years ago, when I was a second-year medical student, just about your age, my father, who had always been a strong, healthy man of untiring energy, and whom I worshipped, fell ill. The doctors diagnosed diabetes, one of the most horrible and malignant diseases that can ever afflict a human being. For no apparent reason the body ceases to assimilate nourishment, fat and sugar are no longer absorbed, and as a result the person affected wastes away and dies a lingering death from starvation. I won't harrow you with all the details; three years of my own youth were embittered by this dread disease.

And now listen to this. In those days no cure whatever for dia-betes was known to so-called medical science. The patient was subjected to all the tortures of a strict diet, every ounce of food was weighed, every mouthful measured, but the doctors knew—and I, as a medical student, of course also knew—that it was merely a matter of postponing the inevitable end, that for two, possibly three, years my father would starve slowly and miserably to death in a world teeming with food and drink. You can imagine how I, as a medical student, rushed from specialist to specialist, pored over all the books and monographs on the subject. But the only answer I could extract from either books or people was the one word that has ever since been unendurable to me: 'incurable', 'incurable'. Ever since that time I have loathed the word, for I had to stand by, in full realization of my utter powerlessness to help, and watch the person I loved best on earth meet a more pitiable end than an insentient beast. He died three months before I qualified.

And now pay careful attention to what I say. The day before yesterday one of our foremost biochemists read a paper to the Medical Society in which he told us that in America and in the laboratories of one or two other countries attempts to find a gland extract for the cure of diabetes had met with considerable success. In another ten years, he affirmed with certainty, diabetes would be a curable disease. You can imagine how upset I was by the thought that had there been in existence at that time a few hundred grammes of a certain substance, the person I loved best on earth would not have suffered such torture, would not have died, or at least we should have had some hope of saving him. Try to understand what a terrible effect the verdict 'incurable' had on me at that time, for I had dreamed day and night that a remedy would, should, must, be found, that someone would succeed in discovering it, perhaps I myself. Syphilis, which at the time when we students entered the university was, as we were warned in a specially printed memorandum, 'incurable', has also since then become curable. Nietzsche and Schumann and Schubert and I know not how many more of its tragic victims did not by any means die, therefore, of an 'incurable' disease, but of a disease that was not curable at the time when they lived—yes, if you like, it was in a double sense that they died prematurely. What new, unhoped-for, fantastic discoveries, which but yesterday were inconceivable, does not each day bring to us doctors. Every time, therefore, that I come across a case that other doctors have given up with a shrug of the shoulders, my heart is constricted with anger at the thought that I have as yet no knowledge of the cure that tomorrow, the day after tomorrow may bring, but it beats too with the hope that perhaps I shall find it, that perhaps someone will discover it in time, just in time, to cure my patient. Everything is possible, even the impossible—for where the medical science of today stands before a locked door another door is sometimes unexpectedly opened. Where our present methods fail, efforts must be made to discover fresh ones; and where science is of no avail, there is always the chance of a miracle. Yes, miracles happen even today in the world of medicine, miracles that are performed in a blaze of electric light, in the face of all logic and experience, and sometimes one can perform them oneself. Do you think I would torture that child and let myself be tortured, did I not hope ultimately to do her some real good, to pull her through in the end? Hers is a difficult case, I admit, a stubborn case; I have been working on it for years without making as much headway as I should like. But for all that I shall not give it up."

I had listened with rapt attention, and had understood clearly all that he had said. But without realizing it, I had been infected by old Kekesfalva's obstinacy, his anxiety and fear. I wanted to be told more, something more definite, more precise. And so I proceeded to question Dr Condor.

"You think there is a possibility of an improvement, then—that is to say ... you have already achieved a certain degree of improvement, haven't you?"

Dr Condor was silent. My remark seemed to annoy him. He stumped along more and more vigorously on his short legs.

"How can you say that I have achieved a certain degree of improvement? Have you remarked it? And what do you know about the whole thing, anyway? You've only known the patient for a few weeks, whereas I've been treating her for five years."

And suddenly he stood stock-still. "I had better tell you once and for all: I have achieved practically nothing, nothing of what I hoped to. I have experimented with her and tried this, that and the other thing just like a quack, to no purpose, utterly in vain. As yet I have achieved nothing whatever."

His vehemence startled me; obviously I had touched him on the raw.

"But Herr von Kekesfalva has told me how refreshing Edith has found the electric baths, especially since the injections ... " I said, trying to placate him.

But Condor cut me short.

"Nonsense! Utter nonsense! Don't let the old fool talk you into believing that. Do you really believe that spinal paralysis can be cured with electric baths and a lot of mumbo-jumbo? Don't you know our old dodge? When we doctors don't know which way to turn, in order to gain time we stuff the patient full of all sorts of gibberish and nonsense so that he shouldn't realize we are at our wits' end. Fortunately for us, in the case of most patients Nature helps in the deception and becomes our willing accomplice. Of course Edith feels better. Any form of treatment, whether it's eating lemons or drinking milk, being ordered hot compresses or cold, at first brings about a change in the organism, and that provides a fresh stimulus, which the eternally optimistic patient mistakes for improvement in his condition. That form of auto-suggestion is our best ally, and even helps the biggest fools of doctors. But there's a snag in the business. As soon as the novelty has worn off a reaction sets in, and then a rapid change of treatment is necessary, another fake cure must be invented. In 'incurable' cases we doctors go on pulling off that sort of swindle until perhaps quite by chance we hit upon the right method. No, no compliments, please, I myself know best how little of what I hoped to do I have done for Edith. Everything that I have tried so far—make no mistake about it—all this tomfoolery, this electrical treatment and massage, has literally failed to put her on her feet."

So vehemently was Condor inveighing against himself that I felt compelled to defend him against his own conscience.

"But . . . I have seen for myself that she can walk," I interposed shyly, "thanks to your apparatus . . . those stretching appliances."

But at this point Condor no longer spoke, he positively shouted at me, so indignantly and hysterically, moreover, that two passers-by turned and looked at us curiously.

"A swindle, I tell you, a swindle! Appliances to help *me* and not *her!* Those appliances are toys to keep her quiet, and no more. It isn't the child who needs them, but I, because the Kekesfalvas refuse to be patient. It was only because I couldn't stand his insistence that I had to inject the old man with another dose of confidence. What else could I do but hang those great weights on the child, as one puts shackles on the feet of a rebellious prisoner? They're quite unnecessary . . . that is, they may strengthen the sinews a little . . . but I couldn't help myself . . . I had to gain time. I am not in the least ashamed of these tricks and subterfuges; you can see for yourself how successful they are. Edith persuades herself that she can walk much better since she has worn the appliances, her father exults at the thought that I have done something for her, everyone is full of admiration for the marvellous genius and miracle-worker, and you yourself consult me as though I were an oracle!"

He broke off and removed his hat in order to pass his hand over his moist brow. Then he gave me a malicious sidelong look.

"I fear you're not altogether pleased, eh? I've destroyed your conception of a doctor as a helper of mankind and fount of truth? You in your youthful enthusiasm had had a very different notion of medical morality, and are now—oh, I can tell—disillusioned and even revolted at the thought of such practices. I am sorry, but medicine has nothing to do with morals; every illness is in itself an anarchistic phenomenon, a revolt against Nature, and one must therefore employ every means to fight it, every means. No, no pity for the sick—the sick person places himself outside the law, he offends against law and order, and in order to restore law and order, to restore the sick person himself, one must, as in the case of every revolt, attack ruthlessly, employ every weapon at one's command, for goodness and truth have never yet succeeded in curing humanity or even a single human being. If a deception helps, then it is no longer a shabby deception but a first-class remedy, and so long as I am unable to do any actual good in a particular, case, I must try at least to help the patient to carry on. It's no easy task, either *Herr Leutnant*, to keep on breaking fresh ground for five whole years, particularly when you're not too pleased with your own skill. In any case, I beg you to spare me your compliments."

The plump little man stood there confronting me in such a state of agitation that I felt that if I dared to contradict him he would fall upon me. At that moment a blue flash ran like a vein along the darkened horizon, and was followed by a dull roar and rumble of thunder. Condor suddenly broke into a laugh.

"There, you see, the heavens' wrath is your answer! Well, well, you poor lad, you've had a thoroughly bad time of it today; one illusion after another has been cut away with the dissecting knife: first the one about the Hungarian aristocrat, then the one about the kindly, infallible doctor and helper of humanity. But surely you can understand how the old fool's eulogies got on my nerves? In Edith's case, particularly, all this sentimental slobbering goes against the grain, because it angers me to be making such slow progress, because I am ashamed to think that in her case I have not yet hit upon anything conclusive."

He walked on a few paces in silence. Then he turned to me and addressed me in a more cordial tone.

"By the way—I don't want you to think that in my own mind I have 'given up the case', as we doctors so charmingly put it. On the contrary, it's just at this point that I refuse to give in, even if things continue as they are for another year, another five years. Curiously enough, moreover, it so happens that only yesterday, the day after that lecture I spoke of, I read in a Parisian medical review a description of the treatment of a case of paralysis, a very curious case of a fourteen-year-old boy who had been bedridden for two whole years, unable to move a limb; and Professor Viennot managed to effect such an improvement in his condition that four months later he could climb five flights of stairs again with ease. Just imagine, he was able to effect a cure like that in four months in a case exactly similar to Edith's, a case with which I have been fiddling about for five whole years. It positively knocked me flat to read about it. Of course the aetiology of the case and the methods employed are not quite clear to me; Professor Viennot seems in some strange way to have combined a number of methods—sun treatment at Cannes, some kind of apparatus, and a certain course of remedial exercises; from the brief case history I can, of course, form no idea as to whether and how far any of his new methods would be practicable in our case. But I have written straight off to him to ask for more precise data, and it was with this in mind that I plagued poor Edith today with another thorough examination—one must, after all, have data in order to make comparisons. You see, therefore, that I am by no means lowering my flag, but, on the contrary, clutching at every straw. There may perhaps be some hope for us in this new treatment—I say *perhaps*, no more than that, and in any case I've been chattering far too much. That's, enough of my confounded 'shop talk'."

We were now nearing the station. Our conversation would have to end soon; and so I said insistently: "You think then, that ... "

But the plump little man pulled up with a jerk.

"I think nothing!" he hissed at me. "And there's no 'then'; about it. What is it you all want of me? I'm not in telephonic communication with Almighty God. I've said absolutely; nothing. Nothing definite whatever. I have pronounced no opinion whatever, and I believe and think and promise you, nothing. I've been chattering far too much in any case. And now no more of it. Many thanks for your company. You'd be well advised to hurry back, or you'll get a thorough drenching."

Without shaking hands, and obviously put out—I could not

understand why—he rushed off on his short legs and, as it seemed to me, somewhat flat feet, to the station.

Condor had been right in his prediction. The storm which had long been perceptible to our senses was unmistakably approaching. Great clouds seemed to clatter against one another like heavy black chests above the tremulous, quivering tree-tops, which were lit every now and then by pale darting tongues of lightning. There was an acrid smell in the damp air, which was tossed hither and thither by squally gusts. The town seemed quite changed, the streets were quite different, as I now hurried home. A few minutes before they had lain with bated breath in the pale moonlight; now the street signs clanked and clattered as though startled out of an oppressive dream, doors rattled uneasily, chimney-pots groaned, in some of the houses inquisitive lights were turned on, and here and there white-clad figures could be seen cautiously shutting the windows against the approaching storm. The few belated passers-by, scurried from street-corner to street-corner as though driven along by the very breath of fear. Even the big main square, where at night a fair number of people were usually to be seen, lay completely deserted; the illuminated town-hall clock looked down stupidly and blankly upon the unwonted emptiness. The main thing was that, thanks to Condor's warning, I should get home before the storm broke. Only two more streets, and then across the municipal park to the barracks. Once in my room, I could ponder over all the astonishing things that I had heard and experienced in the last few hours.

The little park in front of our barracks lay in complete darkness. The air was heavy and dense beneath the restless foliage; sometimes a short, snaky gust of wind would hiss, among the leaves, and then the turmoil would give place to an even more uncanny stillness. I walked faster and faster. I had almost reached the entrance when a figure broke away from behind a tree and emerged from the shadows. I faltered, but did not stop—it was probably only one of the prostitutes who habitually waited for soldiers here in the darkness. But to my annoyance I could hear the stranger slinking rapidly after me, and I turned round to give the impudent wretch who was so shamelessly trailing me a piece of my mind. But in the glare of a flash of lightning which at that moment cleft the darkness I saw to my infinite dismay that it was a shuffling old man who was panting after me—the bald head bare, the gold-rimmed spectacles glittering orbs in the darkness. It was Kekesfalva!

In the first shock of astonishment I could not believe my eyes. Kekesfalva in our barrack-grounds? Impossible, for had not Condor and I left him, dead-tired, three hours ago at his house? Was I the victim of an hallucination, or had the old man taken leave of his senses? Had he got out of bed in a fever and was he now wandering about like a sleepwalker in that thin jacket, without overcoat or hat? But it was undoubtedly he. I should have recognized that dejected, bowed, timid, slinking figure among thousands.

"In God's name, Herr von Kekesfalva!" I cried. "How did you get here? Didn't you go to bed?"

"No ... or rather ... I couldn't sleep ... I felt I must ... "

"But you must go home, quickly. Can't you see that the storm may break any moment now? Haven't you got your car here?"

"It's over there ... waiting for me, to the left of the barracks."

"Splendid. But hurry, hurry. If your chauffeur drives fast you'll get back just in the nick of time. Come along, Herr von Kekesfalva." And since he hesitated, I seized him unceremoniously by the arm to drag him along. But he wrenched himself free.

"In a moment. In a moment ... I'm going, *Herr Leutnant* ... but ... tell me first ... what did he say?"

"Who?" My question, my astonishment were genuine. The wind howled above our heads ever more wildly, the trees groaned and bent over as though to tear themselves up by the roots; any moment now the rain might come pelting down, and I naturally thought only of one thing: how to get this old, obviously half-demented man, who seemed to be quite oblivious of the approaching storm, back to his home. But he stammered almost indignantly:

"Dr Condor ... You spoke to him, didn't you?"

And now at last I understood. This encounter in the dark was, of course, no accident. In his impatient longing for certainty the old man had waited, had lain in wait for me in the park just outside the entrance to the barracks, where he knew I could not escape him. For three whole hours he had paced up and down in a state of terrible anxiety, barely concealed in the shadow of the dingy little park, which, as a rule, was frequented at night only by servant girls meeting their lovers. Evidently he had assumed that I should accompany Condor the short distance to the station and then return immediately to barracks, whereas I had quite innocently let him wait, wait, wait for three whole hours while I had sat with the doctor in the wine-bar, and the ailing old man had waited, just as in the past he had waited for people who owed him money, stubbornly, patiently, relentlessly. There was something about this fanatical persistence that irritated and yet touched me.

"Everything is quite all right," I said reassuringly. "Everything will be all right, I am confident of that. Tomorrow afternoon I will tell you more, I'll tell you every word that was said. But now we must get you to your car, quickly. You can see for yourself there's no time to lose ... "

"Yes, I'm coming." Reluctantly he allowed himself to be led along. I managed to urge him ten, twenty paces farther. Then I felt him dragging at my arm.

"Just a moment." he stammered. "Just a moment ... over there on the bench. I can't ... I *can't* go on."

And, indeed, the old man was swaying back and forth like a drunken man. The growling of the thunder drew nearer and nearer, and it took all my strength to haul him over to the bench, where he sank down, breathing heavily. It was plain that all this waiting had been too much for him, and no wonder. For three hours the old man with his weak heart had paced up and down, for three hours he had stood there on his weary old legs, keeping an uneasy look out for me, and only now, when he had succeeded in catching me, had he realized the effort it had cost him. Exhausted, and almost in a state of collapse, he leaned back on the paupers' bench, that bench where at midday workmen munched their snacks, where in the afternoons old pensioners and pregnant women rested, and where at night harlots accosted soldiers—this old man, the richest man in the town, leaned back and waited, waited, waited. And I knew what it was he was waiting for, I realized at once that I should never be able to get the stubborn old man to budge from this bench (how annoying if one of my fellow officers were to catch me in this strange company) unless I were to raise him up spiritually, as it were, unless I reassured him. And once more I was assailed by a feeling of pity, once more that confounded hot wave of emotion surged up within me, sapping my strength and will. I bent over him and began to talk to him.

All around us the wind hissed, roared and spluttered. But the old man did not notice it. For him there was no sky and no wind and no rain—all that existed for him on this earth was this child and her recovery. How could I possibly have brought myself to report to him nothing but the blunt, naked truth, which was that Condor was as yet by no means certain of being able to effect a cure? He needed something, after all, to cling to, just as he had clung to my outstretched arm as he sank down on the bench. And so I hastily scraped together the few words of consolation that I had with difficulty wrung from Condor: I told him that Condor had heard of a new treatment which had been tried out with great success in France by Professor Viennot. Immediately I could feel a rustling and stirring at my side in the dark, and the body that until now had seemed lifeless and inert edged closer, as though to get warmth from mine. I ought really to have said nothing further at this stage, but my pity urged me further than I had any right to go. Yes, this treatment had been carried out in several cases with remarkable success, I said, encouraging him further and further; in three or four months quite astonishing cures had been effected, and probably, no, almost certainly, a cure would be effected in Edith's case. Gradually a positive craving to exaggerate came over me, for it was wonderful to observe the effect of my reassuring words. Every time that he inquired avidly, "Do you really think so?" or "Did he really say that? Did he really say that himself?" and I in my impatience and weakness answered with an eager affirmative, the body that was pressed against mine seemed to grow lighter. I could feel the old man's confidence increasing as I spoke, and for the first and last time in my life I had some inkling of the elation that accompanies all creative activity.

What I said to Kekesfalva on that paupers' bench I no longer know, and never shall know. For just as my words intoxicated my avid listener, so did his blissful hanging on my words rouse in me a lust to promise him more and yet more. We neither of us heeded the lightning that flashed blue all around us, nor the ever more persistent menace of the thunder. We stayed closely pressed together, talking, listening, listening, talking, and again and again I assured him, in tones of honest conviction, "Yes, she will get well soon, quite well," merely in order to hear him stammer out once more, "Ah!" and "Thank God!" and to share his ecstatic gratitude. And who knows how long we might not have gone on sitting there, had there not suddenly come that final gust of wind that heralds, prepares the way, as it were, for a violent storm. The trees bent double so that the wood creaked and snapped, the chestnuts rained down their bursting missiles upon us, and we were enveloped in a great, whirling cloud of dust.

"Home—you must go home!" I said, pushing him to his feet, and he offered no resistance. My words of consolation had strengthened, healed him. He no longer swayed as before, but rushed headlong with me to the car, where the chauffeur was waiting to help him in. Now at last I felt relieved, for I knew he was safe. I had comforted him. At last the poor, broken old man would be able to sleep—a deep, dreamless, blissful sleep.

But just as I was about to spread the rug over his feet so that he should not catch cold, an appalling thing happened. He suddenly gripped my wrists and, before I could prevent him, raised both my hands to his mouth and kissed them, first the right and then the left, then the right and then the left again.

"Till tomorrow, till tomorrow," he stammered, and the car shot off as though borne away by the raging, icy wind. I stood rooted to the spot. But at that moment the first drops came splashing down, the rain drummed, pelted, beat like hailstones on my cap, and I ran the last four or five dozen steps over to the barracks in a downpour. Just as, dripping wet, I reached the entrance, there came a blinding flash, lighting up the stormy night far and wide, and in its wake crashed the thunder as though bringing the whole heavens down with it. It must have been quite near, for the earth trembled, and there was a clatter as though all the window-panes had been splintered to atoms. But although I winced at the sudden blinding flash, I was not half so startled as I had been a few minutes previously, when the old man in his frenzy of gratitude had seized my hand and kissed it.

After experiencing profound emotions one sleeps profoundly. It was not until I awoke next morning that I realized how completely bemused I had been both by the sultriness preceding the storm and by the overcharged atmosphere of my conversation of the night before. Starting up out of unfathomable depths, I stared at first in bewilderment at my familiar room, and made vain efforts to recollect when and how I had fallen into sleep of this depth.

But there was no time to collect my thoughts, for with the part of my mind that functioned, so to speak, as a mere cog in the military machine, quite independently of my ego, I remembered that a special exercise had been ordered for today. From below in the courtyard came the sound of bugles and the stamping of horses' hoofs, and I realized from the way in which my batman was bustling about that it was high time to be on the move. I scrambled into the uniform which was laid out ready for me, lit a cigarette, and rushed down the stairs into the courtyard. A moment later the waiting squadron moved off.

When riding along as part of a column of cavalry one does not exist as a separate entity; the clatter of hundreds of hoofs prevents one from either thinking clearly or day-dreaming, and as we trotted along briskly I was oblivious of all else but the fact that we were jogging along into the most perfect summer's day imaginable. The rain had washed every trace of mist and cloud from the sky, the sun shone warm, and yet there was no sultriness in the air, every contour of the landscape, stood out in sharp silhouette. In the far distance every house, every tree, every field was as real and palpable as if one held it in one's hand; every bunch of flowers in a cottage window, every ring of smoke above a roof-top, seemed to be confirmed in its existence by the vivid and yet pure colours. I could scarcely recognize this tedious highroad along which we trotted week after week at the same pace towards the same objective, so much greener and more exuberant was the freshly painted leafy roof that arched above our heads. I felt marvellously buoyant and carefree as I rode along; gone was all the uneasiness, the despondency, the uncertainty that had so frayed my nerves in the last few days and weeks, and seldom do I remember having carried out my duties more efficiently than on that radiant summer morning. Everything went off like clockwork, everything smiled on me: the sky and the meadows, the steaming horses, which obediently responded to every pressure of the thigh and every tug of the reins, and even my own voice when I shouted words of command.

Now states of profound happiness, like all other forms of intoxication, are apt to befuddle the wits; intensive enjoyment of the present always makes one forget the past. And so when, after those refreshing hours spent in the saddle, I once more took the familiar road to Kekesfalva, it was only dimly that I remembered my nocturnal encounter. I revelled in my own blissful lightness of heart and the happiness of others, for when one is happy oneself, one can only picture the rest of the world as happy.

And, indeed, no sooner had I knocked on the familiar door of the *Schloss* than the usually so obsequiously impersonal Josef welcomed me in particularly radiant tones. "May I take the *Herr Leutnant* up to the tower?" he burst out eagerly. "The young ladies are waiting up there."

But why were his hands so impatient, why did he beam at me so? Why did he rush on ahead so officiously? What was the matter with him? I could not help wondering as I began to climb the spiral staircase that led up to the terrace. What was up with old Josef today? He was burning with impatience to get me to the top as quickly as possible. Whatever was the matter with the honest fellow?

But it was good to feel happy, good, too, on this brilliant June day, to climb up the winding stairs on fresh young legs, and from the mullioned windows to see, now to the north, now to the south, now to the east, now to the west, the summery landscape stretching out into infinity. At length, when I had only ten or eleven steps more to climb to reach the terrace, something unexpected gave me pause. For, strange—there suddenly came floating down the dark well of the winding staircase the faint, far-off strains of a lively dance-tune, lilted by shrill violins, echoed by deep-throated cellos, and warbled by sparkling female sopranos. I was surprised. Whence came this music, at once so near and yet so far, so eerie and yet so earthly, a popular musical air wafted down to me as it were from heaven? Was there an orchestra playing somewhere in a nearby inn, and was the wind carrying the faint dying notes of the melody across to me? But the next moment I realized that the strains of this airy orchestra were coming from the terrace and proceeded from a simple gramophone. How stupid of me, I thought, to detect magic, to expect miracles everywhere today. It would be impossible to install a whole orchestra on so narrow a terrace. But a few steps farther and I once more grew uncertain. Without a doubt it was a gramophone that was being played up there, but the voices, those voices, were too free and too genuine to come from a little whirring box. They really were young girls' voices, vibrating with youthful exuberance.

I paused and listened more intently. The rich soprano, that was Ilona's voice, lovely, full, voluptuous, soft as her arms. But the other voice, to whom did that belong? It was one I did not know. Evidently Edith had invited a friend to tea, a saucy, sparkling young thing, and I was extremely curious to see this twittering swallow that had so unexpectedly alighted on our tower. Hence I was all the more startled to find when I set foot on the terrace that there was no one there but the two girls, and that it was Edith who was laughing and warbling away in an entirely new voice, a free, rapturous, silvery voice. I was taken aback, for this transformation from one day to another somehow seemed to me unnatural. Only a healthy, self-assured person could sing so blithely, out of sheer high spirits. On the other hand it was quite out of the question that the invalid should have been restored to health unless a veritable miracle had occurred between evening and morning. What I wondered in astonishment—had so intoxicated her, what had so gone to her head, that these blissfully confident notes could suddenly burst forth from her throat, from her soul? I can only with difficulty explain my first emotion; it was a feeling of discomfort such as I might have felt had I surprised the girls in a state of nudity, for either Edith had hitherto concealed her true nature from me or—but why and wherefore?—a new being had blossomed forth within her overnight.

To my amazement, however, neither of the two girls was in the least confused when they caught sight of me.

"Come along," Edith called out to me. "Turn off the gramophone, quickly," she ordered Ilona, and then beckoned me to come nearer.

"At last, at last! I've been waiting ages for you. Now be quick, tell me everything, everything, mind, every word. Papa got everything so mixed up that I didn't know where I was. You know what he's like when he's excited, he can never tell a straightforward story. Just think, he came up to my room in the middle of the night! I couldn't sleep in that terrible storm, I was absolutely freezing, there was an awful draught coming from the window and I hadn't the strength to get up and shut it. I kept wishing to myself the whole night that someone would wake up and come to me, and then suddenly I heard steps coming nearer and nearer. At first I was frightened, for it was two or three o'clock in the morning, and in my first gasp of astonishment I didn't recognize Papa, he looked so different. He came straight over to me and was beside himself with joy … You should have seen him, he laughed and sobbed … why, just fancy Papa actually laughing, laughing loudly and gaily, and dancing first on one foot then another like a great big schoolboy! And then, when he began to tell me the whole story, I was so flabbergasted that I couldn't take it in at first. I thought that either Papa had been dreaming or I was dreaming myself. But then Ilona came up too, and we chattered and laughed until morning. But now you must tell us everything … tell us … what this new cure is."

Just as when a strong wave hurls itself upon you and you stagger and try in vain to keep your feet, so now did I vainly attempt to struggle against the boundless dismay that overwhelmed me. Those last words had enlightened me in a flash. It was I, I alone, who had inspired her with this disastrous faith in a cure. Kekesfalva must have told her what Condor had confided to me.

But what was it that Condor had actually told me? And what was it that I had passed on? Condor, after all had expressed himself in the most cautious terms, and I, what could it have been that I, foolish slave of my pity, had read into his words that a whole household was made merry, that an old man was made young again, that a sick girl believed herself to be hale and hearty? What could it have been?

"Well, what's the matter ... why are you hesitating?" said Edith in persistent tones. "You must know how important every word is to me. Well—what did Condor say to you?"

"What did he say?" I echoed, so as to gain time. "Er ... you know already ... he was very optimistic ... Dr Condor hopes in time to get the best possible results. He proposes, if I'm not mistaken, to try a new treatment and is already making inquiries about it ... a most efficacious treatment ... if ... if I understood him rightly ... of course I don't understand anything about it, but in any case you can depend on him if he ... I believe, in fact, I'm quite sure, he'll put everything right."

Either she had not noticed my evasiveness or her impatience would brook no contradiction.

"I always said we wouldn't get any advance with the present treatment. After all, one knows oneself best ... Do you remember my telling you that it was all a lot of claptrap, all this business of massage and electrical treatment and surgical appliances? It's all much too slow; how can one go on waiting for ever? I took off those silly appliances this very morning, I tell you, without asking him ... you can't imagine what a relief it was. I was able to walk far better ... I believe it is only those confounded weights that have so handicapped me. No, you've got to attack the whole business quite differently—I've felt that for a long time. But ... but tell me quickly, what is this French professor's treatment? Shall I really have to go away to have it? Can't it be done here? Oh, how I hate, how I loathe those sanatoriums. And what's more, I just can't bear the sight of invalids. I've got quite enough to put up with from myself ... Well, tell me all about it ... Out with it! How long is it supposed to take? Is it really as quick as all that? Papa said that this professor had cured his patient in four months and that he can now walk up and down stairs and move about quite freely. That ... that would be incredible ... Well, don't sit there like a stuffed dummy, do tell me the whole story. When is he going to start, and how long is it supposed to take?"

Pull her up, I said to myself. Don't let her get caught up in this crazy illusion that everything is quite sure and certain. And so I adopted cautious tactics.

"No doctor can say beforehand how long it will take. I don't think it's possible to say anything definite for the moment ... and then ... Dr Condor only talked of the treatment in general terms. It's supposed to have achieved excellent results, he said, but whether it's absolutely reliable ... I mean, it can only be tried out in each individual case ... in any case, we shall have to wait until he ... "

But in her burning enthusiasm she swept aside all my feeble defences.

"My dear boy, you simply don't know him! One can never get anything definite out of him. He's so terribly overcautious. But once he makes even a half-promise, you can bank on his keeping it. One can depend on him, and you don't know how much I need to be done once and for all with the whole business, or at least to have some definite prospect of being done with it. Patience, they keep on telling me, patience. But one simply must know how long one has got to go on being patient. If I were told it would take another six months or a year—good, I should say, I'll see it through, and would do what was expected of me. But thank God we've at least got to this stage! You can't think how light-hearted I have felt since yesterday. I feel as though I had only now really begun to live. This morning we drove into town—yes, you may well be astonished—but now that I've got the worst behind me I don't care what people say or think, or whether they do stare after me and pity me ... I shall go for a drive every day now, just to show myself that I'm coming to the end of all this wretched waiting and holding myself in patience. And for tomorrow, Sunday—you'll be free of course—we've arranged a special treat. Papa has promised me that we'll drive out to the stud-farm. I haven't been there for years, four or five years at least. I never wanted to go outside the house again. But tomorrow we'll drive out there, and of course you'll come too.

You'll be surprised. Ilona and I have thought out a big surprise for you."

She turned with a laugh to Ilona. "Shall I give away the big secret here and now?"

"Yes," laughed Ilona, "let's have no more secrets."

"Well, listen, my dear friend. Papa wanted us to drive out in the car. But that's over too quickly, and besides, it's boring. Then I remembered that Josef had told us about that old fool of a Princess, the woman you know, to whom the *Schloss* used to belong, a horrid person—and how she always drove out in a coach-and-four, in the big travelling-coach, the gaily painted one in the coach-house. Just to show everyone that she was the Princess, she would always have it harnessed even for the short drive to the station. No one else for miles around would have dared to drive out in such style ... Just think what fun it would be to drive out for once like the late lamented Princess! The old coachman is still here—oh, you've never seen the old boy, he's long since been pensioned off, ever since we've had the car. But you should have seen his face when we told him we were going to drive out in the coach-and-four—he staggered up on to his wobbly legs, and wept for sheer joy to think that such a thing should happen to him once again in his life. It's all arranged, we're leaving at eight o'clock. We'll get up very early, and you of course will stay the night here. You simply can't refuse. We'll give you a nice room downstairs, and Piszta will get you anything you want from the barracks—by the way, he's going to be dressed as a lackey tomorrow, as he used to be in the Princess's time ... No, no objections. You simply must give us the pleasure, we won't let you off ... "

And so on and on it went like a spring that has been released. I listened in a daze, still utterly bewildered by this incomprehensible transformation in Edith. Her voice was changed, her speech, usually so jerky, was fluent and easy, the face I knew so well seemed to be transfigured the sickly, pallid flush had given place to a fresh, a more healthy glow, and there was now no trace of angularity in her gestures. It was a slightly intoxicated young girl who was sitting before me, with sparkling eyes and smiling, vivacious mouth. Willy-nilly, I too was infected by this feverish ecstasy, which, like any other form of, intoxication, sapped my inner resistance. Perhaps, I deluded myself, it is true, or *will* be true. Perhaps I haven't deceived her at all, perhaps she really will be cured as quickly as all that. After all, I have not lied outright, or at least not very much. Condor really has read something about an amazing cure, so why should it not be effective in the case of this radiant and pathetically credulous child, this sensitive being who is made so happy, so rapturous, by the mere mention of recovery? Why seek to dispel this exuberance which so lights up her whole being, why torture her with one's doubts? After all, the poor child has tormented herself long enough. And just as a speaker finds himself genuinely carried away by the enthusiasm aroused by his own hollow phrases, so now did the confidence which was born solely of my own exaggeration take firmer and firmer root in my own mind. And when at length Kekesfalva appeared, he found us all in the most light-hearted of moods, chattering away and making plans just as though Edith were already restored to health. Where could she learn to ride again? she asked; and would we officers of the regiment supervise her lessons and help her? Yes, and would not her father now give the priest the money which he had promised him for the new church roof? And as she made all these reckless proposals, which took for granted her ultimate restoration to normal health, she laughed and joked away so gaily and irresponsibly that my opposition was completely silenced. And it was only when I found myself alone in my room that night that I heard a faint warning knock on the wall of my heart: were not her hopes a trifle exaggerated? Ought I not to prick the bubble of this dangerous optimism? But I refused to admit the thought to my consciousness. Why worry as to whether I had said too much or too little? Even if I had gone further than in all honesty I should have done, my lies, those lies born of pity, had made her happy; and to make a person happy could never be a crime.

The great day of our expedition was ushered in at a very early hour with a little fanfare of hilarity. The first thing I heard on awakening in my cosy room, into which the morning sun was pouring its bright rays, was the sound of merry laughter. I went

175

to the window and saw the whole staff standing about in the courtyard, gaping at the old Princess's vast travelling-coach, which had obviously been taken out of the coach-house during the night. It was a marvellous museum piece, built in Vienna for an ancestor of Prince Orosvár a hundred or perhaps even a hundred and fifty years previously by the coach-maker to the Imperial Court. The actual body of the coach, which was protected by artistically designed springs against the jolting of the mighty wheels, was painted with the Arcadian and classical scenes to be found in old tapestries; no doubt the colours, which were somewhat crude, had originally been more vivid and had now faded. The inside of the silk-upholstered coach—and we had ample opportunity during our drive of exploring it in detail—contained all kinds of cunning contraptions, such as little collapsible tables, mirrors and scent-bottles. At first of course, this vast plaything of a bygone century struck one as being somewhat unreal, a stage property out of a masquerade, but it was for this very reason that footmen and servants threw themselves so merrily and in such carnival spirit into the task of safely launching the ponderous vessel on wheels. The mechanic from the sugar-factory was oiling the wheels with particular zest and testing the metal frame with his hammer. Meanwhile, the four horses, decked out as though for a wedding with garlands of flowers, were being harnessed—an operation that gave Jonak, the old coachman, ample opportunity for airing his superior knowledge. Dressed in the faded princely livery, and displaying surprising agility despite his gouty legs, he was initiating into the tricks of his trade the younger members of the staff, who, although they might be able to ride bicycles and if need be cope with the mechanism of a motor car, had not the vaguest idea how to drive a four-in-hand. It was he, too, who the night before had pointed out to the cook that when the princely household indulged in *fêtes-champêtres* its honour absolutely demanded that even in the most remote corners of the woods and meadows the refreshments should be served as lavishly and punctiliously as in the dining-room of the *Schloss*. Under his supervision, therefore, the footman was stowing away damask table-cloths, napkins and silver in cases bearing the Orosvár coat of arms. Not until this was done to his satisfaction was the cook, a white linen trencher-cap crowning his beaming features, allowed to bring along the actual provisions: roast chickens and hams and pies, freshly baked bread and whole batteries of bottles, all packed in straw so that they might withstand the perils of the bumpy roads and arrive unbroken. A young lad was sent along as the cook's representative to serve the viands, and was assigned the place on the box where, in the Princess's time, a princely lackey had stood side by side with a liveried servant in a hat with a cockade.

What with all this pomp and ceremony the preparations were by now taking on an air of theatrical gaiety, and the news of our strange excursion having quickly spread throughout the district, there was no lack of spectators to witness the diverting spectacle. Peasants in gaily coloured Sunday costumes had come from neighbouring villages, wrinkled old women and grey-haired manikins with their inevitable clay-pipes from the nearby alms-houses. But above all it was the bare-legged children from far and near who, bewitched and enraptured, let their gaze wander from the garlanded horses up to the driver on the box, into whose withered and yet firm hand ran the mysterious tangle of reins. No less entranced were they by the sight of Piszta, whom they saw as a rule only in his chauffeur's blue uniform and who now, dressed in princely livery, was holding the bright silver hunting-horn in his hand in expectant readiness to give the signal for departure.

When having breakfasted, we at length approached the gaudy vehicle, we could not help noticing with amusement that we presented a considerably less festive sight than the ostentatious coach and the glittering lackeys. Kekesfalva looked a little comical as, dressed in his inevitable black frock coat, he climbed stiffly, like a black stork, into this coach that bore another family's coat of arms. One could have wished to see the young girls in costumes of the rococo period, with powdered hair and patches and gaily coloured fans, and I myself would doubtless have cut a more dashing figure in the dazzling white riding costume of Maria Theresa's time than in my blue Uhlan's uniform. Yet even in the absence of period fancy-dress the whole thing seemed quite festive enough as at length we seated ourselves in the great ponderous

177

casket. Piszta raised the hunting-horn to his lips, and its shrill note sounded out above the excited bows and greetings of the assembled staff; whereupon the coachman cracked his whip dexterously in the air with a terrific flourish and a sound like a pistol-shot. As it moved off, the huge equipage gave a mighty lurch, which threw us laughing into each other's laps, but the valiant driver steered his four horses skilfully through the gateway, which suddenly seemed to us, from our seats in the wide-bellied coach, to be peri-lously narrow, and we landed safely on the high-road.

It was not to be wondered at that we should have caused a considerable sensation and also have aroused prodigious respect all along our route. The princely four-in-hand had not been seen in the district for decades, and to the peasants its unexpected reappearance seemed to herald some almost supernatural event. They probably thought we were driving to Court, that the Emperor had come, or that some other quite incredible event had occurred, for wherever we appeared hats flew off as though mown down with a scythe, and bare-footed children followed us all the way with shrieks and whoops of delight.

Whenever we met another vehicle, a cart laden with hay or a ponytrap, its driver would jump nimbly from the box and, doffing his hat, pull in his horses to let us pass. We were the undisputed masters of the road; to us belonged, as in feudal times, the whole lovely, luxuriant countryside with its waving cornfields, its men and beasts. Our rate of progress in the ponderous vehicle, it is true, was far from rapid, but on the other hand, it afforded us all the more opportunity of looking round us and making merry, an opportunity of which the two girls in particular availed them-selves to the full. Novelty always delights the young, and all these unaccustomed excitements—our strange carriage, the obsequious awe displayed by the people as they beheld us driving along in our anachronistic equipage, and a hundred-and-one other little incidents—raised the spirits of the two girls to such a pitch that they seemed almost as though drunk—drunk on sun and fresh air. Edith in particular, who had scarcely been out of the house for months, lent a brightness to this marvellous summer's day with her unrestrained gaiety and high spirits.

We made our first halt at a little village where the bells were

just being tolled for Mass. We could see the last stragglers making
their way towards the village along the narrow strips between
field and field; all that was visible of them above the tall stooks
of corn was the flat black silk hats of the men and the gaily
embroidered caps of the women. From every direction long lines
of people moved forward like dark caterpillars through the waving
gold of the fields, and just as we drove through the—not altogether clean—main street, scattering in alarm a flock of cackling
geese, the droning of the bell ceased. Mass was about to begin,
and surprisingly enough, it was Edith who impetuously demanded
that we should all get out and attend it.

The fact that so incredible an equipage should pull up in their
unassuming market-place, and that the land-owner whom they
all knew from hearsay should, accompanied by his family—for
they apparently assumed that I was a member of it—wish to
attend Mass in their little church, occasioned intense excitement
among the honest country-folk. The sacristan came running out
just as though the former Kanitz were the late Prince Orosvár
himself, and informed us obsequiously that the priest was going
to hold up the service for us; their heads bowed reverently, the
people made way for us, obviously overcome by emotion when
they noticed Edith's infirmity, for she had to be supported and
helped into the church by Josef and Ilona. It is always simple
people who are most shocked at the realization that misfortune
sometimes does not shrink from laying a grim hand even on the
rich. There was a rustling and a whispering, and then some
women came bustling up with cushions so that the crippled
girl—who was, of course, put in the front pew, which had been
hurriedly vacated—should have as comfortable a seat as possible.
And then, when the service began, it almost seemed as though
the priest were celebrating Mass with ritual solemnity for our
especial benefit. I myself was deeply moved by the touching simplicity of this little church; the clear singing of the women, the
rugged, somewhat self-conscious voices of the men, the naïve
piping of the children, seemed to me to betoken a purer and
more direct faith than the far more sophisticated services I was
used to in the Stefanskirche or the Augustinerkirche in Vienna.
But I was distracted from my own devotions when I chanced to

glance at Edith, who was sitting next to me, and noticed with positive alarm with what burning fervour she was praying. Never yet had I come across anything at all to indicate that she had had a religious upbringing or was religiously inclined; now I perceived that her praying was quite different from that of most people, to whom praying becomes in time a mere matter of habit; her head bowed as though she were walking in the teeth of a storm, her hands tightly clutching the front of the pew, her whole being withdrawn, as it were, into itself, so that she murmured the responses mechanically, her whole attitude betrayed the tense excitement of one who is concentrating and rallying all his forces in a supreme effort to obtain his heart's desire. From time to time as I knelt beside her I could feel the dark wooden pew vibrating, as though something of the trembling fervour and quivering ecstasy of her praying were being communicated to the rigid wood. I realized that she was asking God for some definite thing, that she *wanted* something of Him, and what this crippled, sick girl wanted was not difficult for me to divine.

When, too, the service over, we had helped Edith back into the carriage, she remained for some time lost in thought. She did not utter a word, and no longer gazed about her on all sides with wanton curiosity. It was as though that half-hour of fervent wrestling had exhausted and wearied her spirit. And we, of course, also preserved a discreet silence. It was a silent and drowsy party which, shortly before midday, arrived at the stud-farm.

There, to be sure, a special welcome awaited us. The lads of the vicinity—obviously apprised of our visit—had just rounded up the wildest horses on the farm and came riding bareback towards us at a furious gallop, in a kind of Arabian fantasia. They were a joy to watch, these sunburned, exultant young fellows with their open shirts, wide white cowboy trousers, and low-crowned hats from which streamed long coloured ribbons. They charged down upon us like a horde of Bedouins as though to run us down. Our own horses were by now pricking up their ears uneasily, and old Jonak, tautening his legs, was about to pull sharply at the reins, when suddenly, at the sound of a shrill whistle, the wild band dexterously formed into a closed column and proceeded to escort us in triumph to the bailiff's house.

There, as a cavalry officer, I found all kinds of things to interest me. The two girls were shown the new foals, and were beside themselves with delight at the timid, inquisitive animals with their clumsy, gawky legs and stupid mouths, which were as yet quite incapable of nibbling at the lumps of sugar held out to them. Whilst we were all so pleasantly occupied, the kitchen-boy, under Jonak's careful directions, had laid a magnificent spread for us out of doors. Soon the wine proved to be so potent and so good that our hitherto subdued merriment became more and more unrestrained. We chattered away more garrulously, more unconstrainedly than ever, and just as during all those hours never a cloud darkened the silken-blue sky, so never once was my mind clouded by the thought that hitherto I had known this slender girl, who was now laughing more merrily, more loudly, more happily than any of us, as a suffering, despairing, afflicted creature, or that this old man, who was examining and patting the horses with the skill of a veterinary surgeon, joking with all the stable-lads and slipping them tips, was the same man who two days previously, in a frenzy of anxiety, had waylaid me in the middle of the night like a sleep-walker. I scarcely recognized myself either, so free were my movements, so supple were my limbs. After the meal, while Edith was made to take a little rest in the bailiff's house, I tried out several horses one after another. I raced a few of the young lads over the fields, and as I gave my horse his head and galloped along I was conscious of a feeling of freedom such as I had never yet known. Oh, if only I could stay here for ever, be at no one's beck and call, be free for ever in the open fields, free as air. My heart sank somewhat when, after having galloped some considerable distance, I heard from afar the sound of the hunting-horn, warning me of our imminent departure for home.

For the sake of variety the experienced Jonak had chosen another road for our return journey; presumably, too, because it led for some time through a cool, refreshing little wood. Everything had gone off splendidly on this successful day, and to crown all there now awaited us one last surprise, the best surprise of all. As we entered a homely little village of about twenty houses we found our road—the only road in this out of-the-way spot—

entirely blocked by a dozen or so empty carts and carriages. Oddly enough, too, there was no one about to clear the way for our vast and bulky coach; it was as though all the people of the district had been swallowed up by the earth. This state of more-than-Sunday desolation, however, was soon explained when Jonak cracked his enormous whip in the air with a sound like a pistol-shot and a number of people came running up in alarm. It transpired that the son of the richest peasant in the district was celebrating his wedding with a poor relation from another ham-let; and from the end of the village street, where a barn had been cleared for dancing, there now came rushing up, purple in the face, the somewhat corpulent father of the bridegroom to bid us an obsequious welcome. Perhaps he really thought that the illustrious lord and master of Kekesfalva had had the four-in-hand harnessed for the express purpose of honouring him and his son with his presence at their wedding-feast; perhaps it was only out of vanity that he took advantage of our happening to drive past to raise his standing with the other villagers. At any rate, bowing profusely, he begged that Herr von Kekesfalva and his party would, while the road was being cleared, do him the favour of drinking the health of the young couple in a glass of his own Hungarian home-grown wine. We for our part were in far too merry a mood to refuse his kindly request. And so Edith was carefully lifted out of the carriage, and we marched off like con-quering heroes through a gaping, chattering crowd of respectful village-folk to the improvised dance-hall.

On two sides of the barn a dais, made of loose planks placed on empty beer-casks, had been erected. On the dais to the right the relatives of the family and the inevitable notabilities, the parish priest and the commandant of gendarmerie, were seated in state round the bridal couple at a long table decked with a white linen cloth and covered with an abundance of food and drink. On the opposite dais the musicians, four moustachioed, romantic-looking gypsies, had taken up their position: violins, bass-viol and zither. Guests thronged the dance-floor in the middle of the barn, while a number of children who had been unable to gain entry to the overcrowded room peeped in at the door or sat perched with their legs dangling from the rafters.

Some of the less exalted relatives were obliged to move from the table of honour to make room for us, and they were all visibly astonished at the condescension of the grand ladies and mingled without a trace of embarrassment with the worthy villagers. Reeling with excitement, the bridegroom's father himself fetched an enormous pitcher of wine, filled up the glasses and raised his voice in a toast "To the health of the noble gentleman!" which was echoed enthusiastically in a shout that could be heard in the street. Then he dragged forward his son and the bride, a shy, somewhat broad-hipped young woman, who looked very touching in her gay, festive costume and white myrtle wreath. Crimson with confusion, she curtsied awkwardly to Kekesfalva, and respectfuly kissed Edith's hand. Edith was visibly agitated, for the sight of a wedding always has a disturbing effect on young girls; at such moments a mysterious sense of solidarity with their own sex takes possession of them. Blushing, Edith pulled the bashful young bride to her and embraced her; then, struck by a sudden thought, she took a ring from her finger—a slender, old-fashioned, not very costly ring—and gave it to the bride, who was utterly taken aback by this unlooked-for gift. She glanced up anxiously at her father-in-law, as though to ask if she should really accept such a grand present, and no sooner had he proudly nodded his consent than she burst into tears of sheer joy. Once more we were engulfed in a wave of enthusiastic gratitude. From all sides the simple, unsophisticated folk thronged around us; we could tell from their expressions that they longed to show us some special mark of recognition but that no one dared even to address a word to the "grand gentry". The old peasant-woman, the bridegroom's mother, staggered like a drunkard from one to another with tears in her eyes, utterly dazed by the honour that had been accorded her son's wedding, while the bridegroom in his embarrassment kept goggling first at his bride, then at us, and then at his heavy, polished top-boots.

At this moment Kekesfalva did the wisest thing possible to check this display of reverence, which was by now becoming somewhat embarrassing. He shook hands cordially with the bridegroom's father, the bridegroom and some of the notabilities, and begged them not to let our presence interrupt their splendid wedding-feast. The young people, he said, should go on dancing to their hearts' content; they could give us no greater pleasure than by continuing to enjoy themselves. At the same time he beckoned to the leader of the orchestra, who, his fiddle tucked under his left arm, had been waiting on the dais, his back bent, as it were, in a permanent bow, threw him a note and signalled to him to begin. It must have been a note for some considerable amount, for, as though galvanized into activity, the obsequious fellow rushed back to his dais, and the next moment the four musicians fell to as only Hungarians and gypsies can.

At the first note of the zither all reserve was thrown to the winds. In a trice couples formed, and the dancers whirled away more wildly, more extravagantly than before, for all the lads and lasses were fired with ambition to show us how real Hungarians could dance. In a moment the room that had but now been wrapped in awed silence was transformed into a riotous maze of swaying, leaping, stamping bodies; at every beat all round the room the glasses shook and clattered, with such wild abandon did the enthusiastic young people throw themselves into the tumultuous rhythm of the dance.

Edith gazed with flashing eyes at the happy, noisy crowd. Suddenly I felt her hand on my arm. "You must dance too," she commanded. Fortunately the bride had not yet been drawn into the whirling throng; she was staring as though in a trance at the ring on her finger. When I bowed her an invitation to dance, she blushed at the undue honour that was being paid her, but willingly allowed herself to be led off. Our example inspired the bridegroom, too, with courage. At an urgent sign from his father he requested Ilona to dance with him, and now the zither-player hammered away at his instrument more frantically than ever, and the leader of the orchestra fiddled away like a black-moustachioed Mephisto. Never before or after, I fancy, was there such bacchanalian dancing in the village as on that wedding-day.

But the cornucopia of surprises had not yet been emptied of its contents. Tempted by Edith's extravagant present to the bride, one of those old gypsy women who are never absent from such festivals had pushed her way on to the dais and was using all her arts to wheedle Edith into having her fortune told. Edith was visibly disturbed. Genuinely curious on the one hand, she was on the other hand ashamed of lending herself to such quackery in the presence of so many spectators. I quickly stepped into the breach by gently edging Herr von Kekesfalva and the others away from the dais, so that no one should overhear a word of the old woman's mysterious predictions, and the curious were reduced to looking on in amusement from a distance as the old woman, mumbling all kinds of, gibberish, knelt before Edith and studied her hand. Everyone in Hungary is only too familiar with these old wives' age-old dodge of telling their clients the most agreeable things possible about their future, so as to reap a rich reward as the bearers of good tidings. But to my astonishment what the old crone whispered to Edith in wheezy, insistent tones seemed to throw the young girl into an extraordinary state of agitation. That twitching at the nostrils began which was the inevitable precursor of violent emotion. Bending down lower and lower, she listened intently, now and again looking round anxiously to make sure that no one was listening. At last she beckoned her father to come to her, and whispered something imperiously in his ear, whereupon, compliant as ever, he felt in his breast-pocket and handed the old gypsy a bundle of notes. The amount must, according to village notions, have been simply huge, for the greedy old woman fell on her knees as though mown to the ground, kissed the hem of Edith's skirt like one possessed, and with incomprehensible mutterings and mumblings feverishly stroked the crippled girl's feet. Then she bounded away as though afraid the money might be taken back again.

"Let's go now," I whispered quickly to Herr von Kekesfalva, for it struck me that Edith had turned very pale. I fetched Piszta, and he and Ilona helped Edith back to the coach. Immediately the music stopped, for none of the good folk wanted to lose the opportunity of giving us a triumphant send-off. The musicians stood round the coach to sound one parting fanfare and the whole village shouted and yelled "Three cheers!" Old Jonak had considerable difficulty in controlling the horses, which were no longer accustomed to such a warlike din.

I continued to be a little anxious about Edith, who was sitting opposite me in the coach. She was still trembling from head to foot, and seemed to be in the grip of violent emotion. And suddenly she burst into convulsive sobs. But they were sobs of happiness. She cried and laughed by turns. The artful old gypsy had quite obviously prophesied a quick recovery for her—and no doubt other agreeable things into the bargain.

But "Let me be, do let me be!" the sobbing girl protested impatiently. She seemed to take an entirely new and odd pleasure in this emotional outburst. "Let me be, do let me be!" she kept on repeating. "I know, I know the old woman's a humbug. Oh, I know that myself. But why shouldn't one be foolish once in a while? Why not for once let oneself be thoroughly taken in?"

It was already late in the evening when we once more drove through the gate of the *Schloss*. They all pressed me to stay to dinner. But I did not want to, I felt that I had had enough, too much, for one day. I had been perfectly happy the whole of this long golden summer day; anything more could only diminish my happiness. Better to walk home now down the familiar avenue, my spirit tranquillized like the warm, summer air after the burning day. Better not to hanker for more, better merely to look back on it all and remember it gratefully. And so I took my leave earlier than usual. It was a bright, starry night, and I felt as though the stars were shining down affectionately upon me. The wind, full of sweet breath, soughed softly over the darkling fields, and seemed to be singing to me. There stole over me that mood of serene exaltation in which everything seems good and rapturous, the world and its human beings; that mood in which one has an urge to embrace every tree and stroke its bark as though it were the flesh of a loved one; in which one longs to enter every house, to sit down by the side of its unknown occupants and unburden oneself to them; in which one's own breast is filled to bursting point, and one's emotions are too much for one, in which one would like to open one's heart, to give lavishly of oneself—to spend and squander some of the superabundance of one's happiness.

When I at length reached the barracks, my batman was standing waiting at the door of my room. For the first time I noticed (I noticed everything today as though for the first time) what a guileless, round, apple-cheeked face this Ruthenian peasant boy had. I must do something to make him happy too, I thought. I'll give him something to buy himself and his girl a few glasses of beer. He shall have this evening off, and tomorrow evening, and every evening this week. I put my hand in my pocket to feel for a silver coin, but at this point he stood smartly to attention and announced: "A telegram for the *Herr Leutnant.*"

A telegram? I immediately felt uneasy. Who in the world could want anything of me? It could only be evil tidings that had to be told in such a hurry. I strode across to the table. There lay the ominous missive. With reluctant fingers I tore it open. The message, incisively clear, consisted only of a dozen words: "Am asked visit Kekesfalva tomorrow stop meet me Weinstube five o'clock Condor."

That within the space of a few minutes one can pass from a state of reeling drunkenness to a state of crystal-clear sobriety I had once before had an opportunity of discovering. That had been last year when, a few days before his marriage to the daughter of an immensely rich North Bohemian manufacturer, a fellow-officer had invited us all to a magnificent farewell party. The good chap had done us really proud; he had brought into action battery after battery of bottles of heady, full-bodied Bordeaux and, finally, such enormous quantities of champagne that we grew either rowdy or sentimental, according to our individual temperaments. We embraced each other, we laughed, we brawled, we kicked up a hell of a shindig and sang at the tops of our voices. We drank each other's healths again and again, tossed down glass after glass of brandy and liqueurs, and puffed away at cigars and pipes until the over-heated room was enveloped in a kind of bluish fog by the dense fumes of smoke; in the end none of us noticed that behind the clouded windows day was dawning. It must have been about three or four o'clock in the morning, and by this time most of us could no longer sit up straight in our chairs. Sprawling heavily over the table, we stared up with bleary, glazed eyes whenever a fresh toast was drunk; and any one of us who had to leave the room stumbled and reeled to the door or fell flat like a stuffed sack. We could none of us speak or think clearly any longer.

Suddenly the door was flung open, and the Colonel (of whom I shall have more to say later) came bustling in. Since in the frightful hullabaloo only a few of us either noticed or recognized him, he strode abruptly up to the table, and banged his fist down so violently that the plates and glasses clattered. Then he roared in his most acid, incisive tones, "Silence!"

And instantly, before you could say Jack Robinson, there was complete silence; even the most befuddled of us blinked and came to life. The Colonel announced briefly that the next morning there was to be a surprise inspection by the General commanding the Division. He relied on us to see that everything went off smoothly, and that no one disgraced the regiment. And now a strange thing occurred: in the twinkling of an eye we all came to our senses. Just as though some inner window had been thrown open, all the fumes of alcohol were dissipated, the bleary faces changed, tensed, at the call of duty; in a trice every man pulled himself together. Two minutes later the table with all its wreckage was deserted, and every one of us knew exactly what was expected of him. The men were roused, orderlies were sent posting hither and thither, everything, down to the last pommel, was quickly cleaned and polished. And a few hours later the dreaded inspection went off without a hitch.

It was with the same lightning rapidity that, the moment I had torn open and read the telegram, my soft, drowsy, dreamy mood was dissipated. In an instant I knew what I had been refusing to admit to myself for hours and hours: that all my raptures had been nothing but the intoxication born of a lie, and that in my weakness, my fatal wallowing in my own pity, I had been guilty of deceiving both myself and the others. I realized that Dr Condor was coming in order to call me to account, and that I was now to pay the price for my own, for the others', elation.

With the punctuality born of impatience I found myself standing a quarter of an hour before the time appointed outside the little wine-bar, and punctually to the minute Dr Condor drove up from the station in a two-horse carriage. He came straight towards me, and dispensing with formalities, began:

"Capital that you're punctual! I knew I could depend on you.

Perhaps it would be best if we were to ensconce ourselves in the same corner as before. The things we have to discuss are not for others' ears."

He seemed, somehow, different from the flabby creature of a few days ago. Agitated and yet controlled, he marched on ahead of me into the bar and almost rudely ordered the waitress who came hurrying up: "A litre of wine. The same as we had the other day. And leave us alone. I'll call you when I want you."

We sat down. "Well, to come straight to the point," he began, even before the waitress had had time to put the wine before us. "I'll have to hurry, or those people up at Kekesfalva will smell a rat and get it into their heads we're hatching all sorts of plots. It was a devil of a business to shake off the chauffeur; he was absolutely determined at all costs to rush me out there at once. But let me plunge *in medias res*, so that you may know what's at stake.

"Well then—yesterday morning I received a telegram. 'Please dear friend come earliest opportunity stop all await you with greatest impatience stop fullest confidence and deepest gratitude Kekesfalva.' Those piled-up superlatives, 'earliest opportunity' and 'greatest impatience', were in themselves not to my liking. Why suddenly so impatient? I had examined Edith only a few days before. And then, why assure me of his confidence by telegram, why the special gratitude? All the same, I didn't take the matter in the least seriously, and filed the telegram away. After all, I thought, the old fellow often indulges in such whims. But it was what happened this morning that gave me a shock. I received an interminably long express letter from Edith, an utterly mad and ecstatic letter, saying that she had known from the start that I was the only person on earth who could save her and she just couldn't tell me how happy it made her to know that we had at last reached the present stage. She was only writing to assure me I could count absolutely upon her. She would without fail carry out any treatment I prescribed, however difficult. But I must start her on the new treatment soon, at once, she was burning with impatience. And once again, I could expect anything of her, only I must get started quickly. And so on and so on.

"Well, this mention of a new treatment threw a great light on the whole matter. I realized at once that someone must have been chattering either to the old boy or his daughter about Professor Viennot's cure; there must be something behind it all. And this someone could, of course, be no one but you, *Herr Leutnant*."

I must involuntarily have recoiled, for he went on firmly:

"Now please don't let us have any argument on this point. I haven't breathed a word to anyone except you about Professor Viennot's method. If the Kekesfalvas think that Edith's illness is going to be swept away in a few months as though with a broom, you alone are responsible. But, as I have said, let us dispense with all recriminations—we have both of us gossiped, I to you, and you in your turn pretty freely to the others. It was my duty to be more cautious with you. After all, it's not your job to treat the sick. How should you know that invalids and their relatives have a quite different vocabulary from normal people, that they immediately translate every 'perhaps' into a 'certainly' and that one can only measure out hope to them in carefully distilled drops, or their optimism goes to their heads and makes them quite mad?

"But we won't go into that any further—what's done can't be undone. Let's put *finis* to the whole subject of responsibility. I didn't ask you to come here to lecture you. I merely felt it my duty, seeing that you had already meddled in my business, to enlighten you as to the actual state of affairs. That is why I asked you to come here."

Dr Condor raised his head for the first time and looked straight at me. But there was no sternness in his gaze. On the contrary, I felt that he pitied me. His voice, too, was gentler as he went on:

"I know, my dear Lieutenant, that what I now have to tell you will be very disagreeable to you. But, as I have said, we have no time for sentiment and sentimentality. I told you that when I read that article in the medical journal I wrote straight off to Professor Viennot for further information—more than that, I think, I did not say. Well, this morning I received his answer—as it happened by the same post as Edith's effusion. His information seems, at the first glance, to be positive. He actually has had astonishing success with the patient he described in his article and also with one or two others. But unfortunately—and this is the disagreeable point—his method cannot be applied in our case. His cures have been effected in cases of disease of the spinal cord arising out of tuberculosis, in which—I shall spare you the technical details—the motor nerves can be made to function perfectly again. In our case, where the central nervous system is affected, all the methods employed by Professor Viennot, such as lying motionless in a steel corset, the use of sun-rays, his special system of remedial exercises, are out of the question. His method is—alas, alas—entirely impracticable in our case. To expect the poor child to endure all this elaborate treatment would probably be to torture her quite needlessly. So there it is—that was what I felt bound to tell you. So now you know how things really stand, and how thoughtless you have been in buoying the poor girl up with the hope that she will be able to dance and run about again in a few months. I should never have allowed such a preposterous assertion to pass my lips. But it will be you, who have so rashly promised them the sun, the moon and the stars that they will now fall back upon, and quite justifiably. After all, it is you and you alone who have set the ball rolling."

I felt my fingers stiffen. From the moment when I had seen Dr Condor's telegram lying on my table I had subconsciously anticipated all this, and now that he had summed up the situation so clearly for me, I felt as though I had been dealt a blow on the head with a blunt hatchet. Instinctively I felt impelled to defend myself. I did not want to have to bear the whole responsibility. But the words that I eventually forced out sounded like the stammering of a guilty schoolboy.

"But why? I only meant to act for the best ... If I said something to Kekesfalva it was only out of ... out of."

"I know, I know," interrupted Condor. "Naturally, he forced it out of you, wrung it from you. I know how he can break down all one's defences with his desperate persistence. Yes, I know, I know that you only weakened out of pity, out of the best possible motives. But—and I think I've already once warned you on this score—pity is a confoundedly two-edged business. Anyone who doesn't know how to deal with it should keep his hands, and, above all, his heart, off it. It is only at first that pity, like morphia, is a solace to the invalid, a remedy, a drug, but unless you know the correct dosage and when to stop, it becomes a virulent poison. The first few injections do good, they soothe, they deaden the pain. But the devil of it is that the organism, the body, just like the soul, has an uncanny capacity for adaptation. Just as the nervous system cries out for more and more morphia, so do the emotions cry out for more and more pity, in the end more than one can give. Inevitably there comes a moment when one has to say 'No', and then one must not mind the other person's hating one more for this ultimate refusal than if one had never helped him at all. Yes, my dear Lieutenant, one has got to keep one's pity properly in check, or it does far more harm than any amount of indifference—we doctors know that, and so do judges and myrmidons of the law and pawnbrokers; if they were all to give way to their pity, this world of ours would stand still—a dangerous thing, pity, a dangerous thing. You can see for your-self what your weakness has done."

"Yes ... but one can't ... one just can't abandon a person to despair ... after all, there was no harm in my trying ... "

But Condor suddenly grew vehement.

"Oh, but there was—a very great deal. You take on yourself a confounded amount of responsibility when you make a fool of another person with your pity. An adult person must consider, before getting himself mixed up in such a thing, how far he's pre-pared to go—there must be no fooling about with other people's feelings. Admitted that you have fooled these good people out of the best, the most honourable motives—in this world of ours it's not a question of whether one acts boldly or timorously, but solely of what one ultimately achieves, what one accomplishes. Pity—that's all right. But there are two kinds of pity. One, the weak and sentimental kind, which is really no more than the heart's impatience to be rid as quickly as possible of the painful emotion aroused by the sight of another's unhappiness, that pity which is not compassion, but only an instinctive desire to fortify one's own soul against the sufferings of another; and the other, the only kind that counts, the unsentimental but creative kind, which knows what it is about and is determined to hold out, in patience and forbearance, to the very limit of its strength and even beyond. It is only when one goes on to the end, to the extreme, bitter end, only when one has an inexhaustible fund of patience, that one can help one's fellows. Only when one is prepared to sacrifice oneself in doing so—and then only!"

A bitter note crept into his voice. I could not help remembering what Kekesfalva had told me: that Condor had a blind wife whom he had been unable to cure, and had married by way of penance, and that this blind woman, instead of being grateful to him, was a continual plague to him. But he put his hand on my arm with a warm, almost affectionate gesture.

"Come, come, I don't mean to be unkind. It's just that your feelings got the better of you, and that's a thing that can happen to anyone. But now to business—yours and mine. I haven't dragged you here to babble psychology. We must get down to practical details. It's essential, of course, that we should act concertedly in this affair. I cannot have you interfering with my plans behind my back a second time. Well, listen. After that letter of Edith's I am unfortunately bound to assume that our friends have been swept off their feet by the illusion that Edith's complicated disease can be spirited away by Professor Viennot's treatment as easily as a sum is wiped off a slate. If that crazy notion has taken a dangerous hold of them, there's nothing for it but to eradicate it—the quicker the better for us all. Of course it will be a severe shock to them; truth is always a bitter pill to swallow, but we can't let such an illusion go on flourishing like a weed. Leave it to me to deal with the whole thing in the most humane way possible.

"And now as to you. The most convenient thing for me, of course, would be to put all the blame on you; to say that you had misunderstood me, that you had exaggerated or drawn upon your imagination. Well, I'm not going to do that, I prefer to take the whole responsibility on my own shoulders. Only—I may as well tell you straight away—I can't leave you entirely out of the picture. You know the old man and his terrible pertinacity. If I were to explain the whole thing to him a hundred times over and to show him the letter, he'd still keep on whining, 'But you promised the *Herr Leutnant*', and 'But the *Herr Leutnant* said ... '

He'd go on quoting you *ad infinitum* in order to delude himself and me into thinking that despite everything there was still some hope. Without using you as a witness I'll never convince him. You can't dispel illusions as easily as you shake down the mercury in a thermometer. Once you hold out even a straw of hope to one of those patients who are so cruelly called incurable he will immediately construct a plank out of it, and out of the plank a whole house. But such castles in the air are extremely unhealthy for patients, and it is my duty as a doctor to demolish this particular one as speedily as possible, before sublime hopes take up their abode in it. We must therefore tackle the business in earnest and lose no time."

Condor paused. He was obviously waiting for my assent. But I did not dare to meet his gaze. Memories of the day before raced hither and thither in my brain, driven on by the thumping of my heart; how we had driven through the summer countryside, and how the face of the crippled girl had been radiant with sunshine and happiness; how she had stroked the little foals, how she had sat like a queen at the feast; how the tears had trickled down the old man's face into his laughing, trembling mouth. Was I to shatter all that at one blow? To change back into her suffering self an Edith who had been so transformed, with one word to drive back into the purgatory of impatience the girl who had been so gloriously snatched from despair! No, I knew that I should never lift a finger to do such a thing.

"But couldn't we? ... " I began timorously, faltering beneath his scrutiny.

"What?" he asked sharply.

"I only wondered whether ... whether we shouldn't wait a while before opening up the subject again ... at least a few days, because ... because I gained the impression yesterday, that she had entirely adjusted herself to the idea of this treatment ... I mean adjusted her mind to it ... and she would now, as you expressed it, have the ... the psychical strength ... I mean she would be in a position to get far more out of herself, if ... if one left her for a little time longer in the belief that this new treatment, from which she expects so much, would ultimately cure her. You ... you didn't see, you ... simply can't imagine what an effect the mere mention of it had on her ... I really had the impression that she was able to walk better at once ... and I wonder whether we should not first let that work itself out ... Of course ... "—my voice failed me, for I could tell that Condor was looking up at me in astonishment—"of course, I don't understand anything about it."

Condor kept his gaze fixed on me. Then he growled: "Behold—Saul also amongst the prophets! You seem to have got yourself pretty thoroughly mixed up in the affair—you have even made a note of what I said about 'psychical strength!' And clinical observations into the bargain! Without my knowing it, I've secretly enlisted the services of an assistant and counsellor. By the way"—he scratched his head thoughtfully—"what you suggested isn't altogether a stupid idea—forgive me, I mean, of course, stupid in the medical sense. Odd, really odd—when I received Edith's effusion, I asked myself for a moment whether, now that you had persuaded her that recovery was striding towards her on seven-league boots, we should not exploit this fervent faith she has in an ultimate cure ... Not half a bad idea, my dear colleague. The whole thing would be child's play to stage—I could send her to the Engadine, where I have a friend who's a doctor, and leave her in the blissful belief that we were trying out a new treatment, whereas in reality it would be the old one. At first the effect would probably be astounding, and we should get scores of enthusiastic, grateful letters. The illusion, the change of air, the change of scenery, the increase of energy, all that would actually help no end, and bolster up the illusion. After all, a fortnight in the Engadine would do even you and me a world of good. But, my dear Lieutenant, I as a doctor have to think not only of the beginning of a treatment, but of the next stage, and above all of the ultimate result. I have to take into account the reaction that would inevitably follow such wild and extravagant hopes. As a doctor I have to remain a sober chess-player; I dare not become a gambler, least of all when someone else has to put down the stakes."

"But ... you yourself are of the opinion that an essential improvement could be effected in her condition ... "

"Certainly. At the start we should see considerable progress—

after all, women react amazingly to emotions, to illusions. But just think what the situation will be in a few months when, the so-called psychical forces of which we spoke are exhausted, the will which has been whipped up played out, the fervour used up, and when, after weeks and weeks of wearing emotional tension, there is still no sign of recovery, the complete recovery upon which she now counts as upon a certainty. Just consider what a catastrophic effect that would have on a sensitive person, who is in any case devoured by impatience. In Edith's case it is not a question of a slight improvement, but of something fundamental, of a changeover from slow and sure methods, methods relying on patience, to risky and dangerous ones, based on impatience. How can we expect her ever again to have confidence in me, in any other doctor, or in any human being, when she realizes that she has been so deliberately deceived? Rather, then, the truth, however cruel it may seem. In medicine the use of the knife is often the kinder course. Never procrastinate. I could never take the responsibility for such dissimulation with a clear conscience. Think it out for yourself. Would *you* have the courage in my place?"

"Yes," I answered without hesitation, and the very next moment was startled at my own precipitancy. "That is to say ... " I added cautiously, "I should admit the true state of affairs when she had at least made *some* progress ... Forgive me, *Herr Doktor* ... it sounds somewhat presumptuous ... but you have not had the opportunity I have had of observing during the last few weeks how essential it is for these invalids to have something to help them on, and ... Yes, she must be told the truth ... but only when she is able to bear it ... not now, *Herr Doktor*, I beseech you ... not now ... not immediately."

I hesitated. He was gazing at me with such astonished curiosity that I grew confused.

"But when?" he said meditatively. "And above all, who is to tell her? Some day or other she'll have to be told, and I'm afraid that her disappointment when she hears the truth will be a hundred times more cruel and more dangerous than if we told her now. Would you really take on yourself such a responsibility?"

"Yes," I said firmly (I believe that it was only fear lest I should have to drive out with him there and then to Kekesfalva that inspired me with this sudden resolution). "I will take the responsibility on myself wholly and entirely. I know for certain that it would do Edith an immeasurable amount of good just now if for the moment we left her in the hope that her troubles would soon be at an end. If it eventually proves necessary to explain to her that we ... that I have perhaps promised too much, I shall quite frankly acknowledge my responsibility, and I am convinced that she will understand."

Condor fixed me with his gaze. "My God!" he murmured at length. "You're taking on a hell of a lot, I can tell you. And the curious thing is that you infect other people with your almost religious faith—first those people out at Kekesfalva, and now, by degrees, even me. Well, if you are really prepared to take upon yourself the responsibility of restoring Edith's mental poise in the event of a crisis, that, of course, puts a new complexion on the whole thing ... in that case we might risk waiting a few days until her nerves are in a slightly better state ... But if you take on a thing of that sort, *Herr Leutnant*, there's no turning back. It is my duty to give you due warning beforehand. We doctors are in duty bound, before performing an operation, to draw the attention of all those concerned to the dangers involved—and to promise a girl who has been paralysed for as long as she has that she will be cured in a very short space of time is an action no less responsible than the performing of an operation. I beg you, therefore, to consider carefully what it is you are taking upon yourself. It requires an incalculable amount of energy to restore the faith of a person whom one has once betrayed. I like having things cut and dried. Before I forgo my intention of explaining quite frankly to the Kekesfalvas this very day that Professor Viennot's method cannot be employed in Edith's case, and that we must unfortunately ask her to go on being patient, I *must* know whether I can depend on you. Can I absolutely rely on your not letting me down?"

"Absolutely."

"Good." Condor abruptly pushed his glass away from him. We had neither of us touched a drop. "Or rather, let us hope that the outcome will be a good one, for I don't feel entirely happy about this postponement. I shall now tell you how far I am prepared to go—and that is, not one step beyond the truth. I shall advise her to go to the Engadine for treatment, but I shall explain that Viennot's method has by no means been tried out, and shall point out emphatically that they must not expect a miracle. Should they, pinning their faith on you, nevertheless buoy themselves up with illusory hopes, it will be for you—I have your promise—to put the whole business, *your* business, straight in good time. Perhaps I am taking a certain risk in placing more faith in you than in my professional conscience—ah well, I'll take the responsibility for that. After all, we both mean equally well by this poor sick girl."

Condor rose. "As I have said, I count upon you if any kind of crisis should arise as a result of her being disappointed. Let's hope your impatience will achieve more than my patience. Well then, let us allow the poor child to live in hope for a few weeks longer. And if in the meantime she makes any real progress, then it will have been you who has helped her, and not I. That's settled, then. High time too. They'll be expecting me out there."

We left the wine-bar. The carriage was waiting for Condor at the door. At the last moment, when he had taken his seat, my lips moved involuntarily as though to call him back. But the horses had already moved off. And with the departure of the carriage the die was cast.

Three hours later I found on my table a hastily written note which had been brought by the chauffeur.

"Come tomorrow as early as you can. I have a terrible lot to tell you. Dr Condor has just been. We're going away in ten days. I'm frightfully happy
—EDITH.*"

Odd that I should have picked up that particular book on this night of all nights. I was in general a poor reader, and the rickety shelves of my barrack-room contained, apart from the six or eight military volumes, such as the cavalry drill manual, which are the alpha and omega of army life, the twenty or so classics which, ever since I had been gazetted, I had trailed around from one garrison to another without ever opening perhaps only in order to invest the bare, strange rooms in which I was obliged to take up my quarters with the semblance and shadow of personal ownership. Amongst these were scattered a few still half uncut, badly printed, badly bound books which had come into my hands in a rather odd way. From time to time a little hunch-backed peddler with curiously melancholy watery eyes used to turn up at our café; in an irresistibly importunate manner he would offer for sale notepaper, pencils and cheap trashy volumes, most of them of a kind he hoped to get rid of easily in cavalry circles: tales of so-called gallantry such as the adventures of Casanova, the *Decameron*, the memoirs of an opera-singer, or rollicking stories of garrison life. Out of pity—ever and again out of pity!—and perhaps, too, to keep at bay his melancholy impor-tunity, I had at one time and another bought three or four of these sordid, badly printed volumes and then casually left them lying about on my shelves.

On this particular evening, however, tired and overwrought, unable to sleep and unable, too, to think consistently, I looked about for something to read which would distract my mind and send me off to sleep. I picked up the *Arabian Nights*, in the hope that its naïve, colourful stories, of which I still had a confused memory from childhood, would have the most powerful narcotic effect. I lay down and began to read in that state of semi-somnolence in which one is too lazy to turn over the pages and saves trouble by skipping any pages that happen to be uncut. I read the first story about Scheherazade and the King with lan-guid attention, and then read on and on. But suddenly I started up. I had come to the curious story of the young man who sees a lame old man lying in the road, and at the word "lame" I felt myself wince inwardly as though at a twinge of pain; some nerve in my brain had been touched by the sudden association as though by a fiery ray. In the story the crippled old man calls despairingly upon the young man, telling him that he is unable to walk and asking to be carried on his shoulders. And the young man takes pity on him—pity, you fool, why do you take pity on him? I thought—and in his eagerness to help he actually bends down and sets the old man on his shoulders, piggyback fashion.

But this apparently helpless old man is a djinn, an evil

spirit, a scoundrelly magician, and no sooner is he seated on the young man's shoulders than he clamps his hairy, naked thighs round his benefactor's throat in a vice-like grip and cannot be dislodged. Mercilessly he makes of the young man who has taken pity on him a beast of burden, spurs him on and on, pitilessly, relentlessly, never granting him a moment's rest. The luckless young man is obliged to carry him wherever he asks, and from now on has no will of his own. He has become the beast of burden, the slave, of the old rascal: no matter if his knees give and his lips are parched with thirst, he is compelled, foolish victim of his own pity, to trot on and on, is fated to drag the wicked, infamous, cunning old man along for ever on his back.

I stopped reading. My heart was pounding as though about to burst out of my breast. For even as I had been reading, I had had an unbearable vision of the crafty old man first of all lying on the ground and turning up his tearful eyes imploringly for help, then riding piggyback on the young man's shoulders. He had white hair with a parting, the djinn of my vision, and wore a pair of gold-rimmed spectacles. With the lightning rapidity with which only in dreams as a rule are scenes and faces conjured up and imposed one upon another, I had instinctively lent the old man of the fairy-story Kekesfalva's features, and had myself all of a sudden become the luckless beast of burden which he spurred on and on—yes, the sensation of those legs twined about my throat was so physically vivid that I could scarcely breathe. The book fell from my hands, and I lay there in my bed, icy-cold; I could hear my heart beating against my ribs as though against hard wood. Even in my sleep this grim hunter urged me on and on, I knew not whither. When in the morning I awoke, my hair damp with sweat, I was as weary and exhausted as though I had travelled along an unending road.

It was in vain that I spent the morning with my comrades, that I carried out my duties with due care and attention; no sooner did I find myself, that afternoon, on the inevitable road to Kekesfalva than I could once more feel that ghostly burden on my shoulders, for deep down in my troubled conscience I knew that from this moment on I was assuming a responsibility of an entirely novel and unspeakably difficult nature. That night when, on the bench in the park, I had held out to the old man the prospect of his daughter's imminent recovery, I had exaggerated merely out of a compassionate desire to withhold the truth, without meaning to do so, indeed despite myself, but I had not been guilty of a deliberate deception, a downright fraud. Henceforward, however, now that I knew an early cure was out of the question, I should have, coldly, tenaciously, calculatingly, persistently, to act a part, should have to wear an impenetrable mask and lie in the bland tones of a hardened criminal, who subtly thinks out every detail of his crime, prepares every detail of his defence, weeks and months in advance. For the first time in my life I began to realize that it is not evil and brutality, but nearly always weakness, that is to blame for the worst things that happen in this world.

At the Kekesfalvas' everything turned out exactly as I had feared. No sooner had I stepped out on to the terrace than I was given an effusive welcome. I had brought with me a bunch of flowers on purpose to distract immediate attention from myself. But after an abrupt "Why on earth are you bringing me flowers? I'm not a *prima donna*!" I had to sit down beside the impatient Edith, who began to hold forth without a pause, a certain faraway tone in her voice. Dr Condor—"Oh, that wonderful man, there's no one like him!"—had inspired her with fresh courage, she said. In ten days' time they were going to a sanatorium in the Engadine—why lose even a single day, now that they were going to set about curing her in earnest? She had always known that hitherto they had been going the wrong way about things, that she would never make any progress with all this electrical treatment and massage, all these silly appliances. God knew it was high time. On two occasions—she had never told me before—she had tried to make an end of herself—twice, and each time in vain. You just couldn't go on living like that indefinitely, never really alone for a moment, always dependent on others at every turn and every step, always spied upon and watched and oppressed into the bargain with a feeling that you were nothing but a burden, an incubus, an intolerable nuisance. Yes, it was time, high time, but I should see what a quick recovery she would make if only they set about things properly. Whatever was the use of all these slight improvements in her health which brought about no permanent improvement? One must get well completely, or else one was not really well at all. Oh, how wonderful even the anticipation of it was, how wonderful it would be!

And so it went on and on, a leaping, bubbling, sparkling torrent of ecstasy. I felt like a doctor who listens to the fevered outpourings of a patient suffering from hallucinations, and, since he regards the hot, glowing fantasies as indubitable and disquieting clinical proof of a state of mental disturbance, gazes suspiciously the while at the infallible second-hand of his watch and feels the racing pulse. Whenever a wanton laugh spurted up like fine spray above the racing cascade of words I shuddered, for I knew what she did *not* know—I knew that she was deceiving herself, that we were deceiving her. And when at last she paused, I felt like one who starts up in a train at night because the wheels have suddenly stopped moving. But she had interrupted the flow of her own words.

"Well, what have you to say? Why are you sitting there with such a stupid—I beg your pardon, I mean such a scared—look on your face? Why don't you say something? Don't you share my happiness?"

I felt as though I had been caught out. Now or never was the moment to strike a cordial, a really enthusiastic note. But I was only a wretched tyro in the art of lying, I did not yet understand the technique of deliberate deception. So I laboriously scraped together a few words.

"How can you say such a thing? It's only that I am completely taken by surprise ... Surely you will be able to understand that? And in Vienna we have a saying about great happiness, that it 'strikes one dumb' ... Of course I am frightfully pleased on your account."

It revolted me myself to hear how artificial and cold these words sounded. She too must have noticed my constraint, for her attitude suddenly changed. Her mood of exaltation was overcast by a shadow of ill-humour; she was like someone who has been rudely awakened out of a dream; her eyes, a moment before sparkling with joy, grew suddenly hard, the bow between her brows was stretched taut as though to shoot its arrows.

"Well, I can't say I have exactly noticed your great pleasure." I was conscious of the implied insult and tried to propitiate her.

"My dear child ... "

But at this she flared up. "Don't keep on calling me 'your dear child'. You know I can't bear it. You're not so much older than I am. Perhaps I may be permitted to wonder at your not being very surprised and, above all, not ... not very ... interested. And by the way, why shouldn't you be pleased? After all, you too will be having a holiday, for this place will be shut up for several months. And so you'll be free to sit about and play *tarock* with your friends in the café and be relieved of the boring business of playing the Good Samaritan. Oh yes, I can well believe that you're pleased. You have a nice, easy time to look forward to."

There was something so offensive in her tone that her words got right under my skin. My conscience pricked me. I must have given myself away. In order to divert her anger—for by now I was familiar with the dangerous consequences of her irritability—I tried to introduce a certain spirit of jocularity into the whole discussion

"Easy time—that's what you civilians think! An easy time for a cavalryman—July, August and September! Don't you know that's the very time when one works like a slave and gets hauled over the coals? First of all there are the preparations for manoeuvres, then chasing about here, there and everywhere, to Bosnia or Galicia, then the manoeuvres themselves and all sorts of reviews. The officers in a state of nerves, the men worn out, one long round of parades, drilling, exercises from morning to night. And so the dance goes on until well into September."

"Until the end of September ... ?" She suddenly grew thoughtful. She seemed to have something on her mind. "But when ... " she began at length, "will you come to us?"

I did not understand her. I really did not understand what she meant, and inquired with complete naïveté:

"Come where?"

Once more her brows lifted. "Don't keep asking such idiotic questions. To see us, to see me!"

"In the Engadine?"

"Where do you think? In Tripstrill?"

And only now did I realize what she meant; the idea that I, I who had just spent my last seven crowns in cash on flowers and to whom every trip to Vienna was a luxury despite the fifty per cent reduction on the fare, should go off just like that for a holiday in the Engadine was too absurd even to contemplate.

"So now we know," I said, with a perfectly genuine laugh, "what sort of idea you civilians have of military life: one long round of cafés, billiards, strolling on the promenade, and just when one feels like it, changing into mufti and gadding about the world for a few weeks. The simplest thing on earth, an excursion of that kind. You raise your two fingers to your cap and say, 'Bye-bye, Colonel, I don't feel like playing at soldiers at the moment. See you later, when I'm more in the mood!' A fine idea you civilians have of what it's like on the Imperial treadmill! Don't you know that we soldiers, if we want even an hour's extra leave, have to click our heels smartly when we report and ask *gehorsamst* for the great favour? Yes, I tell you, we have to go through all that mumbo-jumbo and ceremony even to get an hour off. And to get a whole day at least a dead aunt or some other family funeral is necessary. I should just like to see the Colonel's face if I were humbly to inform him bang in the middle of the manoeuvres that I had a fancy to go careering off to Switzerland on a week's leave! I bet there'd be a few expletives flying about that you wouldn't find in any dictionary fit for a young lady. No, my dear Fräulein Edith, you have far too simple an idea of the whole thing."

"Nonsense! Everything is simple if you really set your mind on it. Don't get it into your head that you're indispensable. Someone else would drill your Ruthenian blockheads while you were away. And by the way, Papa could fix up things with regard to your leave in half an hour. He knows a dozen people at the War Office, and at a word from higher quarters you'll get what you want. It really wouldn't do you any harm, either, to see something of the world outside your riding school and parade ground. No more excuses now—the matter's settled. Papa will see to it."

It was silly of me, but her casual tone irritated me. After all, a few years in the army do drill into one a certain consciousness of the dignity of one's calling, and the fact that a mere chit of a girl should be able to dictate, as it were, to the generals at the War Office—whom we looked upon as gods—as though they were her father's employees, seemed to me to cast a slur on the whole profession. All the same, despite my irritation, I preserved my jocular tone.

"Very good—Switzerland, leave, the Engadine—not half bad! Excellent, if it's all actually going to be served up to me on a silver tray, as you seem to imagine, without my having to beg for it *gehorsamst*. But your father would have to wheedle a special travelling scholarship for *Herr Leutnant* Hofmiller out of the War Office, in addition to leave."

And now it was her turn to look up in surprise. She sensed something behind my words which she did not understand. The brows above the impatient eyes were arched more tautly. I saw that I should have to speak even more plainly.

"Now, do be sensible, my child ... I beg your pardon, I mean, let's talk sensibly, Fräulein Edith. The whole thing is not as simple as you think. Tell me, have you ever considered what a trip of that kind costs?"

"Oh, is *that* what you mean?" she said with a lack of embarrassment. "That won't come to so very much. A few hundred crowns at the most. That surely can't make any difference."

And now I could no longer restrain my indignation. For this was a point on which I was highly sensitive. I believe I have already said what a torture it was to me to be one of the officers without private means and to be dependent merely on my pay and the wretched little allowance made me by my aunt. Even in my own circle it always caught me on the raw to hear money spoken of contemptuously in my presence just as if it grew like thistles. This was *my* sore spot. In this respect I was lame, I walked on crutches. It was solely for this reason that I was so immoderately upset by the fact that this spoiled, pampered creature, who herself suffered all the pangs of hell at being at such a physical disadvantage, should not understand my feelings. In spite of myself I was almost rude.

"A few hundred crowns at the most, eh? A trifle, isn't it? A mere trifle for an officer! And you, of course, think it very bad form on my part to mention such a bagatelle? Bad form, petty, niggling? But have you ever considered what we soldiers have to scrape along on? What a struggle we have to make ends meet?"

And as she continued to stare at me with the same puzzled and, as I foolishly thought, contemptuous look, I was suddenly seized with an impulse to expose the full extent of my poverty to her. Just as she, on one occasion, had hobbled defiantly across the room on purpose to torture us, who were sound of limb, to revenge herself on us for our smug good health, so did I now feel a kind of angry pleasure in revealing to her in an exhibitionistic way the restricted and dependent state of my existence.

"Have you the remotest idea what the pay of a lieutenant is?" I snapped. "Have you ever given a thought to it? Well, I may as well tell you; two hundred crowns on the first of the month, which has to last the whole thirty or thirty-one days as the case may be, and what's more he is expected to live up to his station in life. Out of this pittance he has to pay his mess bills, his rent, his tailor's bill, his shoemaker's bill, and buy all the little luxuries incidental to his rank. Not to mention anything that may happen, God help him, to his horse! And if he's managed jolly well, he'll just have a few coppers left for carousing in that paradise of a café which you're always throwing up at me; if he has really pinched and scraped like a labourer, he can purchase all the delights of this world in a cup of coffee."

I know now that it was stupid, criminal of me, to let myself be so carried away by my bitter feelings. How should a seventeen-year-old child pampered and brought up in seclusion, how should this crippled girl, permanently chained to her room, have any idea of the value of money and a soldier's pay and our splendid poverty? But the desire to take my revenge on someone for innumerable minor humiliations had suddenly overwhelmed me, and I struck out, blindly, heedlessly, as one always does in anger, without realizing how hard I was hitting.

But the moment I looked up I realized how brutally I had hit out. With the acute perception of the sick she had immediately sensed that she had unwittingly touched me on a very sore spot. Try as she might—and I could see how she struggled to control herself and how she quickly put her hand up to her face—she could not help flushing; some quite definite thought had evidently sent the blood rushing to her cheeks.

"And then ... and then you go and buy me such expensive flowers."

A painful moment ensued and seemed to last for ever. I felt ashamed in front of her, and she felt ashamed in front of me. We had each of us unintentionally wounded the other and were afraid to say another word. All of a sudden we could hear the wind blowing warm through the trees, the cackling of the hens down below in the courtyard, and every now and then from the distance the faint rumble of carriage-wheels on the road. Then she pulled herself together.

"And to think I was stupid enough to be taken in by all that nonsense of yours. Really, I *am* stupid and I'm still furious with myself. Why need you bother about the cost of the trip? If you come to us, it goes without saying that it will be as our guest. Do you think Papa would allow you to be put to expense if you were so kind as to come to see us? What nonsense! And to think that I let you fool me! Well then, not another word on the subject—no, not a word, I tell you."

But this was the very point on which I could not yield. Nothing—as I have said before—was so intolerable to me as the thought of being taken for a sponger.

"Oh yes! There *is* another word to be said. Don't let's have any misunderstanding. I tell you flatly, I will not allow anyone to wangle leave for me, I will not allow anyone to keep me. It's not my way to ask for special privileges. I want to be on exactly the same footing as my comrades. I don't want special leave or any sort of patronage. I know you mean well and that your father means well. But there are some people who simply cannot have all the good things of this life. Don't let's talk of it any more."

"So you don't want to come?"

"I didn't say I didn't want to. I was merely explaining to you why I can't come."

"Not even if my father begs you to?"

"Not even then."

"And not even ... if I ask you to? If I ask you as a dear friend?"

"Don't do it. It would be useless."

She hung her head. But I had already noticed the ominous quivering and twitching at her mouth which infallibly heralded a dangerous outburst. This poor spoiled child, round whom the whole household revolved, had had a new experience: she had come up against opposition. Someone had said "No" to her, and that was a bitter pill. Impulsively she snatched my flowers from the table and hurled them in an angry arc far over the balustrade.

"Very well," she hissed through her teeth. "At least I now know how far your friendship goes. It's just as well to have put it to the test! Merely because one or two of your friends might wag their tongues in the café, you shelter behind all these excuses. Just because you're afraid of getting a bad mark in the regiment, you ruin a friend's pleasure ... Very well then. The matter's settled. I'm not going to plead with you any more. You don't want to come ... good! That's that!"

I could tell that her agitation had not yet died down completely, for she kept on repeating with a certain obstinate persistence, "Very well. Very well." Gripping the arms of her chair convulsively, she levered herself up, as though about to make a physical attack on me. Suddenly she veered round sharply.

"Very well! The matter's over and done with. Our humble request has been refused. You refuse to come and see us. It doesn't suit your book. Very well. We shall get over it. After all, we've managed quite well without you in the past ... But there's one more thing I should like to know—will you answer me frankly?"

"Why, of course."

"I mean honestly? On your word of honour? Give me your word of honour."

"If you insist—my word of honour."

"Very well then." She kept repeating this harsh, biting "very well" as though hacking away at something with a knife. "Very well. Don't be afraid, I shan't insist any further on your Highness's visit! But there's just one thing I'd like to know—you have given me your word, remember. Just one thing. Well, if it doesn't suit your book to come, either because you don't like the idea or because it's a nuisance—or for some other reason—it's all the same to me. All right, very well. That's that. But now tell me frankly and plainly: in that case why do you come to see us at all?"

I had been prepared for any other question but this. In my confusion, and in order to gain time, I stammered out:

"Why ... why, it's quite simple ... You didn't need my word of honour for that ... "

"Oh, I see ... simple, is it? Good! So much the better! Get on with it then."

And now evasion was no longer possible. It seemed simplest to tell the truth, but I realized that I must put things very tactfully.

"Why, my dear Fräulein Edith," I began with apparent un-constraint, "don't look for any mysterious reasons. After all, you know me well enough to know that I am the sort of person who doesn't think a great deal about his own motives. It has never entered my head to ask myself why I go to see this person and that, why I like some people and not others. On my word ... I really can't give you any more coherent reason than that I come here again and again ... simply because I like coming here and because I feel a hundred times happier here than anywhere else. I think you civilians are rather too apt to picture the life of a cavalryman as something out of light opera, an everlastingly riotous, gay existence, a sort of perpetual feast. Well, from with-in things don't look nearly so splendid and as for all the vaunted *camaraderie*, it sometimes lets you down with a bump. When a few dozen men are harnessed to the same cart, one always pulls harder than the others, and when it's a question of promotion and seniority, it's easy to tread on the toes of the men ahead of you. At every word one utters one has to be on one's guard; one's never quite sure whether it isn't going to arouse the disapproval of the bigwigs; there's always a storm in the offing. The word 'service' comes from serving, and serving means being dependent. And then you can't really feel at home in barracks or an inn; no one, needs you, and no one cares a straw about you. Oh yes, you sometimes have one or two really loyal friends, but you never get a feeling of ultimate security. Whereas when I come to see you people, I shed all my doubts the moment I take off my sword, and when I find myself chatting away so happily with you, then ... "

"Well ... what then?" she rapped out impatiently.

"Then ... well, you'll probably think it cheeky of me to speak so frankly ... I tell myself you like to have me here, that I belong

here, that I am a hundred times more at home here than anywhere else. Whenever I look at you, I have a feeling that ... "

I faltered involuntarily. But she broke in as vehemently as
before; "Well, what about me?"

" ... that here is someone to whom I'm not so terribly unimportant as I am to the fellows in the regiment ... Of course,
there's not a great deal to me, and sometimes I myself keep on
wondering that you haven't long since found me boring. Often
... you don't know how often I have been afraid lest you should
be tired of me ... but then I keep on remembering that you are
all alone in this big, empty house, and that you may enjoy having
someone to come and see you. And it's that, you see, that keeps
giving me courage ... When I find you on your terrace or in your
room, I tell myself that it was a good thing for me to have come
instead of letting you spend the whole day alone. Can't you really understand that?"

Her reaction was most unexpected. The grey eyes grew glassy;
it was as though something in my words had turned her pupils
to stone. Her fingers, on the other hand, grew more and more
restless; they roamed up and down the arms of the chair, and
began, at first softly, then more and more vigorously, to drum on
the polished wood. Her mouth was slightly contorted.

"Yes, I see," she said abruptly. "I understand perfectly ...
Now ... now, I really believe you've told the truth. You've
expressed yourself very politely and very tortuously. But I have
understood you perfectly ... perfectly ... You come here, you
tell me, because I'm so 'alone'—that is, in other words, because
I'm tied to this confounded chaise-longue. That's the only reason
you come trotting out here every day, simply to play the Good
Samaritan to a 'poor, sick child'—that's what you all call me, I
expect, when I'm not there—I know, I know. It's only out of pity
that you come. Oh yes, I believe you—what's the use of denying
it now? You're one of those so-called 'good' people, you like to
be called so by my father. 'Good people' of that kind take pity
on every whipped cur and every mangy cat—so why not on a
cripple?"

And suddenly she sat bolt upright, and a spasm shook her rigid
frame.

"Thank you for nothing! I can do without the kind of friendship that is only shown me because I'm a cripple ... Yes, you needn't screw your eyes up like that. Naturally, you're upset at having let the cat out of the bag, at having admitted that you come to see me only because I 'make your heart bleed', as that charwoman said—except that she said it frankly and straight out. You however, as a 'good person' express yourself far more tactfully, far more 'delicately'; you beat about the bush, and say you come just because I have to sit about here alone all day long. It's simply out of pity that you come, I've felt that in my bones for ages, merely out of pity, and you would like, moreover, to be admired for your noble selflessness—but I regret to have to inform you that I refuse to allow anyone—to sacrifice himself on my behalf. I refuse to tolerate that from anyone least of all from you ... I forbid you to do it, do you hear me? I forbid it ... Do you really imagine that I am dependent on your sitting around with a 'sympathetic', sloppy look in your eyes, or on your 'tactful' conversation? ... No, thank God, I can do without the lot of you ... I can manage all right, I can manage alone. And when I can't stand it any more, I know how to get rid of you all ... Look"—she suddenly thrust out her hand toward me, palm uppermost—"Look at this scar! I made one attempt, but I was clumsy and couldn't sever the artery with my blunt scissors; and the stupid thing was that they came along in time to bind it up, or I should have been rid of you all and your measly pity! But next time I'll do the job properly, you may be sure. Don't imagine for a moment that I'm entirely in your hands. I'd rather die than allow myself to be pitied! There!"—she suddenly burst out laughing, and the sound was as sharp and jagged as a saw—"There, you see, my devoted father forgot one thing when he had the tower fitted up for me ... His idea was simply that I should have a lovely view to look at ... plenty of sun, plenty of sun and fresh air, the doctor ordered. But it never occurred to any of them, neither to my father, nor the doctor, nor the architect ... to what good purpose I might one day be able to put this terrace ... Take a good look ... "—she had suddenly levered herself up and had propelled her swaying body in one convulsive movement towards the balustrade, which she now clutched frantically with both hands—"there are four—five storeys, and down at the bottom hard concrete ... that would do ... and thank God I have still enough strength in my muscles to get over the balustrade—oh yes, hobbling on crutches strengthens the muscles. Just one jerk would be needed and I should be free for ever of you and your cursed pity. And you'd all feel relieved, Papa, Ilona and you—all of you, to whom I'm nothing but a horrible encumbrance and ... look, it would be quite simple! One would just have to lean over a little bit, like this ... just like this ... "

As, her eyes flashing, she leaned dangerously far over the balustrade, I jumped up in an agony of anxiety and seized her quickly by the arm. But she shrank away as though fire had seared her skin.

"Go away!" she screamed at me ... "How dare you touch me! Go away! I have a right to do what I wish. Let me go! Let go of me at once!"

And since I refused to obey her, but tried to drag her away from the balustrade by force, she swung round with the upper part of her body and struck me a blow in the chest. And then a really ghastly thing happened. In striking out she lost her hold on the balustrade and with it her balance. Her knees gave completely, as though mown through by a scythe, and although I put my arms out to save her, I was too late. With a convulsive jerk she collapsed, bringing down with her the table that she had vainly endeavoured to clutch. Vase, plates and cups, spoons, all came smashing, clattering, rattling down upon us; the great bronze bell fell with a loud crash to the ground and, its clapper jangling, rolled the whole length of the terrace.

Meanwhile, Edith lay huddled in a pitiful, defenceless heap on the ground, a quivering bundle of fury, sobbing for very anger and shame. I tried to lift the frail body, but she beat me off.

"Go away, go away!" she sobbed. "You beast, you brute!"

And she thrashed out wildly with her arms, vainly trying to struggle to her feet without my assistance. Every time I went near her to try to help her, she doubled herself up to keep me at bay and screamed at me in mad, helpless rage: "Go away ... don't touch me ... get out of here!" Never had I been through a more ghastly experience.

At that moment there was a faint whirring noise behind us; the lift was coming up. Probably the bell had made enough noise in falling to rouse Josef, who was always on the *qui vive*. Discreetly lowering his startled gaze he hurried up, and, without looking at me, gently lifted up the trembling, sobbing girl—he must have acquired the knack from long practice—and carried her to the lift. In another minute it was gently whirring it's way down again, and I was left alone with the overturned table, the broken cups, the objects that lay scattered about in such confusion that one might have thought a thunderbolt had suddenly fallen out of a perfectly clear sky and sent them flying in all directions.

I do not know how long I stood there among the shattered plates and cups, utterly dumbfounded by this primitive outburst, which I was entirely at a loss to explain. What had I said that was so foolish? How had I called forth this inexplicable rage? But now I could hear, coming from below, that familiar sound as of air rushing through a vent-pipe: the lift was coming up again. Once more Josef approached, his clean shaven features overcast by a strange look of grief. I thought he had merely come to clear away the debris, and felt embarrassed at being in his way. But with lowered eyes he made his way noiselessly towards me, stooping on the way to pick up a napkin.

"Pardon me, *Herr Leutnant*," he said in his discreet hushed voice, which always seemed in itself to be a bow (ah yes, he was a manservant of the old Austrian type!). "Allow me to dry your clothes a little."

Only now, as I watched his busy fingers, did I notice that there was a great wet patch both on my tunic and on my lights summer trousers. Evidently as I had bent down to break Edith's fall, the contents of one of the tea-cups that she had brought down with her had been upset over me, for Josef was rubbing and dabbing away all round the wet patches. As he knelt there I gazed down at his good old grey head with its faithful parting, and I could not rid myself of the suspicion that the old fellow was purposely ducking his head so that I should not catch a glimpse of his dismayed face and his troubled eyes.

"No, it's no good," he said sadly at last, without raising his head. "I had better send the chauffeur to the barracks to fetch another coat for the *Herr Leutnant*. The *Herr Leutnant* cannot go out like this. But the *Herr Leutnant* may rest assured that everything will be dry in an hour's time, and I shall give the trousers a good press."

He stated all this in what appeared to be merely the matter-of-fact tones of an attentive manservant. But there was an undertone in his voice that betrayed his sympathy and consternation. And when I pointed out that it was not in the least necessary, and that I should prefer him to ring up for a carriage, since I was in any case going straight home, he unexpectedly cleared his throat and raised his kind, somewhat weary eyes pleadingly up to my face.

"Oh please, won't the *Herr Leutnant* stay just a little longer? It would be terrible if the *Herr Leutnant* were to go away now. I know for a fact that the *gnädiges Fräulein* would be dreadfully upset if the *Herr Leutnant* did not wait a little longer. Fräulein Ilona is with her now ... and ... has put her to bed. But Fräulein Ilona wishes me to say she will be coming almost immediately, and begs the *Herr Leutnant* to be sure to wait for her."

In spite of myself I was profoundly moved. How they all loved this invalid girl! How they all cherished her and made excuses for her! I felt an irresistible urge to say something reassuring to this good old man who, abashed at his own daring, was busily and ostentatiously dabbing away again at my tunic; and so I patted him gently on the shoulder.

"Let it be, my dear Josef, it doesn't matter. It will easily dry off in the sun, and let's hope your tea isn't strong enough to leave a real mark. Leave it alone, Josef, and gather up the tea-things instead. I'll wait until Fräulein Ilona comes."

"Oh, how good that the *Herr Leutnant* is going to wait!" He positively heaved a sigh of relief. "And Herr von Kekesfalva will soon be back too, and is sure to be delighted to see the *Herr Leutnant*. He desired me expressly to ... "

But at that moment the faint creak of footsteps could be heard on the stairs. It was Ilona. She too kept her eyes lowered, just as Josef had done, as she came up to me.

"Edith asks if you will come down to her bedroom for a moment. Just for a moment. She says you will be doing her a very great favour."

Together we descended the spiral staircase, and without a word walked through the drawing-room and the little sitting-room into a long corridor which evidently led to Edith's bedroom. Now and again our shoulders touched in this dark narrow defile, perhaps by chance or because I was so agitated and upset. At the second door Ilona halted.

"You must be nice to her now," she whispered urgently. "I don't know what happened up there on the terrace, but I know these sudden outbursts of hers. We all know them. But you must not take it amiss of her, really not. It is impossible for healthy people like us to imagine what it means to have to lie about as she does from morning to night. She must, after all, get into a terribly pent-up state, and sometimes it all just has to come out, without her knowing it or meaning it to. Please believe me, no one is unhappier afterwards than she herself, poor thing. And it is at these times when she is so racked with shame and remorse that one must be doubly kind to her."

I made no reply. Nor was it necessary. Ilona must have noticed how shaken and distressed I was. She now knocked cautiously on the door, and from inside came a faint, timorous "Come in."

"Don't stay long. Only a moment," Ilona just had time to warn me.

I pushed open the door, which yielded noiselessly to my touch. At first I could see nothing in the vast room but reddish twilight, for the orange curtains were drawn to shut out the light on the garden side; and only after a moment was I able, to make out in the background the lighter rectangle of a bed, from which a familiar voice issued shyly.

"Come and sit over here, please. On the stool. I'll only keep you a moment."

I went up to the bed. A little face on the pillows gleamed forth wanly out of a shadowy frame of hair. The trail of embroidered flowers on the colourful bedspread crept right up to the thin, childish throat. With a certain anxiety Edith waited for me to sit down. Only then did she venture to speak.

"Forgive me for receiving you here," she said shyly, "but I felt very faint ... I ought not to have lain out in the hot sun so long, it always affects my head ... I really believe I was not quite in my right mind when I ... but ... you'll forget all about that, won't you? You won't go on being offended with me for my ... my rudeness, will you?"

There was such an anxious pleading note in her voice that I broke in quickly: "What are you thinking of? It was I who was to blame. I ought not to have allowed you to stay out so long in that stifling heat."

"Then you're really ... really not offended with me?"

"Not a bit."

"And you'll come again ... just as always?"

"Just the same. But on one condition."

"What condition?" she asked with a troubled look.

"That you'll have a little more confidence in me and stop always being afraid that you've annoyed or offended me. Whoever heard of such nonsense between friends! If you only knew how different you look when you let yourself go and enjoy yourself, and how happy you make us all by doing so, your father and Ilona and me and the whole household. I only wish you could have seen yourself the other day on our excursion, you were so happy and we were all so jolly together—I kept thinking about it the whole evening."

"You thought about me the whole evening?" She gazed at me a little uncertainly. "Really?"

"The whole evening. What a day that was! I shall never. forget it. The whole trip was wonderful, wonderful."

"Yes," she said dreamily, "it was wonderful ... *wonderful!* First the drive through the countryside and then the little foals and the wedding-feast in the village ... everything was wonderful from beginning to end! Oh, I should go out more often on excursions like that! Perhaps it is only this stupid staying indoors, this idiotic imprisonment that has been getting me down. But you're right, I am always too mistrustful ... that is, I have been since my illness began. Before that, good Lord, I can't remember ever having been frightened of anyone! It's only since then that I've been so horribly unsure of myself ... I always imagine that everyone is staring at my crutches, that everyone is pitying me. I know how silly it is, of course, that it's just a kind of silly, childish pride. I know that it's just cutting off one's nose to spite one's face, it only comes back on one, I know that; it only tears one's nerves to pieces. But how is one to help being distrustful when the whole thing drags on and on like this. Oh, if only this dreadful business would come to an end at last, so that I could stop being so wicked, so beastly and bad-tempered!"

"But it's coming to an end soon now. You must just have courage, courage and patience for a little while longer."

She raised herself up slightly. "Do you think, do you honestly think that this new treatment will really cure me? ... The day before yesterday, you see, when Papa came up to my room, I was absolutely certain. But last night, I don't know why, I was suddenly seized with fear lest Dr Condor should have made a mistake and have told me something that wasn't true, because because I remembered something. At one time I trusted Dr Condor as though he were God. But it's always the same. First the doctor observes the patient, but when the whole thing goes on for a long time, the patient learns to observe the doctor, and yesterday—but I wouldn't say so to anyone else—yesterday, while he was examining me, it seemed to me once or twice that he was trying to throw dust in my eyes ... that the whole thing was a farce. He seemed to me to be so unsure of himself, so evasive, not so frank, not so sincere as usual. I don't know why, but I had a feeling that for some reason he was ashamed in my presence. Of course I was frightfully pleased when I heard that he proposed to send me straight off to Switzerland ... and yet ... somewhere at the back of my mind ... I'm only telling *you* this ... an unreasonable fear kept cropping up—but don't for Heaven's sake tell him that—that there was something not quite right about this new treatment ... that he was trying to fool me ... or perhaps merely to pacify Papa. You see, I still can't rid myself of my horrible mistrust. But how can I help it? How can I help being suspicious of myself, suspicious of everyone, when I've so often been persuaded that I was reaching the end of my troubles, and then it has all dragged on as slowly, as horribly slowly, as before? No, I can't, I can't stand this interminable waiting any longer."

In her agitation she had raised herself to a sitting position, and her hands began to tremble. I went over to her quickly. "Now don't, don't ... upset yourself again! Remember, you promised me."

"Yes, yes, you're quite right. It's no use torturing oneself, it only tortures other people. And what can they do about it. I'm a burden enough to them in any case. But no, I didn't mean to talk of it, I really didn't ... I only wanted to thank you for not being offended with me for my stupid tantrums and ... for always being so kind to me, so ... touchingly kind, when I don't deserve it ... and to think that I should have ... but let's forget it, shall we?"

"Of course. Don't worry any more. And now you must really have a good rest."

I got up to shake hands. She looked so pathetic as, half fearful and half reassured, she smiled up at me from her pillows, like a child just about to go to sleep. Everything was all right, the atmosphere was cleared as is the sky after a thunderstorm. With a complete lack of embarrassment, almost gaily, I went up to her. But she gave a sudden start.

"What on earth's that? Your uniform?"

She had noticed the great damp patch on my tunic, and must have realized with a pang of guilt that she alone could have been responsible for the mishap, which had occurred when she had brought the cups crashing down with her in her fall. Her eyes withdrew beneath their lids, and the outstretched hand was timidly withdrawn. But the very fact that she took such a foolish trifle so seriously moved me, and, in order to calm her I took refuge in a playful tone.

"Oh, that's nothing," I said teasingly, "nothing of any consequence. A naughty child upset some tea over me."

Her eyes were still troubled. But she gratefully jumped at the opportunity of turning the whole thing into a joke.

"And did you give the naughty child a good thrashing?"

"No," I replied, keeping the ball rolling. "It wasn't necessary. The child has been good again for a long time now."

"And you're really not angry with her any more?"

"Not a bit. You should have heard how prettily she asked to be forgiven."

"You won't bear her any grudge?"

"No, it's all forgiven and forgotten. But she must go on being a good girl and do as she's told."

"And what is the child to do?"

"To be always patient, always friendly, and always merry. Not to sit in the sun too long, to go out for lots of drives and obey the doctor's orders to the letter. And now the child must go to sleep and not talk or worry her head any more. Good night."

I gave her my hand. She looked enchantingly pretty as she lay there, her gleaming, starry eyes laughing happily up at me.

Then I turned to go, my heart light within me. My hand was on the door-handle when a laugh came rippling after me.

"Has the child been good this time?"

"Perfectly. She shall have full marks. But now she must sleep, sleep, sleep, and not think about any more unpleasant things."

I had half opened the door, when her laugh once more came trilling after me, childish and coaxing.

"Have you forgotten," came the voice again from the pillows, "what a good child gets before going to sleep?"

"A good child gets a goodnight kiss."

Somehow or other I did not feel altogether comfortable. There was a teasing note flickering and flaring up in her voice that I did not care for; I had already fancied that there had been a too-feverish sparkle in her eyes as she had looked at me. But I did not want to risk putting her in a bad humour.

"Ah yes, of course!" I said with apparent nonchalance. "I had nearly forgotten that."

As I walked the few paces back to her bedside I could tell from the sudden silence that she was holding her breath. Her eyes were fixed steadily on me as I moved towards her, her head was motionless on the pillows. She did not move a hand, a finger, but her eyes followed me and would not leave me.

Quickly, quickly! I thought, in growing discomfort. And I bent over her as hurriedly as possible, my lips rested lightly and fleetingly on her forehead. Quite deliberately, I scarcely touched her skin, and only from nearby inhaled the faint fragrance of her hair.

But her hands, which had evidently been lying in wait on the pillow, shot up, and before I could turn my head away, seized me by the temples in a vice-like grip, tore my mouth from her forehead and pulled it down to her lips, which she pressed so hotly and greedily to mine that teeth touched teeth, while her breast strained and arched and thrust upwards to touch, to feel my body as I leaned over her. Never in my life had I received such a wild, despairing, thirsty kiss as the one given me by this crippled girl.

And it was not enough, not enough! With a kind of drunken strength she held me clasped to her until her breath gave out. Then her grip relaxed, and her hands began feverishly to wander from my temples and to bury themselves in my hair. But still she did not let me go. Only for a moment did she relax her hold in order to lean back and stare as though bewitched into my eyes; then she pulled me to her afresh, and pressed hot, blind kisses on my cheeks, my forehead, my eyes, my lips, with wild and yet impotent avidity. And every time she pulled my head down, she stammered, groaned, "You silly ... you silly ... oh you great silly, you!" Ever more avid, ever more passionate was her onslaught, ever more vehemently, convulsively did she seize me and kiss me. And then suddenly a spasm rent her frame. Her hold on me relaxed, her head fell back on the pillows, and only her eyes continued to sparkle triumphantly at me.

Turning abruptly away from me, she whispered, at once exhausted and ashamed: "Now go, go, you old silly ... go!"

I went—no, I staggered—out of the room. Before I had reached the end of the dark corridor the last remnants of my strength left me, and my senses reeled so that I had to steady myself by holding on to the wall. So *that* was it! This was the secret, so belatedly revealed, of her restlessness, her hitherto inexplicable aggressiveness. I was appalled. I felt like one who, stooping innocently over a flower, is stung by an adder. If the hypersensitive creature had struck me, reviled me, spat at me, I should have been less disconcerted, for in view of her uncertain temper I was prepared for anything but this one thing—that she, an invalid, a poor, afflicted cripple, should be able to love, should desire to be loved; that this child, this half-woman, this immature, impotent creature, should have the *temerity* (I cannot express it other wise) to love, to desire, with the conscious and sensual love of a real woman. I

220

had envisaged every possibility but this: that a being whom Fate had so maimed, who had not the strength to drag herself along, could dream of a lover, a beloved, that she should so horribly misunderstand me, who, after all, visited and went on visiting her simply out of pity. But the next moment I realized with a fresh shock that it was my own burning pity that, more than anything else, was to blame if this lonely girl, cut off as she was from the outside world, should fancy that she perceived in me, the foolish slave of my pity, the only man who was sympathetic enough to visit her day after day in her prison, signs of tender emotion. Whereas I, fool, hopeless simpleton that I was, had only seen in her a sufferer, a cripple, a child and not a woman. Not even for a fleeting moment had it occurred to me to think that under that concealing coverlet there breathed, felt, waited, a naked body, a female body which, like any other, desired and longed to be desired. Never had I, even in my wildest dreams, imagined that invalids, cripples, the immature, the prematurely aged, the despised and rejected, the pariahs among human beings, *dared* to love. For a young and inexperienced person almost invariably forms a picture of real life and experience that is a reflection of the world of which he has heard about or read in books; before he has experienced life at first-hand he inevitably moulds his ideas of it on second-hand experience. In books, in plays, or in films, where you get a levelling down, a simplification of reality, it is always and without exception the young, the beautiful, the elect of this world, who desire one another; and so I had assumed—hence my shrinking from many a love-affair—that one had to be specially attractive, specially privileged, specially favoured by fortune, to arouse the passion of a woman. It was only because it had seemed to me that anything of an erotic nature was precluded in our relations from the start, and because I had never so much as suspected that Edith could look upon me as anything more than a nice boy, a good friend, that I had been able to preserve such an innocent, light-hearted friendship with the two girls. Even if I had sometimes been stirred by Ilona's sensual beauty, I had never even thought of Edith as a member of the opposite sex; it had never even so much as crossed my mind that her crippled body was possessed of the same organs, that her soul harboured the same urgent desires, as those of other women. It was only from this moment that I began to have an inkling of the fact (suppressed by most writers) that the outcasts, the branded, the ugly, the withered, the deformed, the despised and rejected, desire with a more passionate, far more dangerous avidity than the happy; that they love with a fanatical, a baleful, a *black* love, and that no passion on earth rears its head so greedily, so desperately, as the forlorn and hopeless passion of these stepchildren of God, who feel that they can only justify their earthly existence by loving and being loved. That it is precisely from the lowest abysses of despair that the panic cries and groans of those hungry for love ring out most gruesomely—this was the dread secret which I, in my raw inexperience, had never ventured to suspect. It was not until this moment that the knowledge penetrated my consciousness like a red-hot knife.

"Silly!"—now too I understood why this particular word had risen to her lips in the midst of her emotion, as she had pressed her immature breast to mine. "Silly!"—she had been right to call me that. They must all have seen through the whole thing from the very start—the old man and Ilona and Josef and the other servants. They must all long since have suspected her love, her passion, viewed it with alarm, no doubt with foreboding. I alone had had no inkling of it, I, the foolish slave of my pity, who had played the role of the good, kind, blundering comrade, who had joked like a clown and never noticed that my blindness, my incomprehensible lack of perception, had been excruciating torture to her ardent soul. Just as in a cheap farce the sorry hero is the centre of an intrigue, the ramifications of which everyone in the audience has long since realized, and only he, poor innocent, goes on playing in deadly earnest, blissfully unaware of the net in which he is entangled (although the others have known its every thread and every mesh from the outset)—so everyone at Kekesfalva must have seen me blundering about in this foolish blind man's bluff of the emotions until at last she had torn the bandage violently from my eyes. But just as a single flash of light suffices to illuminate a dozen objects in a room simultaneously, so now in retrospect—too late, alas, too late!—did innumerable details of the past few weeks become embarrassingly plain to me. Only now did it occur to me why it was she had been so infuriated whenever I had blithely called her "my dear child"—she, who wished to be regarded by me of all people not as a child but as a woman, to be yearned for as a lover. Only now did I realize why her lips sometimes quivered so ominously when she saw that her lameness so visibly affected me, why my pity so enraged her. Obviously she had realized with a woman's clairvoyant instinct that pity is far too lukewarm and fraternal a feeling, and but a sorry substitute for real love. How the poor creature must have waited for a word, a sign of understanding that never came, how she must have suffered from my easy garrulity while she lay on the burning spit of impatience, and with trembling soul waited, waited, for the first tender gesture, or at least for me to become aware of her passion. And I, I had said nothing and yet had not stayed away, ever giving her fresh strength by my daily visits and at the same time driving her to distraction by my spiritual deafness. How easy it was to understand, then, that her nerves should at last have got the better of her and that she should have pounced upon me as her prey! A hundred and one scenes and pictures chased through my mind whilst, as though struck down by an explosion, I leaned against the wall, the breath knocked out of me and my legs almost as impotent as hers. Twice I tried to grope my way onwards, but only at the third attempt did I succeed in grasping the door-handle. This leads to the salon, I thought to myself quickly; to the left is the door into the hall, where I left my sword and cap. Quickly then, across the room; and away, away before Josef comes! Straight down the stairs and away, away! Get out of the house before meeting anyone to whom you will have to give an account of yourself. You must get away, avoid running into the old man, or Ilona, or Josef, or any of those who have let you foolishly run your head into this noose. Away, you must get away!

But it was too late. There in the salon Ilona was waiting; evidently she had heard me coming. At the sight of me her face changed.

"Mother of God, what's the matter? You're as pale as death! Has ... has anything happened to Edith again?"

"No, nothing, nothing," I just had the strength to stammer out, and prepared to go. "I believe she's sleeping now. Excuse me, I must go."

There must, however, have been something alarming in my brusque behaviour, for she seized me resolutely and forced, nay, pushed me, into an armchair.

"There—sit down for a moment. You must recover ... And your hair ... what *does* it look like? You're all dishevelled ... No, stay," she ordered, as I tried to jump up. "I'll fetch you a brandy."

She ran to the cupboard and poured out a glass; I gulped it down. She gazed at me uneasily as I put down the glass with shaking hand (never in my life had I felt so weak, so utterly shattered). Then she quietly sat down beside me and waited in silence, occasionally stealing a sidelong, cautious, uneasy glance at my face, as though I were ill.

"Did Edith ... say anything?" she asked at length. "I mean, anything as regards ... yourself?"

I could tell from her sympathetic manner that she had guessed everything, and I was too weak to put her off. So I merely murmured a faint "Yes".

She neither stirred nor spoke. I merely noticed that her breath suddenly came and went more violently. Cautiously she leaned towards me.

"And ... had you really only just noticed it?"

"How could I possibly have had any idea of such a thing, of anything so preposterous? So crazy? How was it that she? ... Why me ... me of all people?"

Ilona sighed. "Oh my God! And she always thought that you came only on her account ... that that was the only reason you came to see us. I ... I never believed it, because you ... you were so much at your ease ... and so friendly in quite a different way. From the very first I was afraid that you felt no more than pity. But how could I warn the poor child, how be so cruel as to rob her of an illusion that made her happy? For weeks she has lived only on the thought that you ... And when she kept on asking and asking me whether I thought that you were really fond of her, I simply couldn't be brutal ... I had to comfort and encourage her."

I was unable to contain myself any longer. "Well, you must disillusion her, without fail. It's madness on her part, a fever, a childish whim ... nothing but the usual teenage infatuation for a uniform, and if another officer were to turn up tomorrow, it would be transferred to him. You must explain that to her ... you must disillusion her while there's still time. It's only by chance that I came along, and not another of my fellow officers, a better man. One gets over these things quickly at her age ... "

But Ilona sadly shook her head. "No, my dear friend, don't deceive yourself. In Edith's case it's serious, dreadfully serious, and it gets more dangerous every day. No, my dear friend, I can't smooth out a difficult situation like this for you all in a moment. Oh, if you only knew what goes on in this house! Three times, four times a night her bell rings, ruthlessly waking us all up, and when we rush to her bedside in a panic lest something should have happened, we find her sitting there, bolt upright, distraught, staring into space. 'Do you think he's just a little bit fond of me, just a very little?' she asks over and over again. And then she asks for a mirror, but throws it aside again, and then she herself realizes that she's behaving crazily. And then two hours later, the whole thing begins all over again. In her despair she cross-questions her father and Josef and the maids, and yesterday she got that gypsy—you remember the one we met the other day?—to come secretly and tell her the same things all over again. Five times she's written letters to you and torn them up again. From morning to night, from dawn to dusk, she thinks and speaks of nothing else but you. Sometimes she asks me to go to see you and find out if you're fond of her, just a little bit fond, or if ... if she's a nuisance to you, since you're always so silent and evasive. I have to go off to find you that very minute, stop you on your way home, and the chauffeur has to go rushing off to fetch the car. Three, four, five times she makes me repeat by heart what I am to say to you, to ask you. Then, at the last moment, when I'm in the hall, her bell shrills out again, and I have to go back in my hat and coat and swear to her by all that I hold dear never to make the slightest allusion to the matter. Oh, how should you know all this! For you the whole thing's over when you shut the door behind you, but no sooner have you left than she repeats to me every word that you have said to her, and asks me if I believe this and think that. And if I say to her, 'Surely you can see how fond he is of you?' she shrieks at me, 'You're lying! It's not true. He didn't say a single kind word to me today,' but all the same she wants to hear it all over again, and I have to repeat it three times over and swear it's true. And then there's my uncle into the bargain. Ever since she's been in this state he's been at his wits' end; he loves and worships you, by the way, as though you were his own son. You ought to see him sitting hour after hour by her bedside, his eyes utterly weary, stroking and soothing her until at last she falls asleep. And then he himself paces up and down his room all night long. And you—do you mean to say you've noticed nothing of all this?"

"No," I shouted in my uncontrollable despair. "No, I swear, to you, nothing! Nothing whatever! Do you think I would have gone on coming, that I could have sat playing chess and dominoes with you, or listening to gramophone records, if I had had the slightest notion of what was going on? But how could she run away with the crazy idea that I … I of all people … how expect me to fall in with such nonsense, such childishness? No, no, no, I tell you!"

I was on the point of jumping up, so excruciating was the thought of being loved against my will, but Ilona seized me firmly by the arm.

"Calm down! I beg you, dear friend—don't get excited, and do please be a little quieter. She has a way of hearing through the very walls. And for Heaven's sake don't be unfair. The poor child took it as a good omen that it was you who brought the good news, that it was you who were the first to tell her father about this new treatment. You know how he rushed straight up to her in the middle of the night and woke her up. Can't you really picture to yourself how they both sobbed and thanked God that these horrible times were at an end and how they were both convinced that as soon as Edith was cured, was just like other people, you would—well, I needn't tell you. *That* is why you *must* not plunge the poor child into despair at the very moment when she needs all her nervous energy to cope with this new treatment. We must be exceptionally careful, and God forbid that she should suspect that you find it all so … so *horrible*."

226

But desperation had made me ruthless. "No, no, no!" I said, hammering violently on the arm of the chair. "No, I *can't* ... I *won't* be loved, loved like this. And I can't go on behaving as though I had noticed nothing, I can't go on sitting about unconcernedly and playing the cavalier. I *can't*! You don't know what happened there in her room ... she's under a complete misapprehension about me. I really only felt pity for her. Only pity, nothing else, nothing else whatever."

Ilona was silent and gazed straight ahead.

"Yes," she sighed at last. "I feared that from the start. I could feel it in my bones the whole time. But my God, what's going to happen now? How are we going to break it to her?"

We sat there in silence. All that there was to be said had been said. We both knew that there was no way out at all. Suddenly Ilona sat up, and seemed to be straining her ears to listen, and almost at the same moment I could hear the crunching sound of a car on the gravel outside. That must be Kekesfalva. She jumped up quickly.

"It's better that you shouldn't meet him now. You're too upset to talk to him calmly ... Wait, I'll fetch your cap and sword, and you can creep out through the back door into the park. I'll find some excuse for your not staying on to dinner."

In one bound she had fetched my things. Fortunately Josef had hurried out to the car and so I was able to slip past the estate buildings unnoticed. Once I was in the park, my panic lest I should have to stop and speak to anyone lent me wings. For the second time I fled, as stealthily and furtively as a thief, from this fateful house.

In my youth and comparative inexperience I had always regarded the yearning and pangs of love as the worst torture that could afflict the human heart. At this moment, however, I began to realize that there was another and perhaps grimmer torture than that of longing and desiring: that of being loved against one's will and of being unable to defend oneself against the urgency of another's passion. Of seeing another human being seared by the flame of her desire and of having to look on impotently, lacking the power, the capacity, the strength to pluck her from the flames. He who is himself crossed in love is able from time to time to master his passion, for he is not the creature but the creator of his own misery; and if a lover is unable to control his passion, he at least knows that he is himself to blame for his sufferings. But he who is loved without reciprocating that love, is lost beyond redemption; for it is not in his power to set a limit to the other's passion, to keep it within bounds, and the strongest will is reduced to impotence in the face of another's desire. Perhaps only a man can realize to the full the tragedy of such an undesired relationship, for him alone the necessity to resist it is at once martyrdom and guilt. For when a woman resists an unwelcome passion, she is obeying to the full the law of her sex; the initial gesture of refusal is, so to speak, a primordial instinct in every female, and even if she rejects the most ardent passion she cannot be called inhuman. But how disastrous it is when Fate upsets the balance, when a woman so far overcomes her natural modesty as to disclose her passion to a man, when, without the certainty of its being reciprocated, she offers her love, and he, the wooed, remains cold and on the defensive. An insoluble tangle this, always; for not to return a woman's love is to shatter her pride, to violate her modesty. The man who rejects a woman's advances is bound to wound her in her noblest feelings. In vain, then, all the tenderness with which he extricates himself, useless all his polite, evasive phrases, insulting all his offers of mere friendship, once she has revealed to him her weakness! His resistance inevitably becomes cruelty, and in rejecting a woman's love, he takes a load of guilt upon his conscience, guiltless though he may be. Abominable fetters that can never be cast off! Only a moment ago you felt free, you belonged to yourself and were in debt to no one, and now suddenly you find yourself pursued, hemmed in, prey and object of the unwelcome desires of another. Shaken to the depths of your soul, you know that day and night someone is waiting for you, thinking of you, longing and sighing for you—a woman, a stranger. She wants, she demands, she desires you with every fibre of her being, with her body, with her blood. She wants your hands, your hair, your lips, your manhood, your night and your day, your emotions, your senses, and all your thoughts and dreams. She wants to share everything with you, to take everything from you and to draw it in with her breath. Henceforth, day and night, whether you are awake or asleep, there is somewhere in the world a being who is feverish and wakeful and who waits for you, and you are the centre of her waking and her dreaming. It is in vain that you try not to think of her who thinks always of you, in vain that you seek to escape, for you no longer dwell in yourself, but in her. Of a sudden a stranger bears your image within her as though she were a moving mirror—no, not a mirror, for that merely drinks in your image when you offer yourself willingly to it, whereas she, the woman, this stranger who loves you, she has absorbed you into her very blood. She carries you always within her, carries you about with her, no matter where you may flee. Always you are imprisoned, held prisoner somewhere else, in some other person, no longer yourself, no longer free and light-hearted and guiltless, but always hunted, always under an obligation, always conscious of this "thinking-of-you" as though it were a steady devouring flame. Full of hate, full of fear, you have to endure this yearning on the part of a being who suffers on your account; and I now know that it is the most senseless, the most inescapable, affliction that can befall a man to be loved against his will—torment of torments, and a burden of guilt where no guilt is.

Not in the most fleeting day-dream had it ever seemed conceivable to me that I too could be so boundlessly loved by a woman. I had, it is true, heard my friends brag how this woman or that "ran after" them; I may even have joined in the general amusement aroused by such indiscreet revelations of female importunacy, for at that time I had had no idea that every form of love, even the most ridiculous and absurd, is the destiny of someone, and that even by one's indifference one can incur a debt to love. But all that one has heard and read passes one by; it is only from personal experience that the heart can learn the true nature of its emotions. I had to experience for myself the burden of misery that the hopeless love of another imposes on one's conscience in order to feel pity with either the woman who forces her love upon a man, or the man who vigorously defends himself against her unwelcome passion. But how inconceivably greater was the responsibility that had fallen to my lot! For if in itself it is cruelty, brutality almost, to disappoint a woman where her emotions are concerned, how much more horrible, then, was the "No" that I should have to utter to this passionate child. I should have to hurt a cripple, to wound more deeply than ever one who had already been grievously wounded by life, to snatch from one who was inwardly unsure of herself the last crutch of hope with which she kept herself erect. I knew that by fleeing from her love I should perhaps imperil the life and the reason of this girl who had aroused in me so pure an emotion of pity. I was gruesomely aware of the monstrous crime that I should, against my will, be committing if, incapable though I was of returning her love, I did not at least make some show of responding to it.

But I had no choice. Even before my mind had consciously realized the danger, my body had revolted against that sudden embrace. Our instincts are always more prescient than our waking thoughts; in that very first moment of horror, when I had torn myself away from her violent caresses, I had dimly foreseen this, known that I should never have the selfless strength to love the crippled girl as she loved me, and, probably, not even enough pity simply to *bear with* this un-nerving passion. At the first recoil I had divined that there was no way out, no middle course. Either the one or the other of us, perhaps both, was bound to be made unhappy by this futile love.

How I reached the town that day I shall never be able to explain to myself. I only knew that I walked very quickly and that one thought alone kept beating through my mind with every throb of my pulse: away! away! Away from this house, away from this entanglement, flee, escape, vanish! Never again enter that house, never again see those people, or any people at all! Hide yourself, make yourself invisible, never again be under an obligation to anyone, never again be ensnared! I know that I tried to carry my thoughts a stage further; that I said to myself that I must leave the army, get money from somewhere and then flee into the world, so far away that I should be out of reach of this crazy desire. But all these plans were dreamed rather than thought out clearly, for that one word kept hammering at my temples: away, away, away!

From the dust on my shoes and the tears brambles had made

in my trousers I realized later that I must have rushed pell-mell across fields and meadows and lanes. However that may be, when I finally found myself on the highway the sun was already setting behind the roof-tops. And I started like a sleepwalker when someone unexpectedly slapped me on the back.

"Hallo, Toni, so there you are! It's high time we ran into you. We've been searching for you in every nook and cranny, and we were just going to ring you up at your baronial hall."

I found myself surrounded by four of my friends, among them the inevitable Ferencz, Jozsi, and Captain Count Steinhübel.

"Look lively now! Just imagine! Balinkay's suddenly drifted in on us, from Holland or America or God knows where, and he's invited all us officers to dinner this evening. The Colonel's coming and the Major. There's going to be a grand do at the Red Lion at half-past eight. It's a jolly good thing we ran into you. The old man would have really made a fuss if you'd been missing! You know how he dotes on Balinkay. When he turns up, everyone has to answer the roll."

I had not yet collected my scattered thoughts. "Who's come?" I asked, still in a daze.

"Why, Balinkay! Don't look so stupid. I suppose you'll be telling us next you don't know who Balinkay is!"

Balinkay? Balinkay? My head was still in a whirl and I had to drag the name out laboriously as though from a pile of dusty lumber. Oh yes, of course, Balinkay—at one time he had been the black sheep of the regiment. Long before my transfer to this garrison he had served here as second and then first lieutenant. He had been the best rider, the maddest fellow in the regiment, an incorrigible gambler and Don Juan. But then there had been some unpleasant incident, I had never inquired what it was. At any rate, within twenty-four hours he had taken off his uniform, and had gone wandering about all over the world. All sorts of strange rumours of his doings had reached the regiment. At length he had got on his feet again by hooking a rich Dutch woman at the Excelsior Hotel in Cairo, a widow with pots of money, the owner of a shipping line with seventeen ships and vast plantations in Java and Borneo. Ever since then he had been our invisible benefactor and patron.

Colonel Bubencic must have got Balinkay out of the dickens
of a scrape, for Balinkay's loyalty to him and the regiment was
really touching. Whenever he returned to Austria, he made a
point of paying a visit to the garrison, and he would throw his
money about so wildly that it would be the talk of the town for
weeks afterwards. It seemed to be a sort of emotional necessity
for him to put on the old uniform for one evening, to be accepted
once more by the officers as one of themselves. When he sat,
entirely at his ease, at the familiar table, one felt that he was a
hundred times more at home in the smoky room at the Red Lion
with its grubby walls than in his feudal palace on an Amsterdam
canal. We were and always would be his children, his brothers,
his real family. Every year he offered a prize for our steeplechase,
regularly every Christmas he would send along two or three
cases of Bols and of champagne, and every New Year the Colonel
was able to pay a nice fat cheque into the mess account at the
bank. Anyone who wore the Uhlan's tunic and our facings on his
collar could depend on Balinkay if ever he got into difficulties—
a letter, and the whole thing was cleared up.

At any other time I should have been genuinely overjoyed at
the opportunity of meeting this celebrity. But the thought of a
binge with all the attendant rowdiness and toasts and after dinner
speeches seemed to me, in my overwrought state, about the most
intolerable thing on earth. I tried, therefore, to get out of it, saying that I did not feel quite up to the mark. Ferencz, however,
promptly seized me by the arm with a flat "Nonsense! No slinking
off for you today, my lad!" and I had no option but to yield.
They dragged me along and I listened in a daze as he told stories
of people whom Balinkay had got out of a tight spot, and how he
had found a job for his brother-in-law and if any member of the
regiment, he said, was unable to get promotion quickly enough,
he simply took the next boat to Alexandria or to the Dutch
Indies, where Balinkay was entirely at his service. That lean,
morose fellow Jozsi punctuated good old Ferencz's hymn of
grateful praise with an occasional acid comment. Would the
Colonel receive his "blue-eyed boy" so cordially, he jeered, if
Balinkay had not hooked that fat Dutch shellfish? Incidentally,
she was said to be twelve years older than he. "If you're going to

sell yourself, you should at least get a good price!" laughed Count Steinhübel.

Now, in retrospect, it seems odd to me that in spite of my bemused state my memory registered every word of this conversation. It is not uncommon, indeed, for a state of subconscious nervous excitement to exist side by side with a paralysis of one's conscious mind, and even when we arrived in the big dining-room of the Red Lion, I did what I had to do, thanks to the hypnotic power of discipline, more or less competently. And there was plenty to do. The whole array of bunting, flags and emblems, which usually only graced a regimental ball, were brought out, orderlies were hammering away noisily and cheerfully at the walls, and in the next room Steinhübel was instructing the bugler as to when and how to sound the fanfare. Jozsi, who happened to have the neatest handwriting, was given the task of writing out the menu, in which all the dishes were given humorously suggestive names, while I was fobbed off with the job of arranging the places at table. In the meantime the houseboy was getting ready chairs and tables, and the waiter was setting out rows of bottles of wine and champagne, which Balinkay had brought in his car from Sacher's in Vienna. Curiously enough, this noisy whirl of activity did me good, for it drowned the dull, insistent throbbing at my temples.

At last, by eight o'clock, everything was ready. All that remained to be done was to go over to the barracks, have a quick wash, and change. My batman had been forewarned, and my dress uniform and patent-leather shoes were put out ready. I quickly plunged my head into cold water and then glanced up at the clock. Another ten minutes at the most, for we had to be confoundedly punctual for the Colonel. I rapidly undressed, and kicked off my dusty shoes. But just as I was standing in front of the mirror in my underclothes in order to brush my tousled hair, there was a knock at the door.

"I'm not at home to anyone," I told Kusma, my batman. He rushed off obediently, and there was a moment's whispering outside in the ante-room. Then he returned with a letter in his hand.

A letter for me? Standing there in shirt and pants, I took the square blue envelope—it was fat and heavy, almost a small package—and it was like a live coal in my hand. I had no need to look at the handwriting to know who it was that was writing to me.

Later, later!—a sudden instinct warned me. Don't read it, don't read it now. But against all the dictates of my reason I tore open the envelope and read, read the letter, which seemed to crackle more and more violently in my hands.

It was a letter sixteen pages long, written in tearing haste, in an unsteady hand; a letter such as a person writes only once, and receives only once, in a lifetime. The sentences were poured out unremittingly like blood from an open wound; there were no paragraphs, no punctuation; one word overtook, outstripped, tumbled headlong over the next. Even now, after years and years, I can see every line, every character before me. Even now I could repeat that letter by heart, page by page, from beginning to end, at any time of the day or night, so often have I read it. For months and months after that day I carried that folded blue packet about in my pocket, again and again taking it out—at home, in barracks, in the trenches and by the camp-fires during the war. And it was not until the retreat in Volhynia, when our division was being trapped on both flanks by the enemy, that, seized with anxiety lest this confession made in a moment of exaltation might fall into strange hands, I tore the letter up.

"I have already written you six letters," the letter began, *"and torn them all up. For I did not want to give myself away, I did not want to. I held myself in as long as I had any powers of resistance. For weeks and weeks I struggled to hide my feelings from you. Every time you came to see us, in all friendliness and innocence, I commanded my hands to keep still, my gaze to feign indifference, so as not to upset you; often, even, I deliberately treated you harshly and contemptuously, so that you should have no inkling of how my heart burned for you—I tried everything that lies in the power, and beyond the power, of a human being. But today it happened, and I swear to you that it came over me against my will, it took me by surprise. I myself no longer know how I could let such a thing happen; afterwards I felt like beating and punishing myself, I felt so desperately ashamed. For I know, oh, I know, how mad, how crazy it would be to force myself upon you. A lame creature, a*

234

cripple like myself, has no right to love. How should I, broken, shattered being that I am, be anything but a burden to you, when to myself I am an object of disgust, of loathing. A creature such as I, I know, has no right to love, and certainly no right to be loved. It is for such a creature to creep away into a corner and die and cease to make other people's lives a burden with her presence. Oh yes, I know all that—I know it, and it is because I know it that I am a lost soul. I should never have dared to throw myself at you, but who except you has ever given me any assurance that I should not continue for ever to be the wretched monstrosity that I am? That I should be able to move, to walk about, like other people, like all the millions of superfluous people who simply don't know that every unimpeded step they take is a blessing and a glory? I had made an iron resolve to preserve silence until I had really reached the point when I was a human being, a woman like other women, and perhaps—perhaps—worthy of you, beloved. But my impatience, my hunger, to get well, was so frantic that at the moment when you bent over me I believed, genuinely believed, honestly and foolishly believed, myself to be that other, that new, that well person! You see, I had wanted and dreamed of being so too long, and then you were near me—and for a moment I forgot my wretched legs, I saw only you, felt myself to be what I wanted to be for your sake. Can't you understand one's losing oneself in a day-dream for a moment, when one has dreamed only one dream day and night, year in year out? Believe me, beloved—it was only the crazy illusion that I had cast off my deformity that so went to my head; it was only my impatient yearning not to be an outcast, a cripple, any longer that caused my heart to run away with me so madly. Do understand—I had wanted you so long and so interminably.

But now you know what you ought never to have known until I was literally on my feet, and know too for whom it is I want to be cured, for whom alone on this earth—for you alone! For you alone! Forgive me, my heart's beloved, for this love, and above all I implore you—do not be afraid of me, do not shrink from me! Do not think that because I have once been importunate I shall trouble you again, that I, infirm and abhorrent to myself as I am, will try to hold you. No, I swear to you—you shall never find me forcing myself upon you, I shall try to hide my feelings from you. I only want to wait, wait patiently, until God takes pity on me and makes me well. And so I implore you—do not be afraid, dearest, of my love. Remember, you who have taken pity on me as no one else has, remember how horribly helpless I am, chained to my chair, unable to take a single step by myself, powerless to follow you, to rush after you. Remember that I am a prisoner who has to wait in my prison, to wait always in impatient patience, until you come and bestow an hour of your time upon me, until you permit me to look at you, to hear your voice, to know we are breathing the same air, to feel your presence, the first and only happiness that has been granted to me for years. Remember it, picture it to yourself: there I lie and go on lying, waiting, waiting, day and night; and every hour stretches out endlessly until the tension is unbearable. And then you come, and I cannot jump up like another woman, cannot go to meet you, cannot seize you, cannot hold you. I have to sit and control myself, master my feelings and keep silent, have to keep a watch upon my every word, my every look, every tone of my voice, so that you shall not think that I presume to love you. And yet believe me, beloved, even this agonizing happiness has nevertheless been happiness, and I have praised myself, loved myself every time I have succeeded in restraining myself, and you have gone away, unsuspecting, free and untrammelled, knowing nothing of my love. My only torture then has been the realization of how hopelessly I have fallen under your spell.

But now it has happened. And now, beloved, that I can no longer deny and dissimulate my feelings for you, do not be cruel to me, I implore you. Even the most wretched, the most pitiable creature has her pride, and I could not bear it if you were to despise me because I could not keep my heart in check. I do not expect you to return my love—no, by God, who is to heal and save me, I have not the audacity to expect that! Not even in my dreams do I dare to hope that you could love me as I am—I do not want, as you know, any sacrifice, any pity from you. All I ask is that you should let me wait, wait in silence, and not spurn me utterly. I know that even this is asking too much of you. But is it really too much to grant a human being this pitiful modicum of happiness, which one willingly allows to any dog, the happiness of gazing up dumbly now and then at his master? Is it necessary to thrust it away violently, to drive it away scornfully with a whip? For the one thing, I tell you, that I could not bear, would be that I, wretched creature that I am, should become repellent to you through having given myself away, that you should punish me; for my own shame and despair are punishment enough to me. In that case I should have only one way out, and you know what that is. I have already shown it to you.

But no, don't be alarmed, I don't want to threaten you! I don't want to frighten you, to extort from you, instead of love, pity—the only thing that you have hitherto given me of your own free will. You must feel quite free and unhindered—God knows I don't want to burden you with my burden, weigh you down with guilt of which you are guiltless—all I want is that you should *forgive and forget what has happened, forget what I have said, what I have revealed to you. Give me just this reassurance, just this pitiful little certainty! Tell me now—a word will suffice—that I have not become repugnant to you, that you will come to see us again as though nothing had happened. You can have no idea of how I dread losing you. Ever since that moment when the door closed behind you I have been in an agony of fear that it was for the last time. You were so pale, you had such a look of horror in your eyes as I let go of you, that in the midst of my ardour I suddenly felt icy cold. And I know— for Josef told me—that you rushed straight out of the house, seized your cap and sword and were off in a moment. He searched for you in vain, in my room and all over the house, and so I know that you fled from me as from the plague, the pest. But no, beloved, I am not reproaching you—I understand. I of all people, who recoil in horror from myself when I see the great weights on my feet, I alone, who know how beastly, how petulant, how impossible, how intolerable I have become in my impatience, I of all people should be able to understand why others should recoil in horror from me. Oh, I can understand only too well why they flee from me, shrink back when they come upon such a monstrosity! And yet I implore you to forgive me, for there is no night and no day without you, but only despair. Send me just a note, a little hurried note, or a blank sheet of paper, a flower—but something, some sign or other. Just something by which I shall know that you are not spurning me, that I have not become repellent to you. Remember that in a few days I shall be going away for months, that in a week or ten days your torture will be at an end. And if mine is increased a thousand-fold, the torture of having to do without you for weeks, for months on end, don't think of that, think only of yourself, as I think always of you, only of you. In a week's time you will be released—so come again, and in the meantime send me a word, give me a sign. I cannot think, cannot breathe, cannot feel until I know that you have forgiven me. I will not, I cannot go on living if you deny me the right to love you!"*

I read and read. I read the letter over and over again from the beginning. My hands trembled and the hammering at my temples grew more and more insistent; my consternation and dismay at being loved so desperately were boundless.

"Well, I'm damned! There you are still in your underclothes, and they're all waiting anxiously for you. The whole crowd's already at table, dying for things to begin, even Balinkay; the

237

Colonel may turn up any moment now, and you know what a song and dance the old buffer makes when any of us is late. Ferdl sent me over specially to see if anything had happened to you, and there you are mooning about reading a *billet doux* ... Well, look sharp, or we'll both get a deuce of a dressing down!"

It was Ferencz who had burst into my room. I had not noticed his presence until he gave me a hearty slap on the back. At first I couldn't take in what he was saying. The Colonel? Ferdl had sent him over? Balinkay? Ah yes, ah yes, I remembered now: the dinner in honour of Balinkay! Hastily I reached for my trousers and tunic, and with a speed acquired after years at the cadet school, I mechanically threw on my clothes, without really knowing what I was doing.

"What's up with you?" asked Ferencz, looking at me oddly. "You're behaving absolutely crazily. Have you had bad news or something?"

"No, of course not," I hastened to protest. "I'm coming." Three bounds and we were on the landing. Then I tore back again to my room.

"God bless the boy, what's wrong now?" Ferencz roared after me indignantly. But I had merely gone to pick up the letter I had left lying on the table and stow it away in my breast-pocket. As it was, we were only just in time. The noisy crew were assembled round the long horse-shoe table, but, like schoolboys waiting after the bell has gone they none of them really dared to let themselves go until the senior officers had taken their seats.

And now the orderlies flung open the doors; the Colonel and his staff entered, their spurs jingling. We all rose and stood for a moment at attention. The Colonel sat down on Balinkay's right, the senior Major on his left, and the whole table instantly became animated; plates clattered, spoons rattled, everyone chattered away and fell to with a will. I alone sat in a kind of trance amidst my jovial companions and kept feeling for the place where, beneath my tunic, something was hammering and thumping away like a second heart. Every time I touched it I could feel the letter crackling through the soft, yielding cloth like the flames of a newly kindled fire; yes, it was there, it moved and stirred close to my breast like a living thing, and while the others babbled away happily over their food I could really think of nothing but the letter and the desperate plight of the girl who had written it.

In vain the waiter placed food before me; I left everything untouched. This listening to my inner self paralysed me. It was as though I was asleep with my eyes wide open. To right and left of me I heard people talking as through a fog, without understanding a word of what they were saying; they might have been speaking a foreign language. Before me, beside me, I saw faces, moustaches, eyes, noses, lips, uniforms, but saw them dimly as one sees things through the plate-glass of a shop window. I was there and yet not there, immobile and yet occupied, for I kept murmuring with soundless lips the individual phrases of the letter, and sometimes, when I could not remember how it went on or I got mixed up, my hand would move stealthily towards my pocket, as though I were a cadet, bringing out proscribed books during the lecture on tactics.

Then a knife was rattled vigorously against a glass, and there was a sudden hush, as though the sharp steel had cut right through the din. The Colonel had risen and was about to make a speech. Gripping the table with both hands, he swung his stocky body backwards and forwards as though he were on horseback. Starting off with a harsh and strident *Kamerraden*, he barked out his well-prepared speech, rhythmically accentuating the syllables. I listened attentively, but my brain refused to function. I could hear only isolated phrases vibrating through the room: " ... hon'r of the *army* ... spirit of the Austrian *cav'lry* ... loyalty to the *reg'ment* ... old *comr'de*."But in between these I could catch the ghostly whisper of other words, soft, pleading words, coming as though from another world: "My heart's beloved ... do not be afraid ... I cannot go on living if you take from me the right to love you ... " And in between these, again the Colonel's crisp syllables: " ... has not forgotten his *comr'des* ... so far away ... or the Fatherland ... or his native Austria ... " And once again the other voice, like a sob, like a stifled scream: "All I ask is that you should let me love you ... all I ask is that you should give me a sign ... "

And now there rattled and thundered out a salvo, "*Hoch, hoch,*

239

hoch!" As though dragged to their feet by the Colonel's raised glass, my comrades sprang to attention, and from the next room there rang out the prearranged fanfare: "Here's health to Balinkay!" Everyone clinked glasses and drank a toast to Balinkay, who had only been waiting for the shiver of breaking glass before replying in mellow, easy, jocular vein. He wanted to say only a few modest words, he said; merely that, despite everything, there was nowhere in the world where he felt so much at home as among his old comrades. He ended up with the toast: "Long live the Regiment! Long live His Majesty, our most gracious Commander-in-Chief, the Emperor!" Steinhübel once more signalled to the bugler, another fanfare was sounded, and the National Anthem boomed forth from all throats. Then came the inevitable song of every Austrian regiment, in which each mentions its own name with the same boastful pride:

> *Wir sind vom k und k,*
> *Ulanenregiment ... * *

Glass in hand, Balinkay strolled round the table to clink glasses with each of us. All of a sudden, pushed forward energetically by my neighbour, I found myself gazing into a pair of bright friendly eyes: "*Servus*, Comrade!" I nodded back in a stupor; and only when Balinkay had passed on to the next man did I realize that I had omitted to clink glasses with him. But everything had already vanished in the rainbow mist in which faces and uniforms were so strangely blurred and jumbled together. Good heavens!—whatever was that blue smoke before my eyes? Had the others already begun to puff away at their cigars? I suddenly felt suffocatingly hot. I must drink something, drink quickly! I gulped down one, two, three glasses, without knowing what I was drinking. At all costs I must get this bitter, nasty taste out of my mouth! And I must smoke too. But as I felt in my pocket for my cigarette-case I was once more conscious of that crackling under my tunic: the letter! My hand drew back. Once again I could hear nothing amid the confusion of voices but those sobbing, pleading words: "All I ask is that you should let me love you ... I know that it is madness to force myself upon you ... "

*We are the –th Regiment of his Royal and Imperial Majesty's Uhlans.

But at this moment a fork was tinkled against a glass to call for silence. Major Wondraczek, who seized every opportunity of displaying his poetic talents by declaiming humorous verses and extempore doggerel, had got to his feet. The moment he rose, rested his comfortable little paunch on the table and tried to assume a sly, knowing expression, we all knew that the "matey" part of the evening had begun, and that nothing could stop it.

And now, pushing his spectacles up above his somewhat longsighted eyes, he struck an attitude and ostentatiously unrolled a sheet of foolscap on which was written the inevitable poem with which, as he fondly thought, he graced every festive occasion. This time it was an effort to embroider Balinkay's life story with all kinds of telling witticisms. Several of my neighbours, either out of courtesy to a senior officer or because they themselves were already a little tipsy, tittered obligingly at every allusion. At last a point really did get home, and a volley of bravos thundered out from the whole company.

But suddenly I was seized with a feeling of revulsion. This ribald laughter clawed at my heart. How could they laugh like that when somewhere someone was groaning in despair, suffering boundless torments? How could they crack smutty jokes when someone was in agony of soul? The moment Wondraczek had come to an end of his silly twaddle, the real orgy, I knew, would begin. There would be songs; they would bawl out *The Good-wife on the Lahn*, they would recount funny stories, they would laugh uproariously. All of a sudden I felt unable to bear the sight of all these good-humoured, glowing faces. Had she not asked me in her letter to send her just a note, just one word? Ought I not to go to the telephone and ring her up? One couldn't leave a person in suspense like that. One ought to send *some* message, one ought ...

"*Bravo, bravissimo!*" Everyone applauded, chairs were pushed back noisily, the floor groaned, and a cloud of dust flew up as forty or fifty rowdy and slightly tipsy men suddenly shuffled to their feet. Proudly the Major stood there, removed his spectacles and rolled up his manuscript, nodding good humouredly and a little vainly at the officers who had crowded round to congratulate him. I, however, seized the opportunity of this hullabaloo to rush off without saying any farewells. Perhaps they wouldn't notice my absence. And even if they did, it was all the same; I simply could not stand it any longer—could not stand this laughter, this smug merriment, which seemed, as it were, to be patting itself on its full belly. I could not, simply could not.

"Is the *Herr Leutnant* going already?" asked the orderly at the cloakroom in amazement. "Go to the devil!" I murmured under my breath, and pushed past him without a word. Across the road, round the corner and up the stairs to my room. Oh to be alone, alone!

The corridors reeked of desolation. Somewhere a sentry was pacing to and fro, a tap was running, a boot fell to the ground, and the only human sound came, faint and far-off, from one of the men's dormitories, where, according to the regulations, lights had already been put out. Involuntarily I listened; a few of the Ruthenian lads were either singing or humming a melancholy song in low voices. Every night before going to sleep, when they took off the strange bright uniform with the brass buttons and were once again no more than the peasants who lay down naked at home among the straw, they would remember their native land and its pastures, or perhaps a girl they were fond of, and then they would sing these mournful tunes in order to drown their home-sickness.

As a rule I paid no heed to their humming and singing, because I did not understand the words. But this time its strange melancholy moved me, and I felt as though these men were my brothers. Oh to sit down by one of them, to talk to him! He would not understand, and yet, perhaps, as he gazed sympathetically at me out of his mild, cow-like eyes, he *would* understand everything far better than those revellers at the horse-shoe table. Oh to have someone who would help me out of this hopeless entanglement!

So as not to wake Kusma, my batman, who was snoring away loudly in the ante-room, I crept on tiptoe into my room, threw my cap down in the darkness, and tore off my sword and the collar which had long been choking me. Then I lit the lamp and went over to the table in order at last, at last, to read the letter in peace—the first heart-breaking letter which I, a young, unsophisticated fellow, had ever received from a woman.

But the next moment I gave a start. There on the table lay, in the circle of lamplight—how was it possible?—the very letter I had thought was still hidden in my breast-pocket! Yes, there it lay, the blue, square envelope, the familiar handwriting.

For a moment I reeled. Was I drunk? Was I dreaming with my eyes wide open? Had I lost my senses? Had I not just now, as I took off my tunic, distinctly heard the letter crackling in my breast-pocket? Was I so distraught that I had taken it out without remembering anything about it a moment afterwards? I felt in my pocket. No—of course I was right—the letter was still safely there. And only now did I understand what had happened. Only now did I become fully awake. This letter on the table must be a fresh letter, a second letter, one that had arrived later, and my good Kusma had thoughtfully placed it by the thermos flask so that I should find it on my return.

Another letter? A second letter within two hours? My throat immediately went dry with vexation and anger. So this was to go on every day, every day, every night, letter after letter, one upon another. If I wrote to her, she would write back to me, and if I did not answer, she would want to know why. She would always be wanting something of me, every day, every day! She would send me messages, she would telephone me, she would watch out for me and have me spied upon at every turn; she would want to know when I went out and when I returned, whom I was with and what I said and did. I could see that I was lost—she would never let me go again.

Oh, the djinn, the Old Man of the Sea, old Kekesfalva and the cripple—I should never be free again, those greedy, desperate creatures would never let me go until one of us was destroyed, she or I, by this futile, fatal passion.

Don't read it, I told myself. Don't read it today on any account. Don't get involved any further. You haven't sufficient strength to resist this pulling and tugging, it will tear you to pieces. Better destroy the letter or send it back unopened. Don't let the knowledge that a total stranger loves you force itself upon your consciousness, your conscience. To the devil with all the Kekesfalvas! I used not to know them and I don't want to know them any more. But then I was suddenly petrified by the thought that perhaps because I had not answered her she had done herself some injury. One could not leave a desperate person without a reply of any kind. Ought I not, after all, to wake Kusma and quickly send some word of reassurance, of acknowledgement, out to Kekesfalva? I must not incur any guilt, whatever happened. And so I tore open the envelope. Thank God, it was only a short letter! Only a single sheet, only ten lines without any heading.

"Destroy my previous letter at once. I was mad, completely mad. All that I wrote was untrue. And DON'T come to see us tomorrow. Please DON'T come. I must punish myself for having abased myself so horribly to you. So on no account come tomorrow, I don't want you to, I forbid it. And don't answer my letter on any account. Destroy my previous letter without fail, forget every word of it. And think no more about it."

Think no more about it—a childish command! As though over-wrought nerves could ever be bridled by the will! Think no more about it—when your thoughts were chasing about like wild, stampeding horses in the narrow space between your temples. Don't think about it—when your memory was feverishly projecting picture after picture on the screen of your brain, when your nerves were tingling and your senses were keyed up to resist the attack. Think no more about it—when those letters were still scorching your fingers with their burning words, the first letter and the second, which you picked up and put down again and re-read and compared, the first and the second, until every word was branded into your brain. Think no more about it—when you could think of only one thing—how to escape, how to resist, how to save yourself from this greedy importunity, from this unwelcome and immoderate passion.

Think no more about it—that is just what you yourself would like to be able to do, and you put out the light, because light makes all your thoughts too vivid, too real. You try to creep away, to hide yourself in the dark, you tear the clothes from your body so as to breathe more freely, you throw yourself on your bed to try and deaden all feeling. But your thoughts, they will not rest; they flutter like bats in ghostly confusion round and round the exhausted brain, they gnaw and nibble their way like rats through your leaden weariness. The more quietly you lie there, the more restless is your memory, the more agitating the flickering pictures in the dark; and so you get up and light the lamp again to scare away the ghosts.

But the first thing that the lamp cruelly seizes upon is the bright square envelope of the letter, and there on the back of the chair hangs your tunic, the one stained by the tea; everything reminds and admonishes you.

Think no more about it—you yourself don't want to think about it, but it's beyond your will to do otherwise. And so you pace up and down the room, to and fro, fling open the cupboard and the drawers in the cupboard, one after another, until you find the little glass ampoule containing a sleeping-draught and then stagger back to bed. But there is no escape. The dark thoughts, those restless rats, gnawing their way through the black shell of sleep, burrow even into your dreams, the same thoughts over and over again, and when you awake in the morning you feel as though you have been drained and sucked dry by vampires.

What a solace then is reveille, what a solace your duties, that far milder form of bondage! What a comfort to vault into the saddle and to have to trot along with all the others, to have to be unceasingly on the *qui vive*! You have to obey, you have to give orders. For three hours, perhaps four, you escape, ride away from yourself.

At first all went well. We had—thank God!—a very full day, carrying out various movements in preparation for the manoeuvres and ending up with the march past, in which the regiment rides past the commanding officer in line of squadron column, every horse's head, every sword-point dressed dead straight. At such parades there is always a confounded lot to do—ten, twenty times, you have to start all over again from the beginning, to keep your eye on every single Uhlan, and such an extreme effort of attention was demanded on the part of every one of us officers that my mind was entirely concentrated on my duties, and I forgot everything else.

But when we broke off for ten minutes to let the horses have a breather, my gaze happened to wander over the horizon. Far and wide the fields, with their sheaves and harvesters, gleamed forth in the steely blue light, the flat horizon stretched away in an unbroken semi-circle against the sky. Only beyond the patch of woodland was silhouetted, slender as a toothpick, the quaint outline of the tower. There it is, I thought with a start—*her* tower, with its terrace! The thought kept returning with all the force of a compulsion—I felt an irresistible urge to stare at it and think: it is eight o'clock now, she's just waking up and thinking of me. Perhaps her father is at her bed-side and she is talking of me, perhaps she is pestering Ilona or Josef to tell her whether a letter has come containing the news so greedily awaited (I really ought to have written to her), or perhaps she has already gone up to the tower and, clutching at the balustrade, is peering out and staring across at me just as I am staring across at her. And no sooner did I remember that someone was yearning for me over there than I felt that familiar hot tugging and tearing, that confounded clawing at my own breast, and although we had fallen in again, although words of command were being shouted out on all sides, and the various units were carrying out the prescribed movements at the gallop, closing up, scattering and closing up again, and I myself was shouting into the hubbub, "Left wheel," "Right wheel," my thoughts were far away. In the very depths of my consciousness, in the secret places of my mind, I was thinking only of that one thing of which I did not want to think, of which I ought not to have been thinking.

"God blast my soul, what the hell are you at! Back! Re-form, you rabble!" It was Colonel Bubencic who, purple in the face, had come galloping up, and was bellowing right across the parade-ground. And he had every excuse. Someone must have given a wrong word of command, for two troops, which ought to have wheeled and formed squadron column, had charged down upon one another and become dangerously entangled. One or two horses shied and got completely out of hand, others reared, one Uhlan was thrown and fell beneath the horses' hoofs; and above all the confusion the steeds could be heard screaming and whinnying. The clatter of weapons, the neighing of horses, the thundering and stamping of hoofs were as deafening as though a real battle were in progress. The officers who came charging up took

246

some time to disentangle passably the turbulent confusion of horses and men, and at a shrill bugle-blast the squadrons once more formed line. And now ensued a ghastly silence; everyone knew that someone or other was in for a hot time. The horses, still foaming from the excitement of the *mêlée*, perhaps, too, feeling the restrained agitation of their riders, twitched and trembled, and a faint quiver ran down the long line of *czapkas* as though down a tautly stretched steel telegraph wire. The Colonel rode forward into this dismayed silence. From the very way in which he sat in the saddle, raising himself stiffly in the stirrups, striking his top-boots restlessly with his riding-crop, we could tell that a storm was brewing. A sharp tug at the reins and his horse pulled up. Then there vibrated sharply across the whole parade-ground (as though an axe had descended): "Lieutenant Hofmiller!"

It was not until now that I realized what had happened. Indubitably it was I who had given the wrong word of command. My thoughts must have been wandering. I had been thinking of that terrible thing that so completely distracted me. I alone was to blame. Mine was the sole responsibility. A slight pressure of my knees, and my gelding trotted past my comrades, who looked away in acute embarrassment, towards the Colonel; he was waiting motionless some thirty paces from the regiment, and I reined in my horse at the regulation distance away from him. The rattle and clatter had now completely died down, and that final, soundless, yet deathly stillness had set in which precedes the order to fire at an execution. Everyone, even the peasant lads at the very back, knew what was in store for me.

I would rather not remember what followed. The Colonel, it is true, lowered his dry, grating voice so that the men should not hear the coarse language that he levelled at me, but, despite this, every now and then one of his juiciest expressions, such as "bloody stupidity" or "damn-fool order" was pitched on a high note so that it shrilled out through the silence. And in any case everyone, down to the very last man, must have noticed from the way in which, crimson in the face, he let fly at me, accompanying every staccato phrase with a resounding slap on his riding-boots, that I was getting a more ignominious dressing-down than any schoolboy. I could feel hundreds of curious, ironic glances piercing my back as the choleric old veteran poured forth his torrent of abuse on my head. For months and months no such hail-storm had descended on any of us as that which I had to face on that steely-blue radiant day, loud with the wings of blithe and care-free swallows.

As they held the reins my hands trembled with suppressed indignation. I felt like striking my horse on the hind-quarters and galloping off. But I had to sit there motionless, without moving a muscle of my face, while Bubencic rapped out in conclusion that he did not propose to let the whole parade be ruined by a wretched bungler like me. Tomorrow I should hear more of this; for today he did not wish to set eyes on me again. Then, giving his boots a final whack with his riding-crop, he barked out a contemptuous "Dismiss!" with all the brutality and suddenness of a kick.

And I had to raise my hand respectfully to my *czapka* before I could turn round and ride back to the ranks. Not one of my comrades ventured an overt glance in my direction; they all kept their eyes lowered in embarrassment, so ashamed were they all on my account, or at least so it seemed to me. Fortunately a word of command cut short the agony for me. At a bugle-call the drill began anew, each squadron wheeling off in turn. And Ferencz seized the opportunity—why is it that the stupidest people are always the most good-natured?—to urge his horse forward as if by chance and to whisper to me: "Don't let it get you down. A thing like that might happen to anyone."

But he was out of luck, poor chap. "Will you kindly mind your own business," I flared up at him, and turned away abruptly. In that moment I had learned for the first time, and at first-hand, how deeply one can be wounded by tactless pity. For the first time, and too late.

To hell with it! To hell with it all! I thought to myself as we rode back to the town. Oh to get away, away, to some place where no one knew me, to be rid of everyone and everything. Oh to get away, to escape, to flee! To see no one any more, never to let oneself be idolized, be humiliated again. Away, away!—the word became part of the rhythm of my horse's trot. Arrived at the barracks, I hastily threw the reins to an Uhlan and left the court-yard. I was determined not to go into mess today, I was determined not to let myself be jeered at, much less pitied.

But I had no idea where to go. I had no plan, no objective. My position had become impossible in both my worlds, the world of my regiment and the world of Kekesfalva. Oh to get away! my pulses hammered. Away, away! they thundered at my temples. Right away, anywhere, away from these confounded barracks, away from the town! Down the dingy main street and then on and on! But suddenly, from quite nearby, a friendly voice called out, "*Servus!*" Involuntarily I looked across the road. Who was that hailing me so familiarly? A tall man in mufti: breeches, grey coat and Glengarry hat. Never seen him before, can't remember him. He was standing, this stranger, beside a car, at which two mechanics in blue overalls were busily tinkering away. Evidently quite oblivious of my confusion, he came up to me. It was Balinkay, whom I had never before seen out of uniform.

"The damn thing's got bladder trouble again," he laughed across at me, pointing at the car. "It happens on every trip. I fancy it'll be another twenty years before one can really depend on these puffing billies. It was much simpler with our good old nags. At least we cavalrymen knew something about their works."

I could not help being conscious of a strong bond of sympathy with this stranger. There was something so self-assured about the way he moved, and he had the clear, warm-hearted gaze of a devil-may-care, happy-go-lucky sort of fellow. And no sooner had his unexpected greeting fallen on my ears than the thought suddenly flashed across my mind: here's a man you can confide in. And within the space of a second a whole chain of thoughts joined themselves on to the first with that rapidity with which the brain functions at moments of extreme tension: He's in mufti, he's his own master. He's been through the same sort of thing. He helped Ferencz's brother-in-law, he's only too pleased to help anyone, so why shouldn't he lend me a helping hand too? Before I had time to get my breath this fleeting, flickering chain of lightning reflections was welded into a sudden resolve. I plucked up courage and went up to Balinkay.

"Excuse me," I said, astounded at my own *sans gêne*, "but I suppose you couldn't spare me five minutes?"

He was somewhat taken aback, but his teeth gleamed out in a smile.

"With pleasure, my dear Hoff ... Hoff ... "

"Hofmiller," I said.

"Entirely at your service. It would be a fine thing if one hadn't time for a comrade! Shall we go into the restaurant, or would you rather come up to my room?"

"Up to your room, if it's all the same to you, and I really mean only five minutes. I won't keep you."

"As long as you like, old chap. It'll take half an hour in any case for the old bus to be repaired. But it's not very comfortable up there. The landlord always wants to give me the royal suite on the first floor, but, being sort of sentimental, I always take my old room, where I once—but we won't talk about that now."

We went upstairs. And the room really was a damned poor one for such a rich fellow. It contained a single bed, and had no wardrobe, no armchair, nothing but two mangy wicker chairs between the window and the bed. Taking out his gold cigarette-case, Balinkay offered me a cigarette and made things delightfully easy for me by coming straight to the point himself.

"Well, my dear Hofmiller, what can I do for you?"

No beating about the bush, I thought to myself, and so blurted out:

"I'd like to ask your advice, Balinkay. I want to leave the service and get out of Austria. I wonder if you know of a job for me?"

Balinkay grew suddenly serious. His face straightened, and he threw away his cigarette.

"Nonsense—a chap like you! What's come over you?"

But I was seized with a sudden obstinacy. I could feel the resolution which had been born only during the last ten minutes hardening like steel within me.

"My dear Balinkay," I said in that brusque tone which precludes all argument, "do me the favour of asking for no explanations. Every man knows what he wants and what he's got to do. No one can understand from outside. Believe me I've got to make a fresh start."

Balinkay must have realized that I was serious.

"Well, I don't want to interfere, but believe me, Hofmiller, you're making a mistake. You don't know what you're doing. You are, I fancy, somewhere about twenty-five or twenty-six, and not so far off promotion to first lieutenant. And that's something not to be sneezed at. Here in the army you've got your rank, you're *somebody*. But the moment you try to launch out into a new career, the dirtiest ragamuffin and lousiest counter-jumper will rate more than you, for the very reason that he hasn't got to trail around our fool prejudices like a knapsack. Believe me, when we military chaps take off our uniform there's not much left of what we once were, and I only beg one thing of you: don't be deceived merely because I've succeeded in getting out of the mire. That was a pure chance, one in a thousand, and I wouldn't like to think of what's happened to all the others to whom the Lord hasn't been so kind as He has to me."

There was something convincing about the firm way in which he spoke. But I felt I must not give in.

"I know," I agreed, "that it's a downward step. But I've just *got* to go away, I've no choice. Don't try to dissuade me, there's a good chap. I'm nothing out of the ordinary, I know that, and I've got no particular ability, but if you're willing to give me a recommendation I can promise not to let you down. I know I'm not the first chap you've helped; you found a job for Ferencz's brother-in-law."

"Oh, Jonas?"—Balinkay snapped his fingers contemptuously. "But I ask you, what sort of chap was he? A little provincial official. It's easy to help a man like that. All you have to do is to move him from one stool to a better one, and he thinks he's God Almighty. What does it matter to him whether he wears his trousers out on one stool or another, he's never known anything better. But to wangle a job for someone who's once had a star on his collar—why, that's a different kettle of fish! No, my dear Hofmiller, the top floors are already occupied. Anyone who wants to make a start in civilian life must start at the bottom, right down in the cellar, and that doesn't smell of roses, I can tell you."

"That doesn't matter a damn to me."

I must have spoken with extreme vehemence, for Balinkay regarded me first with a curious and then with a fixed look, as though from a great distance. Finally he drew his chair up closer and laid his hand on my arm.

"Look here, Hofmiller, I'm not your guardian, and it's not for me to give you a lecture. But believe a comrade who's been through the mill. It *does* matter, it matters a very great deal when you go slithering in one fell swoop from top to bottom, from your officer's horse straight into the mire ... and the man who is telling you this once sat here in this dingy little room from noon till dusk, saying exactly the same thing to himself—'it doesn't matter a damn to me'. Just before half-past eleven I reported to the Colonel for the last time. I didn't want to sit down with the others in the mess, nor did I want to walk through the streets in mufti in broad daylight, and so I took this little room—now you'll understand why I always like to have the same one—and waited here until it was dark so that no one should be able to cast an eye of pity on Balinkay as he slunk off in his shabby grey coat and a bowler hat. I stood over there at the window, that very window, and took one last look at the crowd in the street. There they were, my fellow-officers, striding along in uniform, erect and free, every one of them a little tin god, and each of them knew who he was and where he belonged. It was then that I felt for the first time that I was nothing more than a speck of dust on the face of the earth; it was as though in stripping off my uniform I had stripped off my skin. Of course, you'll be thinking it's all nonsense, one piece of cloth is blue and another is black and another grey, and it doesn't matter two hoots whether one carries a sword or an umbrella. But I still shudder when I remember how I crept off to the station, and how two Uhlans passed me at the corner and neither of them saluted. And how I carried my little trunk myself into a third-class carriage and sat among sweating peasant women and workmen. Oh, yes, I know it's all stupid and all wrong and that our so-called code of honour is all my eye—but it's in your blood after years of service and four years at the military academy. At first you feel like a man who's lost an arm or a leg or has a boil bang in the middle of his face. God forbid that you should ever have to go through all that! I wouldn't go through that evening again for all the money in the world—that evening when I slunk away and avoided every street lamp until I reached the station. And that was only the beginning."

"But, Balinkay, that's just why I want to go far away from here, where all that sort of thing doesn't exist and no one knows anything about me."

"Exactly what I told myself, Hofmiller, exactly what I thought. I just wanted to get away, and then I thought everything would be wiped out—*tabula rasa!* Better, I thought, be a boot-black or a dishwasher in America, like the big millionaires whose life-stories you read of in the newspapers. But, my dear Hofmiller, even to get to America you need a hell of a lot of money, and you've no idea what it means for the likes of us to have to kow-tow. The moment an old Uhlan no longer feels the collar with its stars round his neck, he can no longer stand squarely on his feet, still less talk as he has been used to. He sits there, tongue-tied and embarrassed even in the presence of his best friends, and when the moment comes to ask a favour, his pride chokes him. Yes, old man, I went through a good deal that I'd rather not think about—disgrace and humiliations I've never mentioned to anyone."

He got up and threw his arms wide as though he suddenly felt his coat too tight for him.

"There's no reason, by the way, why I shouldn't tell you. For I'm no longer ashamed, and I should probably only be doing you a good turn by removing your rose-coloured spectacles before it is too late."

He sat down again and drew up his chair.

"I suppose you've been told the whole story of my marvellous catch, of how I got to know my wife at the Excelsior Hotel in Cairo? I know they bandy the story about in every regiment, and no doubt would like to have it included in a book of golden deeds performed by His Imperial Majesty's officers. Well, it wasn't as marvellous as all that! There's only one thing about the story that's true, and that is that I really did meet her at the Excelsior, but *how* I met her only she and I know, and she's told no one, and neither have I. And I'm only telling *you* so that you may realize that the streets aren't paved with gold for the likes of us

... Well, to cut a long story short—when I met her at the Excelsior I was—yes, don't be shocked—I was a waiter there; yes, my dear chap, an ordinary common or garden waiter, running up and down stairs with trays. Naturally I wasn't doing it for my own amusement, but out of sheer stupidity and inexperience. I had met an Egyptian at my dingy *pension* in Vienna, and the fellow had boasted to me that his brother-in-law was the manager of the Royal Polo Club in Cairo, and that if I gave him two hundred crowns commission he could get me a job there as trainer. Breeding and a good name would get you on no end there; I had always been a first-class polo-player, and the salary he mentioned was excellent—in three years' time I should have scraped together enough to start some really decent business. Besides, Cairo was a long way off, and in polo I would be mixing with pukka sahibs. And so I agreed enthusiastically. Well, I won't bore you with the story of the dozens of doors on which I had to knock and how many embarrassed excuses I had to hear on the part of old friends before I scraped together the few hundred crowns I needed for the journey and my kit—after all, you've got to have riding-things and evening-clothes for a smart club like that, you've got to keep up appearances. Although I travelled steerage, it was a devil of a squeeze to manage it. When I got to Cairo, I had exactly seven *piastres* jingling merrily away in my pocket. When I rang the bell of the Royal Polo Club, a negro came out and goggled at me and said he didn't know Mr Efdopulos or his brother-in-law, and they didn't require a trainer, and in any case the Polo Club was being wound up. You'll have guessed by now that the Egyptian was a lousy blackguard who had swindled me, poor mug that I was, out of my two hundred crowns, and I hadn't been sufficiently on the ball to get him to show me all the letters and telegrams he said he had received. Yes, my dear Hofmiller, we're no match for such scum, and what's more, it wasn't the first time I had been hoaxed in my search for jobs. This time it was a real knock-out blow. For, my dear chap, there I was in Cairo, not knowing a soul, with the grand sum of seven *piastres* in my pocket, and it's not only a hot, but a confoundedly dear, place to be stranded in. I shall spare you the details of how I lived and what food I picked up during the first six days—it's a miracle to me myself how one gets through such an experience. Another chap, of course, would go along to the Consulate in such a case and ask to be repatriated. But there's the rub—we officers can't do that sort of thing. We can't go and sit in a waiting-room with dockers and coolies who've lost their jobs, and I couldn't have stood the sort of look the two penny-halfpenny Consul would have given me as he spelt out the name on my passport: 'Baron Balinkay'. Chaps like us would rather go to the dogs; and so you can imagine what a stroke of luck in the midst of all my bad luck it was for me to hear by chance that they needed a *sous* waiter at the Excelsior. As I had a suit of evening-clothes—a new one, what's more (I had lived for the first few days on the proceeds of my riding-kit)—and as I knew French, they condescended to give me a trial. Well, on the surface that sort of job seems quite bearable; there you stand, with gleaming shirt-front, you wait and serve at table, you cut a good figure. But to have to sleep in an attic right under the burning hot roof with two other waiters and seven million fleas and bugs, and in the morning to wash in the same tin basin as the two others, and to feel the tips scorch your hand and so on— we'll draw a veil over all that. Enough that I went through it, that I managed to survive.

"And then came the business with my wife. She had recently been left a widow and had gone to Cairo with her sister and brother-in-law. This brother-in-law was about the lowest type of fellow you can imagine, stocky, fat, podgy, impudent. Something about me got his goat. Perhaps I was too elegant for him, perhaps I didn't bow sufficiently low for Mynheer, and so one day, because I didn't bring him his breakfast to the minute, he shouted: 'You ***** lout!' . . . That sort of thing gets under your skin when you've been an officer. It had the effect on me of a jerk at the reins. I pulled up sharp and was within an inch of punching him in the face. Then at the last moment I held myself in, for in any case, don't y'know, all this business of being a waiter seemed a bit of a masquerade, and the next moment—I don't know whether you can understand me—it gave me a kind of sadistic pleasure to think that I, Balinkay, should have to put up with such an insult from a lousy cheesemonger. And so I merely stood still and just smiled faintly at him—*de haut en bas*, you know, look-ing down my nose—and the fellow went a sickly green in the face with rage, for he felt that somehow or other I was more than a match for him. Then I marched out of the room as cool as a cucumber, with an exaggerated, ironical bow, and he nearly exploded with anger. But my wife, that is to say, the lady who is now my wife, was present; she must have guessed the situation between the two of us and she realized—she admitted it to me later on—from the way in which I had drawn myself up, that no one had taken such a liberty with me before. And so she followed me into the corridor and explained that her brother-in-law was a little on edge, I mustn't take it amiss, and—well, I may as well tell you the whole truth, old chap—she even tried to slip me a bank-note to smooth things over.

"When I refused her note, she must have realized for the second time that there was something fishy about my being a waiter. And there the whole thing might have ended, for I had scraped together enough in the few weeks I'd been there to be able to get home without having to go whining to the Consul. I only went there to get some information. And then I had a stroke of luck, the sort of luck that only comes your way after you've drawn a hundred thousand blanks: the Consul happened to walk across the waiting-room, and who should he turn out to be but Elemèr von Juhácz, whom I had met God knows how many times at the Jockey Club. He seized me by both hands and immediately invited me to his club, and then, by another stroke of luck, one stroke after another—I'm only telling you all this so you can see how many strokes of luck are needed to pull chaps like us out of the mire—my present wife was there. When Elemèr introduced me as his friend, Baron Balinkay, she blushed crimson. She recognized me at once, of course, and was horri-fied at the thought of that tip. But I realized straight away what sort of person she was, what a fine, decent soul, for she didn't try to act as though she had forgotten all about it, but was quite frank and outspoken. Everything else happened in a whirl, and does not concern what I have to say. But believe me, such a sequence of accidents doesn't happen every day, and despite my money and despite my wife, for whom I thank God a thousand times over every morning and evening of my life, I shouldn't like to go through a second time what I went through then."

Impulsively I held out my hand to Balinkay.

"Thanks awfully for warning me. Now at least I have a clearer idea what's in store for me. But upon my word, I see no other way out. Don't you really know of any job for me? I'm told that you and your wife are in a big way of business."

Balinkay was silent for a moment; then he sighed sympathetically.

"Poor fellow, you must have been through it—oh, don't worry, I'm not going to cross-examine you. I can see for myself. When things have got to such a pass, persuasion and dissuasion are of no more use. One's got to hold out a helping hand, and there's no need for me to tell you I'll do my very best. There's only one thing, though, Hofmiller; you must be sensible and not get the idea into your head that I can push you up to the top of the tree straight away. That sort of thing's out of the question in a decent business; it only makes bad blood if one man is promoted over the heads of the others. You'll have to begin right at the bottom. You may even have to sit at a desk in the counting-house for a few months before we can send you out to the plantations or fit you in somewhere else. Anyway, as I have said, I'll fix up something for you. My wife and I are leaving tomorrow, and after a week or ten days in Paris we're going for a few days to Le Havre and Antwerp to have a look at our agencies. But in about three weeks we shall be home again, and I'll write to you directly we get to Rotterdam. Don't worry—I shan't forget. You can rely on old Balinkay."

"I know that," I said. "It's damned good of you."

But Balinkay must have sensed a trace of disappointment behind my words (only those who have been in a jam themselves acquire an ear for such half-tones).

"Or ... or is that too long to wait?"

"No," I faltered, "of course not, so long as I know for certain. But I would have preferred it if ... "

Balinkay reflected for a moment. "I suppose you've no time today? I mean, my wife's still in Vienna, and since the business belongs to her and not to me, the final decision rests with her."

"Oh yes—of course I'm free," I said quickly. I had suddenly remembered that the Colonel had expressed a wish not to see my face again today.

"Excellent! Splendid! In that case, the best thing would be if you came along with me in the old bus. There's room in the front next to the chauffeur. I'm afraid you can't sit at the back, for I've offered to give my old friend Baron Lajos and his better half a lift. We shall be at the Bristol by five, and I'll speak to my wife straight away, and then we'll have turned the corner. She's never yet refused when I've asked her for anything for a friend."

I gripped his hand. We went downstairs. The mechanics had already taken off their blue overalls, and the car was waiting. Two minutes later we rattled off along the high road.

Speed has at once a stimulating and a numbing effect on both the mind and the body. No sooner had the car left the streets of the town and reached the open country than a remarkable feeling of relief and release came over me. The chauffeur drove at a furious pace; the trees and telegraph poles receded as though lopped off obliquely, houses staggered into each other as in a distorting mirror, milestones sprang up white and dived out of sight before one could read the figures on them, and from the violence of the wind on my face I could tell at what a terrific pace we were going. But even greater, perhaps, was my amazement at the speed at which my own life was rushing along: what decisions had been taken in these last few hours! As a rule, until dawning purpose and final action follow on vague desire, the mind hovers, vacillates, swings back and forth between countless shades of emotion, and it is one of the most secret pleasures of the heart to try to dally with resolves before putting them into effect. Now, however, everything has descended upon me with dream-like rapidity, and just as villages and streets, trees and meadows, fell away in the wake of the throbbing car into nothingness, finally and beyond recall, so now was all that had hitherto been my daily life, the barracks, my career, my comrades, the Kekesfalvas, the *Schloss*, my rooms, the riding-school, the whole of my apparently secure and well-regulated existence, rushing away at full speed. One single hour had changed the whole of my world.

At half-past five we drew up outside the Hotel Bristol, thoroughly jolted about and covered with dust from head to foot, yet wonderfully exhilarated by having been whistled along at such a speed.

"You can't come up and meet my wife in your present condition," laughed Balinkay. "You look as though someone has emptied a sack of flour over you. And anyway, it might be better if I had a word with her alone; I can speak much more freely, and you'll have no need to feel embarrassed. I suggest you go to the cloak-room, have a thorough wash and brush up, and then go and sit in the bar. I'll come down in a few minutes and report to you. And don't worry. I'll manage things."

And I must say he didn't keep me waiting long. In five minutes he was back, smiling all over his face.

"There, what did I tell you! It's all fixed up—that is, if it suits you. You can take your time to think it over, and call it off at any time. My wife—she really is a brilliant woman—has had a brainwave as usual. Well, the idea is that you should join one of our ships, mainly to learn the necessary languages and take a look at things over in the Dutch East Indies. You'll be enrolled as assistant purser, be given a uniform, eat at the officers' table, make the round trip several times, and help with the clerical work. Then we'll fit you in somewhere, at one end or the other, whichever suits you—my wife has given me her word on it."

"Oh, thanks ... "

"No need to thank me. Naturally I would lend you a hand. But let me beg you once more, Hofmiller, don't take a step like this on the spur of the moment. As far as I'm concerned you can report for duty the day after tomorrow—in any case, I'll wire our manager to make a note of your name. But it would be better, of course, if you were to sleep on the whole thing. Personally, I'd rather see you in the regiment, but *chacun à son goût*. As I've said, if you come, you come, and if not, we won't hold it against you. Well then"—he held out his hand to me—"whether it's yes or no, however you decide, it's been a real pleasure to me to be of service. *Servus*."

I felt deeply moved as I looked at this man whom Fate had sent to my aid. In his marvellously light-hearted, casual way he had taken the heaviest part of my burden off my shoulders, the asking of favours, the hesitation, and the torturing doubt and agony attendant on the taking of momentous decisions. All that was left for me to do was to carry out one small formality—to write out and hand in my resignation. After that I should be free, saved.

The so-called "chancery double", a folded sheet of paper of prescribed dimensions and format, was perhaps the most indispensable requisite of the Austrian civil and military administration. Every request, every memorandum, every report, had to be sent in on this neatly trimmed form, which, owing to the uniqueness of its format, enabled official documents to be distinguished at a glance from private correspondence. From the millions and millions of such forms piled up in government offices it may one day be possible to glean the only reliable account of the history and misfortunes of the Habsburg monarchy. No communication is officially recognized unless it is made on this white rectangle of paper, and so my first task was to buy two such forms at the nearest tobacconist's, an envelope, and, in addition, one of those so-called "guides" which you place underneath so that the lines show through. The next thing was to go across to a café, the place in Vienna where all business, the most serious as well as the most frivolous, is transacted. In twenty minutes' time, that is to say by six o'clock, I should have my resignation written out, and I should once more belong to myself and myself alone.

I can remember with uncanny clarity, for, after all, the most important decision of my life was being taken, every detail of this upsetting procedure; the little round marble table by the window in the café in the Ringstrasse; I can remember carefully spreading out the form on my briefcase, and folding the paper over carefully with the help of a knife, so that the fold should be dead in the middle. I can still see before me, with all the definition of a photograph, the blue-black, somewhat watery ink, can feel the slight squaring of the shoulders with which I prepared to lend the first letter the correct fullness and melodramatic flourish. For I got a certain kick out of performing my last act as a soldier with ultra-correctitude; and since the contents were prescribed by formula, the only way in which I could mark the solemnity of the occasion was by writing in a particularly neat and artistic hand.

But even as I was writing the first few lines a strange dreaminess came over me. I put down my pen and began to think of what would happen tomorrow when my resignation reached the regimental office. At first, no doubt, there would be a look of bewilderment on the face of the sergeant-major, then astonished whispering among the clerks, for, after all, it was not every day that a lieutenant threw up his commission just like that. Then the document would pass through the usual official channels until it reached the Colonel himself. I could suddenly see him before me as large as life, clamping his pince-nez before his long-sighted eyes, giving a start as he read the first few words, and then in his choleric way banging his fist down on the table; the churlish old buffer was only too accustomed to seeing junior officers whom he had hauled over the coals fairly wagging their tails with joy when he gave them to understand the next day by some genial remark that the thunder-cloud had passed. This time, however, he would realize that he had come up against as tough a nut as himself, namely, little Lieutenant Hofmiller, who was not going to let himself be bullied. And when it came out later that Hofmiller had resigned his commission, twenty or thirty heads would involuntarily be jerked up in amazement. My fellow-officers would each think to himself: Well, I'm damned, there's a chap for you! He's not going to stand for that sort of thing! Confoundedly disagreeable it might be for Colonel Bubencic! In any case, no one had taken a more honourable farewell of the regiment, no one had got out of a scrape more decently, for as far back as I could remember.

I am not ashamed to confess that as I pictured all this to myself a curious feeling of self-satisfaction came over me. In all our actions vanity is, after all, one of the most powerful driving forces, and weak natures in particular succumb to the temptation to do something which, viewed superficially, makes them appear strong, courageous and resolute. For the first time in my life I had an opportunity of showing my comrades that I was someone with some self-respect, in fact no end of a fellow. Writing more and more quickly and, as I thought, more and more resolutely, I completed the twenty lines or so of my resignation, and what at first had been merely an irksome duty had suddenly become a positive pleasure.

Now for the signature—and the whole thing would be finished. A glance at the clock: half-past six. Call the waiter and pay the bill. Then once more, for the last time, parade my uniform in the Ringstrasse, and take the night train home. Hand in the scrap of paper tomorrow morning, so that my decision should be irrevocable and a new existence be ushered in.

Taking the fateful document, I folded it first lengthwise and then across, so as to stow it away carefully in my breastpocket. At this moment an unexpected thing happened.

It was like this: during that half-second when, assured, self-confident, even happy (for every task accomplished makes one happy), I pushed the somewhat bulky envelope into my breastpocket, I became aware of a crackling resistance within. Whatever is this? I thought, feeling inside the pocket. But even as I did so my fingers shrank back as though they had realized before my brain what this forgotten packet was. It was Edith's letter, her two letters, of yesterday.

I cannot accurately describe the emotion that overwhelmed me at this sudden recollection. I believe it was not so much a feeling of horror as of boundless shame; for at this moment a fog seemed to lift within me. In a flash I realized that all I had done, thought, and felt in the last few hours had been completely unreal: my rancour at having been reprimanded no less than my pride in my heroic manner of leaving the army. If I were clearing out, it was not because the Colonel had cursed me (after all, that happened to someone every week). In reality I was running away from the Kekesfalvas, from my own dishonesty, my responsibilities. I was running away because I could not bear to be loved against my will. Just as a man in the throes of a mortal illness forgets his torturing, agonizing pangs because of a chance toothache, so had I forgotten (or tried to forget) what was really tormenting me, what was turning me into a cowardly runaway, and had advanced as the motive for my resignation that trivial mishap on the parade-ground. But now I realized that this was no heroic farewell I was taking out of a sense of wounded honour. This was cowardly, contemptible flight.

But there is a certain finality about any act once it is carried out, and now that I had written my letter of resignation I did not want to go back on it. What the devil does it matter to me, I said angrily to myself, if she's waiting and whining? They've worried me quite enough, upset me quite enough. What does it matter to me if some strange woman is in love with me? With all her millions she'll soon find someone else, and if she doesn't it's not my business. It's quite bad enough that I should have to chuck up everything, throw up my commission. What concern of mine is all this hysterical speculation as to whether she's going to get well or not? Damn it, I'm not a doctor!

But at this significant word *doctor* my thoughts stopped dead, just as a furiously whirling machine comes to a halt at a given signal. At that word doctor the thought of Condor came into my mind. It's his business, his affair, I said to myself. He's paid to cure the sick. She's *his* patient, not mine. He must reap what he has sown. The best thing will be to go straight to him and tell him that I am washing my hands of the whole business.

I glanced up at the clock. A quarter to seven, and my train didn't leave till after ten. Plenty of time, then. I shouldn't need to say very much; simply that I personally had finished with the whole thing. But where did he live? Hadn't he given me his address, or had I forgotten it? But surely, as a doctor, he must be in the telephone directory. I flew across the road to a telephone booth and hurriedly turned over the pages. Be ... Bi ... Bu ... Ca ... Co ... there they all were, the Condors: Condor Anton, general dealer ... Condor Dr Emmerich, general practitioner, Vienna VIII, Florianigasse 97, and no other doctor on the whole page—that must be he. As I ran out I repeated the address twice, three times, to myself—I hadn't a pencil on me, I had forgotten everything in my tearing haste—shouted it to the driver of the nearest cab, and while it bowled off smoothly and rapidly on its rubber-tyred wheels, I worked out my plan. The great thing was to be brief, to come straight to the point. On no account must I behave as though my mind were not entirely made up. I must not let him suspect for a moment that I was decamping because of the Kekesfalvas, but simply refer to my resignation from the start as a *fait accompli*. The whole thing had been planned months ago, I should say, but this excellent job in Holland had only just turned up. If, nevertheless, he went on cross-examining me, I must hedge and say nothing further. After all, had he been entirely frank with me? I must put a stop to all this business of eternally considering other people.

The cab drew up. Had the driver made a mistake or had I in my haste given the wrong address? Could Condor really live in such a poor district? He must get colossal fees from the Kekesfalvas alone, and no doctor of standing would live in such a slum. But no, he really did live there, for there in the entrance hall was his name-plate: *Dr Emmerich Condor. Second court, third floor. Hours of consultation 2 to 4 p.m.* Two to four—and now it was getting on for seven. All the same, he'd have to see me. Quickly paying off the cabman, I crossed the ill-paved courtyard. What a dingy staircase it was—worn stairs, peeling walls scribbled all over, a smell of cheap food from the kitchens, the stench of half-open lavatories, women in grubby dressing-gowns who stood gossiping in the corridors and cast suspicious glances at the cavalry officer who went clanking past somewhat sheepishly in the dusk.

At last I reached the third floor, where there was another corridor with doors to right and left and one in the middle. I was about to feel in my pocket for a match, so that I could see which was the right door, when a somewhat slatternly maid came out of the door to the left, an empty jug in her hand. Probably she was on her way to fetch some beer for the evening meal. I asked for Dr Condor.

"Yes, 'e live 'ere," she said, in the broken accents of a Czech, "but 'e not 'ome yet. 'E go to Meidling, 'e come back soon. 'E tell the mistress 'e come back for supper. You come in and wait."

Before I had had time to reflect, she had ushered me into the hall.

"You put your things there"—she pointed to an old wardrobe of cheap wood, the only piece of furniture in the dark little hall. Then she opened the door of the waiting-room, which was somewhat more imposing; at any rate there were four or five armchairs round the table, and the wall on the left was lined with books.

"You sit there," she said, pointing with a certain condescension to one of the chairs. And I now realized that Condor must have a working-class practice; rich patients were received very differently from this. A rum fellow, I thought, a very rum fellow. He could make pots of money, if he wanted to, out of the Kekesfalvas alone.

Well, I waited. Waited in a state of nerves as you always do in a doctor's waiting-room. Without really wanting to read, you keep turning over the pages of well-thumbed, long since out-of-date periodicals, so as to conceal your uneasiness under an appearance of being absorbed. You keep getting up and sitting down again and looking up at the clock, which ticks away in the corner with its sleepy pendulum—twelve minutes past, fourteen minutes past, a quarter past, sixteen minutes past seven—and staring as though hypnotised at the door of the consulting-room.

At last—twenty minutes past—I could no longer contain myself; I had already warmed the seats of two chairs. I got up and went to the window. Down below in the courtyard an old man with a limp, evidently a porter, was oiling the wheels of a hand-cart; behind the lighted windows of a kitchen a woman was ironing, in another a woman was bathing her child in a tub. Somewhere, I could not make out on which storey it was, either just above me or just below me, someone was practising scales, the same thing over and over again. Again I glanced at the clock—twenty-five past seven, half-past seven. Why didn't he come? I couldn't, I wouldn't, wait any longer. I could feel this waiting sapping my resolution, throwing me into a state of confusion.

At last I heaved a sigh of relief, for a door banged in the next room. I immediately drew myself up. Put a bold face on things and behave easily in front of him, I kept urging myself. Tell him quite nonchalantly that you have just called on him, in passing, to say goodbye and to ask him, incidentally, if he will pay a visit to Kekesfalva in the next few days and, if they should be suspicious, explain to them that you have had to go to Holland and leave the service. Good God Almighty, confound it all, why was he keeping me waiting like this? I could distinctly hear a chair being drawn up in the next room. Had that silly trollop of a maid forgotten to announce me?

I was just about to go out and remind her of my presence when I suddenly faltered, for the person who was walking about next

door could not be Condor. I knew his step. I knew exactly—
from that night when I had walked to the station with him—how
he stumped along, short of leg and short of breath, in his squeaking shoes, whereas those footsteps in the next room, that kept
approaching and receding, were quite different, more hesitating,
more uncertain, more dragging steps. I don't know why I listened in such agitation, with such inner intentness, to those
strange footsteps. But it seemed to me as though the person in
the next room were listening just as uneasily and anxiously as I
was. Suddenly I heard a faint rustling at the door, as though
someone were turning, or toying with, the handle; and lo! it
moved. The thin brass bar moved visibly in the twilight, and the
door opened just perceptibly. Perhaps it's only the draught, the
wind, I told myself, for no normal person, unless it be a burglar
in the night, opens a door so stealthily. But no, the crack widened.
A hand must have been pushing the door very cautiously, and
now, even in the darkness, I could make out a human shadow.
Spellbound, I stared at it. Then through the crack a woman's
voice asked timidly:

"Is ... is anyone there?"

The answer died on my lips. I knew at once that only a blind
person would talk in that way. Only the blind walked and shuffled
and felt their way about so quietly, only the blind spoke in such
uncertain tones. And in a flash I remembered. Had not Kekesfalva
mentioned that Condor had married a blind woman? It must be
she, it could only be she, this woman who stood there behind the
crack of the door and questioned, and yet could not see me. I
stared hard in the effort to take in her shadow in the darkness,
and at last I distinguished a thin woman in a flowing dressing-
gown, with grey, somewhat untidy hair.

Good God, could this unattractive, plain woman be his wife!
Horrible to feel oneself being stared at by those sightless orbs
and to know that one was not seen. At the same time I could tell
from the way in which she craned her neck to listen that she was
straining all her senses to form a picture of the stranger in this
room which it was beyond her power to take in. The effort contorted her heavy, large mouth so that it was more unlovely than
ever.

For a moment I remained silent. Then I stood up and bowed—yes, bowed, although it was quite pointless to bow to a blind person.

"I ... I'm waiting for Dr Condor," I stammered.

She had now opened the door to its full extent. With her left hand she continued to hold on to the handle, as though seeking support in the darkness which enveloped her. Then she groped her way forward, her brows drawn more tautly over the sightless eyes.

"It's long past consulting hours," she rapped out at me in another, a harsh voice. "When my husband comes home he must have a meal and rest. Can't you come tomorrow?"

At every word her features grew more and more restless. I could tell that she was scarcely able to control herself. A hysteric, I thought at once. I mustn't provoke her. And so I murmured—stupidly bowing once more into empty space:

"Forgive me ... naturally I have no intention of consulting your husband professionally at this late hour. I merely wanted to tell him something ... concerning one of his patients."

"His patients? Always his patients!" The exasperation in her tone verged on the tearful. "He was called out last night at half-past two, and at seven o'clock this morning he was out again, and ever since his consulting hours he's not been back again. He'll be ill himself if he's given no peace. But I'll have no more of it. Consulting hours are over for today, I tell you. They're over at four. You can leave a note for him, or, if it's urgent, go to another doctor. There are doctors enough in this town, four in every street."

She groped her way nearer, and with a feeling of guilt I shrank back at the sight of the angry face, in which the wide-open eyes suddenly gleamed like glowing white marbles.

"Go away, I tell you! Go away! let him eat and sleep like other people. Take your claws out of him, all of you! In the middle of the night, early in the morning, the whole day long, patient after patient. He's expected to wear himself out, and all for nothing. Just because you all realize that he's weak, you cling to him and to him only ... oh, you're a pack of brutes! You think of nothing but *your* troubles, *your* illnesses. But I won't stand it, I won't allow it. Go away, I tell you, go away at once! Leave him in peace, let him have one hour to himself in the evening!"

She had groped her way to the table. By some instinct she must have found out more or less where I was standing, for her eyes stared straight at me as though they could see me. There was so much genuine and at the same time so much irrational desperation in her anger that I could not help feeling ashamed.

"Why, certainly, *gnädige Frau*," I said apologetically, "I perfectly understand that the *Herr Doktor* must have a little peace ... I won't trouble you any further. Will you allow me just to leave a note, or perhaps to ring up in half an hour's time?"

"No," she shouted at me in desperation. "No, no, no! You mustn't ring up. The telephone rings the whole day long, everyone wants something of him, asks this and complains of that. No sooner has he taken a bite of food than he has to jump up. Come tomorrow during consulting hours, I tell you. It can't be as urgent as all that. He must have a little time to himself sometimes. Now be off! Be off, I tell you!"

Feeling and groping her way uncertainly, the blind woman came at me with clenched fists. It was horrible. I felt that she was about to seize me with her outstretched hands. But at that moment the hall door clicked and banged to. That must be Condor. She listened, she started. Immediately her face changed. She began to tremble from head to foot, and the hands, clenched but the instant before, were now clasped imploringly.

"Don't keep him now," she whispered. "Don't say anything to him. He's sure to be tired, he's been on his feet the whole day ... Please have some consideration. Do have pity ... "

The door opened and Condor entered the room.

He obviously took in the situation at a glance, but not for a moment did he lose his composure.

"Ah, I see you've been entertaining the *Herr Leutnant*," he said in the hearty manner which, I had come to realize, he assumed to conceal violent emotion. "How sweet of you, Klara!"

He went up to the blind woman and tenderly stroked her grey, rumpled hair. At his touch her whole expression changed. The anxiety that had distorted her large, heavy mouth was conjured away at this tender caress, and with a helpless, shamefaced,

positively coy smile she turned to him; her somewhat protuber-
ant forehead gleamed clear and bright in the electric light. It was
breathtaking, this expression of sudden calm and assurance after
the outburst of violence. Apparently she had completely forgotten
my presence in the joy of feeling him near her. Her hand,
attracted as though by a magnet, groped towards him through
empty space, and when her gently exploring fingers found his
coat, they kept stroking his arm, up and down, up and down.
Realizing that her whole body was yearning for him, he went
nearer, and now she leaned against him, relaxing her limbs as
though utterly exhausted. Smilingly he put his arm round her
shoulders and repeated, without looking at me:

"How sweet of you, Klara!" And even his voice seemed like a
caress.

"Forgive me," she said, obviously anxious to excuse herself,
"but I had to explain to the gentleman that you must have a
meal first; you must be dreadfully hungry. Rushing about the
whole day long, and while you were away there've been at least
a dozen telephone calls for you ... Forgive me for telling the
gentleman he'd much better come tomorrow, but ... "

"This time, my child," he laughed, stroking her hair again (I
realized that he was doing this so that she should not be hurt by
his laugh), "you were wrong to put the gentleman off. Lieutenant
Hofmiller is, I'm glad to say, not a patient, but a friend who has
long promised to look me up when in town. He can only get off
in the evenings, for he's on duty all day. And now the main thing
is: have you anything nice to give us for supper?"

The anxious, drawn look came back into her face, and I could
tell from the way in which she involuntarily started that she
wanted to be alone with the husband who had been so long
away.

"Oh, no, thank you," I hastened to say. "I must go soon. I
mustn't miss the night express. I really only came to bring you
greetings from the Kekesfalvas, and that'll only take a minute or
two."

"Is everything all right out there?" asked Condor, gazing
searchingly into my eyes. And he must somehow have realized
that something was not quite right, for he quickly added: "Now

269

listen, my friend, my wife always knows how things are with me, usually better than I do myself. I must confess I am ravenously hungry, and until I've had something to eat and have lit a cigar I'm no use to anyone. If you don't mind, Klara, we two will go and have some supper and let the *Herr Leutnant* wait a little. I'll give him a book to read or he can have a rest—you've probably had a heavy day," he said, turning to me. "When I've got to the cigar stage I'll come back to you, in dressing-gown and slippers if you've no objection—you won't expect me to dress formally, will you, *Herr Leutnant*?"

"And I'll really only keep him ten minutes, *gnädige Frau*. I shall have to rush off to the station then."

At this her face lit up again. She turned to me almost cordially.

"What a pity you won't have supper with us, *Herr Leutnant*! But I hope you'll come another time."

She stretched out her hand towards me, a delicate, slender, somewhat faded and wrinkled hand, and I kissed it respectfully. And with a genuine feeling of reverence I watched Condor cautiously steering the blind woman towards the door, skilfully preventing her from knocking into anything either to left or right; it was as though he were holding something infinitely fragile and precious in his hands.

For two or three minutes the door remained open, and I could hear the shuffling steps recede. Then Condor came back again. There was quite a different expression on his face; that alert, keen expression which I had noticed on his face at moments of mental tension. He had obviously realized that I had not turned up at his house so unceremoniously without some pressing reason.

"I'll be back in twenty minutes. Then we can talk the whole thing over quickly. I suggest that in the meanwhile you lie down on the sofa or make yourself comfortable in this arm-chair. I don't like the look of you, my boy. You look frightfully fagged out. And we must both be fresh and clear-headed."

And quickly changing his voice he added loudly, so that he was audible in the room across the passage:

"Yes, my dear Klara, I'm just coming. I was just giving the *Herr Leutnant* a book to read, so that he shouldn't be bored."

Condor's trained eye had not deceived him. It was not until I mentioned it that I myself realized how horribly exhausted I was after my disturbed night and all the excitements of the day. Following his advice—I felt myself completely under his sway— I stretched myself out in the big armchair in his consulting-room, my head thrown back into its depths, my hand resting slackly on the padded arms. During my uneasy period of waiting night must have fallen; I could make out scarcely anything around me but the silver gleam of the instruments in the tall glass cupboard, and the alcove where I was sitting was a vault of pitch-black darkness. Involuntarily I closed my eyes, and immediately there appeared before them, as though projected by a magic lantern, the face of the blind woman; I beheld once more that unforgettable transition from dismay to sudden rapture as Condor's hand touched her, as his arm was thrown round her. What a wonderful doctor! I thought. If only he could help me like that! I felt dimly that I was trying to think of someone else, someone who had been just as uneasy and distracted and had had the same worried gaze, to think of a certain definite thing which had been the cause of my coming here. But try as I would I could not.

Suddenly I felt a hand on my shoulder. Condor must have entered the pitch-dark room with the lightest of steps, or perhaps I had really fallen asleep. I was about to get up, but he pushed me down gently, yet vigorously, by the shoulders.

"Stay where you are. I'll come and sit by you. It's easier to talk in the dark. I only beg one thing of you—speak softly. Very softly. In some magical way, you know, the hearing of blind people often becomes more acute, and they acquire, too, a mysterious instinct for putting two and two together. Well then,"—and his hand brushed my arm hypnotically from the shoulder down-wards—"tell me all about it, and don't be shy. I saw at once that something was the matter with you."

Odd—at that moment a memory suddenly came back to me. At the cadet school I had had a friend, Erwin he was called, frail and fair as a girl; I believe that I was even, unwittingly, a little in love with him. In the daytime we hardly spoke to one another, or else talked merely of casual things; we were probably both ashamed of our secret and unconfessed fondness for each other. Only at night, in the dormitory, when the lights were turned out, did we sometimes pluck up courage. Propping ourselves up on our elbows in our adjoining beds, we spoke to each other in the all-protecting darkness, whilst the others were asleep, of our childish thoughts and dreams, only to fight shy of each other again the next morning and display the same inevitable embarrassment. For years and years I had not thought of those whispered confessions, which had been the secret delight of my boyhood years. But now, as I lay stretched out in the sheltering darkness, I completely forgot my resolve to dissimulate before Condor. Without wishing to be so, I was completely frank; and just as in those far-off days in the cadet school I had told my friend of all the little vexations, the wild, fantastic dreams of childhood, so now did I tell Condor—and it gave me a secret thrill to do so—of Edith's unexpected outburst, of my dismay, my fear, my distraction. I told him everything in the silent darkness, in which nothing stirred but the lenses of his pince-nez, which, when from time to time he moved his head, flashed out indistinctly.

Then a silence ensued, and after the silence I heard a queer sound. Condor had obviously pressed his fingers so hard against each other that the joints cracked.

"So that was it!" he growled in a tone of self-dissatisfaction. "And to think I was fool enough not to see it all. It's always the same—you cease to see the patient for the illness. What with all this careful examining and exploring of the symptoms, the essential feature of the situation, what's going on inside the patient, eludes you. That is to say—I felt at once that something was the matter with the girl. You remember how after my examination of her the other day I asked the old man whether another doctor had not been called in—I was quite nonplussed by that sudden, feverish desire to be well all in a moment. I had guessed quite rightly that some stranger had been meddling in the case. But, dunderhead that I am, I thought only of a quack or a hypnotist; I imagined that her head had been turned by some sort of hocus-pocus. But I never thought of the most simple, the logical, explanation, the one that was staring me in the face. The girl's at the very age for falling in love. The pity of it is that it should have to

272

happen just at this moment, and with such violence. Oh God, the poor, poor child!"

He had risen, and I could hear him taking short, sharp steps up and down the room.

"Dreadful!" he sighed. "To think that this tiresome business should happen just now when we have fixed up the trip to the Engadine. And the devil of it is that no power on earth can put back the clock—now that she has persuaded herself that she must get well for you and not for herself. It'll be terrible when the reaction sets in. Now that her hopes and expectations are placed so high, she won't be satisfied with a modicum of improvement, a slight advance in her condition. My God, what a terrible responsibility we have taken upon ourselves!"

A feeling of rebellion suddenly assailed me. I was furious at being dragged into the affair. After all, I'd come here to free myself.

"I'm entirely of your opinion," I broke in resolutely. "The consequences are unpredictable. We must put a stop to this madness in good time. You'll have to be firm. You'll have to tell her ... "

"Tell her what?"

"Why ... that this infatuation is mere childish nonsense. You must talk her out of it."

"Talk her out of it? Talk her out of what? Talk a woman out of being in love? Tell her she ought not to feel as she does feel? Not to love when she does love? That would be about the worst thing one could possibly do, and the stupidest into the bargain. Have you ever heard of logic prevailing against passion? Of anyone's being able to say to a fever: 'Fever, cease raging!', or to a fire, 'Fire, stop burning!' A fine, a really kindly thought, to shout at an invalid, a cripple: 'For heaven's sake don't get it into your head that you can be allowed love like other people! It's presumptuous of you, a cripple, to show feeling, to expect people to show feeling for you—it's for you to lie low. Go and stand in the corner. Give up, renounce, all thought of love!' That, apparently, is what you want me to tell the poor girl. But have the goodness to consider the glorious effect of such a step!"

"But it is you who must."

"Why me? You expressly took all the responsibility on yourself. Why should I now assume it?"

"Well, I simply can't tell her myself that ... "

"Nor *should* you. Nor *must* you. First drive her mad, and then expect her at one fell swoop to come to her senses ... that would be the last straw! It goes without saying that you must not by word or sign let the poor child suspect that you find her fondness for you distasteful—that would be tantamount to—striking her down with a hatchet."

"But ... "—my voice failed me—"someone's got to make her see ... "

"See what? Do you mind expressing yourself more precisely."

"I mean ... that ... that it's quite hopeless ... quite absurd ... so that she won't ... if I ... if I ... "

I faltered. Condor too was silent. He was evidently waiting for me to go on. Then, quite unexpectedly, he took two vigorous strides to the door and put his hand on the electric light switch. Harsh and pitiless—the shrill blaze forced me to close my eyes—three white flames sprang to life in the bulbs, and the room was bright as day.

"Aha!" exlaimed Condor. "Now we have it, *Herr Leutnant*! I can see now that it doesn't do to make you too comfortable. It's too easy to hide away under cover of the darkness, and in certain cases it's better for people to look each other straight in the eye. Let's have no more of this dithering, *Herr Leutnant*—there's something wrong here. You're not going to persuade me you came here merely to show me this letter. There's something else behind all this. I can tell that you've got some definite plan. Either come out with it honestly or I shall have to ask you to take your departure."

His pince-nez flashed at me; I was afraid of the gleaming lenses, and lowered my eyes.

"It doesn't impress me very favourably, this silence of yours, *Herr Leutnant*. It doesn't exactly point to a clear conscience. But I have a shrewd idea what's in the wind. No evasions, if you please. Is it your intention, because of this letter ... or the other, to break off your so-called friendship?"

He waited. I did not raise my eyes. His voice took on the challenging tone of an inquisitor.

"Do you realize what you would be doing if you suddenly beat a retreat? Now that you've turned the girl's head with your precious pity?"

I was silent.

"Well, in that case I will venture to give my personal opinion of such behaviour. Running away like that would be a pitiable act of cowardice ... Oh come on, let's cut out all that military stuff! Let's leave an officer's code of honour out of it! There's more at stake here than all that mumbo-jumbo. The happiness of a young, living, valuable human being is at stake, of someone, what is more, for whom I am responsible. In such circumstances I am in no mind to be polite. In any case, so that you may be under no misapprehension as to what you will be taking on your conscience if you make off now, let me tell you quite bluntly: for you to decamp now at this critical moment— please don't turn away—would be a dastardly crime against an innocent creature, and I fear even more than that—it would be murder!"

Clenching his fists like a boxer, the portly little man advanced upon me. He might perhaps in other circumstances have presented a ridiculous appearance in his woolly dressing-gown and sloppy slippers, but there was something majestic about his genuine indignation as he shouted at me again:

"It would be murder, murder! Yes, murder, I tell you, and you know it! Do you imagine that that hypersensitive, proud creature could bear to go on living if, the first time she opened her heart to a man, the gallant fellow responded by running away in a panic as though he had caught a glimpse of the devil? A little more imagination, if you please! Didn't you read her letter, or have you no heart at all? Even a normal, healthy woman would be unable to stand such a slight. A blow like that would upset even *her* balance for years. And this girl, who is only kept going by the vain hope of a cure which you have dangled before her eyes—this hapless, forlorn creature, do you think she'd ever get over it? If the shock itself didn't do for her, she would do away with herself. Yes, that is what she'll do, a creature in her desperate state won't endure such a humiliation—I'm convinced she won't get over such brutal treatment, and you, *Herr Leutnant*, know that as well as I do. And because you know it, to run away now would

275

be not only an act of weakness and cowardice, but vile, wilful murder."

Involuntarily I retreated still further. At the moment when he had uttered the word "murder" I had seen everything in a lightning vision: seen the balustrade on the terrace of the tower and the poor girl clutching at it with both hands; seen myself seizing her and pulling her back just in time. I knew that Condor was not exaggerating; that was exactly what she would do, hurl herself down—I could see the paving-stones far below, could see everything at that moment as though it were really happening, as though it had already happened, and there was a roaring in my ears as though I myself were plunging down those five storeys into the depths below.

"Well? Can you deny it?" Condor went on persistently. "Let us see something of that courage which you profess as a soldier!"

"But, *Herr Doktor* ... what am I to do? ... I can't be forced ... can't say something I don't mean ... How could I possibly manage to behave as though I encouraged her crazy delusion? ... No, I can't bear it, I can't bear it!" I burst out. "I can't, I won't and I can't!"

I must have shouted at the top of my voice, for I felt Condor seize my arm in an iron grip.

"Quietly, for heaven's sake!" He sprang to the switch and turned the light off again. Only the lamp on the desk shed a dim cone of light from beneath its yellowish shade.

"Damnation take it! One's got to treat you like a patient. There—sit down quietly; far more serious matters have been discussed in that chair."

He came closer to me.

"Now don't work yourself up, and please—quietly, slowly, one thing at a time. First of all: here are you groaning, 'I can't bear it!' But that doesn't tell me enough. I must know what it is you can't bear? What is it you find so horrifying about the fact that this poor child has fallen head over heels in love with you?"

I drew a deep breath and made ready to answer, but Condor quickly went on:

"Don't be in a hurry. And above all, don't be ashamed. I can understand a man's being horrified when a passionate declaration of love is sprung on him. Only a numskull is pleased at being a so-called 'success' with women, only a dunderhead is puffed up by it. A real man is much more likely to be dismayed at realizing that a woman has lost her heart to him when he can't reciprocate her feelings. I can understand all that. But since you're so exceptionally, so very exceptionally upset, I am bound to ask whether there is not some special factor at work in your case—I mean the special circumstances?"

"What circumstances?"

"Well ... the fact that Edith ... it's difficult to put such things into words ... I mean ... does her ... her deformity inspire you with a certain repugnance ... a feeling of physical disgust?"

"No ... absolutely not," I protested vehemently. Had it not been her very helplessness, her defencelessness, that had so irresistibly attracted me to her? And if at certain moments I had felt for her an emotion that in some mysterious way bordered on the tenderness of a lover, it had only been because her suffering, her forlorn and crippled state had so moved me. "No, never !" I repeated in tones of almost indignant conviction. "How can you think such a thing!"

"So much the better. That reassures me to some extent. As a doctor, you see, one has plenty of opportunity of observing such psychological inhibitions in the case of apparently completely normal people. I must admit I have never been able to understand those men in whom the slightest physical abnormality in a woman produces a kind of pathological aversion, but there *are* a great many men for whom the slightest aberration in a single one of the millions and millions of cells that go to make up a body, a human being, immediately excludes all possibility of a sexual relationship. Unfortunately such aversions, like all the instincts, can never be got over—and that is why I am doubly glad to hear that in your case it is not the fact of her lameness in itself that repels you. In that case, to be sure, I can only assume that ... may I speak frankly?"

"Why, of course."

"That your feeling of horror was not aroused by the fact itself, but the thought of the consequences ... I mean, that it is not so much that you are appalled at this poor child's falling in love with you as that you're afraid that other people may hear of it and sneer ... In my opinion your exaggerated distress is nothing but a kind of fear—if I may say so—of appearing ridiculous in the eyes of others, of your fellow-officers."

I felt as though Condor had stabbed me to the heart with one of his fine, sharp needles. For I had long since subconsciously felt what he was now saying, but had not allowed myself to think it. From the very first I had been afraid lest my fellow-officers might jeer at my strange relationship with the crippled girl, and indulge in that good-humoured and yet devastating *badinage* for which Austrians are famous. I knew only too well how they ridiculed anyone whom they had once come upon in the company of ugly and unpresentable women. It was for that reason alone that I had instinctively drawn a dividing line in my life between the one world and the other, that of the regiment and that of the Kekesfalvas. Condor had conjectured aright; the moment I had become aware of her passion, I had felt ashamed chiefly on account of what other people would think—her father, Ilona, Josef, my fellow-officers—had even felt ashamed before myself of my disastrous feelings of pity.

At this point I felt Condor's magnetic touch on my knee.

"No, don't be ashamed. If anyone can understand a man's fear of his fellow-men the moment their preconceived ideas are flouted, I can. You've seen my wife, haven't you? No one could understand why I married her. Everything in life that deviates from the straight and, so to speak, normal line makes people first curious and then indignant. It immediately got about among my colleagues that I had bungled my treatment of her and had only married her out of panic. My so-called friends, on the other hand, spread it abroad that she had a lot of money or was expecting a legacy. My mother, my own mother, refused for two years to receive her, for she had had another match in mind for me, a marriage to the daughter of a professor—one of the most famous specialists of the day—and had I married her, I should within three weeks have got a lectureship in the university, have become a professor, and have sat pretty for the rest of my life. But I knew that my wife would go under completely if I left her in the lurch. She believed in me, me alone, and had I taken her faith from her, she would have been incapable of going on living.

I may as well confess to you that I have never regretted my choice, for, believe me, a doctor, of all people, seldom has a clear conscience. One knows how little one can really do to help; as an individual one can't cope with the infinite wretchedness that exists all around us in the world. One merely bales a few drops out of the unfathomable ocean of misery with a thimble, and those whom one imagines one has cured today have a new malady tomorrow. One always has a feeling of having been remiss, negligent, and then there are the mistakes, the professional mistakes, that one inevitably makes—and so it's always good to know that one has saved at least *one* person, kept faith with *one* person, made a good job of *one* thing. One must know, after all, whether one has lived a dull, useless existence, or lived to some purpose. Believe me"—and I was suddenly conscious of the warmth and tenderness that seemed to emanate from him—"it's worth while taking a hard task upon oneself if thereby one makes life easier for another person."

The deep, vibrant tone in his voice moved me. I felt a faint burning in my breast, that familiar pressure, as though the heart were expanding or being distended; I could feel the pity welling up within me once more at the thought of the desperate plight of the unfortunate child. In a moment, I knew, that turbulent emotion against which I was powerless would surge up within me. But—don't give in, I said to myself. Don't let yourself be caught up in it, be dragged back into it again. And so I looked up resolutely.

"*Herr Doktor*, every man knows to some extent the limits of his own strength. I must therefore warn you not to count on me. It rests with you and not with me to help Edith now. I have already gone much further in this matter than I originally intended, and I tell you frankly—I am not so ... so good, so self-sacrificing as you think. I have reached the end of my strength. I cannot stand being adored, being idolized, cannot endure having to behave as though I desired or tolerated it. It's better that you should understand the situation now than be disappointed later on. I give you my word of honour as a soldier that I am absolutely sincere when I warn you not to count on me, not to over-estimate me."

I must have expressed myself very firmly, for Condor gave me a somewhat baffled look.

279

"That sounds almost as though you had made up your mind to some definite course of action."

He suddenly got up.

"The whole truth, if you please, and not half of it! Have you already taken some ... irrevocable step?"

I too stood up.

"Yes," I said, pulling my resignation from my pocket. "Here. Please read it for yourself."

Hesitatingly Condor took the document, throwing me an uneasy look before going over to the tiny circle of lamplight. He read it slowly, and in silence. Then he folded it up and said quite calmly, in perfectly matter-of-fact tones:

"I take it that after what I have said to you you are fully aware of the consequences. We have just decided that the effect on the child of your running away would be murder—or would lead to suicide ... and you are, I assume, quite clear as to the fact that your ... your flight involves not only your resignation but a sentence of death on the poor child."

I did not answer.

"I have addressed a question to you, *Herr Leutnant*. And I repeat that question: Are you aware of the inevitable consequences? Will you take full responsibility upon your conscience?"

Again I was silent. He came nearer, the folded document in his hand, and handed it back to me.

"There you are. I wash my hands of the whole thing. There— take it!"

But my arm was paralysed. I had not the strength to lift it, and I had not the courage to withstand his searching gaze.

"Then you do not propose ... to proceed with this death sentence?"

I turned away, and put my hands behind my back. He understood.

"Then I may tear it up?"

"Yes," I replied, "please do."

He went back to the desk. Without looking up, I could hear the paper being torn sharply across, once, twice, a third time, could hear the rustle as the torn fragments fell into the waste-paper basket. In some strange way I felt a sense of relief. Again—

for the second time on this fateful day—a decision had been taken on my behalf. I had not had to take it myself.

Condor came up to me and urged me gently back into the armchair.

"There—I think we have prevented a great tragedy ... a very great tragedy. And now to business. I have, I hope, to some extent learned to know you over this affair—no, don't protest. I don't over-estimate you, or by any means look upon you as a 'wonderful and good person', as Kekesfalva so eulogistically refers to you, but as one who, because of the instability of his emotions, because of a certain impatience of the heart, is a thoroughly unreliable colleague. Glad as I am to have put a stop to your senseless project, I am not at all pleased by the hasty way in which you take decisions and are then deflected from your purpose. People who are so much at the mercy of their moods should never be given serious responsibilities. You would be the last person to whom I should entrust a task that required perseverance and unwavering resolution.

"So listen, I'm not going to ask much of you. Merely the most essential, the absolutely essential thing. We have persuaded Edith to try a new treatment—or rather one that she thinks is new. For your sake she has decided to go away, to go away for months, and, as you know, they're leaving in a week's time. Well, for that one week I need your help, and to relieve your mind I'll tell you straight away, for that one week only. I ask no more of you than that you should promise me not to do anything precipitate during this week before their departure, not to betray by word or gesture that the poor child's infatuation is a nuisance to you. For the moment I shall ask nothing more of you, and I think it is the very least one can ask: one week of self-control when the life of a human being is at stake."

"Yes ... but what about afterwards?"

"We won't think of that for the moment. When I have to perform an operation for the removal of a tumour, I daren't waste time in asking whether it will not come back in a month or two. When I am called in to help, there is only one thing it is my duty to do: to act, without hesitation. That's the only right course in every case, because it's the only humane course. Everything else is in the hands of Providence or, as more pious people would put it, of God. Anything can happen in the space of a few months. Perhaps her condition really *will* improve more rapidly than I thought, perhaps her passion for you will die down—I can't foresee all the possibilities, nor must you try to do so. Concentrate all your energy on not betraying to her during this decisive period that you find her love for you so irksome. Keep on saying to yourself: a week, six days, five days, and I shall save a human being; I will not wound, offend, upset, discourage that human being. A week of bearing up manfully and resolutely—do you really think you can't manage that?'

"Oh yes, I could," I said spontaneously. And added even more resolutely: "Certainly! Certainly I could!" From the moment I knew that there was a limit to what was expected of me I felt a kind of fresh strength.

I heard Condor breathing heavily.

"Thank God for that! Now I can tell you how worried I was. Believe me, Edith would never have got over it if, in reply to her confession of love, you had taken to your heels. It is the next few days that are so important. The rest will work itself out later. Let us give the child a few days' happiness to start with—a week of unsuspecting happiness. You'll vouch for this one week, won't you?"

For reply I held out my hand.

"Well, then, I think everything's settled, and we can now join my wife."

But he did not get up. I could tell that he was troubled by a doubt.

"One more thing," he added in a low voice. "We doctors are always compelled to bear in mind even the unforeseen, we must be prepared for all eventualities. If by any chance—I am stating a hypothetical case—something should occur in the meantime—I mean, should your strength give out or Edith's suspicions lead to some crisis, you must let me know at once. Not at any price must anything irrevocable happen during this short but critical period; on no account must she have a sudden shock. The slightest thing might be fatal. If you should not feel equal to your task, or if during this week you unwittingly give yourself away, don't be ashamed—for heaven's sake don't be ashamed to tell me. I've seen enough <u>naked bodies and broken spirits</u>. You can call on me or ring me up at any time of the day or night; I shall always be ready to come to your aid, for I know what's at stake. And now"—the chair beside me creaked and I realized that Condor was getting up—"we had better go across to the other room. We have been talking for rather a long time, and my wife easily gets disquieted. Even I, after all these years, have still to be on my guard against upsetting her. Those whom Fate has dealt hard knocks remain vulnerable for ever afterwards."

Again he strode across to the switch, and the light blazed forth. As he now turned to me his face looked different; perhaps it was only the glare that made its contours stand out, but at any rate I noticed for the first time the deep furrows on his forehead, realized from the whole bearing of the man how tired, how exhausted he was. He is always giving of himself to other people, I thought. All at once my desire to run away the moment I came up against disagreeable realities seemed to me despicable, and I looked at him with grateful emotion.

He seemed to notice it, and he smiled.

"How splendid," he said, patting me on the shoulder, "that you came to me and we have been able to talk the matter over. Just think what would have happened had you simply run away from the problem without reflecting! It would have been on your mind for the rest of your life, for one can run away from anything except oneself. And now let us go into the other room. Come—my dear friend."

The warmth in his voice as he called me "my dear friend" moved me profoundly. He knew how weak, how cowardly I had been, and yet he did not despise me. He was an older man, a man of experience, I a mere youngster, a blundering beginner, and with those words he gave me back my confidence. A load fell from my mind, and I followed him with a light heart.

We crossed the waiting-room, and Condor opened the door leading to the room beyond. His wife sat knitting at the table, which had not yet been cleared. Nothing would have led one to suspect as she worked away busily that the hands which plied the needles so nimbly were those of a blind woman; the little basket containing her wool and the scissors were arranged neatly by her side. Only when she raised her vacant pupils to us, and the electric lamp was reflected in miniature in their smooth orbs, did their sightlessness become obvious.

"Well, Klara, we've kept our word, haven't we?" said Condor, going up to her affectionately, and speaking in that soft vibrant tone that came into his voice whenever he addressed her. "We weren't long, were we? And if you only knew how glad I am that the *Herr Leutnant* looked me up. I ought to tell you, by the way— but sit down for a moment, my friend—that he is garrisoned in the town where the Kekesfalvas live—you remember my little patient, don't you?"

"Oh, you mean that poor lame child?"

"Yes. And, you see, I hear from time to time from the *Herr Leutnant* how she's getting along, instead of having to go there myself. He goes there almost every day to cheer the poor child up, and to sit with her for a while."

The blind woman turned her head in what she guessed was my direction. A sudden gentleness seemed to smooth out her harsh features.

"How good of you, *Herr Leutnant*! I can just imagine what a comfort that must be to her," she said, nodding at me, and impulsively reaching out her hand to me across the table.

"Yes, and good for me too," Condor went on. "Otherwise I should have to go there far more often myself, to keep up her spirits. It's a great relief to me to know that Lieutenant Hofmiller is going to keep an eye on her during this last week before she goes off to Switzerland. She's not always easy to deal with, but he's amazingly clever with her, and I know he won't let me down. I can rely on him more than on all my assistants and colleagues."

I realized that, by exacting a promise from me in the presence of this other helpless woman, Condor was trying to bind me more firmly than ever. But I gave the promise willingly.

"Of course you can depend on me, *Herr Doktor*. I shall see her every day of this last week and shall ring you up if the slightest thing happens. But I'm pretty certain"—I gave him a meaning look over the head of the blind woman—"that nothing *will* happen, and that there will be no difficulty."

"So am I," he agreed with a faint smile. We understood each other perfectly. But his wife's mouth began to work. It was plain that she had something on her mind.

"I have not yet made my apologies to you, *Herr Leutnant.* I am afraid I was a little ... a little unfriendly to you just now. But that stupid girl didn't tell me anyone was there; I had no idea who was in the waiting-room, and Emmerich has never mentioned you to me. And so I thought it must be some complete stranger who wanted to buttonhole him, and he's always dead-tired, you know, when he gets home."

"You were quite right, *gnädige Frau,* and you should be even firmer, I am afraid—forgive my presumption—that your husband gives out far too much of himself."

"He gives everything," she broke in vehemently, eagerly drawing her chair up nearer to mine. "Everything, I tell you—his time, his nerves, his money. He doesn't eat, doesn't sleep on account of his patients. Everyone takes advantage of him, and I, with my blind eyes, cannot relieve him of any of his responsibilities, cannot lighten his burdens. If you only knew how I worry about him! The whole day I keep thinking: he's not had anything to eat yet, now he's in the train again, or in the tram, and in the middle of the night they'll be waking him up again. He has time for everyone except himself. And, who thanks him for it, I should like to know? No one, no one!"

"Really no one?" he said, bending over her with a smile.

"Oh yes, of course," she replied with a blush. "But I'm unable to do anything for him. When he comes home from his work, I'm always in an agony of anxiety. Oh, if only you could have some influence over him! He needs someone to restrain him a little. One simply can't help the whole world ... "

"But one must try," he said, with a glance at me. "That's what one lives for. For that alone." The shot went home, but since I had now made up my mind I was able to meet his eye. I rose. At this moment I had taken a vow.

No sooner did the blind woman hear my chair being pushed back than she raised her eyes.

"Must you really go?" she asked with genuine regret. "What a pity, what a pity! But I hope you'll come again soon, won't you?"

I felt very strange. What is there about me, I wondered to myself, that everyone should have confidence in me, that this blind woman should raise he sightless eyes so joyfully to me, that this man, who is practically a stranger to me, should put a friendly arm round my shoulder? And as I went down the stairs I could no longer understand what it was that had brought me here an hour before. Why had I wanted to run away? Because a cross-grained old colonel had given me a dressing-down? Because a poor crippled creature had fallen in love with me? Because a human being wanted to cling to me, to get consolation from me? Was it not the most wonderful thing on earth to be able to help one's fellow-creatures? I now knew that it was the only thing that was really worth while. And this realization was driving me to do of my own free will what I had yesterday regarded as an intolerable sacrifice: to show my gratitude to a sick girl for her great, her burning love for me.

A week! Ever since Condor had set a time-limit to what was expected of me I had once more felt sure of myself. I felt apprehensive only at the thought of that one moment when I should encounter Edith for the first time after her confession of love. I knew that complete lack of embarrassment after that passionate embrace would be impossible—her first glance at me would be bound to hold the question: have you forgiven me? And perhaps that still more critical question: will you bear with my love, and can you return it? That first moment when she would gaze up with a blush, a look of controlled and yet uncontrolled impatience, might be at once the most hazardous and decisive. One single maladroit word, one false gesture, might reveal in all its cruel truth what I must on no account reveal, and she would irrevocably have received that sudden shock, that blow to her feelings, against which Condor had so earnestly warned me. But once that first moment had been got over, I should be saved, and, moreover, should have saved her for ever.

But no sooner had I set foot next day in the Kekesfalva house than I realized that Edith, prompted, no doubt, by the same anxiety as myself, had wisely taken the precaution to see that our first meeting should take place in company. While still in the hall, I heard the sound of animated female voices; it seemed that in order to bridge the awkwardness of the first critical moments of meeting she had invited friends to the house—at an hour of the day when as a rule we were left undisturbed together.

Even before I entered the salon, Ilona—either at Edith's instigation or on her own initiative—came rushing up to me with unwonted impetuosity, led me up to other guests and introduced me to the wife of the Prefect of the district and her daughter, an anaemic, freckled, pert creature, whom, I happened to know, Edith detested. And so that first glance, which I had so dreaded, was, as it were, deflected. Ilona led me up to the table, where we sipped our tea and chatted away. I talked vivaciously to the saucy, freckled little provincial Miss, while Edith conversed with her mother. Because of this by no means haphazard disposal of the guests, the emotional undercurrent between us was short-circuited, and I was able to avoid looking at Edith, although I could feel her gaze sometimes resting somewhat uneasily on me. Moreover, when at length the two ladies got up to go, Ilona put us at our ease by means of a skilful and rapid manoeuvre.

"I'll just see the ladies to the door. In the meantime you two can start your game of chess. I've got one or two matters to settle with regard to our journey, but I'll be with you again in an hour."

"Would you care for a game?" I was able to ask Edith in a casual tone.

"I'd love one," replied Edith, lowering her eyes as the others left the room.

She kept her gaze fixed on her lap as I got out the chess-board and set out the pieces, methodically, so as to gain time. As a rule, in order to decide who should start I held a white and a black chessman behind my back, one in each fist, according to the rules of the game. But this method of deciding would have necessitated the uttering of the word "Right" or "Left," and even this one word we avoided by tacit agreement. We must avoid speaking at all costs! All our thoughts must be imprisoned within this chequer-board with its four-and-sixty squares. Our eyes must be riveted on the pieces, not even on the fingers that moved them. And so we simulated that absorption which is characteristic only of the great masters, who forget everything around them and concentrate their whole attention on the game.

Very soon, however, the game itself gave us away. Edith's play broke down completely. She made a number of false moves, and from the way her fingers twitched it was obvious that she could endure the strained silence no longer. In the middle of the third game she pushed the board away.

"That's enough! Give me a cigarette."

I passed her the chased silver box, and attentively struck a match. As it flared up I could not avoid her eyes.

They were staring fixedly ahead, neither turned to me nor gazing at anything in particular; as though frozen with anger, they gazed steadily and coldly into space, although above them her brows were raised in a tremulous arch. I was quick to recognize the ominous signs of an approaching outburst.

"Don't!" I warned her in genuine alarm. "Please don't!"

But she threw herself back in her chair. I saw a tremor run through her frame, and she dug her fingers deeper and deeper into the arms of the chair.

"Don't, don't!" I begged again, unable to think of anything but that one word of entreaty. But the pent-up tears had already gushed forth. This was no wild, turbulent sobbing, but—far worse!—a silent, heart-rending fit of weeping through clenched teeth, weeping which she was ashamed of yet was unable to control.

"Don't, don't, I implore you!" I said, and, bending over her, laid my hand on her arm to calm her. It was as though an electric current had run up her arm to the shoulder and then right through her whole contorted body.

And suddenly the spasm ceased; she grew rigid again and did not stir. It was as though her whole body were straining to understand what this touch indicated, to know whether it was a gesture of tenderness or of love or merely of pity. It was terrible, this waiting with bated breath, this waiting of a tense, motionless body. I had not the courage to withdraw the hand which had with such marvellous suddenness stilled the paroxysm of sobs, and on the other hand I had not the strength to force from my fingers the caress that Edith's body, her burning flesh—I could tell—so urgently awaited. I let my hand lie there, as though it were not a part of me, and I felt as though all the blood in her body came surging in a warm pulsating stream to this one spot.

My hand rested slackly on her arm for I know not how long, for during those few minutes time stood still as the air in the room. Then I felt a faint tension in her muscles. Her gaze averted, she pushed my hand gently away from her arm with her right hand, and drew it slowly towards her heart; now her left hand, too, shyly and tenderly closed on it. Her two hands very softly clasped my huge, heavy, bare masculine paw, and began, very, very gently and timorously, to caress it. At first her fingers merely strayed as though out of curiosity over my defenceless, motionless palm, flitting as lightly as a puff of wind over the surface. Then I could feel her light, childish touch venturing cautiously upwards from the wrist to the fingertips, feel them tenderly exploring the shapes of my fingers, inside and out, outside and in, feel them coming to a startled halt at the hard nails, only to grope round them too, and then to glide along the veins down to the wrist again, and then up again, and down—a tender search that never made so bold as to seize my hand firmly, to press it, to grasp it. It was no more insistent than the lapping around one of tepid water, this playful fondling, at once reverent and childish, marvelling and abashed. And I felt that in embracing this one small part of me which I had yielded up to her she was embracing the whole of me. She had let herself sink further back into her chair, as though to enjoy more rapturously this gentle stroking of my hand; she lay there as though asleep, as though in a dream, her eyes closed, her lips softly parted, on her features a tranquil radiance that came of perfect peace, as again and again, with renewed rapture, her frail fingers stroked my hand from wrist to fingertips. There was no avidity in this fervent stroking, only serene, awestruck bliss at being allowed at last to take fleeting possession of some part of my body and to show it her boundless love. Never have I been so moved by a woman's embraces, however passionate, as I was by this delicate, almost dreamy, playful caress.

How long this lasted I do not know. Such experiences cannot be measured in terms of ordinary time. This shy fondling and stroking, which affected and agitated me more profoundly than that first sudden, burning kiss, had a hypnotic, bewitching, narcotic effect on my senses. I was still unable to summon up the strength to withdraw my hand. I remembered those words of hers, "I only ask you to bear with my love," and in a dim dream, as it were, I enjoyed the rippling of her fingers over my skin, the tingling of my nerves—I let it happen, powerless, defenceless, yet subconsciously ashamed at the thought of being loved so infinitely, while for my part feeling nothing but shy confusion, an embarrassed thrill.

But gradually my own immobility became unbearable to me; it was not that her fondling, the warm straying and exploring of her affectionate fingers, her timid, light touch, wearied me, but it was a torment to me to let my hand lie there inert as though it did not belong to me, as though this person who was caressing it had no part in my life. Just as in a half-sleep one hears church bells pealing, I knew that I must respond in some way—either repulse this display of affection or return it. But I had strength neither for the one nor the other. Make an end of this dangerous game, came an urgent prompting from within. And so, cautiously, I tensed my muscles.

Slowly, very, very slowly, I began to release my hand from her gentle hold—imperceptibly, as I hoped. But with her acute sensitivity she realized at once, even before I myself was aware of it, that I was about to withdraw my hand; and with a sudden startled movement she let go of it. Her fingers limply fell away—suddenly I could no longer feel the tingling warmth on my skin. It was in some embarrassment that I took back my now deserted hand, for Edith's face had clouded over, and her mouth had once more begun to pucker up in a childish pout.

"Don't, don't!" I whispered to her. I could think of nothing else to say. "Ilona will be here in a moment." And seeing that at those empty, feeble words she began to tremble all the more violently, I was seized once again with a sudden access of burning pity. I bent over her and gave her a fleeting kiss on the forehead.

But her eyes stared sternly, coldly and forbiddingly at me and, as it were, through me, as though they could divine the thoughts behind my brow. I had been unable to deceive her, so quick were her perceptions. She had realized that in withdrawing my hand I had withdrawn myself from her caresses, and that this hasty kiss was no proof of real love, but merely of embarrassment and pity.

That was the fateful mistake I made and continued to make during the next few days—an irreparable, unforgivable mistake: despite all my desperate efforts I did not muster the very last reserves of my patience, the very last ounce of my strength, in an effort to hide my feelings. It was in vain that I resolved not to betray by a single word, glance or gesture that her love was irksome to me. Again and again I called to mind Condor's warning as to what a dangerous situation I might precipitate, what a responsibility I should be incurring, were I to wound this vulnerable creature. Let her love you, I said to myself, conceal your feelings, dissimulate for this one week, to spare her pride. Don't let her suspect that you are betraying her, doubly betraying her, by talking so blandly of an early prospect of a cure, while you are inwardly trembling with embarrassment and shame. Behave easily, naturally, I kept admonishing myself; try to put warmth into your voice, affection and tenderness into your touch.

But between a woman who has once let a man see her desire and that man the atmosphere is charged with mysterious, dangerous tension. It is characteristic of those who love to have an uncanny insight into the true feelings of the beloved; and since love, according to the inmost laws of its being, ever desires the illimitable, all finiteness, all moderation, is repugnant, intolerable to it. In every sign of constraint, of restraint, on the part of the other it suspects opposition; any reluctance to yield utterly it rightly interprets as secret resistance. And there must have been a trace of embarrassment and confusion in my behaviour, of disingenuousness and gaucherie in what I said, for all my efforts were no match for her alert expectancy. I failed in my ultimate task: that of convincing her, and in her mistrust she divined with growing disquiet that I was failing to do the one thing, the only thing, she desired: to reciprocate her love. Sometimes, in the middle of a conversation, and at a moment when I was most eagerly making a bid for her confidence, her friendliness, she would throw me a keen look out of her grey eyes, and I would be obliged to lower my gaze. I would feel as though she were sounding the very depths of my heart.

And so it went on for three days; it was torture to me, torture to her. The whole time I was conscious of the mute, avid expectancy in her gaze, in her silence. Then—I think it was on the fourth day—I became aware of a curious hostility, which at first I was at a loss to understand. I had gone to see her as usual in the early afternoon and had taken her some flowers. She accepted them without really looking at them and laid them casually aside, as if to show me by her studied indifference that I need not imagine I could buy myself off by giving her presents. "Dear me, why these lovely flowers?" she said almost contemptuously, and proceeded to entrench herself once more behind a barrier of demonstrative and hostile silence. I tried to make light conversation. But she answered with a curt "Oh?" or "Is that so?" or "How odd!" She plainly and insultingly implied that my conversation bored her. By her behaviour, too, she deliberately emphasized her indifference: she toyed with a book, turned over the leaves, laid it aside, dallied with all sorts of objects, ostentatiously yawned once or twice, and then, while I was in the middle of saying something, summoned Josef to ask if he had packed her Chinchilla coat; only when he had replied in the affirmative did she turn to me again with a cold "What was it you were saying?" which suggested only too obviously that what she would have liked to add was, "It's all the same to me what you prattle on about."

At length I felt my powers of resistance weakening. More and more often I looked towards the door to see whether someone, either Ilona or Kekesfalva, were not coming to release me at last from this desperate "monologue". But even this glance did not escape her. "Are you looking for anything?" she asked, in apparently sympathetic tones, but with ill-concealed scorn. "Do you want anything?" And to my shame I could only stammer quickly, "Oh no, nothing at all." My wisest course would probably have been to accept her challenge and burst out, "What is it you want of me? Why are you torturing me like this? If you don't want me here, I'll go away." But I had promised Condor to avoid saying anything that would give her a shock or lead to an argument; and so instead of abruptly breaking through this sullen silence I was fool enough to drag the conversation out for two hours, as though across hot, unresponsive desert sand, until at last Kekesfalva appeared, nervous as ever during these last few days and perhaps even more embarrassed. "Shall we go in to dinner?" he asked.

And then we sat round the table, Edith opposite me. Not once did she look up, not a word did she address to any of us. We all three felt how aggressively offensive was this stubborn silence of hers. All the more strenuous, therefore, were the efforts I made to brighten things up. I told them about our Colonel, who, like a man subject to bouts of drinking, had an attack of "manoeuvre-itis" every June and July, and how as the date for the manoeuvres drew nearer he became more and more excitable, and in order to spin out the silly story I embroidered it with more and more absurd details, although all the time I felt as though my collar were strangling me. But only Kekesfalva and Ilona laughed, constrainedly, in an obvious endeavour to cover up Edith's painful silence, for she was now yawning ostentatiously for the third time. At all costs go on talking, I said to myself; and so I told them how we should be chivvied about all summer and hardly know whether we were on our heads or our heels. Although two Uhlans had fallen off their horses yesterday from sunstroke, the fanatical old martinet drove us harder every day. No one could ever tell when we should dismiss, for in his maniacal zeal he would have the silliest evolution repeated twenty or thirty times over. It was only with the greatest difficulty, I said, that I had succeeded in getting off in time today, and whether I should be able to turn up punctually tomorrow only God knew and the Colonel, who for the time being regarded himself as the Almighty's representative on this earth.

This was, to be sure, a perfectly innocent remark, which should not have offended or upset anyone. I had been speaking in a light and cheerful tone to Kekesfalva, without looking at Edith, for I had long since ceased to be able to bear the way in which she was staring vacantly into space. Suddenly there was a clatter. She had thrown her knife, with which she had been fidgeting the whole time, right across her plate, and as we started in alarm she snapped out:

"Well, if it's such a bother for you to come, you'd better stay in your barracks or your café. We can get along perfectly well without you."

We all stared and held our breath; it was as though a shot had been fired through the window.

"Edith!" stammered Kekesfalva, moistening his dry lips.

But she threw herself pettishly back in her chair.

"Well, one can't help being sorry for someone who has such an awful time!" she sneered. "We really ought to give him a day off! I for my part will certainly not grudge him a holiday."

Kekesfalva and Ilona looked at one another in distress. They both realized that I was quite unreasonably being made the victim of her long-pent-up feelings; and from their anxious glances at me I could see that they were afraid that I might return rudeness for rudeness. And for that very reason I made a special effort to control myself.

"Do you know, I really think you're right, Edith," I said as cordially as my hammering heart would permit me. "When I turn up so dog-tired I'm really not awfully good company. I've been feeling the whole time today that I've been boring you stiff. But you should be able to put up with a poor fagged-out fellow for a few days. After all, I shan't be able to come to see you much longer. The house will be empty very soon and you'll all be gone. I simply can't believe that we've only got four more days—four, or rather three and a half, before you ... "

But at this she burst into a sharp, shrill laugh, which sounded like the tearing of a piece of calico.

"Just listen to him! Three and a half days! Ha-ha! He's worked out even to the last half-day when he'll be rid of us at last! I expect he's bought himself a calendar and marked the day of our departure in red. But you'd better look out! Sometimes people can be very much out in their calculations. Ha-ha! Three and a half days, three and a half—a half—a half ... "

She laughed more and more uproariously, glaring at us as she did so. But she trembled as she laughed; this was hysteria rather than genuine merriment. I could tell that she longed to jump up, and indeed that would have been the most natural thing for her to do in her state of extreme agitation, but her powerless legs fettered her to her chair. This enforced immobility lent her anger something of the viciousness and tragic helplessness of a caged animal.

"One moment, I'll fetch Josef," whispered Ilona, who had blenched. For years she had been accustomed to anticipating Edith's every movement. Kekesfalva too went up to his daughter anxiously. But his fears proved to be superfluous, for when Josef entered the room Edith allowed herself to be led away quietly by him and her father, without a word of farewell or apology to me. Evidently it was only our embarrassment that made her realize what a scene she had made.

I was left alone with Ilona. I felt like a man who has fallen from an aeroplane and staggers to his feet dazed and frightened, not knowing what has happened.

"You *must* try and understand," Ilona whispered to me hurriedly. "She never gets a night's sleep now. The thought of going away upsets her terribly and ... you don't know ... "

"Oh yes, I do, Ilona," I said. "I know everything. That's why I'm coming again tomorrow."

Hold out! Stand fast! I told myself firmly as, thoroughly upset by this whole scene, I walked homewards. Stand fast at all costs! You promised Condor you would. Your honour is at stake. Don't let yourself be deflected because of her nerves and her moods. Remember always that this hostility is only the desperation of a person who loves you, and to whom you are in debt because of your coldness and hardness of heart. Stand fast until the very last moment—only another three days, three and a half days, and you will have stood the test, you will be able to slacken off, you will he relieved of your burden for weeks, months! Patience, have patience—just for this last lap, these last three, three and a half days.

Condor had been right. It is only the immeasurable, the limitless that terrifies us. That which is set within defined, fixed limits is a challenge to our powers, comes to be the measure of our strength. Three days—I shall manage that, I felt, and the knowledge inspired me with confidence. Next day I carried out my duties in exemplary fashion, which is saying a good deal, for we had to parade an hour earlier than usual and drill for all we were worth until the sweat poured down our necks. To my own astonishment I was even able to extract an involuntary "Well done!" from our testy old Colonel. This time the storm of his wrath descended with all the more violence on the head of the unfortunate Count Steinhübel. Mad about horseflesh as he was, he had acquired, only a few days before, a new, high-stepping chestnut, a young, unmanageable thoroughbred, and in his confidence in his own equestrian skill he had been so imprudent as to neglect to put him through his paces beforehand.

While the Colonel had been discussing the orders of the day with us, the villainous beast, startled by the shadow of a bird, had reared up madly, and later, during the attack, had simply bolted. Had Steinhübel not been such a marvellous horseman the whole regiment would have been privileged to see him take a tumble. It was only after a positively acrobatic struggle that he was able to get the whip-hand of the furious beast, a redoubtable feat for which he was not exactly congratulated by the Colonel. Once and for all, growled the old martinet, he was not going to tolerate circus tricks on the parade-ground; if Count Steinhübel knew nothing about horses by this time he should at least break them in properly beforehand in the riding-school, and not make such a disgraceful exhibition of himself before the men on the parade-ground.

This caustic remark infuriated the Captain beyond measure. All the way home and later at mess he kept on complaining of how unjustly he had been treated. It was merely that the beast was mettlesome; we should see what a fine figure the chestnut would cut once he'd been thoroughly broken in. But the more he got worked up, the more his friends chaffed him. He'd been sold a pup, they jeered, and this made him absolutely wild. The argument became more and more heated. During this stormy scene an orderly spoke to me over my shoulder. "You're wanted on the telephone, *Herr Leutnant.*"

I jumped up with an uneasy presentiment. During the last few weeks telephone calls, telegrams and letters had meant nothing but endless trouble and nervous worry. What did she want this time? Probably she was regretting that she had given me an afternoon of freedom. Well, if that was so, all the better; it meant everything was smoothed over. At any rate I slammed the padded door of the telephone booth as firmly behind me as though I were completely cutting off all contact between my two worlds. Ilona was at the other end.

"I only wanted to say," she said, speaking, it seemed to me, in a somewhat strained voice, "that it would be better if you didn't come today. Edith doesn't feel very well ... "

"Nothing serious, I hope?" I interrupted her.

"Oh no ... but I think we'd better let her have a good rest today, and then ... "—she hesitated for a remarkably long time—"and then one day doesn't matter so much now. We shall have to ... we shall have to postpone our departure."

"Postpone it?" I must have sounded very alarmed, for she added hastily:

"Yes ... but only for a few days, we hope ... Anyhow, we can discuss that tomorrow or the day after ... Perhaps I'll give you another ring ... I only wanted to let you know ... So don't come today, if you don't mind, and ... and ... good-bye and best wishes."

"Yes, but ... " I stammered into the receiver. But there was no further answer. I went on listening for a moment or two. No, there was no answer. She had rung off. Odd—why had she broken off the conversation in such a hurry—as though she were afraid of being questioned any further? There must be something behind it all. And why put off the journey? The date had been settled.

A week, Condor had said. A week— I'd completely adapted myself to the idea, and now I should have to ... Impossible ... it was impossible! I couldn't stand this eternal shilly-shallying ... After all, I had nerves too.... I must be left in peace some time ...

Was it really so hot in this telephone booth? I pushed open the padded door as if I were suffocating, and staggered back to my seat. Apparently my absence had not been remarked. They were still arguing away and ragging the wretched Steinhübel, and the orderly was hovering patiently behind my vacant chair with the meat course. Mechanically, to get rid of the fellow, I helped myself to two or three slices, but I made no move to take up knife or fork, for there was a violent pounding at my temples, as though a little hammer were pitilessly knocking out the words on my skull: "Postpone! Postpone our departure." There must be *some* reason for it. Something must have happened. Had she really been taken ill? Had I offended her? Why had she decided all of a sudden not to go? Condor had promised me that I should have to hold out only for a week, and I had already struggled through four days ... But I couldn't go on any longer ... I simply could not!

"A penny for your thoughts, Toni? Our homely fare doesn't seem to be to your taste. Well, well, that's what comes of living in such style! As I keep on saying, we can't live up to Toni these days."

There was that confounded Ferencz again with his good-natured chaff, his beastly innuendoes, and hints that I was sponging on the Kekesfalvas.

"Can't you give me a rest from your damn silly jokes, blast you!" I burst out. Something of my pent-up fury must have crept into my voice, for the two ensigns opposite looked up in surprise. Ferencz put down his knife and fork.

"Now look here, Toni," he said threateningly, "I don't like your tone. Surely we can go on cracking our little jokes in the mess! If you like it better elsewhere, all right, that's your affair, not mine. But I still have a right to remark at our table that you're not touching your lunch!"

Our neighbours looked at the two of us with interest. The clattering and scraping of cutlery on the plates suddenly died down. Even the Major frowned and looked sharply across at us. I realized that it was high time to make some amends for my outburst.

"And you, Ferencz," I said, forcing a laugh, "will perhaps kindly allow me to have a splitting headache and to feel out of sorts once in a while."

"Oh, sorry, Toni!" Ferencz immediately interposed. "How was I to know? Yes, now I come to think of it, you really do look washed out. I've been thinking for the last few days that you were a bit under the weather. But—you'll pick up again. I'm not seriously worried."

The incident was happily closed. But I continued to fume inwardly. What were the Kekesfalvas up to? This way, that way, hot and cold—no, I wasn't going to let them play me up like this! Three days, I had said, three and a half days, and not a moment longer. It was all the same to me if they postponed their journey or not. I wasn't going to let my nerves be torn to pieces any longer. I wasn't going to be tortured any longer by this cursed pity. It was driving me mad.

I had to keep a tight hold on myself so as not to betray my inward fury. I felt like picking up the glasses and crushing them between my fingers or smashing them down on the table; I felt I must do something violent to relieve my feelings. I just couldn't go on waiting with my nerves on edge, waiting to know whether they were going to write or ring up, to postpone or not postpone their journey. I simply couldn't go on. I felt I had to do something.

Meanwhile my comrades were arguing just as heatedly as before. "I tell you," sneered the lanky Jozsi, "that fellow Neutitscheiner did you down thoroughly. I know something about horses, and you'll never get the better of that rascal, no one'll ever master that one."

"Is that so? Well, I'd just like to see!" I suddenly burst in upon the conversation. "I'd just like to see whether one couldn't get the better of the beast. I say, Steinhübel, d'you mind if I take your chestnut in hand for an hour or so and give it him hot and strong till he submits?"

I don't know what put the idea into my head, but the urge to vent my fury against someone or something, to have a tussle, a real scrap, was so overpowering that I eagerly jumped at the first opportunity that offered. They all looked up at me in astonishment.

"Good luck to you!" laughed Count Steinhübel. "If you've got the nerve, you'll be doing me a favour. I've positively got cramp in my fingers today, I had to pull the beast in so hard. It would be a jolly good thing if someone fresh took a hand with the rogue. If you like, we'll go along straight away. Come along, quick march!"

Everyone jumped up in pleasant anticipation of some real fun.

We went to the stables to fetch Caesar—for this was the invincible name that Steinhübel had somewhat prematurely bestowed on the intractable animal. Caesar, seeing us gathered in a noisy group round him, scented mischief. He snorted and pawed the ground and frisked about in the narrow confines of his box, tugging at his halter until the boards groaned. It was not without considerable difficulty that we managed to manoeuvre the suspicious beast into the riding-school.

In general I was only an average rider, and far from being the equal in prowess of so redoubtable a rider as Steinhübel. Today, nevertheless, he could not have found anyone better than myself, and the unmanageable Caesar could not have met a more dangerous antagonist. For my muscles were tensed with fury, and in my perverse craving to get the better of, to master, someone or something, I took an almost sadistic pleasure in showing at least this stubborn animal (for one cannot let fly at what is out of one's reach) that there were limits to my patience. It little availed the doughty Caesar to zoom about like a rocket, to pound the walls with his hoofs, to rear and do his best, by suddenly leaping sideways, to throw me. My blood was up; I tugged mercilessly at the curb-rein as though trying to break all his teeth, I dug my heels into his ribs. And at this treatment he soon began to stop his antics. I was excited, elated by his stubborn resistance, and the approving remarks of my fellow-officers, "My stars, he's giving him what for!" or "Just look at old Hofmiller!" inspired me with more and more daring and confidence. The feeling of self-assurance derived from physical achievement always transfers itself to the mental sphere. After half an hour of ruthless wrestling with the animal I still sat victorious in the saddle, and the exhausted brute beneath me was gnashing his teeth and steaming and sweating as though he had come out of a hot shower. His neck and bridle were flecked with foam, and his ears drooped submissively. After another half-hour the invincible Caesar was pacing up and down mildly and obediently at my will; I no longer needed to squeeze him firmly with my legs and was now able to dismount at my leisure and receive the congratulations of my fellow-officers. But there was still so much fight left in me, and I had felt so fine during this trial of strength, that I asked Steinhübel to allow me to ride out to the parade-ground for an hour or two at most, at the trot of course, to allow the sweating beast to cool off a little.

"Why, with pleasure," Steinhübel laughed his consent. "I can see you'll bring him back as meek as a lamb. He won't try any of his tricks again. Bravo, Toni, my congratulations!" And so, followed by the thunderous applause of my friends, I rode the conquered Caesar out of the riding-school and, letting the reins hang loose, through the town and into the meadows. The horse's movements were light and easy, and I too felt light and easy. In that one hour of struggle I had taken out on the recalcitrant animal all my anger and exasperation. And now he trotted along meekly and peaceably, and I had to admit that Steinhübel was right, he really stepped wonderfully. More beautifully, more gracefully, more smartly, it would have been impossible to canter; and gradually my original ill-temper gave way to a voluptuous and almost dreamy feeling of well-being. For a good hour I rode him hither and thither, and at length, at about half-past five, walked him slowly back. We had both of us had enough for one day, Caesar and I. I was a little somnolent as I rode back to the town along the familiar high-road at a comfortable jog-trot. Suddenly I heard the sound of a motor-horn behind me, loud and shrill. The excitable chestnut immediately pricked up his ears and began to tremble. Realizing in good time that the horse was likely to shy, I pulled in the reins and urged him under a tree by the side of the road, to allow the car to pass.

The chauffeur must have been a very considerate driver, for, correctly interpreting my caution, he came driving along at a most leisurely pace, and the engine could scarcely be heard. As the car now passed us, Caesar stood fairly still, and I was able to glance up at my leisure. But the moment I raised my eyes, I became aware that someone was waving to me from the open car, and I recognized Condor's spherical bald head side by side with Kekesfalva's egg-shaped skull with its frame of scanty white hair.

I could not tell whether I myself was trembling or the horse was trembling under me. What was the meaning of this? Condor here, and he had not let me know! He must have been to see the Kekesfalvas, for the old man was sitting next to him in the car.

But why had they not stopped to say a few words to me? Why had they driven past me so coldly? And how was it that Condor had suddenly come out here again? Surely his consulting hours in Vienna were between two and four? They must have sent for him very urgently and, moreover, very early in the morning. Something must have happened. It must have something to do with what Ilona had said on the telephone about their postponing their journey and my not going that afternoon. Something *must* have happened, something that they were keeping from me. Had she done herself some injury? Yesterday evening there had been an air of resolution about her, an air of scornful confidence, such as a person only wears when planning something dreadful, something desperate. She must have done something to herself. Ought I not to gallop after them? Perhaps I might catch Condor at the station?

But perhaps, I quickly bethought myself, he's not going away at all. No; if something dreadful has happened, he will on no account go back to Vienna without leaving a message for me. I expect he's left a note at the barracks. He would, I knew, do nothing without my knowledge, nothing against my interests. He would not leave me in the lurch. The main thing was to get back quickly. I was certain to find a message, a letter, a note from him, or the man himself. I must hurry.

Arrived at the barracks, I stabled the horse as quickly as possible and rushed up the stairs so as to avoid the chatter and congratulations of my friends. And there, to be sure, I found Kusma—waiting outside my door. From his anxious expression, his drooping shoulders, I realized something was wrong. A gentleman in mufti was waiting in my room, he told me in some consternation; he had not liked to turn the gentleman away, because his business had seemed to be so urgent. As a matter of fact, Kusma had strict instructions to let no one into my room, but probably Condor had given him a tip—hence his fear and uneasiness, which, however, quickly changed to astonishment when, instead of cursing him, I merely murmured a jovial "That's all right" and made for the door. Thank God Condor had come! He would tell me everything.

As I threw open the door a figure stirred, seemed to take shape out of the shadows of the darkened room (Kusma had pulled down the blinds because of the heat). I was just about to give Condor a hearty greeting when I realized—this was not Condor at all. It was someone else waiting for me, the very person whom I had least expected to find here—Kekesfalva. Even had the darkness been denser I should have recognized him among thousands by the timid way in which he got up and bowed. And even before he spoke, I imagined I could hear his dejected, despondent tones.

"Forgive me, *Herr Leutnant*," he said with a bow, "for bursting in upon you like this, but Dr Condor asked me to present his compliments and to apologize for our not stopping the car ... we hadn't a moment to lose, he simply had to catch the Vienna express because this evening he has to ... and ... and ... so he asked me to let you know at once how sorry he was ... That's the only reason ... I mean that's why I have taken the liberty of coming up to your room."

He stood there before me, his head bowed as though beneath an invisible yoke. His bony egg-shaped skull with its scanty hair gleamed in the darkness. The completely uncalled-for servility of his bearing began to exasperate me. I had an uneasy feeling— and I knew I was not mistaken—that behind all this hum-ing and ha-ing there was some quite definite purpose. An old man with a weak heart did not climb three storeys merely in order to convey someone else's compliments. He could just as easily have rung up or saved his breath until tomorrow. Be careful, I told myself. This old man wants something of you. Once before he appeared like this out of the darkness; he starts off humbly like a beggar and ends by forcing his will upon you like the djinn, the Old Man of the Sea in your dream. Don't yield! Don't let yourself be trapped! Don't ask, don't inquire about anything, but get rid of him, get out of his clutches, as quickly as possible.

But the man who stood before me was an old man, and his head was meekly bowed. I could see the parting in the thin white hair, and it conjured up a vision of my grandmother bending over her knitting and telling us youngsters fairy-stories. One could not turn away an old, sick man without a kindly word.

And so, as though all my experience had taught me nothing, I motioned him to a chair.

"Most kind of you, Herr von Kekesfalva, to take all this trouble! Really most charming of you! Won't you take a seat?"

Kekesfalva made no reply. Probably he did not hear me distinctly, but at least he had understood my gesture. Timorously he perched himself on the extreme edge of the chair I had offered him. He must have sat down just so timidly in his youth, I thought in a flash, when eating the bread of charity in the homes of strangers. And there he sat now, the millionaire, in my shabby, worn-out cane-bottomed armchair. Deliberately he removed his spectacles and, foraging in his pocket for his handkerchief, began to polish the lenses. Aha, my friend! I thought, I've learned a thing or two, I know what that polishing means, I know your tricks! I know you're only polishing your spectacles to gain time. You want me to begin the conversation, want me to ask all the questions, and I know, moreover, what you want to be asked—whether Edith is really ill and why your trip is being postponed. But I'm going to be on my guard. If you have anything to say to me, you can begin. I won't go a step to meet you. No, I refuse to be dragged into the whole thing again—there must be an end of this accursed pity, an end of this eternal cry for more and yet more! An end of all this secretiveness and disingenuousness! If you want anything of me, then ask me straight out, but don't sit there meekly polishing your glasses. I'm not going to walk into your trap again, I'm fed up to the teeth with all this pity.

At length, as though he had heard the unuttered words behind my closed lips, the old man put down the now shining spectacles on the table in front of him. He evidently realized that I was not going to help him and that he would have to open the conversation himself. Keeping his head obstinately lowered, he began to speak, without looking across at me, and addressing his words to the table as though he hoped to wring more pity from the hard, cracked wood than from me.

"I know, *Herr Leutnant*," he said with a gulp, "that I have no right, no right whatever, to take up your time. But what am I to do? What are we to do? I can't go on any longer, we none of us can ... God knows what's come over her! One can't talk to her, she won't listen to anyone now ... And yet I know she doesn't mean it ... she's simply unhappy, desperately unhappy. She is only doing this to us in desperation ... believe me, in desperation."

I waited. What did he mean? *What* was she doing to them? What? Out with it! Why was he talking in riddles? Why didn't he say straight out what was the matter?

But the old man was staring vacantly at the table. "And everything had been settled, all the arrangements had been made— the berths in the sleeping-car booked, the best rooms engaged ... and only yesterday afternoon she was still looking forward impatiently to going away. She had looked out the books she wanted to take with her, tried on all the new clothes and the fur coat that I had sent for from Vienna; and then suddenly, yesterday evening after dinner, this came over her—I don't understand it. You remember what a state she was in. Ilona doesn't understand, nor anyone else, what it's all about. But she screams and vows that she won't go away on any account, and that nothing on earth will make her. She will stay, stay, stay, she says, even if the house is burned over her head. She's not going to lend herself to all this humbug, she's not going to be duped, she says. This treatment is simply an excuse to get rid of her, to get her away. But we are all making a mistake, she says. She flatly refuses to go away, she's going to stay, stay, stay!"

I felt a cold shudder run down my spine. So that was what had been behind her angry laughter yesterday. Had she realized that I was at the end of my tether, or was she merely staging all this to get me to promise to follow her to Switzerland?

Don't let yourself be drawn into it, I said to myself. Don't let the old man see that the news agitates you. Don't let him see that the thought of her remaining is agony to you. And so I deliberately feigned obtuseness.

"Oh, that'll soon pass," I said with some indifference. "You should know by now how capricious she is. And Ilona told me over the telephone that it was only a matter of postponing your departure for a day or two."

A hollow sigh escaped from the old man; it was as though the last ounce of strength were being torn from his breast.

"Oh God, if only that were so. But the dreadful thing is that I'm afraid ... we're all afraid ... that she'll never go away at all now ... I don't know, I can't understand it—but suddenly she's lost all interest in the new treatment, in whether she gets well or not. 'I'm not going to put up with this torture any longer, I won't allow myself to be experimented on—it's all a lot of nonsense!' That's the sort of thing she says, says it in such a way that one's heart stands still. 'You can't deceive me any longer!' she screams and sobs. 'I see through it all, I see through it all, all of it!' "

I quickly reflected. Good heavens, had she noticed anything? Had I given myself away? Had Condor been imprudent? Could some heedless remark have made her suspect that there was something fishy about this new treatment in Switzerland? Had she with her intuition, her terribly acute intuition, realized that we were sending her away to no purpose?

"I can't understand that," I said guardedly. "Your daughter until now has had such absolute confidence in Dr Condor, and if he has recommended this new treatment so emphatically ... well, I simply don't understand it."

"That's just it! That's the crazy part of it all; she refuses to have any more treatment at all, she refuses to be cured. Do you know what she said? 'I'm not going away on any account,' she said. 'I'm tired of all these lies! I'd rather be the cripple that I am and stay here ... I don't want to be cured now, there's no point in it now.' "

"No point?" I repeated in utter bewilderment.

But now the old man bowed his head still lower. I could see his swimming eyes, but could no longer see his spectacles. Only by the fluttering of his thin white hair did I realize that he had begun to tremble violently. Then he murmured almost inaudibly:

" 'There's no point in my being cured now,' she says, and bursts into sobs, 'for he ... he ... ' "

The old man drew a deep breath as though preparing for some great effort. Then at last he jerked out "For he ... he ... all he feels for me is pity."

An icy shiver ran through me as Kekesfalva uttered that word "he". It was the first time that he had made any allusion to his daughter's feelings. It had long struck me that of late he had been avoiding me more and more, that he scarcely ventured to approach me nowadays, whereas formerly he had fluttered around me so persistently. But I knew that it was shame that kept him away from me; it must, after all, have been dreadful for the poor old man to see his daughter throwing herself at a man who shunned her attentions. Her secret confessions must have been agony to him, her unconcealed desire must have caused him infinite embarrassment. He, like myself, was no longer free of constraint. A man who has something to hide loses the candour of his gaze.

But now it had all come out, and the blow had struck with equal force at both our hearts. After this revelation we both sat there mute, avoiding each other's gaze. Silence hovered in the motionless air, in the narrow space above the table that divided us. But gradually this silence expanded, surged like black vapour up to the ceiling and filled the whole room; from above, from below, from all sides this emptiness pressed down and thrust itself upon us, and I could tell from Kekesfalva's laboured, convulsive breathing that the silence was almost suffocating him. Another moment and this pressure would choke us both unless one of us started up and shattered it with a word—this oppressive, murderous emptiness. Then something happened: I only saw at first that he was making a movement, a curiously clumsy and awkward movement. And then I saw the old man drop from his chair in an inert, flaccid heap. The chair fell with a loud crash after him.

A fit, was my first thought, a stroke. Condor had told me he had a weak heart. Horror-struck, I rushed to lift him up and lay him on the sofa. But as I did so I realized that the old man had not really fallen from his chair; he had thrown himself down. He had deliberately sunk to his knees—in my first start of dismay I had failed to notice this. As I now went to raise him up, he shuffled nearer to me, and seized my hands.

"You must help her!" he implored. "You are the only one who can help her ... even Condor says so—you and no one else ... I beseech you, have pity on her! Things can't go on like this ... She'll do something desperate, she'll do away with herself!"

Violently as my hands trembled, I dragged the old man to his feet. But he seized my arms, and his fingers dug desperately like claws into my flesh—the old Man of the Sea, the djinn of my dream, who ensnared the young man who took pity on him.

"Help her," he panted, "for God's sake help her! She can't be left in the state she's in now ... I swear to you, it's a matter of life and death! You can't conceive what wild things she says in her despair ... She will have to make an end of herself, put herself out of the way, she sobs, so that you may be left in peace and we shall all be rid of her ... And it's not just idle talk, she's in deadly earnest ... She's made two attempts already—once she severed the arteries in her wrists and another time she tried a sleeping draught. If she makes up her mind to a thing, no one can shake her, no one ... Only you can save her now, only you ... no one but you, I swear it."

"Why, of course, Herr von Kekesfalva ... Please calm yourself ... Of course I'll do everything that's in my power. If you like we'll drive out to your place straight away, and I'll try to talk her round. I'll come with you now. Just tell me what I'm to say to her, what I'm to do."

He suddenly let go of my arm and stared at me. "What you're to do? Do you really not understand, or do you not want to? Hasn't she opened her heart to you, offered herself to you? And the poor child is tormenting herself to death for having done so. She wrote to you, and you didn't answer, and now she's tortured day and night by the thought that you're having her sent away, trying to get rid of her because you despise her ... she's quite frantic with fear that she's repugnant to you ... because she ... because she ... Don't you realize that it means death to a proud, passionate creature like this child to be left in suspense? Why don't you give some hope? Why is it that you don't say a word to her, why are you so cruel, so heartless to her? Why do you torture the poor, innocent child so horribly?"

"But I've done everything I could to calm her ... After all I've told her ... "

"You've told her nothing! You must surely realize yourself that you are driving her mad by your visits, by your silence,when she's waiting only for one thing ... for that one word that every woman awaits from the man she loves ... After all, she would never have dared to hope so long as she had no prospect of being cured ... But now that she's definitely going to be well, quite well like other people, in a few weeks' time, why shouldn't she expect the same as any other young girl? Why not? She has shown you, hasn't she—told you, that she is only waiting for a word from you? She *can't* do more than she has done ... She can't humble herself any more ... And you, you don't say a word, don't say the one thing that can make her happy ... Is the thought really so abhorrent to you? After all, you'd have everything a human being could wish for on this earth. I'm an old man, a sick man. All that I possess I should leave to you both, the *Schloss* and the estate and the six or seven millions I've made in the course of forty years. It would all be yours ... You can have it tomorrow, any time you like, I no longer want anything for myself ... All I want is someone to look after my child when I'm gone. And I know that you're a good man, a decent man, you'll look after her, you'll be good to her."

His breath failed him. Impotent, helpless, he slumped back into his chair. But I too had come to the end of my strength, and I sank into the other chair. And there we sat opposite each other just as we had sat before, speechless, avoiding each other's gaze, for I know not how long. Only sometimes I could feel the table which he was gripping being gently rocked by the spasms that ran through his body. Then I heard—once more an eternity had passed—a dry sound like the falling of some hard object on another hard object. His bowed head had sunk down on to the table. I could feel how this man was suffering, and a boundless desire to comfort him sprang up within me.

"Herr von Kekesfalva," I said, bending over him, "do have confidence in me. We'll think the whole thing over, think it over calmly ... I repeat, I am entirely at your disposal ... I will do everything that lies in my power. Only the thing ... the thing you hinted at just now ... that's impossible ... utterly impossible!"

He shuddered faintly like a mortally wounded animal at the final death-blow. Dribbling slightly in his agitation, his lips began to move, but I gave him no time to speak.

"It's impossible, Herr von Kekesfalva, so please don't let's discuss the matter any further ... Think it out for yourself ... Who am I? A mere subaltern, who lives on his pay and a small monthly allowance ... One can't undertake responsibilities with such restricted means, they're not enough for two people to live on."

He tried to interrupt me, but in vain.

"Oh yes, I know what you're going to say, Herr von Kekesfalva—that money doesn't come into it, that all that will be arranged. And I know, too, that you're rich, and ... that I could have all I wanted from you. But it's just because you are so rich and I am nothing, a nobody ... that it's out of the question. Everyone would say that I had married for money, that I had ... And Edith herself, believe me, would never rid herself her whole life long of the suspicion that I had accepted her only because of her money and in spite of ... in spite of the special circumstances ... Believe me, Herr von Kekesfalva, it's impossible, genuinely and honestly as I esteem and ... and ... and like your daughter ... But surely you can understand?"

The old man remained motionless. At first I thought he had not taken in what I had said, but gradually his frail body stirred. With an effort he raised his head and stared before him into space. Then he gripped the edge of the table with both hands, and I realized that he was trying to lever up his feeble body, that he was trying to get up, but could not. Twice, thrice his strength gave out. At length he struggled to his feet and stood there, still swaying from the effort, a dark shadow in the darkness, his pupils fixed and rigid, like black glass. Then he said to himself in a far-away, dreadfully casual tone, as though his own, his human voice, had left him:

"Then ... then in that case it's all over."

It was terrible, this tone, this utter resignation. Still staring fixedly into empty space, he groped along the table-top, without looking down for his spectacles. But he did not place them before his stony eyes—what was the point of seeing anymore, of living any more?—he thrust them clumsily into his pocket. Once again his bluish fingers (in which Condor had perceived the signs of death) strayed round the edge of the table until at last they found his battered black hat. Then he turned to go and murmured, without looking at me:

"Forgive me for disturbing you."

Kekesfalva rammed his hat down askew on his head; his legs

310

refused to obey him, they shuffled and tottered feebly. He staggered like a sleepwalker towards the door. Then, as though
remembering something, he took off his hat, bowed and repeated:

"Forgive me for disturbing you."

He bowed to me, the broken old man, and it was this gesture of
politeness in the midst of his utter despair that was my undoing.
Suddenly I felt that warm stream of compassion welling up within me, bringing the burning tears to my eyes, could feel my heart
melting, my will weakening; once more I was at the mercy of my
pity. I couldn't let him go away like this, this old man who had
come to offer me his child, the only thing he held dear on earth. I
could not deliver him up to despair, to death. I could not tear the
very life out of his body. I *must* say something further to him, something comforting, calming, reassuring. And so I rushed after him.

"Herr von Kekesfalva, please, *please* don't misunderstand me.
You mustn't go away like this and tell her ... that would really
be terrible for her at this moment and ... and ... it wouldn't be
true either."

I grew more and more agitated, for I saw that the old man was
not listening to me. Despair had turned him to a pillar of salt; he
stood there rooted to the spot, a shadow in the shadow, a living
corpse. The impulse to comfort him became more and more
urgent.

"It really wouldn't be true, Herr von Kekesfalva, I swear to you
... and nothing would distress me more than to insult your
daughter Edith or ... or to let her think that I was not genuinely
fond of her ... No one has warmer feelings for her than I have, I
swear to you, no one could have more affection for her than I
have. It's really a delusion on her part to think that ... she means
nothing to me ... On the contrary ... on the contrary ... I only
meant that there would be no point in my ... in my saying anything now ... The only thing that matters at the moment is that
she should take care of herself ... that she should really be cured."

"But afterwards ... when she is cured?"

He had turned to me abruptly. His eyes, but a moment ago
frozen and dead, were phosphorescent in the dark.

I was horrified. Instinctively I was aware of the danger that
threatened me. Were I to promise anything now, I should have

committed myself. But at that moment I remembered that all her hopes were illusory. She would not be cured as quickly as all that. It might take years and years. Don't think too far ahead, Condor had said; the thing to do is to pacify her, console her, for the moment. Why not leave her a shred of hope, why not make her happy, if only for a brief spell?

"Why, when she is cured," I said, "then I shall of course ... come and ask you ... "

He stared at me. A tremor shook his body; it seemed to me that some inner force imperceptibly urged him on.

"May I ... may I tell her that?"

Again I scented danger. But I no longer had the strength to withstand his supplicating look.

"Yes, tell her that," I replied in a firm tone, and held out my hand.

His eyes sparkled, and filled with tears of gratitude. So must Lazarus have looked when he rose dazed from the grave and once more beheld the sky and the blessed light of day. I felt the hand that was in mine tremble more and more violently. Then the old man bowed his head, lower and yet lower. I remembered just in time how on a former occasion he had stooped down and kissed my hand. Hurriedly I withdrew it.

"Yes," I repeated, "tell her that, please tell her that. Tell her not to worry. And above all—she must get well, soon, for herself, for all of us."

"Yes," he echoed ecstatically, "she must get well, get well soon. She'll go away at once now, oh, I'm sure of that! She'll go away at once and get well, well *because* of you, *for* you ... From the very first moment I knew that God had sent you to me ... No, no, I can't thank you. May God reward you! I'm going now ... No, stay where you are, please don't trouble. I'm going." And with quite a different gait from the one I knew, a light, springy step, he positively ran, his black coat-tails swinging behind him, to the door, which banged behind him with a clear, almost joyous sound. I stood alone in the dark room, slightly bewildered, as one always is when one has taken a decisive step without having made up one's mind to it beforehand. But what it was that I had actually promised in my weakness and my pity became clear to me in all its implications an hour later, when my batman, knocking timidly on the door, brought me a letter, written on the familiar blue paper.

"We're leaving tomorrow. I have given Papa my word. Forgive me for the last few days, but I was distracted by the fear that I was a burden to you. Now I know for WHAT and for WHOM I must get well. Now I no longer have any fear. Come tomorrow as early as you can. Never have I waited your coming with more impatience. Always, your E."

"Always." I shuddered as I read that word, which binds a person irrevocably and for all eternity. But there was no turning back now. Once more my pity had been stronger than my will. I had yielded myself up. I no longer belonged to myself.

Pull yourself together, I told myself. That is the very utmost that she can force from you, that half-promise that will never have to be fulfilled. One more day, two days, and they will go away, and you'll belong to yourself again. But the nearer the afternoon approached, the more I fretted, the more tormenting became the thought of having to meet her tender, trusting gaze with a lie in my heart. It was in vain that I tried to chatter unconcernedly with my comrades—I felt a hammering at my temples, my nerves tingled, and there was a sudden dryness in my mouth as though a half-extinguished fire were smouldering and flickering up within me. On a sudden impulse I ordered a cognac and gulped it down. It was of no use, my throat was still parched. And so I ordered a second cognac, and not until I had drunk a third did I become aware of my subconscious motive: I was drinking to inspire myself with courage so that when I reached Kekesfalva I should be neither cowardly nor sentimental. There was something in myself that I wanted to anaesthetize before-hand—perhaps fear, perhaps shame, perhaps some very good, perhaps some very evil, emotion. Yes, that was it, that was all it was—that was why soldiers were given a double ration of rum before going into battle; I wanted to deaden, to blunt my senses so as not to be too clearly aware of the equivocal, perhaps criti-cal, situation I was going to face. But the first effect of those three glasses was merely that my feet felt as heavy as lead and that there was a humming and vibrating in my head like that made by a dentist's drill before the last agonizing thrust. It was by no means a self-confident, clear-headed, still less joyful, young man who made his way hesitatingly, with pounding heart, along the interminable road—or was it merely that it seemed so to me today?—towards the dreaded *Schloss*.

Everything, however, went off far more easily than I had expected. Another, a better, kind of intoxication awaited me, a more sublime, a purer form of drunkenness than I had sought in the crude spirits. For vanity, too, inebriates; gratitude, too, intoxicates; tenderness, too, can blissfully confuse the senses. At the door good old Josef started back with an exclamation of delight. "Oh, the *Herr Leutnant*!" Swallowing hard, he almost pirouetted from one foot to the other in his excitement and looked up furtively—I cannot express it otherwise—as one gazes up at the image of a saint in church. "Will the *Herr Leutnant* kindly step across to the salon. Fräulein Edith has been expecting the *Herr Leutnant* the whole afternoon," he whispered in the flustered tones of one ashamed of his emotion.

Why was the old retainer looking at me so ecstatically? I asked myself in amazement. *Why* was he so fond of me? Were people really made so kind and happy by seeing others display kindness and pity? If that were so, Condor was right; if that were so, anyone who made a single person happy had fulfilled the purpose of his existence; it was really worth while to devote oneself to others to the very limit of one's strength, and even beyond. If that were so, every sacrifice was justified, and even a lie that made others happy was more important than truth itself. Of a sudden I felt my step grow firm, for a man who knows that he is bringing happiness with him has a new lightness in his tread.

At this moment Ilona came to meet me. She, too, was radiant. Her dark gaze seemed to embrace me with tender affection. Never yet had she pressed my hand so warmly, so cordially. "Thank you," she said, and her voice seemed to come through a warm summer shower. "You don't know what you've done for the poor child! You've saved her, really saved her. But come quickly, I can't tell you how eagerly she's awaiting you."

Meanwhile the other door moved softly. I had a feeling that someone was standing behind it, listening. The old man entered, and his eyes were no longer filled with the deathly horror of yesterday, but with a tender radiance. "How good that you've come! You'll be astonished at the change in her. Never in all the years since her illness began have I seen her so glowing, so happy. It's a miracle, a real miracle. Dear God, what you have done for her, for us!"

He broke down as he said these words. He swallowed and sobbed, ashamed of his emotion, which gradually began to affect me too. For who could be unmoved by such gratitude? I don't believe I have ever been a vain man, one who admires or over-estimates himself, and even today I have little faith either in my own goodness or my own strength. But the wild and frenzied gratitude of these two sent out a warm wave of confidence that carried me away irresistibly. Of a sudden all my fear, all my cowardice, was swept away as by a golden summer wind. Why should I not let myself be loved in all heedlessness, if it made others so happy? I grew positively eager to enter the room which the day before yesterday I had left in such despair.

And behold, there sat a girl in a chaise-longue whom I scarcely recognized, so gaily did she look up, such brightness emanated from her. She was wearing a dress of pale blue silk which made her look more girlish, more childish than ever. In her auburn hair gleamed white blossoms—were they myrtle?—and arranged round her chair were baskets of flowers, a gaily coloured hedge. She must long since have known that I was in the house, and had doubtless heard the delighted greetings of the others and my approaching footsteps. But this time there was no sign as I entered the room of that restless, inquisitorial gaze which was usually directed at me out of half-closed, suspicious lids. She sat there graceful and upright; and now I completely forgot that the rug concealed a deformity, and that the deep chaise-longue was actually her prison. I could do nothing but marvel at this new girlish creature, who seemed more childish than ever in her joy, yet more womanly in her beauty. She noticed my faint astonishment and accepted it as a gift.

"At last, at last!" she said, the old note of carefree comradeship ringing out in her voice. "Come and sit over here by me. And don't say anything. I have something important to say to you."

I sat down, completely at my ease. For how could one be confused, how remain embarrassed, when she spoke in such clear, friendly tones?

"Listen to me just for a moment. And don't interrupt me, please." I could tell that this time she had weighed every word. "I know everything you have told my father. I know what you mean to do for me. And now, please believe me, believe me word for word when I promise you that I shall never—never, do you hear!—never ask why you have done this, whether it is merely for my father's sake or really for me. Whether it is merely out of pity or ... no, don't interrupt me, I don't *want* to know, I refuse to know ... I will not go on worrying and tormenting myself and others. It's enough to know that it is only because of you that I am alive again and can go on living ... that only since yesterday have I begun to live. If I am cured, I shall have only one person to thank—you, you alone."

She hesitated for a moment and then went on: "And now listen to what I for my part am going to promise. I thought everything out last night. For the first time I weighed everything up as clearly as though I were quite well, and not in a fever of impatience as I used to when I was still uncertain. It's wonderful—I've only just realized it—to think without being afraid—wonderful! For the first time I have an idea what it will be like to be a healthy, normal person, and it is you, you alone, whom I have to thank for that. I mean, therefore, to do whatever the doctors ask of me—everything, everything, so as to become a human being instead of the impossible creature I now am. I shall never give in, never stop trying now that I know what depends upon it. I shall strive with every fibre, every nerve of my body and every drop of my blood, and I can't help thinking that when one wants a thing as desperately as I do, one can wrest it from God. All this I shall do for you—that is to say, so as to exact no sacrifice from you. But if things should not turn out well—please don't interrupt me— or not as well as we hope, if I should not be as completely well, as able to get about as other people—then have no fear. In that case I shall go through with it all by myself. There are sacrifices,

316

I know, that one cannot accept, least of all from the person one loves. If, therefore, this treatment, upon which I base all my hopes—all!—should be a failure, then you will never hear from me again, never see me again. In that case I shall never be a burden to you, I swear to you, for I shall no longer let myself be a burden to anyone, least of all to you. There—that's all. And now not another word. There are only a few hours left to us of each other's company, and I want them to be really happy."

This was a different voice in which she spoke to me, an adult voice, as it were. These were different eyes that gazed at me, no longer the restless eyes of a child or the fevered, avid eyes of an invalid. This, I felt, was a different love with which she loved me, not the reckless, the greedy, the tortured love of the early days. And I, too, looked at her with different eyes. It was not pity for her misfortune that moved me now; I no longer had any need to be anxious, to be cautious, I could be friendly and frank. Without being really aware of it myself, I felt for the first time real tenderness towards this frail girl who was so radiant in the anticipation of happiness to come. Without knowing what I was doing, without any conscious intention on my part, I moved my chair nearer to her and seized her hand. She did not, as before, quiver sensuously to my touch. Still and compliant, the cool slender wrist yielded itself to my grasp, and it was with delight that I felt how placidly the little pulse was beating.

We talked without constraint of the journey and of little everyday things; we chatted about what had been going on in the town, in the barracks. I could no longer understand how it was that I had tortured myself when everything, after all, was so simple. You just sat together and held hands, there was no need for you to force yourselves or to hide your real feelings, you showed that you were fond of one another, you did not struggle against your tender feelings, you accepted the other's love for you without shame and with sheer gratitude.

Then we went in to dinner. The silver candelabra gleamed in the candle-light, and the flowers rose up out of the vases like coloured flames. The light of the crystal chandelier was reflected from mirror to mirror, and around us, like an arching shell that holds in its depths a gleaming pearl, was the silent house.

Sometimes I thought I could hear the trees breathing tranquilly outside and the wind playing, warm and voluptuous, over the lawns, for a sweet fragrance was wafted in through the open windows. Everything was lovelier and better than ever. The old man sat there like a priest, erect and solemn, and never had I seen Edith or Ilona so radiant and so young, never had Josef's shirt-front shone so white, never had the smooth skin of the fruit glowed so colourfully. And we sat and ate and drank and talked, revelling in our new-found harmony. Blithe as a twittering bird, the laughter flew from one to the other, the merriment ebbed and flowed in playful ripples. Not until Josef filled the glasses with champagne and I raised my glass to Edith to drink her health was there a sudden silence.

"Yes, health—I must get well," she breathed, looking at me trustingly, as though my wish had power over life and death. "Well for you."

"God grant it!" Her father had risen, unable to contain himself. His spectacles were misty with tears; he took them off and polished them slowly and deliberately. I could tell that he could scarcely keep his hands off me, and I for my part was ready to respond. I too felt impelled to show some sign of my gratitude, and I went up to him and embraced him. As he returned to his seat, I could feel Edith's eyes upon me. Her lips trembled slightly; I realized how much her parted lips were yearning for the same fond touch. I quickly bent over her and kissed her on the mouth.

This was our betrothal. I had not kissed her upon conscious reflection, but upon a sudden impulse. It had happened without my knowledge or will. But I did not repent of the little gesture of sheer affection, for this time she did not wildly strain her heaving breast towards me, did not hold me fast in an ecstasy of happiness. Her lips accepted mine humbly as though receiving some precious gift. The others were silent. Then from the corner came a faint, shy noise. It sounded at first as though someone were clearing his throat in embarrassment, but when we looked up we saw that it was Josef, who was sobbing quietly in the corner. He had put down the champagne and turned away so that we should not notice this unseemly emotion on his part, but we all felt as though his clumsy tears were trickling warm from our own eyes. Suddenly I felt Edith's hand on mine. "Give me your hand for a moment."

I had no idea what she was going to do. Something cool and smooth was slipped on to my fourth finger—it was a ring. "Just to remind you of me when I am away," she said, by way of excuse. I did not look at the ring; I merely took her hand and kissed it.

On that evening I was God. I had created the world, and lo! it was full of goodness and justice. I had created a human being, her forehead gleamed like the morning and a rainbow of happiness was mirrored in her eyes. I had spread the table with riches and plenty, I had brought to maturity the fruit, the wine and the food. Piled up gloriously, these witnesses of my superabundance were offered up to me like sacrificial gifts, they came in glittering dishes and overflowing baskets; the wine sparkled, the fruit shimmered—sweet and delicious, they offered themselves to my mouth. I had brought light into this room and light into the heart of mankind. The chandelier, a glowing sun, was reflected in the glasses, the white damask tablecloth shone like snow, and I felt with pride that mankind loved the light that went forth from me, and I took its love and grew drunk on it. They offered me wine, and I drained my glass to the dregs. They offered me fruits and all manner of good things, and I rejoiced in their gifts. They offered me reverence and gratitude, and I accepted their homage as meat-offerings and drink-offerings.

On that evening I was God. But I did not look down coldly from an exalted throne upon my works and deeds. Kindly and mild, I sat there in the midst of my creatures, and perceived their countenances dimly as through the silvery mist of my clouds. On my left sat an old man; the great light of kindliness that emanated from me had smoothed out the wrinkles on his furrowed brow, chased away the shadows that darkened his eyes; I had removed death from him and he spoke in the voice of one resurrected, gratefully aware of the miracle that I had wrought in him. On my right sat a young girl, and she had been a cripple, chained and enslaved and ensnared beyond hope in her own chaotic misery. But now the light of returning health shed its rays upon her. With the breath of my lips I had raised her up out of the hell of her fears into the heaven of love, and her ring sparkled on my finger like the morning star. Opposite me sat another young girl. She too was smiling in gratitude, for it was I who had given her that beauty of countenance, set the dark fragrant forest of hair about her shimmering forehead. It was I who had bestowed upon them all that they had, and raised them up through the miracle of my presence. They all bore my light in their eyes; and when they looked at one another, I was the radiance in their gaze. When they talked together, I and I alone gave their speech meaning; and even when we were silent, I lingered in their thoughts. For I and I alone was the beginning, the focal point and the origin of their happiness; when they extolled one another, they were extolling me, and when they loved one another, they thought of me as the creator of all love. But I sat in their midst and beheld my works and saw that it was good to have dealt kindly with my creatures. And, in my generosity, with the wine I drank their love and with the food enjoyed their happiness.

On that evening I was God. I had calmed the waters of unrest and driven the darkness from their hearts. But from myself, too, I had chased away the fear, my soul was at peace as never before in all my life. Not until the evening drew to an end and I rose from the table was I assailed by a faint sense of grief, God's eternal grief on the seventh day, when His work is done, and this grief of mine was reflected in their faces, from which the light had suddenly vanished. For now it was time to say farewell. We were all strangely moved, as though we knew that something incomparable was drawing to a close, one of those rare untroubled hours which, like the clouds, never return. For the first time I felt disquieted at parting from Edith; like a lover I kept putting off the moment of bidding farewell to this girl who loved me. How pleasant it would be, I thought, to sit for a while by her bedside, to stroke and stroke her frail, shy hand, to see again and again that rosy smile of happiness light up her face. But it was late. So I merely threw my arms quickly around her and kissed her on the mouth. I felt her hold her breath as I did so, as though to keep for ever the warmth of my breath. Then I moved to the door, accompanied by Kekesfalva. One last look, one more "goodbye" and then I went off, free and confident as one always is after a task successfully accomplished, a meritorious deed.

I went out into the hall, where Josef was waiting for me with my cap and sword. If only I had gone more quickly! If only I had been more ruthless! But old Kekesfalva could not bring himself to part from me. Once more he seized me, once more he patted my arm, kept telling me over and over again how grateful he was to me, and what I had done for him. Now he could die in peace, his child would be cured, all was well now, and it was all my doing, all my doing! I grew more and more uncomfortable at being patted and flattered, in the presence of Josef, who was waiting patiently with bowed head. Several times I had shaken the old man by the hand in farewell, but he kept thanking me all over again. And I, the slave of my pity, I stood there, I stayed, unable to summon up the strength to tear myself away, although an ominous voice within me urged: enough, no more of this!

Suddenly we could hear a disturbance through the door of the room we had just left. I listened intently. Voices could be heard raised in argument and I realized in alarm that Edith and Ilona must be quarrelling. One of them seemed to be wanting to do something from which the other was trying to dissuade her. "Please, please," I could plainly hear Ilona's admonition, "do stay where you are," and Edith's brusque and angry retort, "No, let me be, let me be!" I listened with growing disquiet while the old man chattered away. What was going on behind that closed door? Why had the peace been thus disturbed, my peace, the divine peace of this day? What was Edith insisting upon doing, what was Ilona trying to stop her from doing? Then, suddenly, there came that loathsome sound, the tap-tap, tap-tap, tap-tap of crutches. God help us, surely she wasn't coming after me without Josef's help? But the dry, wooden tapping was faster now, was coming nearer: tap-tap, right, left ... tap-tap, right, left, right, left. I could not help picturing the swaying body; she must be quite near the door now. There was a bang, a thud, as of an inert bulky object being hurled against the door, then a breathless panting; the handle was agitated violently, and the door flew open.

Oh what a ghastly sight! Against the doorpost leaned Edith, still gasping from her exertions. She clung grimly to the post with her left hand so as not to lose her balance, while her right hand grasped the two crutches. Behind her, in obvious desperation, hovered Ilona, evidently trying to support her or to hold her back. But Edith's eyes flashed with impatience and anger. "Let me be, let me be, I tell you!" she shouted, refusing the unwelcome aid. "I don't need help from anyone, I can manage alone."

And then, before Kekesfalva or Josef had come to their senses, a most horrible thing happened. Biting her lips as though preparing for a terrific effort, and gazing up at me with wide-open, burning eyes, Edith gave one thrust against the doorpost, like a swimmer striking out from the shore, and began to walk towards me without the aid of her crutches. As she pushed off, she lurched as though falling into empty space, but quickly swung both hands into the air, the free one and the one that held the crutches, and regained her balance. Then, biting her lips again, she thrust one foot forward and dragged the other after it, her body rent by this spasmodic, marionette-like jerking from right to left. Yet she walked! She walked! She walked, her wide-open eyes fixed on me alone, she walked as though she were being propelled forward on invisible wires, her teeth pressed hard into her lips, her features painfully contorted. She walked, tossed hither and thither like a ship in a storm, it is true, but she walked—walked for the first time alone and without crutches or other aid! A miracle of the will must have brought life into her dead limbs. No doctor has ever been able to explain to me how it was that this crippled girl was able, this one and only time, to throw off the rigidity and weakness of her impotent legs, and I cannot describe what it was like, for we all stared as though petrified at her ecstatic eyes, even Ilona forgetting to go after her and watch over her. She staggered those few steps as though driven forward by an inner tempest. This was not walking, but flight, as it were, just above ground, the hovering, groping flight of a bird with clipped wings. But her will, that demon of the heart, urged her on and on. She was quite near me now, she was holding out her arms, which until now she had kept outspread like wings, longingly and triumphantly towards me; her drawn features relaxed into a smile of ecstatic bliss. She had accomplished it, the miracle! Only another two steps—no, only one, one last step; I could almost feel the breath coming from between the lips that were breaking into a smile—when disaster overtook her. By throwing out her arms prematurely in this violent gesture of longing, of anticipation of the embrace she had earned, she lost her balance. Her knees suddenly gave as though cut through with a scythe. She fell with a crash at my feet, the crutches fell with a clatter on the hard flagstones. And in the first shock of horror, instead of rushing forward and helping her up, as would have been natural, I involuntarily shrank back.

But Kekesfalva, Ilona and Josef had all rushed to her aid as she lay there groaning. Still incapable of raising my eyes, I realized that they carried her away. All I could hear were her stifled sobs, sobs of anger and despair, and their shuffling steps as they cautiously receded with their burden. In that one second the mist of rapture which had hung like a veil over my eyes the whole evening was torn aside, and in a flash I could see everything in all its dread reality. I knew that the hapless girl would never be completely cured. The miracle that they all awaited from me had not happened. I was no longer God, but a puny, pitiable human being, whose blackguardly weakness did nothing but harm, whose pity wrought nothing but havoc and misery. I was conscious, horribly conscious, of my duty; now or never was the time to keep faith with her. Now or never was the time to help her, run after the others, sit by her bedside, reassure her, lie to her, tell her that she had walked splendidly, that she was going to make a wonderful recovery. But I no longer had the strength for such a desperate piece of deception. I was seized with panic, a ghastly fear of those terrible, pleading eyes, those eyes that would once more be hungry with desire; fear of the impatience of this frenzied heart; fear of this catastrophe which was beyond my control. Without stopping to think what I was doing I seized my cap and sword, and for the third and last time fled like a criminal from the house.

Oh for air, a breath of air! I felt that I was suffocating. Was the night really so sultry among the trees, or was it the wine, all the wine I had drunk? My tunic clung stickily to my body; I tore open my collar, I longed to hurl my coat away, it was so heavy on my shoulders. Oh for air, a breath of air! It seemed to me as though my blood were trying to force its way through my skin, so hotly did it surge and beat in my ears. Tap-tap, tap-tap—was that still the horrible sound of crutches or merely the blood hammering at my temples? And why am I running like this? I thought. What has happened? I must try to think. What has actually happened? Try to think calmly, deliberately, don't listen to that tap-tap, tap-tap, tap-tap. Well—I've got engaged, no, they've made me get engaged ... I didn't want to, I never dreamed of such a thing ... and now I am engaged, now I am bound ... But no ... it can't be true ... only if she were cured, I told the old man, and she'll never be cured ... My promise only holds good ... no, it doesn't hold good at all. Nothing has happened, nothing. But did I not kiss her, kiss her on the mouth? I didn't mean to ... Oh, this pity, this cursed pity! Again and again they've ensnared me with it, and now I'm trapped. I've gone and got myself properly engaged, they were all witnesses, the old man and Ilona and Josef ... And I don't want to, don't want to ... What on earth am I to do? Try to think calmly ... Oh, it's revolting, that everlasting tap-tap, tap-tap! It'll go on hammering in my ears for ever now, she'll always be running after me on her crutches ... It has happened, the irrevocable has happened. I have duped them, they have duped me. I have got engaged. They have made me get engaged.

What was that? Why were the trees tumbling about in confusion? And the stars—how my eyes hurt and tingled! There must be something wrong with them! And how everything was pressing down on my head! Oh, the sultriness of the air. I ought to go and cool my head somewhere, and then I could think clearly again. Or drink something, wash the slimy, bitter taste out of my mouth. Wasn't that a fountain just ahead of me on the road—I had ridden past it so often? No, I had long since passed it, I must have been running like a lunatic, hence the terrible hammering, hammering, hammering at my temples. I must drink something, then perhaps I might come to my senses.

At last, when I came to the first group of low houses, I could see the yellow light of an oil-lamp glimmering through the half-covered window-pane. Ah yes, now I remembered it well—that was the little road-side tavern, where the drivers pulled up in the morning to warm themselves with a quick glass of schnapps. I'd ask for a glass of water or something bitter or pungent to wash away the slime from my throat. I must drink something, whatever it was. Without reflecting, and with the eagerness of one parched with thirst, I pushed open the door.

The asphyxiating smell of cheap tobacco came to me from the dimly lit den. At the back of the room was the bar, with its bottles of cheap spirits; in front was a table at which some road-menders were sitting over a game of cards. Leaning against the bar, his back towards me, was an Uhlan, exchanging pleasantries with the landlady. As I entered he felt the draught and turned round; when he saw me his mouth fell open in alarm. Pulling himself together, he clicked his heels. Why was he so frightened? Oh, of course, he probably took me for an officer of the military police, and he ought long since to have turned in. The landlady, too, looked up uneasily, and the workmen paused in their game. There must have been something odd about me. Only now, too late, did it occur to me that this was no doubt one of those taverns only frequented by the rank and file. As an officer I ought not to have set foot in it. Instinctively I turned to go.

But the landlady had already come bustling up obsequiously to ask what she could do for me. I realized that I should have to make some excuse for blindly stumbling in upon them. I did not feel very well, I said. Could she give me a slivovitz and a soda-water? "Certainly, certainly," she replied, scuttling off. Actually I only meant to stand at the bar and gulp the two glasses down, but at that moment the oil-lamp in the middle of the room suddenly began to rock, the bottles on the shelf to bob noiselessly up and down, and the floorboards suddenly to give beneath my feet, to pitch and roll. I reeled. Better sit down, I said to myself. Rallying what strength I still had, I managed to stagger to the empty table. The soda-water was brought to me, and I swallowed it at a draught. Oh, how cool and good it was—for one moment the sickly taste in my mouth disappeared. Then I quickly drained the glass of slivovitz and tried to struggle to my feet. But I could not; my feet seemed to have taken root in the floor, and there was a strange, dull roaring in my ears. I ordered another slivovitz. A cigarette, I thought, and I'll be off.

I lit the cigarette. I'll just sit here for a moment or two, I said to myself, resting my dazed head in my hands, and think, reflect, turn over things in my mind, one after another. Well there it is! I've gone and got myself engaged ... they've pushed me into it ... but it's only binding if ... Oh, it's no use trying to get out of it, it *is* binding, I'm committed ... I kissed her on the mouth, did so of my own free will. But it was only to comfort her, and because I knew that she would never be cured ... Why, didn't she fall to the ground like a log? One can't marry a woman like that, she's not a real woman, she's ... but they won't let me go, no, they'll never release me ... the old man, the djinn, the Old Man of the Sea, the djinn with the mournful eyes and the honest burgher's face and the gold-rimmed spectacles, who clings to me and won't be shaken off ... he keeps seizing me by the arm, he'll always keep dragging me back into the morass of my pity, my cursed pity. By tomorrow it'll be all over the town, they'll put an announcement in the newspapers, and then there'll be no turning back ... Wouldn't it be better if I were to prepare my family for the news, so that my mother and father don't learn of it from other people or from the newspapers? Explain to them how and why I got engaged, and tell them that there's no hurry about it, and that it was unintentional, that I only got mixed up in the whole thing out of pity ... Oh, this cursed, cursed pity! And they certainly won't understand in the regiment, not one of them. What was that Steinhübel said about Balinkay? "If you sell yourself, at least you should get a good price." Oh God, what construction will they put on it? I can't understand myself how I could go and get engaged to ... to that human wreck ... And just wait until Aunt Daisy gets to hear of it—there are no flies on her, you can't throw dust in her eyes! She won't be taken in by a lot of humbug about noble birth and estates, she'll go straight to the *Almanac de Gotha*, and in two days she'll have found out that Kekesfalva was formerly Leopold Kanitz and that Edith is a half-Jewess, and to her nothing could be worse than to have Jewish relations ... As for Mother, she'll get over it, the money will impress her—six or seven million, he said ... But I don't care a damn about his money, I haven't the least intention of really marrying her, not for all the money in the world ... I've only promised that if she's cured ... but how am I going to make them see that? As it is, everyone in the regiment has something against the old boy, and they're deuced fastidious in these matters ... the honour of the regiment and all that ... They haven't even forgiven Balinkay. He sold himself, they sneered ... sold himself to that old Dutch cow. And wait until they see Edith's crutches! No, I'd better not write about it, no one must know anything about it for the moment, no one. I'm not going to have my leg pulled by the whole mess. But how am I to keep out of their way? Hadn't I better go to Holland after all, to Balinkay? That's it— I haven't refused his offer yet, I can clear off to Rotterdam any time, and Condor will have to face the music. He got me into this pickle ... he'll have to find a way of putting matters right, he's to blame for the whole thing ... The best thing would be to go straight to him and tell him plainly ... that I simply cannot ... Oh, it was horrible to see her toppling over like a sack of oats ... one *can't* marry a creature like that! ... Yes, I'll tell him flatly that I'm clearing out ... I'll go to him at once ... Hi! Cabby, cabby! Where to? Florianigasse ... what was the number? Ninety-seven ... Look sharp, and you'll get a fat tip, but hurry ... Lay on to the horse ... Ah, here we are, I recognize it, the shabby house in which he lives, I remember it, the revolting, dirty spiral staircase ... But how lucky it's so steep! Ha-ha! She won't be able to follow me up here on her crutches; at any rate I'm safe here from that tap-tap ... What, is that slattern of a maid still at the door? Does she spend all her time standing at the door, the slut? "Is the doctor at home?" "No, no. But go in,'e come soon." The Bohemian trollop! Well, let's sit down and wait. Always have to wait for the fellow ... he's never at home. Oh God, let's hope the blind woman doesn't come shuffling in again. I can't do with her at this moment, my nerves won't stand it, this everlasting consideration for others ... Mother of God, here she comes! I can hear her step in the next room ... No, thank God, that can't be she, her tread isn't as firm as that, that must be someone else walking about and talking ... But I know the voice ... how's that? Why, that's ... that's my Aunt Daisy's voice, and ... however is it possible? How did Aunt Bella get here, and Mama, and my brother and his wife? Nonsense! Impossible! I'm waiting at Condor's in the Florianigasse ... No one in the family knows him, so why should they all suddenly be meeting at his flat? But yes, it is the family. I know that voice, that screech of Aunt Daisy's ... Good heavens, where can I hide? The steps are coming nearer and nearer ... now the door's opening ... opening on its own and—Good Lord!—there they all are standing in a semicircle as though posing for their photograph, and gazing at me; Mama in the black taffeta dress with the white ruffles which she wore at Ferdinand's wedding, and Aunt Daisy in puffed sleeves, her gold lorgnette poised on her sharp, arrogant nose, that revolting beak that I hated even as a child of four. My brother in a tailcoat ... why ever is he wearing tails? And his wife, Franzi, with her fat, podgy face ... Oh, it's revolting, revolting! Look at them all staring at me, and what a malicious smile Aunt Bella has on her face, just as though she were waiting for something ... There they are all standing round in a semicircle, as though at a reception, waiting and waiting ... What on earth are they waiting for?

And now "Congratulations," says my brother, coming solemnly up to me; I see that he's holding his top hat in his hand ... and I seem to detect a note of offensive contempt in his voice ... And "Congratulations, congratulations!" echo the others, nodding and bowing ... But how ... how have they all got to know about it, and how is it they're all here together? ... I thought Aunt Daisy had fallen out with Ferdinand ... and *I* haven't told anyone.

"Congratulations, by Jove! You've done pretty well for yourself—seven million, that's fine! Seven million, the whole family can come in on this." They all chatter away at once broad grins on their faces. "Splendid, splendid!" says Aunt Bella, smacking her lips, "Carli will be able to go on with his studies. An excellent match!" "I hear, moreover, it's one of the oldest families in the country," bleats my brother from behind his top hat, but Aunt Daisy screeches like a cockatoo: "Well we shall have to look into that!" And now my mother comes up and lisps timidly, "Aren't you going to introduce your bride to us?" Introduce her?

That's the last straw, they'll all see her crutches, see what a hell of a mess I've got into with my infernal pity ... I shall have to head them off ... And then, how can I possibly introduce her when we're in Condor's flat, up on the third floor of a building in the Florianigasse? The poor lame creature could never in all her life climb up eighty stairs ... But why are they all turning round as though something were happening in the next room? I can tell myself by the draught at my back ... that someone must have opened the door ... Is someone coming, then? Yes, I can hear someone coming ... I can hear something groaning and creaking and squeaking on the stairs ... there's something pulling and dragging and snorting Its way up ... tap-tap, tap-tap ... great heavens, surely she's not coming up? She wouldn't go and disgrace me like that with her crutches! I should sink through the floor with shame in front of this sneering crowd ... but my God, this is awful, It really is she! It can only be she ... tap-tap, tap-tap ... I know that sound ... tap-tap, tap-tap, it's coming nearer and nearer ... she'll be right up in a moment ... I'd better lock the door. But my brother has taken off his top hat and is bowing over his shoulder in the direction of the tap-tapping ... To whom is he bowing, and why is he bowing so low? And suddenly they all burst out laughing so loudly that the window-panes rattle. "A-a-h, now we know, now we know! A-ha! a-ha! ... So that explains the seven million, that explains it! A-haa! a-haa! So the crutches are thrown in with the dowry!"

Aah! I started up in a panic. Where was I? I stared around me wildly. My God! I must have fallen asleep, fallen asleep in this wretched little tavern. I gazed timidly around me. Had they noticed anything? The landlady was nonchalantly polishing the glasses, the Uhlan had his broad, sturdy back turned pointedly towards me. Perhaps they hadn't noticed anything. I could have dozed off for only a minute or two at the most, for the stub of my cigarette was still glowing in the ashtray.

My confused dream could only have lasted a minute or two. But it had washed away all the warm drowsiness from my body, and suddenly I knew with icy-cold clarity what had happened. Away, I must get away from this grog-shop. Throwing the money down on the table, I made for the door, and the Uhlan immediately stood to attention. I could feel the workmen eyeing me curiously as they glanced up from their game, and I knew that when I closed the door behind me they would begin to chatter about the queer fish in officer's uniform, that from now on everyone would laugh at me behind my back. All, all, all of them, and no one would have pity on the foolish slave of his own pity.

Where was I to go now? Anywhere but home. Anywhere but up to my empty room, where I should be alone with these horrible thoughts.

The best thing would be to have another drink, something cold, something with a bite in it, for once more I had that foul, bitter taste in my mouth. Perhaps it was the thoughts I wanted to spew up—oh, if only I could swill them away, burn them, deaden, obliterate them all! Oh, it was ghastly, this horrible feeling! Into the town! And, wonder of wonders—the café in the Rathausplatz was still open. Light shone through the gaps between the curtains of the windows. Oh for a drink—a drink !

I stepped inside, and could see from the door that they were all sprawling round our usual table, Ferencz, Count Steinhübel, the regimental doctor, the whole gang of them. But why was Jozsi staring at me in such consternation, why did he give his neighbour a furtive nudge, and why were they all goggling at me like that? Why had the conversation come to a sudden stop? They had just been having a violent argument and shouting at one another so loudly that I heard the noise on the doorstep; and now, no sooner did they see me than they all sat mute like a lot of stuffed fish. There must be something the matter.

Well, I couldn't turn back now that they had seen me. So I sauntered up to them as nonchalantly as possible. I didn't feel at all comfortable, and I hadn't the slightest desire for a lot of ragging and chatter. And, moreover, I felt a certain tension in the atmosphere. Usually they waved to a fellow or hurled a "*Servus*" like a cannon-ball across the room, but today they all sat there stiffly like schoolboys caught out in a prank.

"D'you mind?" I said sheepishly, as I drew up a chair.

Jozsi looked at me oddly. "What do you fellows say?" he

inquired, nodding across at the others. "Do we mind? Ever known a fellow stand on such ceremony? Well, well, that's only to be expected of Hofmiller now!"

This must have been a gibe on the wretched fellow's part, for the others either smirked or smothered a malicious laugh. Yes something was definitely the matter. Usually when one of us turned up after midnight he was questioned in detail as to where he had been and why, and the shafts were barbed with pointed innuendoes. Today not one of them said a word to me; they all seemed confoundedly ill-at-ease. I must have broken in upon their comfortable lethargy like a stone hurled into a stagnant pool. At length Jozsi leaned back and half-closed his left eye as though about to take aim.

"Well, may one congratulate you?" he asked.

"Congratulate me—what on?" I was so taken aback that I really did not know at first what he was getting at.

"Why, your friend the apothecary—he's just gone—had some yarn of how the butler had rung up from Kekesfalva and told him that you had ... become engaged to the ... to the ... well, let us say the ... young lady out there."

Now they all looked at me. One, two, three, four, five, six pairs of eyes were all fixed on my mouth; I knew that if I admitted the charge there would be an outburst of whistling, joking, jeering, mocking and ironical congratulations. No, I couldn't admit it. Impossible in front of these mockers.

"Nonsense!" I growled, trying to get out of it. But this attempt to extricate myself was not enough for them. Ferencz, genuinely curious, patted me on the back.

"Tell me, Toni, I am right after all? It isn't true, is it?"

He meant well, the good, loyal fellow, but he shouldn't have made it so easy for me to say "No". I was seized with an unutterable feeling of disgust at this unabashed, bantering curiosity. I felt how absurd it was to try to explain at this café table something I could not explain even in the privacy of my own soul.

"No, not a word of it!" I protested irritably, without pausing to reflect.

For a moment there was silence. They all gazed at one another in surprise and, I imagine, in some disappointment. I had obviously spoilt their fun for them. But Ferencz proudly propped his elbows on the table and roared triumphantly:

"There, what did I tell you! I know old Hofmiller as well as my own trouser-pockets! I told you straight away it was a lie—a dirty lie on the part of that damned apothecary. Well, I shall have a thing or two to say to him tomorrow morning, the lousy pill-mixer. He'd better palm his muck off on someone else and not on us ! I'll give him a piece of my mind, and a thick ear into the bargain! Infernal cheek! To go and drag a decent fellow's name in the dirt like that! To go and blabber out a low-down story like that about one of us! But you see—I said at once Hofmiller wouldn't do a thing like that! He wouldn't sell his good pair of legs, not for a mint of money!"

He turned to me and gave me a friendly slap on the back with his heavy hand.

"Really, Toni, I'm damned glad it isn't true. It would have disgraced you and all of us, disgraced the whole regiment."

"And how!" added Count Steinhübel. "Just fancy, the daughter of that old moneylender, who ruined poor old Uli Neuendorff with his dirty tricks. Quite bad enough that people like that are allowed to make a pile and buy estates and titles. It'd just suit him to get one of us tied up with his daughter. The low hound! He knows very well why he avoids me when he meets me in the street." As the din increased, Ferencz grew more and more excited. "That rogue of an apothecary—upon my soul, I've a good mind to go and ring his nightbell and rout him out and punch him on the jaw. Blasted impudence! Just because you'd been out to their place a few times, to go and tell a dirty lie like that about you!"

And now Baron Schonthäler, a slender, aristocratic greyhound of a fellow, joined in.

"I say, Hofmiller," he said, "I didn't like to interfere—*chacun à son goût* ! But if you want my frank opinion, from the start I wasn't too pleased when I heard that you were spending so much time with those people. We officers have got to consider whom we're honouring by going to their houses. What his business is, or was, I don't know, and it's not my affair. I don't go about checking up on people. But we fellows must maintain a certain reserve—you can see for yourself, before you know where you are all sorts of gossip goes flying around. We simply can't mix with people we don't really know. We must keep our hands clean, always. You can't touch pitch without being defiled. Well, I'm jolly glad you haven't got yourself into a worse mess."

They all talked excitedly at once, they let fly at the old man they dug up the most fantastic stories, they made merry at the expense of that "monstrosity", his daughter; and again and again one of them would turn to me to commend me for not really having got myself mixed up with "that riff-raff". And I— I sat there mute and motionless; their beastly praise was such martydom to me that I felt like roaring at them. "Shut your filthy mouths!" or yelling, "I'm the blackguard! The apothecary told you the truth! He wasn't lying, but I am. I am the cowardly, pitiable liar!" But I knew it was too late, too late to do anything. I couldn't draw back now, couldn't go back on my denial. And so I sat there mute and motionless, staring straight ahead, the cigarette extinguished between my tightly closed lips, and was horribly aware of the dastardly act of treachery that, by my silence, I was committing against the poor, innocent Edith. Oh, if only the earth would open and swallow me! If I could do away with myself! Finish myself off! I did not know where to look, did not know what to do with my hands, which might any moment betray me by their trembling. Cautiously I clasped them to me and twisted my fingers together till they hurt, in order to master my extreme agitation for a few minutes longer.

But even as my fingers were convulsively intertwined I felt a hard, foreign object between them. Involuntarily I groped for it. It was the ring which Edith had blushingly slipped on my finger only a few hours ago. The engagement ring that I had accepted from her. I no longer had the strength to tear this glittering proof of my mendacity from my finger. With the cowardly furtiveness of a thief I quickly turned the stone inwards before holding out my hand in farewell to my friends.

The Rathausplatz stood out in ghostly relief in the glacial white-ness of the moonlight, every contour of the cobblestones sharply outlined, every line traced cleanly from cellar to roof-top. I felt the same icy clarity within me. Never had my thoughts been more lucid and clear-cut than at that moment: I knew what I had done, and knew what it was my duty to do. At ten o'clock in the evening I had got engaged, and three hours later I had cravenly repudiated that engagement. In the presence of seven witnesses—a captain, two lieutenants, a regimental doctor, two second lieutenants and an ensign of my regiment—I had, with the engagement ring on my finger, allowed myself to be commended for my blackguardly lie. I had perfidiously compromised a girl who loved me passionately, a suffering, helpless, unsuspecting creature; I had without a protest allowed her father to be blackguarded, and a stranger who had told the truth slanderously to be called a liar. By the morning the whole regiment would know my shame, and then all would be over. Tomorrow the very men who had this evening patted me cordially on the back would cut me dead. As one who had been exposed as a liar I should no longer be able to wear the epaulettes of an officer, nor should I ever be able to go back to those I had betrayed, slandered. Even as far as Balinkay was concerned I was done for. Those three minutes of cowardice had ruined my life; the only thing left for me was a revolver. Even while I had been sitting at the table I had been clearly aware that there was only one way to retrieve my honour; and what I now pondered as I wandered alone through the streets was merely the manner in which I should put my resolve into effect. The thoughts arranged themselves quite clearly in my head, as though the white moonlight had penetrated my cap, and I portioned out the next two or three hours, the last of my life, as casually as though it were a matter of taking a rifle to pieces. I must see that everything was settled up decently, must not forget anything, overlook anything. First a letter to my parents apologizing for the pain that I was having to cause them. Then a written request to Ferencz not to have a row with the apothecary, since the matter would be settled by my death. A third letter to the Colonel, requesting him to prevent as far as possible all publicity; I should like to be buried in Vienna, no representatives from the regiment, no wreaths. Perhaps a few brief lines to Kekesfalva, asking him to assure Edith of my warmest affection and to tell her not to think too hardly of me. Then put my room in perfect order, make a note of all my little debts, and leave instructions for my horse to be sold to cover any outstanding bills. I had nothing to leave. My watch and the few clothes I possessed were to go to my batman—oh yes, and the ring and the gold cigarette-case I should like returned to Herr von Kekesfalva.

What else? Ah, of course, burn Edith's two letters, in fact all letters and photographs. Leave behind nothing of myself, no memory, no trace. Disappear, as I had lived, as inconspicuously as possible. All the same, there would be more than enough to do in the two or three hours left to me, for each letter must be carefully written so that no one should be able to attribute my action either to fear or an unbalanced mind. Then the last, the easiest, thing of all: lie down in bed, pull two or three blankets closely over my head and pile the heavy eiderdown on top of them so that the detonation should not be heard in the next room or in the street—that's how Captain Felber had done it. He had shot himself at midnight, and no one had heard a sound; it was not until next morning that they had found him with his brains blown out. Then press the barrel right up against my temple underneath the blankets. I knew I could rely on my revolver, for I happened to have oiled the bolt quite recently, and I knew I had a steady hand.

Never in my life—I must repeat—had I made clearer, more precise, more exact arrangements for anything than I did that night for my death. When, after an hour of apparently aimless wandering, I arrived outside the barracks, the whole programme was worked out in my mind, minute by minute, with all the precision of an official instruction. My step during the whole of that time was unhurried, my pulse regular, and I noticed with a certain pride how steady my hand was when I put the key into the lock of the little side-door which we officers always used after midnight. Even in the darkness I did not miss the little opening by a single inch. Now all I had to do was to cross the courtyard and climb three flights of stairs. Then I should be alone with myself, and could begin—and end—everything.

But as I approached the dark entrance from the moonlit quadrangle a figure moved in the doorway. Confound it! I thought. One of the fellows getting back just before me; he'll buttonhole me and keep me talking for God knows how long! The next moment, however, to my extreme discomfiture, I recognized the broad shoulders of Colonel Bubencic, my commanding officer, who had given me such a dressing-down only a few days before. He seemed deliberately to have stationed himself in the doorway; I knew that the old martinet did not care to see us subalterns arriving back late. But hell, what did it matter to me now! I should be reporting to someone very different tomorrow. And so I was about to go doggedly on my way, as though I had not noticed him, when he stepped forward out of the shadow. His grating voice pulled me up sharply.

"Lieutenant Hofmiller!"

I went up to him and stood to attention. He looked me up and down keenly.

"The latest fashion among you young gentlemen, I suppose, wearing your coats half open. D'you imagine you can wander about after midnight like a sow dragging her teats on the ground? The next thing will be you'll be slouching around with your flies open as well. I won't have it, I tell you! I expect my officers to go about properly dressed even after midnight. Understand?"

I clicked my heels smartly. "Yes, *Herr Oberst.*"

He wheeled round with a look of contempt and stamped off towards the staircase without saying goodnight, his broad back massive in the moonlight. But I was seized with fury to think that the last word I was to hear in my life should be a reprimand, and to my own surprise, acting involuntarily, as though merely obeying the dictates of my own body, I took a few hasty steps and hurried after him. I knew that what I was doing was completely absurd. Why try, an hour before my last hour on earth, to explain things to this obstinate old buffer, to set things right? But it is an absurdly inconsequential characteristic of suicides that, ten minutes before they are to become mangled corpses, they yield to the vanity of trying to make as tidy an exit from life as possible (from that life of which they will no longer know anything); that they shave themselves and put on clean underlinen (for whom?) before putting a bullet through their heads: indeed, I even remember hearing of a woman who made up her face and had her hair waved and scented with the most expensive

perfume before throwing herself from the fourth floor of a building. It was only this logically inexplicable impulse that urged my
legs forward, and if I now ran after the Colonel, it was—I must
emphasize—in no sense from fear of death or from sudden
cowardice, but simply from an absurd instinct for tidiness, a
desire not to vanish into nothingness leaving behind a lot of loose
ends.

The Colonel must have heard my step, for he turned round
abruptly, and his little piercing eyes stared at me in bewilderment
from beneath their bushy brows. The fact that a young subaltern
should dare to follow him without permission was an enormity
beyond his powers of comprehension. I came to a halt two paces
away from him, saluted and, braving the danger in his eye, I
said—and my voice must have been as wan as the moonlight:

"I beg your pardon, *Herr Oberst*, but may I have a word with
you?"

The bushy brows expanded into an astonished arch. "What?
Now? At half-past one in the morning?"

He looked morosely at me. The next moment, I felt, he would
burst out at me or order me to report on parade next morning.
But there must have been something in my face to disquiet him.
For one minute, two minutes, the hard, piercing eyes looked me
up and down.

"Fine thing, I must say!" he growled. "But as you please. Well
then, come up to my room and be quick about it!"

Colonel Svetozar Bubencic, whom I followed like a shadow up
the dimly-lit corridors and barrack stairs which, although they
now rang hollow and empty, still reeked of masculinity, was a
thorough-going martinet and the most feared of all the senior
officers. Short-legged, bull-necked, low-browed, he concealed
beneath bristling eyebrows a pair of deep-set, smouldering eyes
which had seldom been known to twinkle. The stocky body and
heavy, ponderous gait unmistakably betrayed his peasant origin
(he came from the Banat). But with his low, ox-like forehead and
iron skull he had slowly and perseveringly worked his way up to
the rank of Colonel. Because of his utter lack of culture, his rude
speech, his crude abusiveness and rough-and-ready manners,

the War Ministry, it is true, had for years transferred him from one provincial garrison to another, and it was taken for granted in higher quarters that he would be retired before reaching the rank of General. But unattractive and plebeian as he was, he had not his equal in the barracks or on the parade-ground. He knew every line of the service regulations as a Scottish Presbyterian knows his Bible; to him, far from being elastic laws to be adapted at discretion, they were almost religious commandments, the meaning or lack of meaning of which it was not a soldier's place to question. His life was dedicated to the service as is that of a believers to God. He had no truck with women, he neither smoked nor played cards, he had scarcely ever in his life been to a theatre or concert, and, like his Imperial Commander-in-Chief, Francis Joseph, he never read anything but the army regulations and the military gazette. Nothing existed for him on earth but the Imperial Army, in that army nothing but the cavalry, in the cavalry nothing but the Uhlans, and among the Uhlans only his own regiment. That everything in his own regiment should be better than in any other was, in a nutshell, the whole aim and object of his existence.

A man of limited vision is hard to bear with in any sphere in which he is invested with power, but in the army is intolerable. Since service in the army consists of the carrying out of a conglomeration of a thousand-and-one over-meticulous, for the most part outmoded and fossilized regulations, which only an out-and-out martinet knows by heart, and the literal carrying out of which only a fanatic demands, no one of us ever felt safe from this worshipper of the sacrosanct army code. As he sat in the saddle his corpulent figure was the very embodiment of military precision, he presided at mess with eyes as sharp as needles, he was the terror of the canteens and the regimental offices. A cold wind of fear invariably heralded his coming, and when the regiment was drawn up for inspection and Bubencic came riding slowly along on his stocky chestnut gelding, his head lowered slightly like that of a charging bull, every movement was stilled in the ranks as though enemy artillery had been brought into action and were already unlimbering and taking aim. At any moment, we knew, the first shot would be fired, and no one could be sure that he himself would not be the target. Even the horses stood as though frozen to the spot; not an ear twitched, not a spur jingled, not a breath stirred. Obviously enjoying the terror that he struck into everyone's heart, the tyrant would ride forward at a leisurely pace, spearing one after another of us, as it were, with his accurate eye, which let nothing escape it. It took in everything, that steely military eye, it spotted the cap that was pulled down a finger's breadth too low, detected the button that was badly polished, spied out the slightest speck of rust on a sword, or a badly groomed horse; and no sooner had the most trifling irregularity come to light than the culprit was for it. Beneath his close-fitting uniform the Colonel's Adam's apple would swell up apoplectically like a tumour, the forehead under the closely cropped hair would turn the colour of beetroot, thick blue veins would stand out on his temples. And then, in his raucous, hoarse voice, he would burst out into a storm, or rather a muddy torrent, of abuse; floods of foul invective would be poured upon the head of the guiltily innocent victim, and sometimes the coarseness of the Colonel's epithets was so embarrassing that we officers would gaze in discomfiture at the ground for very shame in the presence of the men.

The men feared him as though he were the Devil incarnate, for he would shower fatigues and punishments on them, and sometimes, in his fury, would even punch a man full in the face with his great fist. I myself had on one occasion in the stables seen a Ruthenian Uhlan make the sign of the Cross and tremblingly mutter a short prayer when the "old bull-frog"—we called him that because his fat throat swelled to bursting-point in his fury—was rampaging away in an adjoining box. Bubencic chivvied the wretched lads to the point of exhaustion, cuffed them, made them do rifle drill until their arms almost broke, and compelled them to ride the most restive horses until their legs were chafed and bleeding. Surprisingly enough, however, in their obtuse and frightened way these good peasant lads were fonder of their tyrant than of more lenient and yet more aloof officers. It was as though some instinct told them that this severity of the Colonel's had its origin in an obstinate and narrow desire for a divinely ordained state of order. The poor devils, moreover, were consoled by the knowledge that we officers did not come off very much more lightly, for a human being will accept the strictest disciplinary measures with a better grace if he knows that they will fall with equal severity on his neighbour. Justice in some mysterious way makes up for violence. Again and again the soldiers were cheered by the story of young Prince W; related to the Imperial family, he had imagined that he could claim all sorts of special privileges, but Bubencic had sentenced him to fourteen days' detention just as ruthlessly as though he had been a peasant's son; in vain, distinguished personages had rung up from Vienna to intervene; Bubencic had refused to remit a single day of the young aristocrat's sentence—a piece of defiance, incidentally, that cost him his promotion.

But what was odder still, even we officers could not help feeling a certain affection for him. We too were impressed by his blunt, implacable honesty, and above all by his feeling of absolute solidarity with officers and men. Just as he would not tolerate a speck of dust on a tunic, a splash of mud on the saddle of a single horse, so he could not endure the slightest injustice; he felt that any breath of scandal in the regiment was a slur on his own honour. We belonged to him and knew perfectly well that if ever one of us got into a scrape the wisest thing to do was to go straight to him. At first he might abuse us roundly, but in the end he would do his utmost to get us out of it. When there was any question of obtaining promotion or of securing an advance from the special officers' fund for any of us who was in a tight corner, he always took a firm line, went straight to the War Ministry, and forced the matter through with his bullet head. No matter how he might annoy and plague us, we all felt deep down in our hearts that this peasant from the Banat upheld more loyally and honestly than all the sprigs of the aristocracy the spirit and tradition of the army, that invisible glory on which we poorly paid subalterns subsisted far more than on our pay.

This, then, was Colonel Svetozar Bubencic, the arch-slave-driver of our regiment, in whose wake I now climbed the stairs. During the Great War he was to call himself to account in the same manly, blinkered, naïvely honest and honourable way in which he was for ever coming down upon us. During the Serbian campaign, after Potiorek's disastrous defeat, when exactly forty-nine men out of our whole regiment, the Colonel's pride, retreated safely across the Save, he stayed behind to the last on the opposite bank; then, feeling that the panic-stricken retreat was a slur on the honour of the army, he did something that only a very few commanders and senior officers did after a defeat: he took out his service revolver and put a bullet through his own head, so as not to be obliged to witness the downfall of his country which, with his limited perception, he had prophetically foreseen in that terrible moment when he had watched the headlong retreat of his regiment.

The Colonel unlocked his door and we entered his room, which, in its Spartan simplicity, resembled a student's cubicle: an iron camp-bed—he refused to sleep in greater comfort than Francis Joseph in the Hofburg—two coloured prints, on the right the Emperor, on the left the Empress, four or five cheaply framed photographs of inspections and regimental dinners, a pair of crossed swords and two Turkish pistols—that was all. No easy-chair, no books, nothing but four cane chairs round a bare table.

Bubencic stroked his moustache vigorously several times. We were all of us familiar with that gesture of his; it was an obvious sign of an ominous state of impatience.

"Make yourself at home," he growled at length, without offering me a chair; he was still panting for breath. "Let's have no beating about the bush—out with it. Is it money difficulties, or trouble with women?"

It was disagreeable to me to have to stand as I spoke, and, moreover, in the glare I felt too exposed to his impatient gaze. So I merely protested hurriedly that there was no question of money difficulties.

"Women, then! What, again! Why can't you fellows give yourselves a rest ! As though there weren't women enough who make the whole business damned simple. But let's come straight to the point—what's the trouble?"

I told him as briefly as possible that I had got engaged to the daughter of Kekesfalva and three hours later had flatly denied the fact. But he must on no account think that I wished to say anything in extenuation of my dishonourable conduct—on the contrary, I had merely come to inform him privately as my superior officer that I was fully aware of what was incumbent on me in view of my infamous behaviour. I knew what my duty was and would carry it out.

Bubencic stared at me somewhat uncomprehendingly.

"What's all this nonsense? Dishonourable conduct? What's incumbent on you? What the—? How the—? Why the—? Stuff and nonsense! You say you've got engaged to Kekesfalva's daughter? I saw her once. Well, no accounting for tastes—surely she's a crippled, deformed creature, isn't she? And then you thought better of it, I suppose? Well, there's nothing in that. Many a man has done that and couldn't be called a blackguard. Or have you ... "—he came nearer—"have you been having a bit of fun with her, and something's gone wrong? That, I'm afraid, would be a bad business." I was annoyed and ashamed. The airy, almost deliberately casual, way in which he misunderstood everything exasperated me.

"Permit me most respectfully to remark, *Herr Oberst*," I said, clicking my heels, "that I uttered this crude untruth about not being engaged in the presence of seven officers of the regiment at our table in the café. I lied to my fellow-officers out of cowardice and embarrassment. Tomorrow Lieutenant Hawliczek is going to challenge the apothecary who passed on the news, which happened to be perfectly correct. Tomorrow the whole town will know that I told an untruth in the presence of my fellow-officers, that I have disgraced the army."

At this he stared up in stupefaction. His slow-working brain had obviously at last taken in the significance of the whole thing. His face clouded over.

"Where was this, did you say?"

"At our table in the café."

"In the presence of your fellow-officers, you say? They all heard it?"

"Yes, *Herr Oberst.*"

"And the apothecary knows that you've denied it?"

"He'll hear it tomorrow. He, and the whole town."

The Colonel twirled and tugged violently at his moustache, as

342

though trying to tear it out by the roots. I could see that behind his low forehead his brain was busily at work. He began to pace up and down irritably, his hands crossed behind his back—once, twice, five times, ten times, twenty times—back and forth. The floor shook slightly beneath his heavy tread, and his spurs jingled faintly. At length he came to a halt in front of me.

"And what is it you're going to do?"

"There's only one way out. You know that yourself, *Herr Oberst*. I only came to say goodbye and to beg you most respectfully to see that everything is settled up afterwards, with as little publicity as possible. I don't want the regiment to be disgraced on my account."

"Nonsense!" he murmured. "Utter nonsense! Just for a thing like that. A smart, healthy, decent young fellow like you, because of a crippled creature like that! I suppose the old fox got round you and you couldn't decently get out of it. Ah well—I don't care a damn about them, the whole ruddy lot, what do they matter to us! But this business of your comrades and this lousy apothecary fellow knowing of it, that's the devil, of course!"

He began to pace up and down again, more violently than before. Thinking seemed to be a tremendous effort to him, for every time he turned my way in the midst of his pacing his face flushed a shade deeper and the veins now stood out on his temples like thick black roots. At last he came to a resolute halt. "Now then, listen to me. This sort of thing must be dealt with quickly. If the story gets about, we shan't be able to do anything. Now, first of all, who was present from the regiment?"

I mentioned the names. Bubencic took his notebook out of his breast-pocket—the notorious little red leather notebook which, whenever he caught out any member of the regiment in some misdemeanour, he drew out as though it were a sword. Anyone whose name was written in it might as well say goodbye to his next leave. The Colonel moistened his pencil with his lips in peasant fashion before noting down one name after another with his thick, broad nailed fingers.

"Is that the lot?"

"Yes."

"Definitely all?"

"Yes, *Herr Oberst*."

"I see." The Colonel stowed the notebook away in his breast-pocket as though sheathing a sword—and there was the same ring of finality in his "I see."

"I see. Well, we can put that right. Tomorrow I'll order them to report to me, all seven of them, one after another, before they set foot on the parade-ground, and God help the fellow who dare remember, after I've done with him, a word of what you said! I'll deal with the apothecary myself. I'll bamboozle him all right. I'll find a way of squaring him, you leave that to me. What about saying that you wished to ask permission before making the engagement public ... or, wait a minute"—he came so close up to me that I could feel his breath on my face, and his piercing eyes looked straight into mine—"tell me honestly, I mean really honestly: had you been drinking—I mean before you made a fool of yourself like that?"

I felt hot with shame. "Well, *Herr Oberst*, I certainly did have a couple of cognacs before I went out, and then out there ... at dinner I drank a fair amount ... but ... "

I expected an angry explosion. Instead, his face suddenly beamed all over. He rubbed his hands together and burst into a hearty, complacent laugh.

"Capital, capital, now I've got it! That's how we'll clear up the mess. It's clear as daylight. I'll simply tell them all you were as drunk as a lord and didn't know what you were saying. You didn't give your word of honour, I suppose?"

"No, *Herr Oberst*."

"Then everything's alright. You were just one over the eight, I'll tell them. It's happened even to the best people, even to an Archduke. You were dead-drunk, hadn't the ghost of an idea what you were saying, didn't listen properly and simply didn't understand what they were asking you. That's only logical, isn't it? And I'll hoodwink the apothecary into believing that I gave you a deuce of a dressing-down for blundering into the café in such a disgusting state. There we are—that settles point number one."

I seethed with indignation to think that he should so misunderstand me. It infuriated me to find that this fundamentally good-natured blockhead was, as it were, trying to hold the stirrup for me; obviously he thought I had buttonholed him out of fear, and wanted him to get me out of a scrape. Devil take it, why shouldn't he understand? And so I drew myself up.

"With respect, *Herr Oberst*, that won't settle the matter at all as far as I am concerned. I know what I've done, and know that I can't look a decent person in the face again; I've behaved caddishly, and I can't go on living and ... "

"Shut up!" he bawled. "Oh, I beg your pardon—but do let me think in peace and stop jabbering at me—I know my own business, and don't need to be taught it by a young whipper-snapper like you. Do you imagine this matter is your concern alone? My dear fellow, that was only the first point, and now comes point number two: tomorrow morning you'll have to clear out, I can't do with you here. One's got to let the grass grow over an affair of this sort. You mustn't stay here a day longer, or the whole place will be buzzing with gossip, and everywhere you go they'll be asking you questions, and I'm not going to have that. I won't have any officer of mine badgered with questions and looked at askance. I won't have it ... From tomorrow you're transferred to the reserve battalion in Czaslau ... I'll write the order out myself and give you a letter to the Colonel; what's in it will be no business of yours. It's your business to make yourself scarce, and what I do is my business. You and your batman will pack up your kit tonight, and leave the barracks so early tomorrow that not a soul in the whole regiment will set eyes on you. On parade tomorrow it'll simply be announced that you've been sent away on an urgent mission, so that no one will guess anything. How you will eventually settle up matters with the old man and his daughter is no affair of mine. You'll kindly get yourself out of your own mess—my only concern is that the matter shan't lead to a lot of scandal and gossip in the regiment ... Well, that's settled—you'll report to me here at half-past five in the morning, all packed and ready. I'll give you your letter, and then you'll be off! Understand?"

I hesitated. This was not why I had come. I had not been trying to find a way out. Bubencic noticed my hesitation.

"Understand?" he repeated almost threateningly.

"Very good, *Herr Oberst*," I answered in cool, military tones.

Let the old fool say what he likes, I said to myself inwardly. I shall do what I've got to do.

"There—that's that. In the morning, then, at half-past five."

I stood to attention. He came up to me.

"To think that you of all my officers should get yourself into such a blasted mess! I'm very reluctant to let those chaps at Czaslau have you. You've always been my favourite among the young fellows."

I could tell that he was considering whether to offer me his hand. His gaze had softened.

"Anything else you want? If I can be of any help to you, don't fail to come to me, I'll be glad to do what I can. I shouldn't like people to think you're in disgrace or anything like that. Is there anything you want?"

"No, thank you, *Herr Oberst.*"

"So much the better. Adieu. In the morning, then, at half-past five."

"Very good, *Herr Oberst.*"

I looked at him as one looks at a person for the last time. I knew that he was the last person I was to speak to on this earth. Tomorrow he would be the only one to know the whole truth. Clicking my heels smartly and squaring my shoulders, I marched out of the room.

But even the obtuse old buffer must have noticed something. There must have been something suspicious in my gaze or in my walk, for, "About turn, Hofmiller!" he ordered sharply.

I wheeled round. Raising his eyebrows, he looked me up and down keenly, and then murmured at once acidly and kindly:

"I do not much like the look of you, young fellow. Something's the matter with you. I have an inkling you're going to make a fool of me, you're planning some mischief. But I won't have you doing anything silly over such a business ... with a revolver ... or anything else ... I won't have it ... d'you understand?"

"Very good, *Herr Oberst.*"

"Oh, cut that out! You can't deceive me. I wasn't born yesterday." His voice softened. "Give me your hand."

I held it out to him. He gripped it firmly.

"And now"—he looked me keenly in the eyes—"your word of

honour, Hofmiller, that you won't do anything silly tonight! Your word of honour that you'll report here at half-past five and leave for Czaslau."

"My word of honour, *Herr Oberst*."

"That's all right then. You know, I was a bit afraid that in the heat of the moment you'd go and do something silly. One never knows with you impetuous young fellows ... you're always in a hurry to finish matters, even if it means using a revolver ... Later on you'll get some sense into your head. One gets over these things. You'll see, Hofmiller, nothing will come of the whole affair, nothing at all. I'll smooth it out to the very last crease, and you won't make a fool of yourself like that a second time. Well— you can go now—it would have been a pity, a fine young chap like you."

Our decisions are to a much greater extent dependent on our desire to conform to the standards of our class and environment than we are inclined to admit. A considerable proportion of our reasoning is merely an automatic function, so to speak, of influences and impressions which have become part of us, and anyone who has been brought up from childhood in the stern school of military discipline is particularly apt to succumb to the hypnotic and compulsive force exercised by an order or word of command; a force which is logically entirely incomprehensible and which irresistibly undermines his will. In the strait-jacket of a uniform, an officer will carry out his instructions, even though he is fully aware of their absurdity, just like a sleepwalker, unresistingly and almost unconsciously.

I too, who, out of a lifetime of twenty-five years, had spent the really formative fifteen years first at a military academy and then in the army, ceased, from the moment I heard the Colonel's order, to think or to act independently. I no longer reflected. I simply obeyed. My brain only registered one thing—that I had to report, ready to march, at half-past five, and by that time to make all my preparations without fail. Waking my batman, I informed him briefly that we had received urgent orders to leave for Czaslau in the morning, and helped him to pack up all my belongings. With some difficulty we managed to be ready in time, and on the stroke of half-past five I was duly standing in the Colonel's room, waiting to receive the relevant official documents. In accordance with his orders, I left the barracks without being observed.

This hypnotic paralysis of the will, it is true, only lasted as long as I was still within the four walls of the barracks and I had not completely carried out my instructions. With the first jolt of the train, I threw off the stupor that had come over me, and started up like a man who, after having been hurled to the ground by a violent explosion, staggers to his feet and finds to his surprise that he is unhurt.

My first shock of surprise was to find that I was still alive; my second that I was sitting in a moving train, snatched out of my ordinary daily existence. And no sooner had I begun to remember the events of the night before than everything rushed at feverish speed through my mind. I had been about to make an end of things, and someone had knocked the revolver out of my hand. The Colonel had said he would put everything right. But only, as I realized to my consternation, in so far as the regiment and my so-called "reputation" as an officer were concerned. At this very moment, perhaps, my fellow-officers would be standing before him, and it went without saying that they would all swear on their honour not to breathe a word about the incident. But no order could affect their inward thoughts, they would all be bound to realize that I had slunk off like a coward. The apothecary would, no doubt, let himself be talked round at first—but what of Edith, Kekesfalva and the others? Who was going to let them know, to explain the whole thing to them? Seven o'clock: she would just be waking up, and her first thought would be of me. Perhaps she was already on the terrace—ah, that terrace, why did I always shudder every time I thought of the balustrade?—gazing out through her binoculars at the parade-ground, watching our regiment trotting along, not knowing, not suspecting, that someone was missing. But in the afternoon she would begin to wait, and I should not come, and no one would have told her anything. I had not written her a line. She would telephone, would be informed that I had been transferred, and she would not understand, would not take it in. Or more terrible still: she *would* understand, understand straight away, and then ...

Suddenly I could see Condor's eyes gazing out menacingly from behind his gleaming pince-nez. Once more I could hear him shouting at me: "It would be a crime, a murder!" And immediately another picture was superimposed upon the first; a picture of Edith as she had levered herself up out of her chaise-longue and hurled herself against the balustrade—suicide, the abyss, mirrored in her eyes.

I must do something, do something at once! I must send a wire to her from the station, send her some message. I must at all costs prevent her doing something rash, irrevocable, in her despair. No, it was I who must not do anything rash, anything irrevocable, Condor had said, and if anything dreadful happened I was to let him know at once. I had promised him faithfully, and my word was my bond. Thank God, I should have two hours in Vienna to put this right, for my train did not leave until midday. Perhaps I should find Condor at home. I *must* see him.

On arrival I handed over all my luggage to my batman, telling him to go straight to the North-West Station and to wait for me there. Then I rushed off in a cab to Condor and kept praying (I am not as a rule religious): "O God, let him be in, let him be at home! He's the only person I can explain things to, the only one who can understand, who can help."

But the maid came shuffling towards me, a gaily coloured handkerchief tied round her head. The *Herr Doktor* was not at home, she said. Could I wait for him? "'E no come till midday." Did she know where he was? "No, don' know. 'E go many places." Might I perhaps speak to the *Frau Doktor*? "I go ask," she said, shrugging her shoulders.

I waited. The same room, the same long wait as before, and then, thank God, the same soft shuffling step in the next room!

The door was opened, timidly, uncertainly. As on the previous occasion, it was as though a puff of wind had blown it open, but this time the voice greeted me kindly and cordially.

"Oh, is it you, *Herr Leutnant*?"

"Yes," I said, bowing to the blind woman (foolish as ever).

"Oh, my husband will be sorry. I know he'll be terribly sorry not to have been at home. But I do hope you can wait. He'll be back in an hour at the latest."

349

"I'm so sorry, I'm afraid I can't wait. But ... it's a very important matter ... do you think I could get him on the telephone at the house of one of his patients?"

"No, I'm afraid that's impossible," she sighed. "I don't know where he is ... and then, you see ... the people he likes treating most are not on the telephone. But perhaps you could ... "

She came nearer, and a shy expression flitted over her face. She wanted to say something, but I could see she felt embarrassed.

"I ... I can tell," she managed to say at length, "I can tell that the matter must be very urgent ... and if there were any possibility, I should ... should, of course, tell you how to get hold of him. But ... but ... perhaps I could give him a message the moment he gets back ... I suppose it's about that poor girl out there, to whom you've been so kind ... If you like, I'll gladly undertake to do so ... "

And now an absurd thing happened to me: I did not venture to look this blind woman straight in the face. I don't know why, but I had a feeling that she knew everything, had guessed everything. I felt ashamed, and could only stammer out:

"It's very kind of you, *gnädige Frau*, but ... I don't want to trouble you. If you will allow me, I can leave a note for him. But it's quite certain he'll be back before two, isn't it? For the train goes just before two, and he must go out there, I mean ... it's absolutely essential, believe me, that he should go out there. I'm really not exaggerating."

I could feel that she believed me implicitly. She came nearer still, and I could see her involuntarily raising her hand as though to comfort and reassure me.

"Of course I believe it, if you say so. And don't worry. He'll do what he can."

"And may I write him a note?"

"Yes, do ... Over there, please."

She walked ahead with the remarkable assurance of one who knew every object in the room. A dozen times a day her nimble fingers must have tidied up his desk, for with the precision of one who could see she took three or four sheets of paper out of the left-hand drawer and laid them out quite straight on the blotter. "You'll find pen and ink there," she said, again pointing to the exact spot.

I dashed off five pages. I entreated Condor to go out to Kekesfalva at once, *at once*—I underlined the words three times. I told him everything as briefly and frankly as possible. I had not held out, I had repudiated my engagement in the presence of my fellow-officers. He had correctly surmised from the very beginning that my weakness had been due to my fear of what other people would think, my wretched fear of gossip. I did not conceal from him the fact that I had intended to commit suicide and that the Colonel had saved me against my will. But up to this moment, I said, I had thought only of myself; only now did I realize that I was bringing tragedy upon another, an innocent, person. He must go out there *at once*—once more I underlined the "at once"—he would, I knew, understand how urgent it was, and tell them the truth, the whole truth. He must not gloss over anything. He must not represent me as better than I was, as innocent. If, despite my weakness, she would forgive me, I should regard the engagement as more sacred than ever. Only *now* had it become really sacred to me, and, if she would allow me, I would go with her to Switzerland straight away, I would leave the service, I would stay with her no matter whether she got well sooner or later or not at all. I would do everything possible to atone for my cowardice, my lies; the only point of my life now was to prove to her that it was not she whom I had betrayed, but only the others. He was to tell her all this quite frankly, the whole truth, for only now did I realize how much I was bound to her, far more than to my comrades, to the service. She alone must judge me, pardon me. The decision as to whether she could forgive me was now in her hands, and would he please—it was a matter of life and death—leave everything and go out there by the midday train. He must be there by half-past four without fail, not a moment later, at the time when I was usually expected. It was my last request to him. This was the last time I should ever ask him to help me, and he must go out there at once—four times I underlined the scrawled "at once"—or all would be lost.

It was not until I put down my pen that I felt that I had made an honest decision for the first time. It was only while writing that I had realized what was the right thing to do. For the first time I felt grateful to the Colonel for saving me. I knew that from

351

now on I was bound for life to one person alone, to the woman who loved me.

Not until this moment did I realize that the blind woman had been standing motionless at my side. A feeling, an absurd feeling, came over me that she had read every word of my letter and knew everything about me.

"Please forgive my rudeness," I said, springing to my feet, "I had entirely forgotten ... but ... but ... it was so important to me to let your husband know at once ... "

She smiled at me.

"Oh, it doesn't hurt me to stand for a little while. The other thing was all that mattered. My husband is sure to do whatever you ask him ... I felt at once ... you see, I know every tone in his voice ... that he is fond of you, particularly fond ... And don't torment yourself"—her voice grew warmer and warmer— "don't torment yourself, I beg you ... everything's sure to be all right."

"God grant it!" I said, full of genuine hope, for had it not been said of the blind that they had second sight?

I bent down and kissed her hand. When I looked up, I could not understand how this woman with the grey hair, the harsh mouth, and that bitter look in her blind eyes had at first seemed ugly to me. For her countenance now shone with love and human sympathy. I felt as though those eyes that mirrored nothing but eternal darkness knew more of the reality of life than all those that gazed out, clear and radiant, upon the world.

Like a man cured of an illness I took my leave. The fact that at this moment I had pledged myself anew and for ever to another helpless outcast no longer seemed to me to entail a sacrifice. No, it was not the healthy, the confident, the proud, the joyous, the happy that one must love—they had no need of one's love! Arrogant and indifferent, they accepted love only as homage that was theirs to command, as their due. The devotion of another was to them a mere embellishment, an ornament for the hair, a bracelet on the arm, not the whole meaning and bliss of their lives. Only those with whom life had dealt hardly, the wretched, the slighted, the uncertain, the unlovely, the humiliated, could really be helped by love. He who devoted his life to them atoned to them for what life had taken from them. They alone knew how to love and be loved as one should love and be loved—gratefully and humbly.

My batman was waiting faithfully at the station. "Come along!" I smiled at him. All of a sudden I felt remarkably light-hearted. I knew with a feeling of relief such as I had never known before that I had done the right thing. I had saved myself, I had saved someone else. And I no longer regretted my senseless cowardice of the night before. On the contrary, I told myself, it was *better* so. It was better that it should have happened thus, that those who had faith in me should now know that I was no hero, no saint, no God who had graciously deigned to raise up a poor sick creature to sit beside Him in the clouds. If I now accepted her love, there was no longer any question of sacrifice. No, it was now for me to beg forgiveness, for her to grant it. It was better so.

Never before had I felt so sure of myself. Only once did a fleeting shadow of fear touch me, and that was in Lundenburg, when a fat man burst into the compartment, sank into a seat, and panted: "Thank the Lord I've caught it! If it hadn't been six minutes late I should have missed it."

Anxiety surged up within me for a moment. What if Condor had not returned home at midday after all? Or if he had come too late to catch the midday train? In that case, all would have been in vain! She would wait and wait. Once more there flashed through my mind that horrible scene on the terrace when she had clung to the balustrade and stared down into the depths below. Oh God, she must be told in time how much I rued my treachery! In good time, before she was plunged into despair, before the worst happened! Perhaps it would be best if I sent her a telegram at the next stop, just a few words to set her mind at rest in case Condor should not have given her my message.

At Brünn, the next station, I jumped out of the train and rushed to the telegraph office on the platform. But whatever was the matter? Outside the door was a surging throng, a black, clustering, excited mass of people, all reading a notice. I had to elbow my way roughly through to the little glass door in the post office. Quickly, quickly, a telegraph form. What should I say?

The great thing was to be brief.

"Edith von Kekesfalva, Kekesfalva. Thousand greetings and best wishes. Called away on duty. Back soon. Condor explaining everything. Writing on arrival. Your devoted Anton."

I handed in the telegram. How slow the postmistress was, what a lot of questions she asked: name and address of sender, one formality after another. And my train was leaving in two minutes. Again I had to employ a good deal of force in order to push my way through the curious mob which was standing round the notice and had in the meantime swelled considerably. Whatever was the matter? I was just about to ask, when the whistle blew shrilly, and I just had time to leap into the carriage. Thank God, I had settled that, she could not be suspicious now, could not be uneasy! I was just beginning to realize how exhausted I was after those two nerve-wracking days, those two sleepless nights. And when, that evening, I arrived in Czaslau, I had to rally all my strength in order to stagger up to my hotel bedroom on the first floor, where I plunged into sleep as into an abyss.

I think I must have fallen asleep the moment my head touched the pillow—it was like sinking with numbed senses into a dark, deep flood, deep, deep down into depths of dissolution never otherwise reached. Only much later did I find myself dreaming a dream, of which I no longer remember the beginning. All that I can remember is that I was once more standing in a room, I think it was Condor's waiting-room, and suddenly I could hear that dread wooden sound that for days had been hammering at my temples, the rhythmic sound of crutches, that terrible tap-tap, tap-tap. At first I could hear it in the distance as though it were coming from the street, then it came nearer—tap-tap, tap-tap—and then quite near, loud and insistent—tap-tap, tap-tap—and finally so horribly close to the door of my room that I started up out of my dream and awoke.

Wide-eyed, I stared into the darkness of the strange room. But there it was again: tap-tap—the vigorous rapping of knuckles on hard wood. No, I was not dreaming now, someone really was knocking on my door. I jumped out of bed and hastily opened the door. The night porter was standing there.

"The *Herr Leutnant* is wanted on the telephone."

I stared at him. I? Wanted on the telephone? Where ... where was I, then? A strange room, a strange room ... ah yes ... I was in ... Czaslau. But I didn't know a single soul here, so who could be ringing me up in the middle of the night? Absurd! It must be midnight at least. But "Please hurry, *Herr Leutnant*," insisted the porter. "It's a trunk call from Vienna. I couldn't quite catch the name."

In an instant I was wide awake. It could only be Condor. He must have some news for me.

"Go down quickly," I barked at the porter. "Tell them I'm coming in a moment."

The porter disappeared, and throwing my overcoat as quickly as possible over my nightshirt, I hurried after him. The telephone was in a corner of the office on the ground floor; the porter was holding the receiver to his ear. I thrust him aside impatiently, although he was saying, "They've been cut off," and listened.

But I could hear nothing ... nothing. Nothing but a distant buzzing and humming ... bzz ... bzz ... brrr, a metallic droning as of mosquitoes' wings. "Hallo, hallo!" I shouted, and waited, waited. No reply. Nothing but that contemptuous, meaningless buzz. Was I shivering because I had nothing on over my shirt but my overcoat, or was it sudden fear that was making my teeth chatter? Perhaps there had been a crisis. Or perhaps ... I waited, I listened, the hot rubber ring pressed close up against my ear. At last—krrx, krrx—the line was changed, and I could hear the voice of the operator:

"Did you get your call?"

"No."

"But you were through a moment ago. A call from Vienna! Just a moment, please."

Again that krrx, krrx. Then the line was changed again, and there was a squeaking, a clicking, a whirring, a gurgling, followed by a roaring and a whistling, which gradually died away into the faint humming and singing of the wires. Suddenly a voice, a harsh raucous bass:

"This is Headquarters, Prague, speaking. Is that the War Ministry?"

"No," I shouted in desperation. The voice rumbled on somewhat indistinctly and then faded out, was lost in the void. Once more that stupid singing and murmuring, and then once again a confused buzz of distant voices. Then I could hear the operator.

"Excuse me, I have been making inquiries. The line has been cleared. An urgent official call. I'll give you a ring the moment the subscriber calls again. Hang up your receiver, please." I hung up the receiver, exhausted, disappointed, infuriated. There is nothing more exasperating than to have succeeded in capturing a voice from a distance and to be unable to hold it. My heart was pounding in my chest as though I had climbed up a mountain too quickly. Who could it have been? It could only have been Condor. But why was he telephoning me at half-past twelve at night?

The porter came up to me politely. "The *Herr Leutnant* can perfectly well wait in his room. I'll rush up the moment the call comes through."

But I refused his offer. I mustn't miss the call a second time. I wasn't going to lose a single minute. I *must* know what had happened, for something—I could feel—had happened many kilometres away. It could only have been Condor or the Kekesfalvas. He was the only one who could have given them the address of my hotel. In any case it must have been something important, something urgent, or I should not have been fetched out of my bed at midnight. My tingling nerves told me that I was wanted, that I was needed. Someone wanted something of me. Someone had something extremely important to tell me, something that was a matter of life and death. No, I could not go away, I must remain at my post. I did not want to miss a minute. And so I sat down on the hard wooden chair which the somewhat surprised porter brought for me, and waited, my bare legs hidden under my overcoat, my gaze riveted on the instrument. I waited for a quarter of an hour, half an hour, shivering with anxiety and with cold, again and again wiping away with my shirtsleeve the sweat that kept breaking out on my forehead. At last—rrr—a ring. I rushed to the contraption, snatched up the receiver. Now, now I should hear everything.

But I had made a stupid mistake, to which the porter immediately drew my attention. It was not the telephone that had rung, but the hotel bell, and a pair of late arrivals was admitted. A captain came bustling through the door with a girl, and they threw an astonished look in passing at the strange individual in the porter's lodge who, bare-necked and bare-legged, stared at them from out of an officer's overcoat.

And now I could bear it no longer. I turned the handle and asked the operator, "Hasn't my call come through yet?"

"Which call?"

"From Vienna ... I think from Vienna ... over half an hour ago."

"I'll make inquiries. Just a moment."

That moment lasted an eternity. At last a ring. But the operator merely said reassuringly:

"I'm still making inquiries. Just a moment. I'll ring you again shortly."

Wait! Wait another few minutes? Minutes? Minutes? In the space of a second a human being can die, a fate be decided, a world collapse! Why were they making me wait, wait such a criminally long time? This was martyrdom, madness! It was already half-past one by the clock. I had been sitting about here, shuddering and shivering and waiting, for an hour.

At last, at last, another ring. I strained all my senses to listen, but the operator only said:

"The call has been cancelled."

Cancelled? What did that mean? Cancelled? "One moment, Fräulein." But she had already rung off.

Cancelled? Why cancelled? Why did they ring me up at half-past twelve at night and then cancel the call? Something must have happened of which I knew nothing and which I yet must know. How awful, how horrible, not to be able to penetrate time and distance! Should I ring Condor up myself? No, not now in the middle of the night. His wife would be frightened. Probably it was too late for him, and he had decided to ring up first thing in the morning.

Oh that night, I cannot describe it! Wild thoughts, confused images, chasing madly through my brain, and I myself dead-tired and yet wakeful, waiting and waiting with every nerve in my body, listening to every step on the stairs and in the corridor, to every ring and clatter in the street, to every movement and every sound, and at the same time reeling with weariness, washed out, worn out, and then, at last, sleep, far too deep, too long a sleep, timeless as death, abysmal as nothingness.

When I awoke, it was daylight. A glance at my watch: half-past ten. My God, and I had been ordered by the Colonel to report immediately! Once again, before I had time to think of anything personal, the military part of my brain began to function automatically. I struggled into my uniform and rushed down the stairs. The porter tried to waylay me. No—everything else must wait till later. First I must report, as I had promised the Colonel on my word of honour.

My officer's sash properly adjusted, I entered the regimental offices. But there was no one there but a little red-haired non-commissioned officer, who stared up at me in dismay when he saw me.

"Please go down at once, *Herr Leutnant*. The Lieutenant-Colonel has given express orders that all the officers and men of the garrison must parade at eleven sharp. Please go down quickly."

I raced down the stairs. There they all were, the whole garrison, drawn up in the courtyard. I just had time to take my place next to the chaplain before the Divisional General appeared. He walked at a curiously slow and solemn pace, unfolded a document, and read out in a ringing voice:

"A terrible crime has been committed which has filled Austria-Hungary and the whole civilized world with horror."—What crime? I thought in alarm. Involuntarily I began to tremble, as though I myself were the criminal—*"The most perfidious murder . . . "*—What murder?— *"of the beloved Heir to the Throne, His Imperial Highness Archduke Franz Ferdinand, and Her Imperial Highness the Archduchess"*—What? The heir to the throne had been murdered? When? Ah, of course— that was why there had been such a crowd round that notice in Brunn—that was it!—*"has plunged our Imperial house into deep sorrow and mourning. But it is, above all, the Imperial Army which . . . "*

I could scarcely hear the rest. I do not know why, but the word "crime" and the word "murder" had been like a stab at my heart. I could not have been more horrified had I myself been the murderer. A crime, a murder—those were the words Condor had used.

All of a sudden I could no longer take in what this General in blue uniform with plumes and rows of decorations was babbling and shouting at us. All of a sudden I remembered last night's telephone call. Why had Condor not got in touch with me this morning? Had something happened, after all? Without reporting to the Lieutenant-Colonel, I took advantage of the general confusion after the General's address to slip back quietly to the hotel. Perhaps a call had come for me in the meantime.

The porter handed me a telegram. It had arrived early that morning, but I had rushed past him in such a hurry that he had been unable to give it to me. I tore it open. At first I could make nothing of it. No signature! A completely incomprehensible message! Then I understood: it was merely a communication from the post office to the effect that it had been impossible to deliver the telegram that I had handed in at three-fifty-eight p.m. in Brünn the day before.

Impossible to deliver it? I stared at the words. Impossible to deliver a telegram to Edith von Kekesfalva? But everyone knew her in the little place. Now I could no longer bear the tension. I got a call put through to Dr Condor. "Urgent?" asked the porter. "Yes, urgent."

The call came through in twenty minutes and—melancholy miracle!—Condor was at home and himself answered the phone. In three minutes I heard everything—a trunk call doesn't give one time to mince matters. A devilish freak of fate had frustrated all my plans, and the unfortunate girl had not learned of my remorse, my sincere and honest resolve. All the steps taken by the Colonel to hush the matter up had proved in vain, for Ferencz and the others, instead of going straight home from the café, had gone on to the little bar, where, unfortunately, they had met the apothecary among a crowd of people, and Ferencz, the good-natured bungler, had, out of sheer affection for me, let fly at him. In the presence of everyone he had taken him thoroughly to task and accused him of having spread abominable lies about me. There had been a frightful scene, and the next day it had been all over the town, for the apothecary, feeling his honour called in question, had rushed straight off to the barracks next morning to compel me to bear him out in his story, and on being greeted with the highly suspicious news that I had disappeared, he had driven out to the Kekesfalvas'. Arrived there, he had burst in upon the old man in his office and stormed at him until the window-panes rattled, saying that Kekesfalva had made a fool of him with his idiotic telephone message, and that he, as a respectable citizen, was not going to put up with insults from those impudent young cubs of officers. He knew why I had de-camped in such a cowardly way; they couldn't humbug him into believing that it had merely been a joke; there was some thoroughgoing knavery on my part at the bottom of it all. Even if he had to go to the Ministry of War he would get the matter cleared up; he wasn't going to let himself be abused by a lot of snivelling young-sters in a public place.

It had only with difficulty been possible to calm him down and get him out of the house. In the midst of his consternation Kekesfalva had hoped for only one thing—that Edith should not hear a word of these wild surmises. But, as Fate would have it, the windows of the office had been open, and the apothecary's words had rung out with terrible distinctness across the courtyard and penetrated to the window of the salon, where she was sitting. She had no doubt decided to put her long-planned resolve into imme-diate effect, but she knew how to act a part; she had had her new clothes shown to her once more, she had laughed and joked with Ilona, had behaved charmingly to her father, had asked about a hundred and one details, and had inquired if everything was packed and ready. Secretly she had instructed Josef to ring up the barracks to inquire when I was coming back and whether I had not left a message. The fact that the orderly faithfully reported that I had been indefinitely transferred and had left no message for any-one had tipped the scales. In her impetuosity she had refused to wait a day, an hour longer. I had disappointed her too profound-ly, struck her too mortal a blow, for her to place any more faith in me, and my weakness had endowed her with fatal strength.

' After lunch she had had herself taken up to the terrace. Inspired by some dim foreboding, Ilona had felt disquieted by her unexpected cheerfulness, and had not stirred from her side. At half-past four—at the time when I usually turned up, and exactly a quarter of an hour before my telegram and Condor arrived—Edith had asked her faithful companion to fetch her a certain book, and, as Fate would have it, Ilona had complied with this seemingly innocent request. And the impatient girl, unable to tame her wild heart, had taken advantage of that one brief moment to put into effect her terrible resolve—just as she had told me she would on that very terrace, just as I had seen her put it into effect in my agonized dreams.

Condor had found her still alive. In some incomprehensible way her frail body had borne no external signs of serious injury, and she had been taken away unconscious in an ambulance to Vienna. Until late at night the doctors had hoped to be able to save her, and at eight o'clock, therefore, Condor had put through an urgent call to me from the sanatorium. But on that night of the 29th of June, the day on which the Archduke was murdered, all State departments were in a state of uproar, and the telephone lines were all engaged without interruption by the civil and military authorities. For four hours Condor had waited in vain to get through. Only when, just after midnight, the doctors had decided that there was no more hope, had he cancelled the call. Half an hour later she was dead.

Of the hundreds of thousands of men called to the war in those August days, few, I am certain, went off so nonchalantly, if not impatiently, to the front as I. Not that I was particularly war-minded. For me it was merely a way out, a means of escape. I fled into the war as a criminal flees into the darkness. The four weeks before war was declared I spent in a state of self-loathing, bewilderment and despair which I remember today with even more horror than the most ghastly moments at the front. For I was convinced that through my weakness, my pity, that pity which alternately advanced and receded, I had murdered a human being, the only human being who loved me passionately. I no longer ventured to go out into the streets; I reported sick, I hid away in my room. I wrote to Kekesfalva to express my sympathy (alas, it was really an acknowledgment of my guilt!); he did not reply. I overwhelmed Condor with explanations in self-justification; he did not reply. No word came from my fellow officers, nor from my father—probably because he was overburdened with work in his department during those critical weeks. I, however, saw in this unanimous silence universal condemnation. I became more and more a prey to the delusion that they had all condemned me, as I had condemned myself, that they all regarded me as a murderer, for that was how I regarded myself. While the whole Empire was quivering with excitement, while all over a distracted Europe the wires vibrated, were white-hot, with news of disaster, while markets tottered, armies mobilized and the prudent were already packing their trunks, I could think of nothing but my cowardly treachery, my guilt. To be called away from myself, therefore, meant release for me; the war that drew into its vortex millions of innocent people saved me, guilt-oppressed, from despair (not that I glorify war on that account).

Melodramatic phrases revolt me. So I am not going to say that I sought death. I shall only say that I did not fear it, or at least feared it less than most people, for there were moments when the thought of returning home, where I should meet those who shared the knowledge of my guilt, was more horrible to me than all the horrors of the front. Where, moreover, was there for me to go? Who was there who needed me, who was there who still loved me? For whom, for what was I to go on living? In so far as bravery is no more than not being afraid, I may safely and honestly claim to have been brave in the field, for even what to the most valorous of my comrades seemed worse than death, even the possibility of being crippled, of being maimed, held no terrors for me. I should probably have looked upon it as a punishment, as a just vengeance on the part of Providence, to have myself been made a helpless cripple, the prey of every stranger's pity, because my pity had been so cowardly, so weak. If, then, Death did not cross my path, the fault did not lie with me; dozens of times I went to meet him with the cold eye of indifference. Wherever there was any particularly difficult task to perform, I would volunteer. Wherever there was fierce fighting, wherever there was danger, I felt happy. After being wounded for the first time I transferred to a machine-gun company and then later to the Air Force; apparently I really did perform all sorts of daring feats in our gimcrack machines. But whenever I read the word "bravery" in a despatch in connection with my name, I had the feeling that I was a fraud. And whenever anyone peered too closely at my medals, I turned quickly away.

When those four interminable years came to an end, I discovered to my own astonishment that, despite everything, I was able to go on living in my former world. For we who had returned from hell measured everything by new standards. To have the death of a human being on one's conscience no longer meant the same to a man who had been to the front as to a man of the pre-war era. In the vast blood bath of the war my own private guilt had been absorbed into the general guilt; for I was the same person, it was the same eyes, the same hands, that had, after all, set up the machine-gun at Limanova which had mown down the first wave of Russian infantry to advance on our trenches, and I myself had afterwards seen through my field-glasses the hideous eyes of those whom I had been instrumental in killing, in wounding, and who, impaled on barbed wire, groaned for hours until they died a pitiable death. I had brought down an aeroplane on the outskirts of Görz; three times it had turned a somersault in the air before it crashed in the Alps and went up in a sheet of flames, and then with our own hands we had searched the charred and still gruesomely smouldering bodies for their identity discs. Thousands upon thousands of those who went to the war with me did the same, with rifle, bayonet, hand-grenade, machine-gun and naked fist, hundreds of thousands, millions of my generation, in France, in Russia and Germany—of what moment, then, was one murder more, what mattered private, personal guilt in the midst of this thousandfold, cosmic destruction and wrecking of human life, the most appalling holocaust that history had ever known?

And then—a further relief—in this world to which I returned there was no one left to bear witness against me. No one could reproach with past cowardice one so singled out for his special bravery. There was no one to call me a liar, a weakling.

Kekesfalva had survived his daughter's death by only a few days. Ilona was living as the wife of an insignificant lawyer in a Yugoslav village. Colonel Bubencic had shot himself on the Save. My fellow-officers had either been killed in action or had long since forgotten the trivial episode—everything that had happened before the war had become as trivial, as valueless as the former Austrian currency. There was no one to accuse me, no one to judge me. I felt like a murderer who has buried the corpse of his victim in a wood: the snow begins to fall in thick, white, dense flakes; layer upon layer for months. He knows, this concealing coverlet will hide his crime, and afterwards all trace of it will have vanished for ever. And so I plucked up courage and began to live again. Since no one reminded me of it, I myself forgot my guilt. For the heart is able to bury deep and well what it urgently desires to forget.

Only once did a reminder come to me from the other shore. I was sitting in the Vienna Opera House, in a corner seat of the last row of the stalls, listening to Gluck's *Orphée*, the pure and restrained melancholy of which grips me more than any other music. The overture had just ended, and although the house lights did not go up for the brief interval, one or two stragglers were given an opportunity of finding their way in the dark to their seats. Two of these latecomers, a lady and a gentleman, hovered dimly at the end of my row.

"Excuse me please," the gentleman said, bowing politely to me. Without noticing or glancing at him, I stood up to allow them to pass. But instead of sitting down immediately in the empty seat next to me, he cautiously steered the lady ahead of him with gentle guiding hands; he showed her to her place, paved the way for her, as it were, thoughtfully pulled down the seat for her and helped her into it. This kind of attention was too unusual not to attract my notice. Oh, a blind woman, I thought, and involuntarily looked sympathetically in her direction. Then the somewhat portly gentleman sat down next to me, and with a pang I recognized him—it was Condor!

The only man who knew everything, who knew the very depths of my guilt, was sitting so close to me that I could hear his breathing! The man whose pity had not, like mine, been murderous weakness but selfless, self-sacrificing strength; the only man who could judge me, the only man before whom I need feel ashamed! When, in the interval, the lights went up, he would be bound to recognize me. I began to tremble, and hurriedly put my hand up to my face to be at least safe from discovery in the darkness. Not a bar more did I hear of the beloved music, so violently was my heart pounding. The proximity of this individual, the only man who really knew me, appalled me. As though I were sitting stark naked in the dark among all those well-dressed, respectable people, I shuddered at the thought of the moment when the blaze of light would reveal me. And so in the short space of time before the lights came on, and while the curtain was just falling on the first act, I hurriedly ducked my head and fled up the gangway— quickly enough, I think, for him not to see or recognize me. But ever since that moment I have realized afresh that no guilt is forgotten so long as the conscience still knows of it.

EDUARDO BERTI

Agua

Translated by
Alexander Cameron and Paul Buck

The year is 1920, and Luis Agua, an agent
for an electricity company, arrives in Vila
Natal, an inhospitable village in Portugal.
His objective is to convince the inhabitants of
the benefits of artificial light. Before long Agua
learns that the village and the castle that pre-
sides over it hide dark secrets. The beautiful
widow, shrouded in mystery, who never
leaves her castle, a will that is both puzzling
and cruel, a pioneer of aviation, an epidemic
and a breathtaking finale unite the themes of
love, revenge, humour, death, greed, heroism
and courage in the modern world.

"There is no doubt that Eduardo Berti must be
considered one of the most original, most accomplished novelists writing in Spanish today."
From the Afterword by ALBERTO MANGUEL

PUSHKIN MODERN

ISBN 1-901285-42-1 • 160pp • £10/$14